By the time ⟨...⟩ the pub he be⟨...⟩ laughter bubbled ⟨...⟩ ⟨...⟩ing seemed so funny, and on th⟨...⟩ ⟨...⟩ leading down to the pub, he stepped behind a large tree and let himself have a real belly laugh.

"David, David, is that you?"

Grinning stupidly he came around the tree, "Oh hello Jill." At the furrowing of her brow, through new guffaws of laughter he managed to get out, "Jane's been rocking my boat."

"How many drinks have you had?"

Nonchalantly, he leant back against the tree, and retaliated joyfully, "Sister dear, not a drop has passed my lips."

Grimly she stated, "Well that's not the way it looks to me. And where on earth have you been? Have you seen the state of your clothes?"

He chuckled delightedly. "You'd never believe it if I told you. I'm not sure whether it was here on earth, whether I was in the body or out of it, but it all felt pretty real." At her raised eyebrows, and the shaking of her head, he looked down. Both his short-sleeved, light-blue cotton shirt and beige trousers were covered in brown and green smudges where the branches and stems had slapped against him. Blood from scratches on his bare arms had added to the strange pattern. He muttered to himself, "So much for not wanting to get muddy". That sent him into another fit of laughter, gurgling through that, "Oh my, I really did, I must have, it's true, I've done battle with a maize crop. It was real."

Jill tutted. "Couldn't you have walked down the road like any sensible person?"

RUTH JOHNSON

DAVID

The Heart's Desire Series

BOOK 3

EMANUEL PUBLISHING

First published in Great Britain in 2012
Copyright © Ruth Johnson 2012

The right of Ruth M. Johnson to be identified as the author
of this work has been asserted by her in accordance with
the Copyright, Designs and Patents Act 1988

This novel is entirely a work of fiction.
The names, characters and incidents portrayed in it are the work of the
author's imagination. Any resemblance to actual persons living or dead,
events or localities is entirely coincidental.

ISBN: 978-0-95548-982-2

A catalogue for this book is available in the British Library

Biblical quotes are taken from:
The Living Bible & Revised Standard Version

Songs: used with permission
Title track of the album of the same name:
'Hallowed Ground' by Phil Lawson-Johnston

From the 'Healing Streams' album by Lou Lewis
'Breaking Up' & '(Suddenly) Joy Springs Up'

Printed and bound by:
CPI Group (UK) Ltd, Croydon, CR0 4YY

Published by Emanuel Publishing Ltd
36 Kenmore Crescent, Bristol BS7 0TL
www.emanuel-publishing.com

www.heartsdesireseries.com

Trust in the Lord and do good;
Dwell in the land and enjoy safe pasture;
Delight yourself in the Lord and he will give you
the desires of your heart.
Commit your way to the Lord and
Trust in him and he will do it..
Psalm 37: 3-5

ACKNOWLEDGEMENTS

A 'BIG THANK' YOU FOR

ADVICE
Midwife: Louise Adams
Police Sergeant: Tony Unthank
Dr Stephen Wood

INPUT
Caroline Howe
Naomi Johnson
Christine Parfitt

PROOF READING:
and burning the midnight oil in the hours and hours
it took to read and correct the manuscript.
Graham & Lynne Weakley

ENCOURAGEMENTS
from many friends and readers
to bring out this third book in the Hearts Desire Series
I'm sorry you've had to wait so long!

DEDICATION

To Brian
A husband in a million,
faithful, trustworthy and committed.

In supporting my writing he puts up with
unmade beds, unwashed dishes, uncooked meals
while I tangle with plots and editing.

The finished story only comes to birth as a book
because of his patience to take all those typed words,
and put them in suitable form for the printer.

Oh, for a million words,
to express my thanks and appreciation,
But maybe just five will do.

Thank you

I love you

Ruth
xx

June 1970

CHAPTER 1

Frustrated, David Reinhardt squeezed the steering wheel, and groaned at what appeared to be a never-ending queue of vehicles ahead.

"There's no point scowling. I know you didn't want to make this journey, but I couldn't have anticipated the heavy rain or this traffic jam."

His attention diverted from the road to Jane. Red highlights, lit by a brief appearance of the sun, shone in her brown hair causing a halo around her heart shaped face. Her hazel eyes gazed wide-eyed into his before a small smile curved her lips. He softened his stern expression with a wry smile and reached over to pat her knee. "I've got a lot on my mind!" Jane nodded knowingly. The traffic started to move. He edged the car forward. It was his nature to forge ahead, and he knew he became easily irritated when slowed down. And he pondered again the unsettling and recently recurring dream that forced him to turn from the dawn into darkness. Finally, the road ahead cleared, he negotiated a lane change, accelerated, overtook a bus and headed towards Maidstone.

Jane re-adjusted her sitting position. "I know there's not time to stop for lunch, but I need the toilet and a drink."

Relieved to have a clear road ahead he hid his annoyance by taunting in his booming voice, "Will there ever be a time young lady when you don't turn my well ordered life upside down?"

The retort was more than he expected. "You can't blame me for the weather in London, or the conditions of the roads! A quick stop isn't going to ruin your schedule. And it's not I, but Robert Jones who has upset your well ordered plans by taking over your desk, office, and job, sooner than expected. And you're frustrated because he doesn't want the benefit of your advice or experience. Oh come on, that's the only reason you took today off. I'd have been quite safe travelling with Paul and Jill."

Unable to refute the truth he gave his stock reply. "Is that so?" Jane gave a derisory hum. A few seconds later he commented, "I now know how Harold Wilson felt last week when he was unexpectedly ousted from his office by Edward Heath."

"That's no comparison! Mr Wilson didn't just lose his office, but his job, salary and home all in one day. In losing an office you're gaining a better one, in losing your job you're gaining promotion with a salary raise, and the only part of our home we're losing is your study!"

There was no answer to that! His mind drifted to International Trade Promotions (ITP) where he'd quickly risen from Legal Advisor to Exhibitions Director. And now at only thirty-seven he was about to become Managing Director and Chairman of the Board. "And David, I'll remind you, you started this!" He turned briefly to catch her knowing gaze, wagging finger and cheeky grin, "Everything we do has consequences. You'll soon get used to not gallivanting around the world." In following the signpost on a roundabout he bit back a rejoinder. 'Gallivanting' was not what he did. Although Jane's voice did hold a degree of empathy as she continued, "Oh I know you loved the excitement of international exhibitions, but in managing ITP's infrastructure the adjustments will mean regular hours, freedom to develop the Company, and I expect they'll be the occasional legal wrangle to keep your hand in."

With his eyes on the road, he considered 'the adjustments'. He doubted his new job would excite him, but his home life was bound to keep him on his toes. My, oh my, the little bundle of body sitting beside him had been a constant challenge since the day he'd first set eyes on her! The majority of those working at ITP felt intimidated by his stern looks and position, but not Jane. When their lives converged she'd met him head on, a response so rare it had him reeling and before long he'd fallen in love with the little firebrand. Four years later, and three years of married life was comparable to being on a rollercoaster and more recently riding blindfold! Regular working hours might be a welcome plateau on which to take breath!

Stopped at traffic lights he smiled across at her. Her response was to lean toward him and kiss his cheek. Classically she wasn't beautiful, but she had an inner beauty and a love for him that touched the depth of his being. Against his heavy build, harsh and chiselled features with a height over six feet, her small frame in her stocking feet at five foot, two inches, brought out all his protective instincts. Yet physical desire often sparked through confrontation, the tone of her voice, a toss of her head, or a haughty look.

Jane tugged to adjust the safety belt and wriggled in her seat. "You were right about my being uncomfortable, not helped by your insistence I wear this, but I promised and couldn't let Beatty down." In acknowledgement of her ability to admit when she was wrong, and integrity to do what was right, he squeezed her hand before putting the car in gear and moving forward.

"David, it's just past twelve, the pubs should be open – look there's one."

His eyes followed Jane's finger pointing to a dingy red brick building, and although slowing he felt to ask, "Can't you wait a little longer? It might be called 'The Traveller's Rest' but it doesn't look very inviting."

"Beggars can't be choosers, and a toilet is a toilet."

Obediently he parked in the narrow street of dilapidated Victorian terraced houses as her voice mimicked Lady Penelope of TV series 'Thunderbirds'. "Thank you Parker." Inwardly he smiled for that name Jane also linked to his aquiline nose and his inquisitive nature! Undoing her safety belt she commanded, "While you wait you can buy me a packet of crisps and an orange juice."

Hand to head he saluted, "Yes ma'am."

Jane grinned and added, "Please!"

Gallantly he dashed around the car to help her out and felt to warn her, "I suspect those who frequent this pub live in these houses and work in the local factory, not quite the place I'd choose for you, my lady!"

Jane laughed, but a few minutes later she agreed that the 'Snug bar' was a travesty of its name. Nicotine from cigarette smoke had turned the cream walls to a dingy brown, black smudges blended into the brown and orange pattern carpet and the furniture consisted of battered wooden tables and chairs. A meagre light came from two small, grubby sash windows and a forty watt bulb hung from the ceiling. He and Jane looked at each other, she whispered, "We're here now." But the smell and state of the men's toilet was disgusting and he hoped Jane had faired better.

The brightest area was over the horseshoe counter serving

both the 'Snug' and 'Public' bar. The latter was already filling with a haze of blue smoke from the noisy lunch time crowd. Standing at the bar he felt totally out of place dressed in his dark pin-striped suit. Curiosity reflected in the eyes of the wiry barman with the beaten up face as he asked, "What'll you 'ave" adding as an afterthought, "Sir?"

"A half pint of bitter, an orange juice and two packets of crisps, please."

"Right yer are, coming up." As he pulled the beer he commented, "Yer not from around 'ere."

"No. Driving through. My wife needed a short break."

The man nodded, placed the overflowing half pint dimple glass on to the counter as a loud burst of laughter came from the Public Bar. With a jerk of his head he informed him, "Friday, pay day, it gets a bit rowdy." Decanting a Britvic bottle into a glass he remarked, "We don't often get passers by in 'ere. Not yer sort of place is it?"

Stuck for a reply he asked, "How much do I owe you?" while drawing from his wallet a five pound note.

Before he could blink the money was snatched from his hand with the warning, "Big note! Best not to flash money around 'ere." Not wanting to attract attention David glanced around. The dark area by the door had in it a pile of broken furniture, but a table near the Ladies was out of sight of the other bar. On returning to collect the crisps and his change the barman winked and declared, "'ere comes yer Missus."

Jane, with furrowed brow, was crossing the room her eyes fixed on the noisy crowd. In two strides he was beside her and bent to say in her ear, "Horrible, isn't it? Come over here, drink up and let's be on our way."

About to sit in the seat opposite her, he saw her gaze fixed beyond him and her eyes widening in trepidation. Before he could turn a familiar cultured voice said, "Good grief Reinhardt, it is you!" Shocked he whirled around. His beer slopped on to the filthy carpet as his eyes met those of Andrew Carlton, the man he'd sacked four years earlier for his unwarranted behaviour toward female staff. "Hey man, watch your beer! You nearly had it over me." Andrew smiled in a parody of friendliness. Instability reflected in his jumpy pale and watery blue eyes, the once handsome face had thinned, his suit, expensively cut, was worn and shabby. "Fancy you turning up here. Hardly your kind

14

of place is it?" Andrew's expression hardened as he added, "It wouldn't have been mine, until you ruined my life." Peering around him Andrew exclaimed, "Goodness me! You're with the very bitch that helped you to do that." In recognition his nose wrinkled in a sneer, "And oh dear me Reinhardt, she's looking rather knocked up. Your doing, I fancy. I knew it. So it appears that chivalrous rescue from my clutches opened the way to do what I didn't manage, the taming of the little shrew. And you had the gall to insist to the police that you had no designs on her. You, like me, wanted to..." Andrew's foul and descriptive language caused him to close his eyes as if to block it out. "What's the matter Reinhardt? Are my words going against your sensibilities? Don't tell me, you've become one of those mealy-mouthed, narrow-minded Christians?"

Jane's arm slid through his. "Real Christianity isn't like that. It's a loving relationship with the Father God." Andrew gave a derisive snigger. Jane not put off added, "That's why Jesus died for our sins so we could..."

Contemptuously he interrupted "You've preached it before - we are all sinners and the wages of sin are death. What's sin anyway?"

Promptly Jane answered, "Everything we do that doesn't line up with God's will, His word and ways."

"Still the little zealot I see. Well, that's me, I'm a sinner and I'm not dead."

"It doesn't mean..."

Gently David squeezed Jane's arm against his. "Let's not get into that."

Nastily Andrew observed, "It would seem you've got into her. Bit of a mistake to let that bun develop in her oven."

The tightening of his jaw along with a deep breath and slow exhalation was only outward sign of David's desire to thump the man. Rarely did he consider violence, and the only man who'd ever made him resort to it was Andrew. It still astonished him how on that day his fist had rendered Andrew unconscious. Only afterwards when the repercussions started did he see that his choice to leave Andrew lying on the pavement and drive Jane home hadn't been the wisest action. Now he guessed Andrew's continuing verbiage was trying to provoke him into hitting him again, this time with witnesses. In a cold voice David asserted, "Excuse me, my wife and I are in need of fresh air" and made to move around him.

Andrew sidestepped to stop him. "Oh don't go on my account. Do finish your drinks. There's not much fresh air around here." A malevolent laugh was followed with a mean smile as he goaded, "Wife eh? Foolish man! Fancy you getting caught. That haughty way of hers, so obviously attention seeking. Didn't you see she was out to ensnare you?"

Annoyed he retaliated. "For your information Jane didn't ensnare me. I fell in love with her. I had to persuade her to marry me. Now, please let us pass."

"Persuade her?" Andrew grunted. "That's what she led you to believe, just one of her games playing the innocent. No doubt, she got herself pregnant and landed you with a forthcoming bastard if you didn't do the right thing by her."

Provoked David took a step toward him, stopped, and keeping his clenched fists at his side he levelled a steely gaze into Andrew's mocking face before answering with a calmness he didn't feel, "Not at all. Jane and I have been married three years."

"Really! Good grief! And to think you could have married the beautiful, delectable Felicity? Now there was a peach of a woman - a definite plus on your arm." He nodded his head towards Jane, "Marrying a secretary is a real come down for the heir apparent to the Reinhart millions?"

Determined not to give vent to his inner anger, David turned, picked up Jane's glass, handed it to her and ordered, "Drink up we're leaving." With that he pocketed the crisps, downed his beer and put the glass back on the table. Andrew, feet apart, hands in his pocket, stood as though to block their path. "Excuse us, we've nothing more to say."

"Too bad, for I have." Andrew stepped nearer. David moved to put Jane behind him. "After all Reinhardt, you threw me out of a good job, refused to write me a reference and cast aspersions on my private life. Your interference and high-handedness ruined me. I've always said I'd get even. It would seem that day has come."

Unexpectedly David's anger dissipated, leaving a sadness that such an intelligent man had fallen so low, and he pointed out with genuine regret, "Forget about getting even Andrew because if your life is ruined you can rest assured you did it all by yourself. I don't know how you managed to escape justice and keep your freedom…"

"Freedom, call this freedom!" Andrew's eyes glittered with hate, "Oh believe me Reinhardt, I've paid the price for your interference in my life. The only accountancy work available to me is in industrial firms who aren't interested in my past, but my expertise to lessen their tax bills. I'm reduced to a scabby flat just around the corner from here, all because of you!" Andrew glared at him then snarled towards Jane, "And you started it, you, the little blabbermouth tart! What's the matter little shrew, cat got your tongue?"

A glance at Jane's far away expression indicated she was praying! A good idea for he could do with wisdom, for although he outweighed and outstripped Andrew in fitness, he had no wish to be seen brawling in a public house. In a grim tone he declared, "I see no point in dragging up the past."

Andrew's expression went from derision to rage. "No point! No point in dragging up the past!" A forefinger, near enough to tickle David's nose, jabbed out along with his words, "Oh really 'Mr High and Mighty Reinhardt'! Do you know that's what your dear little wife used to call you, well, let me tell you I've every point, and every right, to drag up the past. And you'll stay until I let you leave." That same hand waved towards the crowd in the Public Bar, "See that tall black guy, he's a heavy weight boxer and a friend of mine."

Despite recognising the veiled threat, David tried to appear nonchalant while considering how to remove Jane from the lurking danger. "Well, Andrew it's always good to have friends." As he spoke he slid his hand in his pocket, pulled out the car keys and turned to instruct Jane, "Go to the car, I'll be right out."

Anxiety etched Jane's face, her eyes questioned him. With a hard stare he strove to convey the need for her obedience, and in that instant Andrew snatched the keys from his hand with a delirious little laugh. Dangling them from his fingers just out of his reach, in a sing song voice he said , "I've got the car keys, I've got the car keys." Malevolently he added with glee, "Now dear little Jane you won't miss seeing your beloved get his nose bloodied, my recompense for last time when you caused my wallet, keys and car to be stolen." Across the room he yelled towards the crowded bar, "Henry!"

The glitter of revenge in Andrew's eyes had to be a madness that came from more than just drink. It was doubtful he'd be able to reason with him, but worth a try. "Andrew, don't be foolish. If you're caught, you'll be arrested and will end up in prison and there's even less freedom there." Anxious that Jane might get hurt he kept his eyes on Andrew as he commanded her to take refuge in the Ladies Toilet.

"She's not going anywhere."

He didn't bother to refute that instead he kept side stepping to block Andrew's path toward her. Through the open Snug door, a big black man in dark workman's overalls entered. Without turning Andrew said, "Henry will deal with you, but I'll start - that baby looks ready to deliver." Before his mind comprehended the threat there was a blur of movement. Instinctively he threw his body against Andrew's arm to deflect the blow. Instantly his mind called, 'God, help me' and then with agility he didn't know he possessed, he twirled, caught Andrew's arm, twisted it and swung him around so fast he stumbled. For them to leave unscathed, and with Henry ready to join in he knew he had to fell Andrew, hold him captive and use him as a human shield. That knowledge kept him turning, the whirlwind effect transmitting to Andrew's arm causing him to cry out as his knees buckled. For David it couldn't have been a better outcome as Andrew's back was towards Henry and the angle in which he held his arm kept him pinned to the floor. He resisted the temptation to twist harder, not to just give pain, but to cause damage. A glance at Henry revealed him standing feet apart, arms folded, in the deep shadow amongst the battered furniture by the door.

From behind Jane exclaimed, "David that was incredible. Where did you learn to do that?"

Through gritted teeth and strained voice Andrew begged, "Okay Reinhardt, you've made your point."

Eyes fixed on Andrew, he bantered, "You know me Jane I make it my business to be full of surprises."

"Reinhardt, let me go."

"Oh no! Not until Jane is safely in the car and you've called off your man."

To his dismay Jane moved around Andrew to take a better look. "It appears you, my knight in shining armour, have the situation under control." David said nothing for if this was a chess game Jane was now a pawn between two rooks, and he, her knight, could only take on one rook at a time! Eyes fixed on

Henry he tightened his grip on Andrew, only to frown as Henry lifted his forefinger and placed it upright against his lips. Andrew struggled, Jane gave a worried cry, then watched bemused at his apparent skill at holding down Andrew's squirming figure. Another glance towards Henry brought a barely perceptible nod indicating the car keys on the nearby table. Anxious for Jane's safety he ordered, "Jane take the car keys from that table and…" Feeling his debilitating grip on Andrew loosening he urged, "Lock yourself in the car." Jane's walk at eight months pregnant was a slow waddle. In the midst of wrestling with Andrew he took a fleeting look at her progress and was caught off guard by Andrew head butting him under the chin. Staggering sideways David's grasp loosened. Andrew pulled free. Desperate that Andrew wouldn't reach Jane, David lunged forward in a rugby tackle at his legs. Andrew hit the floor, his head banged against the side of a table, it tipped causing him to slip down it on to the floor. Stunned, Andrew lay on the carpet with his nose bleeding. Extracting himself from Andrew's legs, David stood, brushed down his trousers, adjusted his jacket and seeing his wallet on the floor he bent to pick it up.

Jane screaming his name was simultaneous to the blow to the back of his head. Unbalanced, with his eyes filled with painful shards of light, he guessed Andrew had hit him with something. Where was Jane? Why was she now silent? Blinded by light, galvanised by terror, he tried to turn towards the door, but tripping over a fallen chair he collapsed heavily over a table. The breath went from his body as their was the sound of breaking glass, then came silence. The eruption of voices, the cacophony of sound, indicated fear and panic. Was that to do with Jane, was she hurt? Panic was as paralysing as his stunned body. And all he could see was the under edge of the bar a few feet from him. Over the top of the bedlam someone shouted, "Has anyone called an ambulance?"

Inside he cried out, 'Oh God, please - not for Jane.' Frantic to find out what had happened, he tried moving from the table, the room spun making him feel horribly sick. If Jane was safe she'd be here beside him? As suddenly as the noise started, it began to diminish. Was the blow so near to his ear bringing deafness? Sheer willpower brought him to grit his teeth and concentrate on getting up. An arm slid under his to hoist him off the table. The barman shorter, and probably several stone lighter, swayed under his weight before lowering him on to a chair. In a voice no more than a raspy whisper, David managed, "My wife?"

"She's alright, she's over there." Anxious to see where the barman was pointing, he turned quickly, and winced as the room spun. But he had glimpsed her in the dark area by the door, her hand resting protectively on her stomach. "Take yer time mate. Good job it was only a 'alf pint dimple glass, 'eavy, but don't easily break. We've called an ambulance if yer like we'll get them to look at the Missus too."

In a stronger voice David protested, "I don't need an ambulance."

"Oh no, not for you Sir, but for Jake."

Confused, and wondering if he had suffered brain damage he queried rather curtly, "Who the hell is Jake?"

Puzzled the barman answered, The chap who came to talk to yer. Fought yer knew 'im. Nasty piece of work. I 'eard yer wife cry out, and jumped the counter because he 'eaded for 'er, and I guessed to 'it 'er. Seeing me 'e only pushed past 'er as he went out the door." That news had David thump his fist into the palm of his hand why hadn't he inflicted pain on Andrew while he had the chance? "Don't worry. Yer wife is only giddy, and Jake's got what 'e deserves. I'll get yer a brandy!"

Cautiously David attempted to stand. His legs felt rubbery, but strong enough to hold him up. The noisy crowd in the Public Bar had disappeared, and besides the slight hum of voices the place seemed eerily empty. Slowly he coordinated his limbs to walk. He'd been against Jane travelling anywhere at thirty-six weeks pregnant, now he could only pray that she wouldn't go into labour and he'd be fit enough to drive away from this place. Standing next to her he cradled her head against him. "Are you alright?"

Clearly shaken Jane's voice was a whisper. "Yes" and then lifting her head to look up at him asked, "But what about you?"

Dazed and nauseous he replied grimly, "I'll survive" and was grateful of the distraction of the barman with a surly smile handing them each a glass. "Drink up, on the 'ouse." Jane politely accepted the brandy, but he knew she wouldn't drink it. He didn't hesitate, knocked it back in one gulp and drew up a chair to sit beside her. Stunned they sat listening to the murmuring of voices in the Public Bar. A warm glow pervaded

David relieving his nausea. He found it difficult to talk of feelings, but Jane frequently chattered about hers. Often it sounded muddled and silly, he'd easily lose the thread causing her to get irritated, but he wished she was speaking now. Had her fears resurfaced that if pregnancy didn't kill her, labour probably would? He placed his hand lightly on top of her baby bulge and felt the tightness there. Not wanting to sound worried he asked, "All well in there?"

Her voice trembled, "My stomach is like a hard ball."

"Is that so!" With a wry grimace he patted her hand. "I expect it's one those Branston Hints, the pre-labour contractions you told me about."

Pleased, he watched Jane's lips curve slightly as she corrected, "Braxton Hicks, David." Unable to keep his face straight, she did her familiar gesture of a light punch against him, saying, "You knew that, you are awful, but I love you." She handed him her brandy, "I'm not sure you need another, but I don't want it." Her look of adoration, and words were more than enough to give him strength. "David, you were amazing. The way you handled Andrew, but oh, when I saw him... I thought..." Tears filled her eyes and threatened to spill over.

"It's alright. We've survived. We're fine."

"But your head? You didn't look fine sprawled across that table."

"Oh it's nothing. The initial blow sent me reeling, but the pain has almost gone."

"Turn around, let me see." To appease her he bent his head sideways. The pain made him flinch. "See you aren't fine." Gently her fingers touched the forming lump. "The skin isn't broken. Do you think you will be able to drive?"

Amused he looked her in the eyes. "A blow to my head hasn't rendered me incapable. And I'll be a good deal safer driving than you with arms that are barely longer than your bulge!" It did his heart good to see her grin. "We're about half way between home and Beatty's house. What do you want to do?"

In the distance they heard ambulance bells. Jane looked at him, "Are they coming for me, or you?"

"Neither! It's for Andrew, known here as Jake." Anxiously he added, "Although if you want them to check you...?"

"No, no! What's happened? I can't make out what is being

said, but I suspect it's to do with that breaking glass?"

David shrugged, "The barman said 'Andrew, or Jake as he's known here, has got what he deserves'!"

Visualizing the earlier scene Jane described it. "After hitting you with that glass Andrew came rushing at me. But I turned from him with a speed I didn't know I had, it made my head spin. His hand caught my back, but only hard enough for me to take a few steps forward before the barman caught me and placed me on this chair."

From the bar area, the same barman's surly voice instructed, "Yer need to get out of 'ere." They turned to see him heading towards them, his expression matching his voice. "Police will be 'ere in a jiffy. Always 'ot foot behind the ambulance, 'specially if people are badly cut up. Lots of knife crime around 'ere. The area is trouble with a capital 'T'."

Horrified David queried, "Knife crime?" and stood to help Jane to her feet. In answer the barman produced a flick knife and pressed it open. As he stiffened, Jane next to him trembled. The barman closed the blade. "These are quite usual around here, and Jake…well…I picked this up from over there." Their eyes followed his finger to the very spot he'd wrestled Andrew to his knees. "Come on, move yerselves. The rest of me customers left by the back door, best yer do the same." Swiftly the barman moved toward the bar, "Follow me. 'urry up."

While supporting Jane to quicken her rolling gait he enquired, "What's happened?"

"Never mind that, best yer get out of 'ere."

Tightening his arm on Jane's he manoeuvred her through into the bar area. The barman mused, "Like usual, no-one saw nothing. Yet his 'ead is through the glass of the Public Bar door." Jane stopped as her hand flew to her mouth. "Forget it Missus. 'e ain't worth it." Leading the way he cautioned, "Be careful through 'ere, it's a bit narrow. Mind them stacked beer crates, we don't want another accident." Walking behind Jane he guessed she'd asked the barman if Andrew was badly hurt, for he'd turned with a grim expression and nodded.

Sickened, David shouted over the loud siren and bells, "I wouldn't have wished that on him."

By the back door the barman stood aside to let Jane waddle across the walled yard, and commented tersely, "Between 'em, Jake and 'enry, 'ave caused some nasty injuries to people." The

22

enormity of the flick knife, and what might have happened, caused a shudder to run through him. "Just count yer lucky stars, that 'e's in a mess not you."

"I prefer to thank God! I managed to restrain Jake from attacking Jane, but when he summoned Henry I didn't know how we could escape without injury, yet Henry didn't get involved and clearly helped us."

"That don't sound like 'enry to me, 'e's always quick to muscle into a fight. Not sure about God either, except perhaps this is divine retribution for the pair of them." The barman drew back the heavy bolts on the wooden gate. Any 'ow I don't remember 'enry leaving the Public Bar."

"Andrew called him, and a big black man came into the Snug?"

Pulling the padlock from the rings on the gate the barman remarked, "Don't know mate. Your brain's fuzzed by the blow to your 'ead. 'enry was in the Public Bar when Jake shot through the glass because…" With a glance at Jane resting against the wall holding her stomach, he murmured, "'e's pretty cut up too."

Bewildered David added, "But Henry was standing in that small dark area by the door watching Jane leave."

With obvious annoyance the barman wrenched the gate open. "I didn't see no-one."

Jane sent him a puzzled look as she went through into the back lane. David rubbed his forehead feeling to do so might clear his memory. And although feeling foolish he felt to state as he went through the gate, "Henry was definitely there, he picked the car keys up from the floor and put them on the table."

The barman surveyed him as though he was mad. "I've got to go" with that he stepped back, shut the gate in David's face and they heard the bolts sprung. If Jane hadn't pulled on his arm he would have remained there trying to figure it out. Leading him down the alley, Jane turned, frowned and asked, "Are you sure you are alright? Only I didn't see a big black man, only you and Andrew."

Mystified he recalled, "But Andrew called Henry. And just after he arrived I did that amazing tackle which floored Andrew." He grinned and squeezed Jane's arm against him, "I must tell Paul how his lessons of self-defence and restraint came in handy. Seriously though, when you stepped in front of me, with Henry standing behind you that definitely wasn't a smart move."

"But I didn't see Henry, only Andrew."

Unable to believe her, he shook his head. "Didn't you think it odd that the car keys in my struggle with Andrew landed on a table?" Jane shrugged. Baffled and about to turn the corner out of the alley David stopped and looked down at her. "When you went to pick up the keys Henry was in the shadows by the door watching you."

"I was concentrating on getting to the keys and had just picked them up, I turned to show you when I saw Andrew, a glass in his hand and his raising it to smash it into the back of your head." Frowning, Jane shook her head, "But I didn't see anyone else."

At her troubled gaze David chuckled, "Do you remember calling me your guardian angel well perhaps today God thought I needed a little help."

Jane's face lightened, "Do you really think…"

Laughter bubbled up in him. "I don't know, but let's get back to the car, it's starting to rain." They looked up at the approaching black and ominous clouds. Seeing those reminded him of his recurring dream, and with that came a sense of foreboding, that they hadn't heard the last of Andrew Carlton.

CHAPTER 2

Within minutes of resuming their journey Jane, lulled by the windscreen wipers, fell asleep. For that alone he felt grateful. Time for her to recuperate and proof she'd no adverse effects. But he felt more shaken now than during the incident. Did God have guardian angels He sent into situations when needed?

He wasn't sure about divine retribution, but divine intervention was something he'd previously considered. If Jane hadn't become pregnant within two weeks of stopping the contraceptive pill she may well have changed her mind. Even before she missed her first period she was arguing about the decision. "I can cope with admin, organising, cooking, it's predictable, it can be worked out in advance, but babies can't. Their constant needs are demanding, and unlike adults you can't reason with them. I don't cope well with lack of sleep."

He'd cajoled, "There are ways around that. I'll be here to help. I can get up at night, we can work it out."

"But that's the problem. You aren't always here at night."

Rashly he'd offered, "I'll change my job" then hurried on to point out that with Paul and Jill living in the downstairs flat, and Rosemary who all loved babies, they'd help her. Changing tack he'd added, "You have to agree William is growing from babyhood into a cute little fellow."

Jane rejoinder was immediate. "Yes, but after an hour I've had enough of looking after him. David, let's wait a bit longer."

But it was already too late. Before she went for the results of her pregnancy test she was already having morning sickness most of the day. Her state of mind only thinly disguised in her telephone announcement to him at the office, "Good news for you David, I'm pregnant." That had curbed that incredible sensation of achievement and excitement bubbling within him, but he'd tempered his response by saying how much he loved her and how much he appreciated what she was doing for him. Later he took home an enormous bouquet of flowers.

With tears in her eyes at seeing his obvious joy she'd said, "Please be patient with me, I really am trying to think positively, but this baby is already taking over my body, and I feel like death. I know that you'll say it's only for nine months, but suppose I come to hate it, not love it?"

At that he'd responded, "Oh that's ridiculous! Of course you won't hate our baby. Whatever next?" But seeing her face puckering to cry he pushed down his irritation, hugged her and injected amusement into his tone. "I'm sure we can arrange times for you to escape."

But as the weeks went by there hadn't been any escape for Jane from her burgeoning body. And at five months pregnant he'd had a phone call at work from Mr Beveridge, the consultant obstetrician at St Mary's Hospital informing him that they had detected two heartbeats, and hoped he'd be delighted to know that his wife was expecting twins. He'd whooped for joy, but the consultant had continued, "I'm afraid your wife is rather shocked, and overwhelmed by the news, and it would be good if you could come and take her home."

On seeing Jane curled up in the chair of the waiting room, her thumb by her mouth, his heart had gone out to her. She was expecting two children, yet in her vulnerability looked little more than a child herself. Mr Beveridge materialising by his side had said, "Ah Mr Reinhardt, I've explained to your wife that there's nothing to fear because we'll take great care of her at St. Mary's. Give her lots of tender, loving care and try to live as normally as possible. We'll monitor her progress, but if either of you have any worries please don't hesitate to contact me." With that he'd shaken his hand and turned into a nearby room.

Eyes that looked too big for her face had stared up at him as he took her hands to draw her to her feet. "Come here my lovely little wife." As he'd hugged her he'd reiterated, "You heard Mr Beveridge. St Mary's is a good hospital, and Dad is insisting you get the best, so you really don't have anything to fear." When she didn't comment he'd drawn back and seen she wasn't convinced. "Come on let's go home, we'll talk about it there." In the car the tense atmosphere was almost palpable. And as his business acumen didn't cover nonreturnable goods, he was left feeling inadequate.

Arriving home, Paul and Jill were in the hall, Jill had looked up from tucking William in the pram to ask, "How did the antenatal go?"

Jane's dour expression was a good enough answer bringing Paul to say kindly, "Don't worry Jane you'll be fine, we'll look after you."

At that Jane had snapped, "Will you? Your first wife died after having Maria, so nothing is guaranteed." Then she'd burst

26

into tears and ran upstairs while Paul blanched, Jill looked bewildered, and he didn't know what to think beyond Jane's rudeness.

After sending Paul a sad, loving look Jill had remarked, "I can't believe Jane's just said that. What, brother dear have you done to upset her?"

Unable to keep a silly grin off his face he'd announced, "We're having twins!"

Stunned they both turned to look up the now empty staircase before Jill stated the obvious. "And Jane has taken the news badly!"

Paul had congratulated him and confessed that as a doctor he'd had his suspicions. His advice was much the same as Mr Beveridge except he added, "Try not to rise to Jane's somewhat irrational behaviour or conclusions. And believe me that since Beth died the care in pregnancy and childbirth has moved on in leaps and bounds." After that Jill had reassured him Jane would adore her babies, and there'd be no shortage of helpers.

Jane was in the kitchen filling the kettle when he'd walked through the dining room towards her to ask, "What are you doing? Put your feet up. I'll make the tea."

Clearly upset she banged the kettle on the stove and bewailed, "I didn't want one baby, let alone two. Why did I let you persuade me to have a child? My Mum's tale of her agony in labour should have kept me sane! If I'd known there was any possibility of conceiving twins I would have insisted on waiting several more years."

"Jane, look at me." With his finger he'd tipped her face upward to brush his mouth against hers before saying gently, "I love you. Look at it as getting our family in one go. You won't ever have to be pregnant again." Her reply was a grunt. "And my dear little wife I think you'll find that the conception of twins is more down to you than me." At her look of disbelief he'd queried, "Wasn't the man in your parents' wedding photos your father's twin who emigrated to Australia? It's my understanding that twins run through families and often missing a generation."

Crossly she'd stated, "Why didn't my mother warn me?"

Cheerily he'd bantered, "I'm glad she didn't."

"That's not funny David." Her eyes narrowed with suspicion, "Obviously you knew the possibility, why didn't you warn me?" At his non committal grimace she'd banged her fists into his chest and sobbed, "Oh how could you do that to me, h...how could you?"

In catching her hands he'd drawn her to him. "I didn't think about it before you were pregnant, but Paul seeing how sick you were, and how quickly you put on weight asked if there were twins in the family. There wasn't any point in upsetting you for nothing, but my delightful little wife, I can't help being thrilled and excited." Jane's expression as she pulled away to reach in the cupboard for the tea cups showed she didn't share his enthusiasm. From behind he'd encircled her thickened waist and gently placed his hands over her stomach. "It's hard to believe that contained in here is the fruit of our love growing into not one life, but two. And this discomfort, this hold on your life won't last forever."

Sharply she retorted, "The discomfort may not, but two children will."

"Well, I'm sure we will both be proud of them." Patting her stomach he added, "This son of mine will be a famous rugby player, none of that football malarkey."

Jane put her hands over his, "How do you know Samson is in there? It could be Jezebel and Delilah who will want their daddy to read stories, play with their dolls, and later need a vast number of clothes for their wardrobe."

Pleased at her more positive response he'd turned her toward him, tapped her nose and said, "I'm not sure they will appreciate those names!"

"And I'm not sure I'll appreciate them. I can't imagine myself as a mother with one child, let alone, two!" What could he say that he hadn't said before? Diversion was always a good tactic, and at the downturn of her mouth, he'd stared into her anxious eyes before slowly bending to nuzzle her lips. For a moment it had worked, before she pushed him away and petulant eyes stared into his. "Is that the only way you can respond?"

Happily he'd countered, "Jane I may often fail your expectations, but this is something I know you appreciate, and on the positive side there's no chance of you getting pregnant."

For a second Jane glared at him, and then laughed, "Oh David, you really are awful, but I do love you."

The kettle had whistled, he'd turned off the gas and pointed out she'd been awful to Paul and needed to apologise for her uncalled for response to his offer of help."

"Immediately Jane agreed, but complained, "Why is pregnancy having such an adverse effect on my mind and body?" To prove everything wasn't adverse he'd began kissing and caressing her until babies and tea were forgotten!

Smiling at that memory he returned to the present to negotiate a roundabout. He grimaced for in recent months it hadn't been that easy to negotiate around Jane's mood swings.

His mind drifted to Paul. Was his coming into their lives a divine act of God? The way his father had immediately liked him and within days had organised his travelling abroad on behalf of his Company, Inhart Pharmaceuticals had been nothing short of a miracle. How quickly Paul had become imbedded in their family. His teenage daughter Maria, had come to share the downstairs flat with Jill and Rosemary, and Paul had become their lodger. Before long Paul became his first valued and trusted friend. Eighteen months older than him, but with a wealth of life experiences to draw on, Paul had brought him fresh perspectives. and understanding in areas that had remained stunted during his formative years.

Ensconced in the rapid growth of Inhart Pharmaceuticals his father had barely interacted with his family, and seemed unable to comprehend the emotional issues that beset his Mum, and sisters' Paula and Jill. When older, he too had escaped the 'foibles of women folk' as his father called them, by immersing his life in study, becoming self sufficient and keeping his social circle to colleagues and acquaintances. But to his astonishment his serious, heavy chiselled features attracted women, and he quickly learnt how to charm, manipulate and use them, leading to numerous sexual liaisons.

At the time he'd no conscience about those, but it was difficult when seeing Jill do much the same not to comment. When finding herself pregnant and alone Jill had determined the age was coming when a child born outside of marriage wouldn't be termed a bastard. But Paul had befriended her, and equally determined, had broken through her resistance, marrying her in a Registry Office only seven days before William's arrival in the hall outside their bedroom door. Recently Paul had declared that their child, due in six months, would have a more dignified entrance into the world.

Jane stirred in her car seat, he glanced in her direction but she didn't awake. Unlike Jill who sailed through pregnancy, Jane had been twice as sick and gained twice as much weight. Two weeks ago in the back garden, they'd celebrated with their respective families, William's first birthday, and Paul and Jill's wedding anniversary. Being unable to help with the catering had exacerbated Jane's frustration. Her life she'd declared was one of monotony. Despite remembering Paul's counsel, 'don't react, let Jane have her say, just empathize to bring comfort' that day he'd retorted, "I don't suppose it's occurred to you that I'm not used to living with constant hormonal changes and swinging emotions, any more than you are by swelling up and looking fit to burst." At the time he'd been leading Jane to a seat under the tree with Bill, Paul's grandfather, when suddenly he was poked in the leg by Bill's stick. Querulously, but with a twinkle in his eye, Bill questioned, "Are you two going to argue all day, or sit down and talk to me?" With apologies, and the excuse to bring them drinks, he'd hurried off, but seeing William between the legs of the guests, he whisked him up on his shoulders. A voice had then commented, "You'll make an excellent father."

William holding and waving his plastic windmill smiled down on Beatty, the white-haired lady, his adopted great-grandmother, who had already clocked up ten grandchildren and eighteen great-grandchildren. Pleased to have such a commendation he gave Beatty one of the smiles Jill described as 'high wattage'. At Jill's calling William he put him down to toddle over to her, and thought how she'd taken to motherhood like a duck to water. Beatty had followed the direction of his eyes, and apparently his thoughts. "I prayed for years that Paul might find another 'soul mate' and have a second chance at fatherhood. William is such a delightful child, with those bright blue eyes and cheeky smile. Bill is so thrilled he has his name. Jill said named also after Ben's grandfather."

"Beatty, your Paul is to be commended for insisting that to keep an identity to his father, his second name be Benson."

Beatty's eyes filled with love for her grandson, "He feels it a privilege to stand in for Ben, as Bob and Lillian did as parents to Maria. We don't like tragedy and suffering, but if we allow them to do their work in us, it softens our hearts and makes us a compassionate people. And now, for Paul being able to combine his skill as a doctor with that of advising your father on ways to support medical issues in third world countries is a dream come true."

'Dreams coming true' was not what David wanted for his recurring dream! It felt as ominous as the black clouds he was continuing to see through the car windscreen. Another torrent of rain fell slowing the cars, and bringing a need to concentrate on the road. When it passed his mind returned to the party two weeks earlier. His conversation with Beatty had led to her pointing out God spoke to biblical characters through dreams and her offer to listen to his. But that day lunch had just been announced and he'd returned to the little group sitting in the tree's shade. But in forgetting their drinks found himself again the recipient of Jane's ire. Apologising and helping Jane to her feet he'd said to Bill, "Beatty's bringing your lunch she says she knows what you like."

Bill, thin and frail, his hand wobbling on the top of the walking stick between his legs gave a cynical smile, "Son, Beatty won't bring what I'd like, but what she feels I need."

Remembering how Jane was continually watching his weight he quickly glanced across where, held by her safety belt, she slept with her head flopped forward almost using her baby lump as a pillow. After Paul and Jill had slipped away for their forty-eight hour, very belated honeymoon Jane had fallen asleep, and he'd decided not to rejoin the party but read the book Paul had lent him on pregnancy and labour. On hearing Beatty coming up the stairs, he'd arisen, put his finger across his mouth and led her into the dining room. Once the door was closed she reported, "Bill's also nodded off, so tell me about your dream."

When he finished recalling it his eyes had connected with hers as he queried, "Is there a message in it? A preparation? A warning? Or perhaps showing our lives are taking a change of direction?" Even as he asked, he thought of how a selfish and self sufficient life style had become a commitment to trust and love the Lord, an engagement to Felicity had become marriage to Jane, and his desire for one baby had produced two!

Expectant that day for answers his hopes were dashed when Beatty's response had been, "I need to analyse, meditate and pray about it." And Jane opening the door and catching the last three words had enquired what she needed to pray about. At Beatty's replying, "David's been telling me about his recurring dream" Jane's eyes had narrowed, with her repeating the last three words as a question.

Beatty had frowned and with both pairs of eyes on him he'd

pulled a face and admitted to Jane, "I didn't know what to make of it. Paul suggested I talk to Beatty."

No-one could mistake Jane's exasperation as she said, "So Paul also knows about this 'dream' yet you haven't thought to share it with me."

With his elbows on the dining room table he'd rubbed his forehead before saying wearily, "Yes Jane, I thought about it. But it could be something or nothing, so as Beatty was here, I though I'd check it out."

Jane grunted, and Beatty suggested he put the kettle on. Obediently he'd moved through the archway to the kitchen beyond to fill the kettle. On lifting the sun blinds and seeing a storm brewing he'd prayed Beatty might circumvent the one developing between him and Jane. As he prepared the tea tray he listened, "…don't begrudge David's friendship with Paul, it's good they confide in each other, it enriches their lives and will enrich yours. Everything influences our minds, what we hear, see, read, eat, and dream! Sometimes it is of the Lord and sometimes its just sheer foolishness."

"So Beatty, do you think this dream of David's is foolishness?" He leant against archway between kitchen and dining room to hear her answer.

Beatty sent him a kindly smile. "When God wants to speak to us He uses different ways, it's good to be open to that. Let's have that cup of tea and I'll pray for you both."

It was the simplest of prayers, but it brought Jane to tears and to blurt out, "I'm sorry David I've got so wound up with how I feel, I've not thought of you and how I've been spoiling this time for you. Will you forgive me?"

Astonished he'd responded, "Good grief, you've never been that difficult. I may have struggled in areas, but you've been the one to suffer all the indignities of being sick, stretching and growing, you certainly haven't spoilt anything for me." With his familiar wry smile, he'd added, "Carrier of my children, I'd forgive you anything and always. And it's me who should be asking you to forgive me."

The response of a haughty, yet impish look preceded the words, "If you must know Mr Reinhardt, the gentleman was forgiven even before he bought the flowers."

He grinned broadly and had to explain to a bemused Beatty that Jane used those words when they first met and it had become their personal 'in' joke when forgiveness was necessary. To that she'd responded, "Forgiveness is the key to a good relationship and a long lasting marriage." After which she'd stood and added, "Now I must get back to Bill he'll be champing at the bit to go home."

Jane had hugged Beatty and said happily, "Like the hymn I feel, 'My chains fell off, my heart is free.' I suppose because I enjoy music the Lord often gives me a song in my heart. I've rather felt on death row, the condemned prisoner since I found out we were having twins. When you prayed I felt such a love rush for David and our babies, so despite feeling I'm racing towards the unknown, I know God is with me." He and Beatty exchanged a glance. Jane noticing asked, "What have I said? What do I need to know? Tell me?"

Before he could answer Beatty had patted her arm and advised, "Let David tell you his dream." Politely he'd jumped forward to open the flat door and Jane in a thoughtful more cumbersome manner, had followed Beatty, standing at the top of the stairs her hand at her back to balance her weight.

A loud clap of thunder had them jump. Below Lillian seeing Beatty descending called, "I'm waiting for Bob he's bringing the car to the door. Bill's so fast asleep even the noise of us rushing inside from the rain didn't disturb him. He has such a lovely smile on his face we left him to it, but I bet after that bang he's awake."

Under the crook of his arm, in the flat doorway Jane smiled adoringly up at him. "You tell me of your dream, and then I'll flex my fingers on the piano."

Cuddled up on the settee he missed out the dream's worrying aspects of feeling caught up and compelled to ride away from the rising dawn. The deafening pounding of thousands of horses' hooves, that brought fear, knowing to fall off would mean to be trampled to death. Instead he told of how each dream had progressed, from a view looking down on what appeared to be masses of ants moving together in the desert below. At a trumpet sound he'd seen the ants move as one in a circle to return from where they'd come. The second dream, instead of watching from above he'd found himself on the desert floor seated on a horse, in a mass of horses. In subsequent ones he'd believed for a destination, perhaps a mission, but as they left behind the dawn the speed of the horses increased and he felt more as if in an army heading for a battle. And as the darkness grew darker he realised even though he couldn't see his fellow riders a light was emanating from their chests. It was only then in looking down he saw he'd a similar beam concentrated like a car lamp on the road ahead. He finished, "So I don't know what to make of it."

Jane's reaction as she rose slowly to her feet and headed to the baby grand piano by the door was, "I can understand Beatty saying she'd pray about it! It could just be your mind is overactive with all the changes going on around you. Although one of the Psalms does say about God's Word is a lamp to our feet, and a light to our path, so there's comfort and truth in that. Jane played a quiet melody before breaking into, "Give me oil in my lamp, and he stiffened as she sang, "Keep me burning 'til the break of day." That seemed very relevant to his dream considering the only light was coming from within him. But as she'd begun to sing 'Amazing Grace' he'd felt peace pervade him.

And now with little traffic on a relatively straight road he put his foot on the accelerator and picked up speed. Peace, was another of God's divine provisions, for despite the altercation with Andrew, Jane had quickly fallen asleep, and besides the discomfort of a lump on the back of his head, he felt quite relaxed. His mind reverted again to two weeks ago and the events leading up to this journey.

CHAPTER 3

Jane's voice had soared over her piano accompaniment to 'Amazing Grace' but her stopping mid-line had his eyes flash open to see Vivienne, Paul's mother standing in the doorway. Distress etched her face as she supported Beatty who suddenly looked her seventy-seven years.

Jumping up, he'd led Beatty to sit down, while Vivienne struggled to speak. "It's Bill." Unsure of the problem they waited as she said haltingly, "He was asleep. Beatty went to wake him."

But as she paused, Beatty quietly announced, "The Lord's called my Bill home."

Jane who had moved to sit beside her, had taken her hand. "Oh Beatty, I'm so, so sorry. What can we do to help?"

She'd answered by patting Jane's hand because Vivienne continued speaking. "Maria confirmed he was…gone. Lillian is comforting her. Bob's making the necessary telephone calls. We left so Mum could say 'goodbye' to Bill. The doctor's just arrived, and Mum on hearing Jane playing asked if she could come up here with you." At that he'd nodded, and gently placed a reassuring hand on Beatty's shoulder. Addressing him Vivienne added, "Your parents and George are clearing up the party debris that's strewn around the basement lounge and kitchen."

About to offer tea, or something stronger, Beatty piped up, "That's the way my Bill would have wanted to go. One minute in the presence of all his family, the next in presence of His Lord. He looked younger, peaceful. And he'd such a smile of contentment as if seeing and welcoming the future he was moving on to." Jane handed her several paper handkerchiefs and after dabbing her tears Beatty looked up and refocused to tell them, "It's not a shock. Paul told me two years ago my Bill could go at any time. We've been so blessed to have such a good innings. Still, it's the same for all of us, we never know when God will call us home, and we should live every day as if our last."

David considered those words because if everyone did that the world might be a better place. He heard Jane ask Beatty if they should contact Paul and Jill. Immediately Beatty, the sprightly old lady, resurfaced with vehemence in her tone. "Good heavens, no. They've waited a year for a honeymoon Bill wouldn't want to spoil that."

Vivienne added, "Rosemary is very capable she's taken William to bath and bed him in Jill and Paul's bedroom, he can remain there until Bill's gone."

Hesitantly Beatty asked, "Jane would you feel it awful, disrespectful even, if I asked you to play again? To hear that music was a great comfort." Jane had smiled, hoisted herself up and while heading for the piano Beatty continued, "I'd like it if you could play at Bill's funeral." Jane had sent him a questioning look to which he'd shook his head believing it would be inadvisable for her to travel several hours in the latter stages of a twin pregnancy. As Jane played he'd made a big pot of tea, and when Lillian and Maria appeared he brought in more cups. After indicating they help themselves and feeling he might be useful downstairs, he'd rested his hand gently on Jane's shoulder, and murmured as he kissed her cheek, "I'll not be long."

He was halfway down when his parents emerged from the flat below. Although a few decibels quieter than usual, his father still boomed, "Sad business, my boy, sad business. This is hardly a time for Jane to be playing the piano."

In the hope of lowering his Dad's voice he pointed to the ground floor bedroom and replied quietly, "William's in there. Beatty asked Jane to play. It's very peaceful."

The booming resonance went to a quieter tone. "Oh right, yes, well, Bill looks peaceful, doesn't he Margaret, almost happy. Bob and George are dealing with everything and we've cleared up as best we can." Behind his Dad's back his Mum raised her eyebrows and shot him a quirky little smile. "It would seem, my boy, everyone is now congregating in your flat, and won't be going home for a while. I said to Margaret we should bring the leftover food up, but she thought it inappropriate with Bill still there."

"Probably right, Dad. There is still a free settee in our lounge for you and Mum. There's tea, but if you'd like something stronger, help yourselves. He paused on his way past Jill and Paul's bedroom and tapped gently on the door. Rosemary opened it with a finger across her lips. He mouthed 'Is everything alright?' as she stepped back so he could enter. Curled up in the double bed, looking so small, with his thumb in his mouth and Jill's teddy clasped against him, was William. Rosemary glided up beside him. He turned to her to whisper,

"Even in sleep there's something irresistible about that little fellow." The unmasked love that shone out of Rosemary's eyes as she looked down on William surprised him, as did a strange sense of companionship as they stood over the bed both adoring a child of which neither of them were its parent! Was Rosemary's expensive, yet understated way of dressing, quiet, cool and somewhat abrupt manner a camouflage for the real Rosemary? With a slight smile he beckoned her outside the door. Her large dark brown eyes widened, giving him a sense of her displeasure. Did she think he was encroaching on her personal territory? Rosemary had never succumbed to the wiles of his charm, but despite that he gave her a 'high wattage smile' before saying, "It seems everyone is congregating in our flat. Do join us. If you leave the door open we'll hear William if he wakes."

Rosemary took a deep breath and replied quietly, "Thank you. I'll stay. The open door and voices might awake William. I don't want him frightened when they take Bill away."

Anxious to encourage her, he agreed ruefully, "Of course. You're right. Forgive me. I'm just naturally bossy! With such a kind and gentle heart you'll make a wonderful mother."

Instantly a deep sorrow filled her eyes, the sculptured lips pursed and head bent the curtain of long dark hair closed over her face as she turned to open the bedroom door. Exasperated for making such a crass remark knowing Rosemary couldn't have children he'd scowled, ran his fingers through his hair and apologised. Rosemary didn't appreciate his overstepping the impersonal relationship they'd established while working together at ITP over the past two years. He was also aware that when upset Rosemary's cultured voice became more pronounced. "I'm sure David that you meant well." She entered the room, then turned, "Jane's playing always brings peace." He nodded at the truth of that. Whenever Jane played his heart and home seemed filled with love, and it had felt right that Bill should leave to such music. Encouraged, he volunteered the information, "Beatty has asked Jane to play at the..."

The door bell had cut off his words. Rosemary said, "That'll be the undertakers" and as he went to let them in Rosemary stepped back and closed the bedroom door.

After that there was a flurry of activity, and when later they gathered the food from the downstairs flat and took it up to their dining room, Rosemary hadn't joined them. Beatty seemed keen to encourage her family to talk of Bill and there was no doubt he and his Dad could learn a tip or two about how to serve their wives from the deceased Bill's life.

A motor bike roared past the car interrupting David's musings, and the noise awoke Jane to murmur, "Are we nearly there?" She winced in discomfort and exercised her neck before readjusting her sitting position.

"Yes, five minutes and we can stretch our legs. Let's hope Lillian has a sandwich and a cup of tea waiting for us."

Jane looked heavenward, "You and your stomach. We'll get Paul to look at the bump on your head."

"Just, as we'll get Paul to check the bump in your stomach." Crossly she sighed, but didn't refuse.

The moment they drew into the church car park Paul's family emerged. William holding Jill and Paul's hands was swinging between them. Bob and Lillian rushed to welcome them and as Bob helped Jane drag her cumbersome body from the car Lillian was offering a visit to the toilet, a cup of tea and a selection from the 'masses of food'." As they ambled towards the church hall door Paul came alongside to query, "Everything okay?"

He drew Paul to one side his tone grim. "I sincerely hope so. Remember that attack on Jane four years ago, well we stopped at a pub to use the toilets and Andrew Carlton was there."

Wide-eyed Paul asked, "No! The police thought he'd gone abroad."

"Apparently not! In wanting vengeance he tried to attack me. You teaching me those restraining techniques came useful. However, afraid for Jane, I lost concentration and he took the opportunity to swing a half pint dimple glass into the back of my head."

"Good heavens - let me see?"

"I'm more worried about Jane. She's been uncomfortable. I've seen her wincing. She says it's only those Braxton Hicks contractions. I've bargained with her, I'd let you check out my bump if she'd let you check hers." Paul chuckled and moved behind him as he explained, "I did see stars on impact, but like a bruise it only hurts now when I either touch it, or move my head."

"Umm, there's lump, but it will go down. Gran has the kettle boiling, so get a cuppa and something to eat while I check out last minute arrangements and Jane's bump."

Beatty poured him a cup of tea, thanked him for coming, told him to help himself to the spread laid on for those not going to the crematorium, and then asked anxiously, "Where's Jane?"

"She's with Lillian." He refrained from saying more, but Beatty nodded thoughtfully and suggested, "Jane must rest after the service. You don't need to stay here, or go to the crematorium. Paul has a key to Bob and Lillian's house. Go there, unpack and make yourselves at home. The family meal at my place won't be until about 7.30 pm, and only come if Jane feels up to it. Now I must change and be ready to greet Bill at the church gate."

Hungry, David consumed several sandwiches, a variety of savoury pastry treats that Jane would tut at him eating, and had poured himself another cup of tea before she appeared. Concerned, he stared at Paul , trying to read his expression.

"The journey has probably aided Jane's discomfort, and of course, at this stage there is always the risk of early labour. It's not unusual for twins to be born early, but I explained that to Jane last week."

Cross he challenged Jane. "You didn't tell me."

Jane's expression was haughty. "I assumed Paul told you."

Paul placed a hand on his back, and put his arm around Jane's shoulders. "Come on you two leave it there. You aren't in labour, and let's believe you won't be until after you return to London tomorrow. David, pour Jane a cup of tea and get her something to eat. We'll need you seated at the piano in about five minutes."

Still annoyed he obeyed Paul, and as she ate he growled, "If I'd have known birth could be that imminent I would have insisted you stay put."

"Oh David you worry too much, what does it matter where I have these babies, one hospital is much like another."

"Forgive me for repeating myself, but few hospitals come up to St Mary's standards, but that's not the point. Imagine the inconvenience. I'd have to stay here, we haven't the clothes for more than a day, and afterwards we'd have to transport two tiny babies on what could be a three hour journey."

Jane gave a heavy sigh, "Well, I'm not in labour, so no point harping on about it." She picked up a chicken wing, munched on it, and changing the subject said, "Bob asked me to stay seated at the piano. He's putting a chair beside me for you." Still fuming he nodded curtly and helped himself to several vol-a-vents and ignored Jane's frown of disapproval.

Entering the church they could see every pew and chair filled, and people standing at the back, Jane stated, "Bill was popular!" The platform was on several levels, and to accommodate the family, each level was being filled with chairs. At the top was the organ, David sighed with relief, that the piano was on the first level, and once Jane had climbed the steps she wouldn't have to negotiate them again until the end of the service. In the small area by the steps, before the stage widened, a chair had been placed behind Jane, for him.

The people quietened, as Jane ran her fingers over the keys, and at the signal she stopped and stood. The minister intoned, "Jesus is the resurrection and life…"

His pique with Jane dissipated as his heart swelled with pride at her musical ability. It was amazing with that huge bump how she managed to play at all let alone with such fluidity. It was a service Jane would call a 'hymn sandwich'! But she also played softly and sensitively as Paul spoke movingly of his Gramps in a blend of sadness and laughter, bringing people to remember a sprightly man, with a quick wit, and a generous nature. From where David sat he could see Jill wiping away tears. She'd become very fond of Bill. Paul returned to her side and put his arm around her as Bob stood to speak. When Bob sat there was a long silence. Puzzled David looked across at Paul who nodded towards Jane, and frowned. Should Jane be playing? Was something wrong? It wasn't obvious from her back view? Then just as he was about to lean forward Jane, without accompaniment sang, her voice ringing out, "*Pausing, listening, hear the voice of Jesus resting in the presence of the Lord, Waiting, ready, spending time together, Holy Spirit, come anoint us as we pray.*" The atmosphere was electric, no wonder she'd paused, it had given the song maximum affect. Jane played the melody to accompany the next verse: "*Touching, healing, like an ointment soothing, Breathing in the fragrance of the Lord, Speaking, revealing, guide us upward believing, In triumph through heaven's open door.*"

Jane's voice slightly faltering in that last line had him sitting up. He heard the continuing strain in her voice as she finished the verse. Was this proving too much for her? He glanced across at Paul, his expression showed his concern. Without hesitation he rose from his seat, took a step forward, and standing behind her placed his hands on her shoulders. His assuring squeeze met with the response of her shoulders rising against them as if gaining comfort or strengthen. At the next line he joined in. *"Remove the shoes from your feet, Lift your eyes to the mercy seat, Can't you see that the veil is torn in two?"* And continued singing until after the refrain in which her voice steadied enough for her to sing alone. The congregation probably thought this was how the song should be sung, and it was amazing how their voices had blended so well in harmony, and he felt to join in with her again to finish the last lines and the refrain, *"We take our place at the Father's feet, Ready for the marriage feast, Join with all creation in heaven's praise. For this is hallowed ground, where we stand, Let us rise before His throne, For this is hallowed ground."* He paused, she sang alone, *"Thou art holy"* before he sang with her, *"Thou art the Lord."* They finished by singing *'Hallelujah'* several times in a gentle wave of rhythm ending with *'Jesus'* sung twice and fading. The hushed reverence that followed caused him to believe they were indeed standing on hallowed ground.

Ten minutes later when the service ended with the enthusiastic singing of 'Amazing Grace', at the end of which the family filed out behind the coffin, he bent forward as Jane continued playing quietly, and whispered in her ear, "Jane Reinhardt, you've done brilliantly, that was a touch of heaven and I am so proud of you." As she continued to play she turned her head towards him. To his dismay tears were pouring down her face. In the small space beside her he pulled in his chair to ask , "What's the matter?"

"Oh David, I do love you." In a few seconds she tailed off her playing and turned to him. Ready with his handkerchief he handed it to her as she commented, "That song is usually awesome, but you joining in just took it to another level. I didn't know you knew the words."

Amused he retorted, "My dear Jane, I'm not deaf. Ever since you bought Phil's LP, you've played it and played it, and I suspect I know the words of most of the songs on it, some mornings I wake up with them echoing in my brain!"

Jane grinned, then with a gasp doubled forward.

"Are you having another of those Braxton contractions?

In a strained voice she said, "Oh David you are going to be

so cross." In the few seconds as he waited for her, head bent, to speak he wondered, what she'd been up to. When she looked up he could see the trepidation in her eyes. "I've been having a few sharp stabbing pains. My stomach is like a hard ball. I nearly stopped singing when the last one hit, and..." A grimace of revulsion filled her face, her voice went to a whisper, Oh no! David, I can't bear it. Up here, where everyone can see me, I'm feeling wet, I think my waters have broken. What am I going to do? This wasn't meant to happen now?"

That same sentiment echoed in his mind, but he knew to voice it wouldn't be helpful. To cover up his apprehension he said cheerily, "Never mind, we've done what we came for. We'd better head straight back home."

"I can't move yet. I've no control. I can't stop it. What are we going to do?"

He rubbed his hand across her shoulders. "Sit tight. When the church is completely empty, we'll go to Lillian's, get you changed and then home. I'll go and find..."

To his relief Paul was heading up the aisle towards them. "Sorry! I tried to get away sooner. Jill and Beatty are waiting in the car."

Despite trying to appear calm David heard the panic in his voice. "Jane's waters have just broken."

Paul's response was a thoughtful hum, nod and to say reassuringly, "These things happen. First step we'll get you to Lillian's. Am I right to say you've had a few brief, but sharp contractions?"

Jane bit her lip and nodded. "Your waters breaking could mean a rupture of either, or both twins' birth sac. Once that happens there is the risk of infection, the next step will be getting you to hospital."

In a quiet, but high pitched squeal Jane declared, "I can't have the babies here!"

"I'm sorry Jane, but despite not much happening in the next couple of hours, I'd not recommend trying to get home." Paul glanced up at his scowling face before pointing out quietly to Jane, "It was a risk you were willing to take." He looked at his watch. "Now the best thing is to get you to Lillian's, put your feet up, have a cup of tea and relax. As soon as we return from the crematorium I'll ring the hospital and ask their advice. It's been several years since I worked with the hospitals around here, but I might be remembered, and to come with you might ease your settling in."

Jane glanced between them and challenged, "If nothing much is going to happen, I've got time to go home."

David gave Paul a questioning look. Paul addressed Jane. "You were uncomfortable getting here. You would be even more uncomfortable getting back. One birth would be a risk, two small babies in need of expert care is not the place for a roadside, or ambulance delivery!"

"But if we go straight away, that's not likely to happen."

He stood. "Jane believe me birth is never predictable. Jill thought she'd a stomach ache then delivered the baby before she could reach the bedroom. Now you will have to excuse me I need to be with Jill and Gran."

"Paul I need directions to Lillian and Bob's house."

Paul rubbed the beard around his chin. "Look I'll tell the funeral car to go on. It will be easier to show you the way. And if I drop you off I can take your car and catch up with the cortege." Before David had time to consider Paul was heading off down the central aisle to the door.

Jane moaned, "My skirt is dripping wet"

Assuaged with guilt at taking Paul from Jill and Beatty when they needed him, he snapped, "Oh for goodness sake Jane. You are causing enough trouble as it is, stop worrying about such a trivial thing." To his consternation Jane burst into tears. and cried out, "But I want to go home. I don't want to stay here."

Paul called across the empty church, "David, bring your car around to the side entrance, we'll take Jane out that way. I'll be right back."

Although exasperated he endeavoured to hide it. "Look Jane we have to make the best of it. You insisted one hospital would be much like another, and let me tell you this will be much more of an inconvenience to me, than you. Now stop crying, I'm going to get the car." By the time he arrived at the side door, it was only a matter of seconds before Jane, with a woeful expression came out with Paul walking behind her. David leapt out to open the car's rear door as Paul suggested "Shall I drive? It would be easier than giving directions." And with a hard stare Paul added meaningfully, "Then you can sit in the back and support Jane."

Outwardly he might appear calm, but inwardly he was

struggling with vacillating emotions. Weeks of planning, expecting and waiting were now coming together, but not as anticipated and planned. How he hated things to be out of his control. Internal frustration and anger fought with the knowledge he should be loving and supportive.

"David will you stop scowling. It's me having these…" she winced and stopped speaking. Automatically his arm went around her. In the driving mirror he saw Paul's sympathetic glance towards him as he tried to settle her more comfortably against him.

Why hadn't he thought this through? Now he was in a predicament not of his making! And on Monday he was supposed to be taking up his new job! But worse, he still hadn't explained to Rosemary that as his personal assistant/secretary her input and experience would best serve Robert than her continuing to work with him. In the course of conversation he told Jill of his decision, her response was to say grimly, "Rosemary will not be happy about that. You know how sensitive she is around men, especially young ones like Robert, how old is he, twenty-eight? At his nod, she'd gone on, "Believe me she'd rather work for the devil she knows than one she doesn't!"

Irritated at Jill's comparison he'd responded with asperity, "Oh that's ridiculous! If she viewed me as the devil she wouldn't have stayed working for me this past two years."

Eyebrows raised Jill had given him a long look. "In which case David, show her some respect, common politeness or better still some care and consideration, by at least telling her your plans and reasons for them, before she finds out by your default."

He'd countered that by saying that he presumed as she enjoyed her job and was good at it, she'd want to stay even if it was working for Robert.

That had been Tuesday night, and on Wednesday he and Robert had been away meeting a group of their Exhibitors. That evening Rosemary had arrived home late, and apparently gone to her bedroom with barely a 'hello' so Jill had advised, "Tell her at work tomorrow." Yesterday several difficult issues took his attention, it had turned out to be one 'hell' of a day and he'd forgotten about Rosemary. Now instead of telling her face to face over this weekend, it looked as if he'd have to explain his decision to her on Monday over the telephone. If Jane knew she'd be exasperated at his lack of thought. Four years ago Jane had shown him that despite Rosemary's vindictive gossip about their engagement that to act with compassion, not condemnation could turn an arch enemy into a faithful friend. A year later Rosemary was sharing the downstairs flat with Jill, and not long after that started working for him. No longer being the bearer of gossip Rosemary had become a quiet, unpretentious female who rarely showed any emotion. When she did make a suggestion, give an opinion, it was swift, sharp and succinct. She then retreated into silence respected his space, and he hers.

Paul's voice interrupted his thoughts as the car drew up outside a semi-detached 1930s style house. "Here we are. Make yourselves at home. I'll get the luggage, you help Jane." Once inside Jane headed upstairs to find the bathroom as Paul called out after her, "The back bedroom is yours, put your feet up. David will bring you some tea." In the kitchen Paul filled the kettle, pointed out where things were and then commented quietly, "Try not to show your frustration, she might have felt brave, but now this is upon her, she will need your love and support. Get her to rest, sleep if possible, because you both have a long night ahead of you. I'll be about an hour. And despite the pains being regular they are very mild, but if you have any cause for anxiety ring for an ambulance, and tell them to go to the Parkfield Hospital. If you aren't here when I get back I'll know where to find you."

Ten minutes later Jane was sitting up on the bed, he'd plumped up all the pillows behind her, the tea was made, he'd eaten the cake, and under Jane's instruction was changing from his suit into his beige trousers, before separating out his things to repack the case for Jane to take to the hospital. A few months earlier frustrated by Jane's complaining he'd commented, "For goodness sake, you are only having a baby, it's a natural process."

To which she'd bitten back, "But David it doesn't feel a natural process and I'm having two babies not one. I didn't know pregnancy would be so difficult, so indulge me because I'm trying hard not to give way to fear."

Now he was trying hard not to give way to fear for having read Paul's medical books on childbirth he knew just what could go wrong, especially with twins. In every respect this was unknown territory and the situation one in which he had no control.

"David, do stop pacing. I saw Jill in the final throes of her very short labour and these babies aren't any where near being delivered. Come and sit down." Jane patted the bed beside her, "And please don't be cross. I'm sorry, I should have listened to you and Paul, but Beatty is so lovely, was so touched and comforted by my playing, how could I refuse her request for me to play at the funeral?"

Sinking on the bed beside her, he took her hand, gave a sympathetic smile while nodding, "I know. And I'm pleased I came with you." Gently he placed his hand over her stomach, it certainly felt hard. "When I went to get the car several people stopped me to say how moved they were by your playing" he smiled down at her, "and were especially touched by our last song!"

"Were they, oh I am pleased." From a bright smile she went to a rueful expression. "I know you wanted me to have all the luxury and expertise of St Mary's, but Paul said all hospitals are well equipped and can cope with any delivery. I didn't expect this, but maybe the upset of this morning set me off." Her hazel eyes filled with anxiety, "You won't leave me. You will stay with me. I can't do this without you."

"Good heavens Jane, you may have thwarted my plans, but you surely don't believe I'd drop you at the hospital and ask them to phone me when my babies are delivered?" Before she could answer he moved his hand from her bump to cup her face and leaned forward to kiss her downturned mouth. When he felt the tension slip from her, he sat back, waited, and then smiled, pleased he still had the skill to cause her eyes to glaze over. From her throat came pleasurable hum before she murmured, "Umm I love you, and I love your kisses."

The smile turned to a grin. "Is that so? Then I suggest you sleep now, and I'll wake you in true Sleeping Beauty fashion."

Just as he stood, she became alert. "David, what about your new job, you start on Monday?"

"Let's get the weekend over first and worry about that later."

"Don't go because there is something I want to ask you." Obediently he sat back down and grasping his right ankle resting on his left knee gave her his attention. "What did Andrew mean when he said today you were heir apparent to the Reinhardt millions?"

46

With consummate skill, practised over years, he kept his face expressionless. Inwardly he'd hoped she hadn't picked up on that! Outwardly he said with a nonchalant shrug. "Hopefully it will be some considerable years before Jill, Paula and I inherit Inhart Pharmaceuticals. Obviously it's a successful business, but as it is I have my job and it provides for us." To end the conversation he stood, lent forward and ran the nub of his finger down her cheek. Now I think you should try and sleep."

Suspicion formed in Jane's eyes as she pointed out, "David I haven't finished drinking my tea. Tell me more about you inheriting Inharts?"

Slowly he settled back down on the bed while considering how to answer. "You know Dad was awarded the MBE because of his continually reinvesting in research to find drugs to combat debilitating diseases. And of course there is his support to third world countries by opening factories and employing local people in the manufacture of drugs."

Impatiently Jane pointed out, "David, that's not an answer. Is Inharts worth millions?"

He shrugged, "I'm not privy to the extent of its profits. Now drink your tea, it's getting cold."

She frowned at him, took several mouthfuls, and commented, "From what I've seen your family isn't poor, so let me ask another way - are they millionaires?"

This time he gave a rueful grimace. "I've told you how Dad has always expected us to stand on our own two feet. But he did release money to help me buy our house, and then to Jill as an investment so we could convert it to two flats." Jane clicked her tongue in frustration so he added, "Dad rarely talks about money, but, yes, that's my understanding." At Jane's wide-eyed stare he rushed on, "But we don't talk about it."

Puzzled she questioned, "Why not?"

"Dad wants us to live independent of any fortune he may have. You know about my drifting towards marriage with Felicity because her family and mine were friends. What you don't know is Felicity and Dad had a massive row. She found out that despite my being 'heir apparent' we would be reliant on my salary, which to her mind, was paltry. My only involvement in that was Felicity's fury at Dad's tight-fistedness with money. Anyway a few weeks later Felicity found an excuse to break off our engagement." He ignored Jane's wide-eyed look and finished, "I was astonished she sent back the ring, but I think it was more a statement of her discontent, and the belief I'd be so upset I'd persuade Dad to part with his money. But she didn't expect me to accept it and say nothing."

"You mean Felicity didn't break off your engagement because you rescued me from Andrew's clutches?"

Surprised he responded, "Is that what you thought?"

"I wasn't sure, and it's never occurred to me to ask." Puzzled she thought aloud, "But Felicity came to ITP's Christmas Party as your partner, and your New Year's Eve housewarming which gave me to believe your engagement might be on again. That was backed up by hearing a group of your friends saying she'd brought you out of yourself, you'd been far too serious for too long."

Amused he chuckled, "I needed a foil for how I felt about you, Felicity obliged. My friends weren't talking of Felicity, but you. At Christmas we'd met up for a meal and several of them noticing I was more relaxed and happy asked, 'Who is she?' I gave them a brief update, but obviously at the party they guessed you were the fiery little lady who had stolen my heart." Bemused she handed him her cup as he went on, "I can also tell you that once Dad had met you, he made it clear he'd prefer you as his daughter-in-law, and I was in agreement with him. But you already thought I wasn't 'in your league' by what you saw as my position at ITP, the house I lived in, and the money I earned. I guessed if you had any ideas of my family's wealth I'd lose you, for the opposite reasons to Felicity. And for once I was pleased Dad had never climbed the housing ladder. When you visited 'Four Chimneys' that first time and saw the size of the house, and what you thought was our wealth you went very quiet. Thanks to a chaotic family weekend revealing people with money were still people with problems, you spoke up, your advice was taken and I saw you blossom under that acceptance. But the truth is Jane, with Dad's investments, here and abroad, and not just Inharts, they could probably buy a stately home, and have money to spare."

Jane sitting up exclaimed, "You're joking?" then winced.

"Another pain?" He looked at his watch, "That's about half an hour. I think you ought to rest."

"No, no carry on. Take no notice of me. What kind of stately home?"

He grinned, "Well, maybe not Hampton Court, or Buck House, but if it came up for sale they could easily purchase Kelston Park, that mansion on the hill by us. Believe me none of us had any idea of Dad's accumulation of wealth until Jill met and tangled with Lord Mallory alias Peter Sanchez. As difficult as all that was it did change Dad, and of late he's been more open to talking about things. And he has admitted that managing his money is a responsibility of magnitude proportions which weighs like a heavy stone around his neck." That thought brought him to grimace. "And when he can no longer bear it, it will, I'm afraid, be passed on to us. But I am grateful I haven't had the responsibility up to now and I wouldn't want to put that burden on our children either. Even knowing money is available can corrupt lives."

To which Jane responded sharply, "Well I assure you it isn't going to corrupt mine. I'm very satisfied with what we have, and have no desire for more. Your Dad is certainly doing good things with his fortune, but had I known I would have questioned how we, from two very different backgrounds, could make a marriage work. I've barely adjusted to living in such a lovely big house, having Mrs P do all the housework, being able to buy whatever we need without thinking about it, and then there's the money you give me to spend."

At that he scowled, "Which is meant to be for you!"

"Exactly, and I spend it when and where I want to."

Grimly he demanded, "Let's not get into that again."

Pursing her lips she gave him a hard look and then commented, "I understand your original motive for not telling me about your father's fortune, but we've been married three years. How long did you intend to keep this information from me?" Unable to answer he shrugged. Jane considered aloud, "I did think they must be richer than I supposed because of that kidnapping business, but millions… That brings me to respect and love them even more for their acceptance of me, and my family who are, in comparison, paupers,"

"Oh Jane, that's an exaggeration. And money doesn't make a person, character does, and you, your Mum and Ted are people of integrity. As far as I was concerned I could see no purpose in telling you until there was a necessity to do so."

"Well my integrity as you call it would agree with that. And certainly I don't want to carry that mill-ion stone…" she grinned at her play on words, "…around our necks, nor inflict it on our babies." Subconsciously she patted her tummy.

"Oh Jane you are indeed priceless, I doubt many would see money as a millstone or it being an infliction! So what would you suggest?"

"It's simple. There are hundreds of organisations all over the world needing money to run their projects. Let's explain to your father we want a family life, and ask him to begin setting up ways to siphon off the excess then it won't be our problem in the future."

He shook his head and explained, "Unfortunately it isn't that simple! With money comes responsibility and influence! The constant accumulation, managing the assets and disposal can be quite a headache! Some people would say money is the kind of headache they'd like. But if you have a family, an interest in research, a desire to help others, it's difficult when you are diverted from what you want to do by the necessity of banking, building and bunting! I think Dad has a lot of regrets and doesn't want them passed on to us."

Immediately Jane retorted, "In which case he'll be willing to release most of the money now so it won't be a burden to his children later. And if he's willing I am sure between us we have the expertise to find a way to simplify the dispensing of the excess funds before that time comes." Snuggling back against the pillows she went on, "But my brain isn't on full function so let's postpone this discussion, I'll think about it as I try to sleep." Her mouth curved into a provocative smile, "I'll look forward to being awakened."

CHAPTER 4

Jane's terminology of "excess funds" had given David an idea. Quietly he closed the bedroom door and bounded down the stairs to the telephone. His father barked his name down the phone, but on hearing David's voice he asked, "What's wrong? It's not like you to ring me at work." David didn't acknowledge that to do so usually brought his father's short, sharp rebuke at disturbing him from something important, and went straight to the point.

"Jane's gone into labour and I'm afraid Dad we're stuck in Kent. Paul doesn't recommend what could be a three hour car journey home."

He held the phone away from his ear as his father boomed, "Kent! You can't have the babies there. Everything is booked at St Mary's. Beveridge is lined up to do the delivery. Does he think Jane will be quick like Jill?"

"I don't think so."

Obviously peeved his father went on, "I don't know why you had to travel all that way in the first place - it's not as though Bill was a relative. You let that girl have too much of her own way. Well, you're just going to have to deal with the consequences. Get her a private room, ensure she gets the best treatment, I'll pay as arranged."

"Thank you Dad, but I wondered if you might consider an alternative."

Barked, into the phone were the words, "Such as?"

Bracing himself for the response he continued, "Hiring a helicopter!"

Almost anticipating the loud retort he held the telephone receiver from his ear. "A helicopter? Good grief boy, what will you think of next? Have you any idea of the cost? Let alone availability, red tape and flying regulations over London. The very thought is preposterous! This isn't a national emergency. I'll get on to Beveridge perhaps he could come there to do the delivery."

To put his father in the picture he explained, "We were staying tonight at Bob and Lillian's, so I can stay here, and once Jane is admitted to hospital I will ring you with news of her progress. Will you tell Mum?"

The answer was snapped, "Of course!" Then clearing his

throat his father added, "If that girl of yours…if there were an emergency, that helicopter, well you could rely on me."

"Thanks Dad, I appreciate that."

Next he rang Jane's mum who understandably was worried and keen to catch the train to be there. With the thought he'd have to return to London once the babies were born he persuaded her to wait a day or so. But unable to sit he paced up and down the lounge watching for Paul's return.

It had been with great foresight that his German grandfather in disliking Hitler had disposed of the majority of his liquid assets before the war. And sent all he could with his son when he came to live in England with his in-laws on a farm near Bristol. Three years later, they heard that his grandparents had lost their lives for hiding Jews, and Hitler had confiscated their small family pharmaceutical business, home and contents. In the meanwhile, in England, his father had wisely invested monies in a Trust Fund for his children, and used the remainder to convert an old barn on the farm into a research laboratory and small manufacturing plant. There Inhart Pharmaceuticals had been born, and after the war with the establishing of the National Health Service demand brought fast expansion, then exports, and now the name Inharts was known in every continent. As children they'd known little about the business except their father was often away, and didn't take kindly to the demands of children, be it his time, or his money. The Trust Fund had provided their education and for the careers of their choice, but his father was quick to point out if they wanted the 'frivolities of life' they had to work for them. However, money had been released when he'd told his mother of the opportunity to buy a cheap, bombed out house in London where the family had died and distant relatives wanted a quick sale.

Later engaged to Felicity and with the house still in need of extensive renovation, the money came forth again this time for Jill to use as an investment in his property. It was only after Jill's unfortunate adventure two years ago that his father admitted the Trust Fund had long been empty, and it had been his gift to invest in their futures.

Felicity's desire for an engagement ring of a large oval sapphire surrounded by diamonds had meant the need to forego some of the planned refurbishment to their upstairs flat. At the time she'd accepted that, but later had a tantrum because he refused to get a loan for a new kitchen and wouldn't approach his father to fund it. But ignoring his wishes she began to drop hints about their need of money. At first his father ignored her, her perseverance received a grim look, but on being asked outright his father had barked, "You are marrying my son, not me. He earns a good salary and is perfectly able to provide more than adequately for you. If you aren't content with that perhaps you'd better consider whether you are marrying him for love, or for the money you think he should have. And, if you want to be accepted by us, then I suggest you refrain from ever bringing up the subject again." Shocked into silence Felicity had later berated him for not 'being on her side' and a few days later returned the ring. That news had brought his father to respond, "Good riddance to the wretched woman. She wasn't in love with you, but what she saw would one day be your money."

To which he'd retorted, "What money? I'm hardly heir to a fortune."

In a gruff voice his father replied, "Inhart Pharmaceuticals has made me a rich man." Astonished he'd wanted to ask more, but his father had marched off indicating the discussion had ended. Yet for his birthday the following January his father had enclosed a substantial cheque with a note, "This is an investment in your future. Finish off the house, propose to Jane and buy her a ring that will reflect the diamond she is."

What a pleasure it had been to meet Felicity a few months later in Bath and his mother announce, "David and Jane have just got engaged, Jane dear, show Felicity your ring." The look Felicity had given him was such to kill, and later she subjected him to a telephone tirade of spite.

Still pacing the room he again looked at his watch wondering how much longer Paul would be when his car drew up outside. Rushing to the front door he opened it before Lillian could put the key in the lock. With a light laugh she exclaimed, "Oh David, you are obviously excited. I haven't given birth myself, but when I became a substitute mother for Paul's Maria and she was placed in my arms, I felt such joy."

Paul smiled at her. "And I couldn't have wished for a more loving couple to step into the breach and be her parents. Now David tell me how is the lady in waiting?" On hearing she was asleep he continued, "Good, we'll leave her there for now. I'll ring Parkfield Hospital. Relax David, your babies arrival will be some while yet."

Unaccustomed nerves, and wanting to hear what Paul was saying on the telephone in the hall, made it hard for him to focus on Bob and Lillian's polite conversation, and they all looked up on Paul's return. Apologising for taking so long he explained, "The Parkfield is only five minutes away, but when they knew you were expecting twins they explained they didn't have a special care baby unit and said if it wasn't urgent to go direct to the 'The General'. That's thirty minutes drive away. I rang them, they've no free antenatal beds at present, but was advised Jane should go there as soon as possible. The Staff Nurse anticipated a bed would be available by the time we arrive."

David nodded. "I've spoken to Dad, he wants to pay for Jane to have a private room and is going to ask Beveridge to do the delivery."

Paul looked sceptical. "Did he indeed! I doubt Beveridge and his team would be persuaded to do a delivery in Kent. Imagine the cost! And private beds - I'm not even sure 'The General' has any of those."

"But cheaper than the helicopter I asked for."

Paul chuckled, "You didn't. I bet he refused. Yet in an emergency, like that military coup in Africa, he did pay for that clinical team to be airlifted out."

Gruffly, not unlike his father he commented, "This feels like an emergency to me."

An hour later Paul drove them in through the hospital gates and, as directed, they reported to the Casualty Department Reception just inside the entrance. In waiting for the transfer to the Maternity Ward Paul chatted to the staff, but ten minutes later returned to tell them he was unable to call in any favours because all the people he knew had moved on. On hearing that he assured Paul they'd be fine and persuaded him to take the car, go to his family meal, and he'd ring Beatty when he needed a lift home.

But once Paul had gone he didn't feel quite so confident with Jane wincing in pain at frequent intervals. In enquiring about private rooms the Receptionist informed him they were reserved for people who needed them. At his arguing that Jane needed one, the woman looked down her nose and informed him that the Ward Sister would be the judge of that. Unused to being thwarted, and having to wait he paced up and down, and twice badgered the Receptionist believing they'd been forgotten. The second time the woman gave him a long look, drew in a deep breath and replied firmly, "Mr Reinhardt your wife is a long way from the last throes of labour, she will be collected as soon as they can spare someone to do so. Now please, sit down, and relax."

Some while later a flustered young nurse burst in with a wheelchair, and dashing over said, "Mrs Reinhardt? I'm Nurse Timmins. I'm so sorry to have kept you waiting, it's the shift change over and…well, it's been hectic. Now we've a bit of a walk so best you sit in this."

As Jane obeyed, David jumped forward. "I'll do that, you direct me."

"Thank you. I believe Mrs Reinhardt you come from London…" As she chatted to Jane his heart sank because on leaving the more modern two storey building housing the Casualty Department their walk took them down a narrow road between row upon row of red bricked single storey buildings with concrete paths between them. He doubted Nurse Timmins' chatter was causing Jane to regularly turn and send him apprehensive looks. Behind his reassuring smile he grimly considered the place, which resembled an army barracks, was aptly named, 'The General'. Their destination indicated by worn looking signs. The 'Maternity Wards' consisted of two long huts linked to a smaller building at the end forming a three-sided square. Nurse Timmins pointed out the wooden benches around the grassed area where mums, babies and visitors could sit outside. Appalled at all he'd seen so far he mocked, "Nice!" at which Jane turned to give him a dark look.

Once through the door marked 'Antenatal' they were in a utilitarian vestibule with several doors. Nurse Timmins stopped and pointed to a door on their left marked 'Day Room' and instructed, "Please wait in there. I'll be back shortly." Ahead through open double doors they could see the Ward where the beds on either side formed a long corridor. However by the entrance there were several glass partitioned rooms. Once inside the Day Room David inwardly groaned. The décor, furniture and lino had seen better days. Admittedly someone had placed a vase of flowers in the midst of the battered dining room table, books were in the bookcase, and the dog-eared magazines on the coffee table were tidy. This wasn't the beautifully appointed room with the comfortable furniture, the quiet music and the atmosphere of calm support giving confidence in the expertise of those around them.

With the parody of a cheerful smile, but lost for words he stood by the metal framed French doors and looked out through one of the square window panes to the uncomfortable looking benches outside. At the sound of people talking in the corridor, the main door opening and closing David realised it was visiting time. His mind recalled seeing a notice, he sighed heavily, visiting was only two hours in the afternoon and one in the evening. This was another consequence of Jane's foolish decision to travel to Kent, he was going to be stuck for hours on end with nothing to do.

"Oh David, please don't scowl. I should have listened to you. Jane looking miserable declared, "One hospital isn't much like another, is it? This place is old and shabby, quite horrible!" Pulling herself up out of the wheelchair she pleaded, "Please don't leave me here?"

At her anxiety he forced himself to say jovially, "Well, it's not what I envisaged, but we'll manage, and look on the bright side in a few days we'll be home with our little family." He drew her to one of the plastic covered green armchairs and sat down beside her. To deflect the problem he took her hand and suggested, "With our babies on the verge of being born we should decide on names." He began with 'Samson and Delilah' and although her eyes pleaded with him he was relieved to receive a small smile as she squeezed his hand. They had just concluded it would be better to name each child after it was born when a smiling, pleasant and buxom young woman opened the door with a file in her hand.

"Mrs Reinhardt I'm Staff Nurse Adams, the midwife. If you come with me I'll take your medical history and examine you to determine how far labour has progressed." In seeing Jane give him tentative look she added, "Your husband can come too."

Nurse Adams friendly chatter as she made notes seemed to relax Jane, but the answering of what seemed endless questions caused David to run his hand through his hair and ask, "Is there much more of this?"

Jane frowned, and then suggested, "Why don't you go for a walk, find a telephone box and bring our Mum's up to date?"

Pleased she was happy to be alone, he agreed and apologised

to Nurse Adams for his impatience. Her response was a nod of understanding with the words, "The waiting is a difficult time for Dad's and especially in these circumstances."

Aimlessly, he wandered along the deserted narrow concrete paths worrying how the next few days might pan out. Eventually directed by a nurse he found the closed WRVS shop and telephone boxes. By the time he'd made his calls the sun had gone down, and in making his way back along the narrow road in the dusk he saw his car coming towards him. Paul came to a halt beside him, but as he rolled down the window David, unable to stop himself, said flatly, "I've just rung Dad, he says Beveridge isn't coming, this place is ghastly, and they don't 'do' private rooms!"

Paul grimaced, "I have to park the car so jump in and tell me about it."

By the time he'd poured out his woes, they'd reached the door of the Antenatal Ward, and Jane waiting on the doorstep demanded, "Where have you been?" Not waiting for an answer, and barely acknowledging Paul, she burst out, "The midwife says I'm only two centimetres dilated and I'll be hours yet. I want to go home." Concerned he looked at Paul for advice.

Cautious Paul inquired, "Did the midwife agree to that?"

"She said it was 'extremely unlikely I'd have the babies in the next few hours. David, I can't stay here, it's just too awful, and I've plenty of time to get home."

Paul questioned, "And the midwife's advice was…?"

Jane grunted before admitting, "That as soon as a bed was available she'd recommend I got in it, and try to sleep for tomorrow would be a tiring day."

At that Paul chuckled, "Good try Jane, so let's go in and see how soon you can take her advice."

In the Day Room Jane introduced them to Stella. She looked between the two men as Jane continued, "Stella said the Sister on the ward is very strict, but I told her David you could be pretty fearsome too." David wondered if he'd unintentionally scowled at Stella for having looked between them she seemed uncomfortable, borne out by her saying awkwardly, "I'd better go. Sister Keenan likes us to be in bed by ten. Woe betide me if I'm not there." They watched her leave and as the door closed Jane explained, "Stella's been here two weeks, she's got high blood pressure. She's never seen the ward this busy. The two girls in her room are in heavy throes of labour, but there's a bottleneck for the delivery room." Jane looking around the room cringed, "I hope they have better equipment than they have furniture." Paul said nothing, but looked thoughtful. Jane, like a drowning woman grasping a life line asked. "Paul are you absolutely sure I'd be better off staying here?"

Paul didn't hesitate, "I'm sure. It's…"

A brusque voice interrupted to question, "What is going on here?" Of one accord they turned. In the doorway stood a big built, middle-aged, woman with a grim expression. "Only fathers are allowed in after visiting hours, so which one of you is Mr Reinhardt?"

Before he could reply, Paul stepped forward, glanced at her badge and said, "Good evening Sister Keenan, I'm Dr Stemmings."

Sister Keenan used her forefinger to push her thick glasses back on her nose as if to see him better. Having stared at him she asked sharply, "Do I know you Dr Stemmings?"

Paul smiled, "It's possible. I worked in Casualty about five years ago and at various times in GP surgeries nearby."

There was derisory grunt before she issued, "Well you have no jurisdiction here! This is my ward, and it's not visiting time. We now have a bed so Mrs Reinhardt come along let's get you installed and asleep." Jane waddled towards the door as Sister Keenan continued, "We'll call you, Mr Reinhardt, when the birth is imminent."

Taken aback Jane stopped to protest, "Oh no! I want David to stay with me."

Sister Keenan pursed her lips, gave her a cold look, and stated to the room, "I rarely allow fathers in my labour ward. If I do it's because the delivery is straightforward. Any problems, they're out! With twins, delivery is never termed as simple." Her eyes rested on him. "Go home Mr Reinhardt, we'll let you know your wife's progress in the morning."

Incensed he boomed, "That's ridiculous. Archaic! I want to be with my wife when she delivers our babies."

"Good heavens Mr Reinhardt, do keep your voice down. And remember this isn't one of your fancy London hospitals. If you wanted one of those then you should have had more sense than to travel with a pregnant wife of thirty-six weeks expecting twins."

A restraining hand on his arm from Paul caused him to bite back his retort. Jane turned towards him, her words choked as she begged, "Don't go. Please... I can't... do this without you."

Aghast, at the developing situation David stepped to Jane's side, and putting his arm around her, sent Sister Keenan the intimidating glare that usually routed any foe. Oblivious, or ignoring him, she summoned Nurse Timmins who was passing to command, "Take this case and Mrs Reinhardt to the ward." Jane burying against him, caused her to snap, "Oh for goodness sake Mrs Reinhardt, you aren't the first woman to have twins and you won't be the last. And believe me, you will be doing it without your husband because those babies will be delivered, there is no 'can't do it' or 'don't want to' about it."

Horrified he and Paul exchanged a glance. The woman was a monster! Paul's almost imperceptible shake of his head warned him not to interfere. Desperate he sought for a solution and hoped Paul, who was stroking his beard, would come up with one.

Jane, at Sister Keenan's rebuke was trying to be brave, and to encourage her he said lightly, "Go with the Sister, I'm sure she'll let me see you safely settled." He bent to give her a hug and with a quick kiss whispered, "I won't be far away." Obediently Jane followed Nurse Timmins, but gave several backward glances, while he determined to keep smiling and nodding encouragingly.

Arms folded Sister Keenan stood in the doorway as though waiting for Jane to be out of earshot. Quietly, but firmly, she said, "Mr Reinhardt you can stay in this Day Room as long as you wish, but you will only enter my ward at visiting times, or to see your offspring once they are born." Screaming from the far end of the corridor took her attention, she tutted as though irritated, then went on, "On this ward what I say goes. Dear me, I'll have to go and deal with that woman, but by the time I get back, I will expect you both to have left." With that she turned on her heel and was gone.

Paul looking around the dreary room commented, "Oh dear!"

"What do you mean, 'oh dear'! Is that all you can say. There must be something we can do?"

"Not at this time of night. From the slow progress Jane is making I doubt she'll be having those babies before lunch time tomorrow."

Appalled he could only echo, "Lunch time tomorrow! I say Paul we risk it and get her home. Jane can't stay here. I have to be with her. I promised her. There are no private beds. Heaven knows what the delivery equipment will be like. When your sister Hazel was in London and her water's broke she made the journey back here."

Paul sighed. "That decision David went against my judgement and she was having one baby, not two. It was known to be a good weight, breathing difficulties weren't anticipated or the need of special care. Twins being smaller usually need incubators for at least the first few hours which was why Parkside wasn't suitable."

Although agreeing with Paul that to relocate Jane could put the twins at risk he groaned before asking, "What other alternative is there? Shall I ring Dad and tell him it's an emergency, for it will be if I can't get past that woman and see my babies born." Thoughtfully Paul stroked his beard. Desperately David questioned, "What about another hospital, not to far away? Surely they don't all have these archaic rules? And have you seen the sign about visiting times?" Exasperated he ran his hand through his hair.

Paul grimaced. "Teaching hospitals, especially in London, are more forward thinking. It didn't occur to me that the more parochial ones might still expect a man to pace the floor awaiting the news of his baby's birth. Visiting restrictions are normal, except of course in the private sector!" Tiredly, he went on "I'll look into it in the morning. There's nothing we can do now, although she might be too far on tomorrow to consider a transfer."

In despair David raked his hair several times asking, "Oh God, if that happens what am I going to do? I can't let Jane down."

"Well then my friend we'd better begin by asking God to help us to find an alternative, or a way to overrule the fearsome Sister Keenan."

Ten minutes later a young, pretty probationer who reminded him of Maria entered, and after apologising for interrupting them, she reported chirpily, "Sister said to tell you your wife is calm, comfortably settled and should get some sleep." Stepping further into the room, she glanced around as if the walls might have ears, and added in a conspiratorial tone, "Sister Keenan told me to get rid of you both. She can be…well she has standards, and is a 'no nonsense' sort of person, but she does have a kind heart. Work with her, and she'll respect you." Paul and David looked at each other wondering what she was getting at. "She's the night-sister, her shift ends at 7.00 am, and she'll not be back again until 7.00 pm!"

Paul spoke first, "Are you saying the rules are more relaxed during the day?" She nodded. "Does that mean David could be with Jane at the birth of the twins?"

Nurse Evans replied, "I don't know about the birth, but Sister Brodie is all for helpful Dad's, she feels it makes her job easier and the mother more relaxed. If you obey Sister Keenan now, and return about 8.00 am she will have gone, and Sister Brodie will have every reason to look favourably on you, and certainly turn a blind eye to you sitting with Jane." At that moment he could have hugged the girl, but instead he thanked the Lord as this could be an answer to their prayers. Nurse Evans was continuing to speak to Paul. "When I heard Sister Keenan mention your name I remembered you. You worked at our doctor's surgery, and were very kind to me when I had measles. You told me you had a daughter about my age, and she'd caught them too."

Paul smiled, "And similarly my daughter, like you, is now interested in caring for others, and hopefully she'll be as helpful to her patients as you've been to us tonight."

A blush defused over Nurse Evans face, but encouraged she offered, "I did think of something else that might be helpful. The Obstetrics Consultant is Mr Freeman. I noted down his telephone number because you being a doctor, well he might at least let you in at the birth, and Sister Keenan wouldn't argue with him." David doubted that, but hoped Paul might be willing to try. "But go now. I'll tell Jane what's afoot and hopefully she'll get some sleep. But if things happen before 8.00 am I'll personally ring the number you've given us." While David grappled with his dismissal without saying 'goodbye' to Jane, Paul had his arm and was heading him out the door saying. "Thank you. We really appreciate your help. Come on David, time to go."

The lights to the Day Room were switched off as they left, the main doors locked behind them. On the way back to the car Paul commented, "Now that was definitely God's provision. I vaguely remember her covered from head to toe with a rash, and it won't do any harm to take up her suggestions. Jill will understand if I'm not around tomorrow." Paul's hand clapped him on the back, "Come on, let's get back to Grans. Cheer up, my friend for tomorrow you become a father."

CHAPTER 5

Beatty's relatives were leaving as Paul and David arrived, but stopped to express concern for Jane, and their admiration of her musical abilities proclaiming it had made the funeral into a beautiful occasion. Paul sent an exhausted Beatty to bed, and Jill serving David a meal said, "I hear you had a run in with Andrew. If I saw Rich Mallory again I'd probably want to kill him." As she and Paul cleared and washed up, David between mouthfuls relayed what happened, and hearing he'd learnt Paul's restraining techniques caused Jill amusement. But both were perplexed by the black man that no-one else had seen, and looked sceptical at his being a guardian angel! Although in the ensuing discussion David felt to proclaim Jane's Mum's theory, 'God takes care of His own, and woe betide those who touch His anointed'."

Jill looking serious commented, "God then had better take care of Jane, for having the twins here is definitely going to be inconvenient, especially if you want to see your babies born."

Paul intervened, "I'd say God's already working on that" and he went on to tell her the latest developments.

David, having finished his meal as Paul and Jill joined him with their cups of hot chocolate, grimaced and said, "Unfortunately from our encounter with Andrew I've another problem. Andrew raved on about me being heir apparent to Dad's millions. I hoped Jane hadn't latched on to that, but she asked me about it at Lillian's."

"I'm surprised two years ago she didn't query why anyone would want to kidnap me."

"I think Jill, because Dad owns Inharts, Jane assumed the ransom money would come through the company. Obviously she sees us as wealthy, but let's face it, none of us know the extent of Dad's fortune. After Felicity's departure Dad said he didn't want to burden us, his children, with the complexity of his investments, but it was sufficient to know that at his death we'd be very rich." With a wry grimace, he added, "Jane's response to that news was that we already have more than enough we should help Dad give his money away before his death!"

Jill gave a loud chortle and clapped her hands. "Now why doesn't that surprise me? Dad made his dislike of Felicity quite clear after she wanted to spend his money. What will be his reaction to Jane wanting to give it away."

With vehemence David replied, "I know my reaction when I found she was giving mine away!" Paul and Jill stared at him so he explained. "We'd been married about eighteen months and in Derry & Toms I suggested she try on a dress she'd admired in the window. She said it was too expensive, but I insisted. Despite my saying it really suited her she seemed unsure, and rejoining me said quietly it wasn't worth it. She tried to draw me from the cash desk, but I stood my ground telling her I liked it, so it was worth it, to write a cheque and be done with it. In the end she had to confess before the sales woman that her bank account was empty. Cross, I asked how was that possible. With a sheepish face she announced others needed it more than she, and she'd given it away. Outraged, I demanded, 'Given it away, given it to whom?' It was then I noticed the shop assistant's interest and steered her into the lift. Jane was livid. She said I'd embarrassed her…"

Jill grinning interrupted, "That makes a change, from my observations it's usually the other way around."

"Um that's as maybe! Anyway I wanted to know where the money had gone. Her retort was, 'You said I could spend it on what I wished. I've done that! And on something far better than an overpriced dress', with that she marched out of the store. I was furious and so was she. For the next few days she'd not tell me, but finally confessed to supplying that large 'miracle box' of food left on the doorstep of the Ryan family when the Sean lost his job. That she was the 'provision of the Lord' for the missionary couple who were going to Nigeria. The remainder she'd loaned to her Mum and Ted to install central heating in their house while waiting for Ted's to sell." He shrugged, "I know they repaid her, but I suspect she gave it away again. Obviously she's kept enough to buy pregnancy clothes, and she assures me she will buy new things once she's back to 'normal'!"

While Jill grinned knowingly, Paul stroking his beard said thoughtfully, "I can't speak on behalf of Jill or Paula, but working for Inharts is one thing, but I don't want to be saddled with the responsibility of one company, or your Dad's personal fortune. I'd say as a family we need to talk about what will be inherited. Even as a tax issue money would be better in a charitable Trust Fund before his death, than after. And why not help needy people and worthwhile organisations now."

Taking the issue more seriously Jill suggested, "We'd need to talk to Paula and Jim before we approach Dad. I'd not thought about us inheriting perhaps millions of pounds, and I doubt they have either. Jane could be our spokeswoman. Dad's got a real soft spot for her. After all he insisted on paying for her to go into the private wing of St Mary's to have the twins."

"But did reject David's suggestion of a helicopter to collect and fly her there!"

Jill wide-eyed questioned, "You didn't…" David nodded, she grinned as Paul pointed out, "And my dear wife he would have paid for you to be in St Mary's. But with your DIY birth, and doctor husband, you insisted in staying at home, and just as I was looking forward to a few nights undisturbed rest."

Jill gave Paul a friendly punch as David yawning said, "Talking of which, I need to drive to Lillian's so I can get some rest while I can."

Despite that resolve, once in bed his mind was crowded with confused worries and anxieties. When he finally slept he dreamt again of being on horseback and riding away from the dawn, only to awake as the birds heralded in a new day. Mulling over the dream he remembered hearing, over the thundering of the horses' hooves, the words, 'the gates of hell shall not prevail'. Sitting up, knowing those words were in the Bible, he lent over to pick it up, found the verse and closed his eyes to ask the Lord what it meant. As if by an unseen hand he felt a thick wad of the Bible's pages turn over. His eyes flash opened to read, "And we know that all things work together for good to them that love God, who are called according to His purposes." It felt like a supernatural reassurance, that whatever the difficulties the Lord would ensure he'd see his twins born. Peace and joy flowed through him. Today he'd become a father, he wanted to sing and shout, but doubted Bob and Lillian would appreciate that at 6.30 am! Instead he crept to their bathroom to shower and shave only to stare at his reflection in the bathroom mirror. His face had its dark morning stubble, his thick, black hair was unruly, but in rubbing his hand over the cleft in his square chin he decided that at thirty-seven his looks and age had now aligned, for when younger, he'd looked older! Ready to apply the razor blade to his soaped face he thought of Jane's reaction to him growing a beard. Without hesitation, she'd declared, "A beard suits Paul. It softens his heavy features and matches his gentle, golden eyes that reflect his calm, kind, yet firm nature. It suits his character, personality and calling as a doctor and in comparison with you he looks, and is, a teddy bear." At his scowl, she'd grinned. "I love you, but that growl and scowl makes you look a wild bear not a cuddly one! And, you use your intimidating features, intuitive character, loud voice and legal calling, to be the tough businessman who doesn't suffer fools gladly."

At that analysis he'd looked at her in disbelief, to which she'd added, "There, that's just what I mean! A cold stare is hardly conducive to your 'open door policy' at ITP. Has anyone ever responded?" A contemplative hum broke from him. Even as a junior secretary at ITP Jane hadn't been deterred by his manner to speak her mind! And she wasn't the only one to point out he'd seem more accessible if he smiled more often. Carefully he scrapped the razor around his sharp nose that Jane had on occasion called his 'sticky beak'. His inquisitiveness he blamed on his serious nature and training as a barrister. Outside of the family Jane and Paul were the only people who had, quite unconsciously, broken through his reserve. Jane had on several occasions embarrassed him by telling people that underneath that stern exterior was a kind, gentle, and romantic man. But he also knew she'd told Jill of his not always listening, being unable to cope with her problems when he had his own, and acting like a bear with a sore head if things didn't work out as he wanted. There was truth in that, but he wasn't sure it was entirely fair.

Anxious to be with Jane he helped himself to breakfast and quietly left the house. There was no sign of Sister Keenan when, having picked up Paul en route, they rang the bell to the Antenatal Ward just after 8.00 am. Paul smiled, addressed Staff Nurse Jury as written on her name badge, and told her who they were. But having let them in, she quickly slipped around him to block the doors to the ward because he was all for marching in to find Jane. "Mr Reinhardt you must wait in the Day Room. I'll have to speak to Sister Brodie about seeing your wife."

Panic gagged at his throat, but his voice still boomed as he asked, "Is there a problem?

The Staff nurse flinched and hurriedly answered. "Just ward protocol. Your wife is fine, her dilation slow, but we will shortly be moving her to the labour ward where we can give her pain relief. She's been clock watching, waiting for you to arrive. I'll

66

tell her you're here. I will come and get you as soon as she is settled. But I have to point out Dr Stemmings although you're welcome to wait with Mr Reinhardt in the Day Room Sister Brodie is strict that out of hours it is father's only." With that she left.

The sun shining in the Day Room made it look even more dilapidated than the night before. As though reading his mind Paul assured him, "This may not be as you envisaged, but hundreds, if not thousands of babies have been successfully delivered here so you've nothing to worry about. I'll wait until you can see Jane, then take the latest news back to Gran and Jill, she can ring both Mums. And I see no harm in my giving Freeman a ring just to tell him your plight if Jane doesn't deliver by the 7.00 pm deadline!

"That's eleven hours away! Surely she will have had the twins by then?"

Paul gave a rueful grimace. "I'd hope so, but first babies can be slow in arriving." There was silence as they pondered that until Paul pointed out, "Pacing up and down, won't help. That won't be acceptable in the labour ward and you're tiring yourself out unnecessarily."

Obediently he sat, grunted, fidgeted and spasmodically asked no-one in particular, "What's keeping that nurse? When am I going to see Jane?"

Each time Paul patiently explained something more of the procedure, and the more nervous he became. After an hour he was on his feet pacing again when Staff Nurse Jury returned. "Your wife Mr Reinhardt is now in the labour ward. Our latest examination reveals she's five centimetres dilated so birth will be a while yet. And turning to Paul she added, "Sister Brodie has, I'm afraid, only given permission for Mr Reinhardt to be there."

Paul arose with a smile, "That's okay, I've got things to do." Giving him a reassuring pat on the shoulder he said, "Give Jane my love. I'll pop back at 2.00 pm the official visiting time." Quickly he added, "I know I won't be allowed in the labour ward, so David I'll meet you in here."

The white-painted labour room with its dark brown linoleum and frosted glass windows was devoid of all comforts except another wooden armed, plastic green padded chair and the bed. Propped up with pillows Jane looked tiny except for the huge swelling in front of her. Hooked up to, and beside her was a machine he assumed was monitoring her and the babies' heartbeat. A nurse was teaching her a breathing technique, which meant counting slowly through the pain. Jane didn't see him enter, but as soon as he moved around the bed, her face lit up, her relief evident by the tears beginning to roll down her cheeks. "David, oh David you're here. Oh thank goodness."

As he bent over the bed to kiss her, her arms came up in the, oh so familiar gesture, to slip around his neck, her hand into his hair and thus to keep his mouth on hers. Embarrassed with the nurse still in the room, he pulled away after a few seconds to say, "I've been so worried about you. How are the pains?"

"Like the worst tummy upset I've ever had."

The nurse smiled across at them. "I'll leave you two alone."

Quickly Jane asked her, "When I was brought in here I was told I'd get some pain relief."

"Yes, and you will. But first try the breathing exercises, they will help. I'll be back in about half an hour."

Once the door closed Jane wailed, "I know Jill delivered William in exceptionally quick time, but it's been sixteen hours since my waters broke, and the pain's been coming every ten minutes. I thought the night would never end. Why is it taking so long?"

From under the window he took the chair and pulled it up to the bed, then took her hand in an attempt to reassure her, said, "Jill is a big girl, built for babies. You are small. Paul said first babies usually take their time appearing." With a sympathetic grimace he asked, "Now what can I do to take your mind off it."

"Did Paul say just how long it could be?"

Not wishing to upset her he avoided a straight answer. "Paul said he'd be back at two."

Dismayed she cried, "Two o'clock! That's nearly five hours away. Surely I'll have had the twins by then?"

The only way to respond was to shrug his shoulders, kiss her hand, and remind her, "Well at least Sister Brodie let me in, unlike the odious Sister Keenan?"

In a conspiratorial whisper Jane lent forward, "Sister Brodie said, 'your husband can stay as long as you behave yourself'." She gave a small smile, "I wasn't sure if that applied more to you than me!"

Until the next contraction came, Jane cheered up, but he

winced with her, and tried to instruct her as he'd heard the nurse do. But wondered if the concentration on breathing wasn't more exhausting than just allowing the pain to wash through.

Once it was over Jane recovered enough to say with amusement, "Oh David, you are priceless. It's breathe 1-2-3 in, 1-2-3 out and 'slow' not 'go'!"

Pleased she'd noticed he bantered, "I know, I was just testing."

In gesture of unbelief she looked up at the ceiling before retorting, "I'll believe you, but thousands wouldn't!" Quickly she reverted to worrying, "Please don't leave me again. You will insist on being here at the birth, won't you?"

The least he could do was confirm what he wanted to happen. "I have every intention of being here." Quietly he told her of Nurse Evans help and Paul's mission. "If Paul can get permission from the consultant to be in here it will over-ride Sister Keenan's authority."

Distraught Jane exclaimed, "Paul is preparing contingency plans for 7.00 pm when Sister Keenan comes back! You said I'd probably have the twins by two, and it's you I want, not Paul!" To be sprawled across the patient's bed probably wasn't considered to be behaving one's self, but with an eye on the door he took Jane in his arms and cradled her against his chest. She felt so frail to have such a huge task ahead of her. "I'm trying to be brave, David, but I'm scared. I keep repeating to myself those words from Psalm 27 you know, 'the Lord is my light and my salvation, therefore I've nothing to dread or fear'. It doesn't help being in such a stark and miserable place. I didn't expect anywhere to be so horrible." In feeling the same way, he struggled to find words as Jane stiffened with the inevitable pain. To support her he stiffened, and breathed slowly with her.

When it was over he cupped her little face in his large hands and gently kissed her. Drawing back he looked into her eyes to declare, "You're the best thing that ever happened to me. And you are giving me so much more than I could have hoped or imagined."

Jane's response was to grunt, "Umm... two babies instead of one!" Then her eyes twinkled with amusement as she added, "But I love your kisses they make me go all squishy! Perhaps they'd help take my mind off the pain? Shall we try it next time?"

"Probably against hospital etiquette!" Amused he continued, "But if it works it could start a new trend in pain relief. I could rent out my services. Let's see…I could call it 'kissalief', or 'panakiss' or 'ukissabirth'. The expected rebuke came with barely disguised laughter. To please her when the next contraction started he tested her suggestion. However, the intensity of the pain over-rode any analgesic effect of a kiss, and he pulled back to let her breath through the pain, but undeterred Jane recommended next time they start before the pain arrived. They were about to test that theory when Staff Nurse Jury appeared with cups of tea. And after the contraction had passed Jane's giggling earned him an approving smile from Nurse Jury for keeping her patient happy.

The kissing experiment didn't really work, but if nothing else it brought a little light-heartedness to help while away the hours. As the day wore on the ten minute contractions gradually increased in ferocity bringing him to run out of distractions and conversation. The books he'd read describing the birthing process said it could take a while, yet hadn't told of the suffering the woman had to endure, or that he would feel so inadequate and helpless.

The injection Jane had to help with the pain didn't seem to do more than make her woozy and unable to talk sensibly. Both times he'd quietly insisted he stay as the Sister checked Jane's dilation, and he'd stifled a groan when she continued to report her progress was less than a centimetre an hour. His stomach was growling in hunger, but it didn't seem right to relieve his own discomfort, while Jane was constantly moaning in agony.

As if in answer to his dilemma Staff Nurse Adams bustled in, gave him a friendly smile, and declared, "Mr Reinhardt you need a break, and Dr Stemmings is in the Day Room. Get something to eat because we can't have you fainting off with hunger." Worried, he looked across at Jane. "Don't worry she'll be quite safe in our hands."

The guilt at being able to escape, and the relief that he could, vied within him as after a quick kiss and smile he left the room. That, and his concern for Jane, had him questioning Paul the minute he set eyes on him. "How did you get on? Did you get hold of Freeman? What did he say?" Raking his hair he exclaimed, "Jane's in agony, I have to be with her. I can't let her down."

Paul patted his shoulder. "Calm down my friend. I know it's awful to see a woman in labour, but believe me the end makes up for the means. Jane will come through this. All will be well. You need some fresh air. He pointed to the benches in the square, "We'll sit on one of those. Gran and Jill knowing you would be in need of sustenance packed you a lunch."

Gratefully he declared, "Thank you. I am starving!" Paul led him out through the open French doors, yet feeling desperate David had to ask, "Is there still time to take her somewhere else?"

"All in good time, my friend. First tell me of Jane's progress, then as you eat I'll tell you of my mornings activities."

Anxious to hear from Paul he obeyed. "She's seven centimetres dilated, in a lot of pain, nothing alleviates it. How much longer will this go on?"

"I'm afraid it could be a while." Once seated Paul took a large plastic box from a rucksack and instructed, "It might be wise to save a couple of rolls for your tea."

Appalled at Jane having to endure even more hours of pain he grimaced, then with hunger overcoming him he bit into the crunchy roll filled with thick ham and pickle. He'd never tasted anything quite so good, and listened as Paul began to fill him in.

"Joshua Freeman wasn't in. I spoke to his wife who told me he was on the golf course. And as he was lunching there he wouldn't be home until late this afternoon." His mouth being full David could only groan in frustration. "Don't worry I drove to the golf course where I found him at the third tee, and to my surprise playing a friend of mine, John Perrington who I knew when working as a police surgeon. He's now up for promotion to Chief Superintendant."

Impatient, he grunted out, "And…"

Paul grinned, "Well he embraced me like a long lost son before introducing me to Freeman who'd been watching our reunion with interest. And he was intrigued to hear I was on a mission to find him, not John! My friendship with John meant Freeman was unconcerned at the interruption to his game of golf and he seemed keen to collaborate. We had to let several groups play through because Freeman wanted to know the details, my qualifications, experience and interest in this birth. I told him I'd delivered probably a hundred babies, including several sets of twins in Africa, but it was you, not me, that needed to be at the birth. His comment was that Peggy Keenan is a real tarter of a woman, but has a knack of urging or cajoling the weakest woman into giving birth naturally, and finds fathers don't like her methods as their sympathy for their wives undermines the job in hand."

About to devour a third roll, David paused to comment, "That doesn't surprise me, I certainly didn't appreciate her attitude last night."

Paul smiled, "I noticed. You did well not to argue. Freeman told me he and Sister Keenan have had some interesting moments over the years, but it was obvious he'd a huge respect for her. Apparently the woman has a sense of humour and he was practically rubbing his hands in glee at the prospect of outmanoeuvring her."

At his fervent 'excellent' Paul grinned, "You haven't heard the best bit. Freeman said he would ring his Registrar, Tony Hanson and I exclaimed, that we trained together in London. That news had Freeman beaming, and immediately he gave me Tony's number with the instruction to work out a plot between us, and any problems, we were to call him."

Unrestrained joy filled David, and raising his arm into the air he couldn't refrain from booming a "Yes!"

Paul looked serious. "Hold on before you get too excited. I've spoken to Tony with Freeman's permission he's happy for you to be there, but not knowing you he wants me there too. "Would you, or Jane, have any objection to that?"

"Of course not, I'd appreciate it. And as far as Jane's concerned as long as I'm there, and those babies get delivered, I rather think the world could be invited."

With a chuckle, Paul pointed out, "Well by the time this is over she may well think the world has been! The delivery of twins' attracts two paediatricians, one for each baby, as well as midwives and nurses." Anyway assuming Jane hasn't delivered by 7.00 pm Tony suggests we gown up before Sister Keenan's shift starts, that way she won't immediately recognise us, and that we aren't part of the team. Freeman seemed to think that even if she did see through our plot she'd be amused at our cunning, and let us stay."

Sceptically he murmured, "Then let's hope he's right!"

"Don't forget Sister Keenan has heard your voice so don't speak unless you have to, our endeavour is to be invisible! Oh and there is one other small detail. Freeman said, for his services to humanity, a nice case of finest malt whisky would be just the ticket for him to wet the babies' heads! And John suggested when it was all over, we should get together for a celebratory drink on you."

With his hunger assuaged and permission to be with Jane assured, he packed up the remaining two rolls while proclaiming, "No problem. I would have given Freeman anything he asked in order to be at the twins births. And, I suspect, a case of malt whisky is considerably cheaper than Beveridge's fees at St. Mary's!

Paul hit his shoulder in a friendly fashion. "As you will have to appear as a doctor the swotting of my medical books about conception, pregnancy and delivery could come in useful."

With a grimace David replied, "How can you be a doctor? I'd hate seeing people in pain. It's so depressing when you can't do anything to help, but with our contingency plan, I'll face anything."

"Good, because I had to assure Freeman that you wouldn't be a problem. Birthing isn't a pretty sight, and believe me if you faint, I will disown you!"

He chortled, "Jane would probably kill me, if after all this, I was to miss that precious moment of a lifetime." He replaced the lunch box in the bag, stood tall and declared, "So let me assure you, my friend, there's no chance of me fainting off. I'm made of sterner stuff than that."

However, after five hours of Jane in excruciating pain in a place that was as welcoming as police cell, her body being strung up like a chicken, and he, dressed in operating garb, did feel queasy! To divert that he concentrated on helping Jane, as too weak to hold the gas and air mask over her face, he did it for her. But when her efforts to push made her face red and bloated, he'd fought the fear she'd not survive.

Then, half an hour ago, Sister Keenan had arrived! And like her name, her keen eye hadn't missed the visitors for she'd asked brusquely, "Tell me, Dr Hanson, who are these gentleman?"

Nonchalantly Tony looked up to say succinctly, "Colleagues. They are doing a survey on childbirth techniques and procedures in hospitals across Great Britain." A snort of laughter from Nurse Evans had turned swiftly into a cough. Sister Keenan had glared at her before demanding, "Has Mrs Reinhardt given permission for these gentlemen to be present?"

As though surprised Tony replied, "Of course" and then turned his head as if he continuing a conversation with them. "I think you are right, the concept of injecting drugs into the spine to numb the lower body during childbirth is something that would be popular, but it will probably be a while before it is perfected for general use."

Paul had taken up the discussion while David, in registering Sister Keenan's surveillance, had tried to appear professional by nodding knowledgeably and taking an interest at the gory end of childbirth. When Paul's amused eyes met his he was suddenly grateful that masks hid their expressions for his was a definite scowl.

Having observed them through several of Jane's contractions Sister Keenan had left, but the tension remained for she could return at any moment.

CHAPTER 6

At the door opening, David jumped to attention. Someone doing an academic survey would not be plumping up the patient's pillows and assisting her to have a drink of water. Sister Keenan entered pushing an incubator. Tony Hanson looked across to comment, "Well timed, the first baby is minutes away." To Jane, oblivious to anything other than the pains ripping through her, he said, "I can just see the baby's head, push again." Despite a groan, she obeyed. In the brief respites Paul and Tony talked of their experiences of childbirth. Feeling Sister Keenan's sharp grey eyes observing him David strove to look intent on their conversation. When he next stole a glance in her direction she was talking with a nurse who just entered the room. With an unexpected sweeping look around the room Sister Keenan's eyes met his. He sent her a perfunctory nod and returned his attention to Tony who was again exhorting Jane to push. The contraction over Sister Keenan reported, "I've spoken to Mr Freeman and understand we have with us a Mr Hyde." Her steely gaze rested on him before moving to Paul, "along with a Dr Jekyll." He and Paul exchanged a glance as she continued, "Nurse Dawson has just reported to me the mother next door has shoulder dystopia. Rather than keep her waiting it seems sensible Dr Hanson, you do the forceps delivery while our visiting doctor delivers Mrs Reinhardt's babies." Their astonishment was reflected in Tony's eyes as Sister Keenan organised her troops. "Evans with me, Adams and Dawson stay with Mrs Reinhardt." With no opportunity for argument she instructed, "Dr Jekyll you're in charge here." With a cursory nod in his direction she said, "Mr Hyde," then turning on her heel she headed to the door from where she commanded, "When you're ready Dr Hanson" before leaving the room.

At Jane's feet, Tony having pulled off his gloves, pushed his stool back. "Good grief, I think she's amused!" As Paul prepared to take over, Tony with laughter in his voice, continued, "David as Mr Hyde, and Paul as Dr Jekyll, very appropriate! Believe me it's quite an accolade to have her permission to take over." A woman's screams pierced the air as Tony opened the door. Pride swelled within David that his Jane was quietly bearing what seemed an inordinate amount of pain. Gently he bent to brush the damp hair from her face, and said encouragingly, "You are doing well. And isn't it wonderful, Paul is going to deliver our babies?"

Through gritted teeth Jane murmured, "I don't care who delivers these…" The onslaught of pain cut her words to a deep growl over which Paul instructed, "Jane, push as hard as you can. That's it, that's it, come on, come on, the baby's head is nearly crowned, not long now."

Red faced and sweating Jane groaned from the exertion finally falling back against the pillows to murmur wearily, "I can't do this."

In feeling it was amazing how women survived this terrible ordeal David admitted, "Paul, I feel so helpless. I know we have to wear these ridiculous garments, but can't I at least take this mask off?"

Paul eyes smiled across at him, "As I'm in charge! I'll let you." Once discarded, he kissed Jane's trembling lips in the wish he could impart his strength into her exhausted body. Laughing Paul called across, "Hey Mr Hyde enough of that."

To which he retorted, "But Dr Jekyll we have the miracle of Sister Keenan's approval."

With unexpected strength Jane snapped, "The only miracle I want is for God to deliver these babies!"

Paul answered, "Oh don't worry Jane, He will. Now David get in between those pillows and support Jane to sit as upright as possible. Baby one is about to arrive." Jane tensed in pain, took a deep breath and through clenched teeth pushed hard. In the brief time between contractions Paul advised, "The head's crowned, and you might feel a sharp sting because I'm going to make a small cut so you don't tear."

Gently David massaged Jane's shoulders as she lay exhausted against him. Paul to help her relax chatted away. "Do you know in Africa the women literally squat, bear down, and gravity does the rest? Some hospitals are beginning to let the mother choose her position of delivery, and this is the …"

He stopped speaking as the door opened to Sister Keenan pushing another incubator, and followed by a man and woman. "Dr Stemmings, these are our paediatricians, Dr Myer and Dr Brown." As Paul gave an acknowledging nod, Sister Keenan said curtly with a wave of her hand, "And the husband, Mr Reinhardt!"

A deep groan alerted them to Jane. Paul encouraged, "Give

it all you can, your baby can be born in this next push."

David forgetting Sister Keenan's presence propped himself up against Jane's back to form a common strength in bringing forth their child. On a growl of effort he felt the vibration of her small frame as racked in pain she pushed with all her might. How much more of this could she take? But he knew they were constantly monitoring her, and the babies for any sign of distress.

Paul's voice rang out in triumphant, "That's it! Relax you've done the hard bit, just breathe slowly, don't push. Now gently bear down and push. Here we are." Seconds later came a faint squeal, not unlike a cat mewing and Paul announced, "Well done Reinhardts' you've got a nice healthy looking boy."

To David's surprise, Sister Keenan took down her mask to smile at Paul and despite her brusqueness of tone turned to say to him, "Congratulations Mr Reinhardt, and on your tenacity and ingenuity to be here at your child's birth."

Eager to see his son, David barely acknowledged her words, because having gently laid Jane back on the pillows he'd leapt forward to where Paul was cutting the umbilical to a black-haired, bloodstained baby. It was he, who now needed to breathe slowly, and Paul catching his expression, instructed, "David sit by Jane. Once the baby has been checked and cleaned up you can hold him" and added as the baby wailed, "Nothing wrong with his lungs!"

Slowly David filled his lungs in a need to control his churning stomach. It would be so embarrassing if he were sick. Sister Keenan obviously satisfied left the room. Nurse Adams approached Jane from the other side of the bed. "Well done! A lovely boy, but I now need to assess the position of number two."

Dr Myers turned to announce, "Mr & Mrs Reinhardt your boy has a good weight of four pounds, twelve ounces, but we'll put him in an incubator so he can adjust to being here, but he's a nice pink and breathing well."

Tony Hanson reappeared. "So baby one safely delivered." He peered over the paediatrician's shoulder. "Excellent, and with a head of hair like his Dad, and so nurse where are we with the second baby?"

Distracted by Dr Brown placing their baby in Jane's arms David didn't hear Nurse Adams reply. "Oh Jane, isn't he just beautiful? Look at those tiny perfectly formed hands." It was obvious Jane was too weak to support the baby, and in putting his arms under hers he pointed out, "I don't think he's going to have your heart shaped face, it's more angular, and it looks as if he's got my nose!"

Tiredly she murmured, "I don't see how you can tell, he's no bigger than two bags of sugar." At the sound of her voice the baby's eyes opened, but as a contraction began Jane relinquished the baby into his arms.

Blue eyes looked straight into his. Love burst from him and jovially he declared, "Hello my son." Jane was already in the throes of pain, but he had to ask, "What shall we name him?"

She managed to say "Joshua" before Nurse Adams held the mask over her face, and Dr Brown indicated it was time for Joshua to go to the Special Care Baby Unit. Loathe to give him up so soon he kissed the small forehead saying quietly, "See you later my son."

Once Jane's contraction had passed, in believing despite her woozy state she could hear him, he commented, "I like Joshua, a Biblical leader and pioneer. I believe as a Reinhardt he will be that."

Jane groaned and squeezed his hand as another contraction started, then the gas and air took hold and her hand slipped from his. David commented as Paul came to stand beside him, "If I'd known that childbirth was such an excruciating tortuous procedure I wouldn't have put Jane through it."

"Women are tougher than you think, and most have told me that the outcome outweighs the hours of agony!" From what he could remember from Paul's books the second baby usually came within about ten minutes, so her suffering wouldn't last much longer. Sister Keenan returned, had a quiet discussion with Nurse Adams, then Tony, before beckoning him and Paul to join them. Sister Keenan spoke. "It appears Mr Reinhardt your second child is not just in the breech position, but high up the abdominal cavity. Your wife is tired, and from our combined experience, even if she pushes the baby down, it will be a forceps delivery. Our recommendation would be to do a Caesarean section." Paul looking at him nodded his agreement as Sister Keenan continued, "You wife may look small and frail, but they are often the fittest and rally around the quickest." In seeing his hesitation, she said abruptly, "Be satisfied that I allowed you to see one of your babies born! Now the operating theatre is free. I'll put the anaesthetist on standby."

Paul patted his back, "Shall I tell Jane, or do you want to?"

"Let's both do it, I can encourage, you can give the technical details."

Jane was dazed and murmuring through a diminishing pain, "How much longer?"

Paul explained the problem and the solution. Despite her exhaustion she begged, "No, no, I want to try, please let me try."

They tried to dissuade her, but despite his saying, "I'm just grateful for having seen Joshua born, this really will be the best way", Jane still insisted she wanted to try. Finally Paul agreed, but explained that at the first sign of distress to her, or the baby, there wouldn't be an option.

After six contractions and much exertion on Jane's part Tony shook his head, and Paul with his hand on Jane's bump advised it was time to give in. "Oh please," she pleaded, "One last try." At the next pain David thought she would break a blood vessel in her effort to push the baby down. An alarm sounded. Terrified he looked at the faces of those around him. Despite, Paul reassuring him it was only a warning, everyone in the room burst into action. Jane's eyes rounded with fright, but in a calm voice Paul said, "Jane it was such a privilege to bring Joshua into the world, Jill's going to be most amused. Now it's just a trip down the corridor, a whiff of anaesthetic, and next thing you know baby two will be in your arms."

Even as Paul spoke, and Jane was bewailing she didn't want to be cut open, they were manoeuvring her bed and equipment out of the door. Dodging around that, and people, he managed to keep pace with the bed, and hold her hand as Sister Keenan reassured Jane. "Mr Freeman, our Consultant is very good. There's nothing to worry about, you and the little one will be fine." That tone of compassion in her voice somehow was more unnerving than the one she used when officiating over her anti-natal ward!

At the door of the theatre he brushed Jane's lips with a kiss, and as the doors closed on her he boomed, "I'll be waiting for you."

Paul directed him to a small room where they could remove their gowns and wash their hands. "Once we've done this we'll go to the waiting room. I'll buy you a cup of tea and you can share with me the remains of your packed lunch."

Anxious, he nodded, for he was envisioning in his mind the pictures in Paul's books, of Jane cut open and the baby pulled out. Paul was rambling on about Freeman, his qualifications, his experience, but he tuned back in at his saying, "...it's his day off. I wonder if he was called in because of it being a twin birth, or he just wanted to bask in our outwitting Sister Keenan." David didn't comment, but remained pacing up and down as Paul munched on the remains of his lunch. Half an hour later a middle-aged, plump man with moustache came striding down the corridor towards them, behind him Dr Myers pushing an incubator.

Hand outstretched, his eyes twinkling with mirth, Joshua Freeman introduced himself. "You must be David Reinhardt, pleased to meet you." David's hand was given a vigorous shake. "Your wife is fine. You have a pigeon pair!" A deep rumble of laughter admitted from him. "Don't look so worried, that's a boy and a girl. Congratulations, and I believe you are naming your son after me, most kind." For a moment David looked blank, as Freeman cheerily went on, "Your daughter weighed in at 4lbs 4ozs, you could call her Francis - it's my middle name." A belly laugh emitted from him. "She's breathing well, but we like to put little ones in the special care unit for a day or two, but you can have a quick cuddle."

Dr Myers handed him a bundle wrapped in a pink blanket while Freeman pumped Paul's hand up and down declaring, "A brilliant night's work. And you earned Peggy Keenan's admiration not only in your birthing technique, but in the way you cleaned up the place after you!" With another guffaw of amusement he added, "Nice episiotomy too, not a sign of tear." Laughter rumbled through him, "Now best to get back to Reinhardt's wife, lots of embroidery to do, eh? I'll send someone to fetch you when she's in recovery. And Reinhardt, I'll look forward to that case of the finest malt whiskey!"

David glanced up to say, "Done! Thank you" and returned to feast his eyes on his daughter. "Look Paul, she's got the sweetest face, heart-shaped like her mother's."

Paul's finger moved back the blanket to see the little screwed up face and commented, "Isn't it awesome that such a perfectly formed baby was so recently tucked up in such a small space? The only difference I can see is she has fine blonde hair and Joshua's was black like yours. Are you going to call her

Frances?"

Adamant he declared, "No, we're not! I didn't want to disappoint Freeman in telling him the choosing of Joshua was coincidence, not design!"

An overwhelming love and protection flowed out from him at such a delicate little body, and sadly he had to part with her all too soon. But as he kissed her 'goodbye' Dr Myers informed him, "Mrs Reinhardt will take a few days to recover, but you are welcome to bottle feed your babies in the Baby Unit. With Mrs Reinhardt having both a 'section' and twins she'll be in a side ward, so you can visit her any time."

Paul patted his back, "There, another answer to prayer."

Grimly he retorted, "But Jane's really suffered for it."

With a grimace Paul proclaimed, "That my friend, is often the way, and has been termed as 'character building'! Sister Keenan calling you Mr Hyde fitted you so well, not just hiding from her, but often you hide your emotions behind a stern mask, but today I've seen compassion, tears, desperation, and there was a moment I thought you might be sick or faint!" Reluctant to admit the truth he hummed as Paul said more seriously, "Jane did have a difficult time, but it will soon be forgotten." Brightening he smiled, "Oh David I was reminded of the pranks I got up to while training. I'm still amazed at Sister Keenan letting me have the privilege of delivering Joshua, what a bonus! I wouldn't have missed it for the world."

The tension of the past hours dissipated in an upward rush of joy. Ecstatic, he boomed, "I'm a father! I've a boy and a girl. We're a family. What more could I want or ask for?"

"Perhaps that last cheese roll, or the Mars Bar in my pocket?"

"You're right for suddenly I'm starving." Boyishly he grinned wickedly, "And there's no chance of Jane catching me eating the latter."

"Even if she did, I think she'd agree you deserve that treat after your performance today."

Once he'd consumed all the food he began a list of phone calls and arrangements he needed to make. After thirty minutes he asked, "How much longer will Freeman be?" Ten minutes later he questioned again, "Why is it taking so long?"

Paul answered, "There's the internal and external stitching to do. I expect he's taking his time and making a neat job of it."

Yet despite Paul's outward calm he sensed his concern. Unable to think further, or sit still he got up and paced the room before voicing his apprehension. "Do you think something has gone wrong?"

Paul didn't answer as with concerned eyes he looked beyond him. Joshua Freeman was walking towards them, but this time without a smile or eyes twinkling in merriment. Everything felt as if it was going in slow motion. His eyes widened in the unspoken question he was too terrified to ask. Freeman's first words were, "Your wife is being transferred to the recovery area" on a gasp he let go of the breath he'd not realized he'd been holding, but tensed as he went on, "However, there were complications."

Apprehensive he barked, "Complications, what kind of complications?"

Freeman admonished, "Please keep your voice down. Your wife had a large post partum haemorrhage. Let me explain."

Immediately the words on the relevant page of Paul's text book came to mind and in a matter-of-fact voice he said, "That's when the uterus blood vessels don't contract as quickly as they should, it happens more frequently in twins, and the mother suffers a heavy blood loss."

Surprised, Freeman nodded. "You've done your homework Mr Reinhardt, I am impressed."

Impatient he retorted, "Don't be - it's the way I am!"

Freeman recoiled slightly, but continued, "Then you'll know we'll keep Mrs Reinhardt under close observation for the next twenty-four hours. We are replacing her blood loss, and will put her on an iron supplement to ensure there isn't any deficiency." Feeling weak he sank on the nearest chair and put his head in his hands. A moment later a hand patted his shoulder and Freeman said, "She's a healthy young woman, she'll soon recover. She's weak and drowsy, but you can see her for a few minutes. I'll check on her in a day or two, but any worries your friend here knows where to contact me. Now you'll have to excuse me."

They watched him amble off down the corridor and Paul suggested, "This would be a good time to go and ring the grandparents with the news."

"But I'm worried about Jane. I'll ring them after I see her?"

"It might be a while. It'll take your mind off the waiting. I'll ring Jill, she can pass the news to the rest of the family."

Grateful for his barrister training he was able to sound confident, draw on the positive evidence and inject information that deflected from his own thoughts and emotions. Both Mums assured him Jane would be fine and childbirth was a nightmare soon forgotten, but when he finally saw Jane anxiety clawed at his throat. He was pleased he'd accepted Paul's offer to come in with him. His voice sounded croaky as he whispered, "She as white as the sheets she's lying between." Drip stands contained a bag of blood, another clear liquid, their tube connections intravenously giving Jane her bodily needs. Under the sheet her stomach was still swollen, her hair although brushed hung limp and lifeless around her face.

Paul picked up the chart at the bottom of the bed. "In a day so she'll perk up. Talk to her, she might not respond, but she'll hear you."

Pulling up the chair beside her he whispered her name. She stirred so he bent over her to kiss her cheek. "Jane Reinhardt you have produced two beautiful babies." Jane's eyes flickered so he moved into her line of vision. Jane's hand slid toward him, he lifted and kissed it. Close to her ear he murmured, "We now have our family, a boy and a girl. No more suffering, time to recuperate, and our little girl has a fine blonde fuzz of hair, her features delicate like yours. I think she looks like a Rebecca." Jane didn't answer, he wasn't sure if she was asleep. Then she stirred, opened her eyes and in a slurred voice murmured, "I'm cold."

"You've lost a lot of blood. The room is warm, but I'll tell the nurse." Not wanting to leave her he relayed their respective Mums' delight and conversation and, feeling Paul's hand on his shoulder, he finished, "All you have to do now is rest." He lent over to brush his lips with hers. "I've got to go, but I'll see you in the morning."

To Nurse Adams he reported Jane was cold. She reassured him that was due to her blood loss, and they'd put plenty of blankets over her to offset that. Drained by the day's activities, neither of them spoke as Paul drove him back to Bob and Lillian's house.

Bob greeted him at the door to pump his hand and congratulate him. Jill appeared, and in a rush of emotion hugged him fiercely. "Congratulations, brother dear. "How's Jane? Paul said she's had a rough time." Lillian, knitting in the corner of the room suggested he sit down, and spoke of everyone's interest in Jane, and the constant ringing of the telephone. At that he smiled inanely, accepted the mug of cocoa Bob handed him and listened to Paul weaving a story out of their ruse. They were so engrossed, and he so tired, that he didn't protest at Paul's exaggerated observation of his reaction to seeing the blood and gore. True that he may have gone a whiter shade of pale, but 'closed his eyes, staggered, sat down quickly, breathing slowly as if to stop being sick' he wasn't sure that was fair!

Jill, watching him grinned. "It's alright David, I don't blame you, with William's delivery I didn't see the messy end, but suspect I would have felt as squeamish as you."

He sent her a grateful smile and stood. "I hope you'll excuse me, but I am dead on my feet."

Bob jumped up. "Of course! Jill's here to take Paul back to Beatty's. Sleep in as long as you like. We'll be off to church about ten o'clock. Lunch is at Beatty's tomorrow, you are welcome, but see how that fits in with your plans. Just help yourself to whatever you need."

Once in bed it took David a while to fall asleep as the events of the day churned through his mind. It felt surreal that he was now the father of two children and that life would never be quite the same again.

CHAPTER 7

After breakfast with Bob and Lillian, David rang the hospital to be told Jane had a comfortable night, was still sedated and advised to wait until visiting time. After congratulating him on the twins the Sister went on, "You rank as one of the few with the tenacity to outwit Sister Keenan." Embarrassed, he remained silent, and she transferred him to the special care unit where a similar conversation took place. Were their exploits the talk of the hospital? He was beginning to feel sorry for Sister Keenan.

The next phone call was to his parents where his father declared, "Bit of a tough time I gather for that girl of yours. Still can't get over your foolishness to gallivant across the country when she was so pregnant. You should have been at St.Mary's with Beveridge's expertise."

Cross, he retorted, "We had Paul's expertise! Without his help I'd not have seen Joshua born. No-one could have anticipated the complications."

At that his father grunted and said gruffly, "No private rooms though, are there?"

Not to be drawn, he said, "True, but she's been promised a side ward."

At that his father conceded, "At least you got past that stuffy woman and her absurd regime. Let me have Joshua Freeman's address I'll send him a case of vintage champagne to go with the one of finest malt whiskey. After all the man saved me a fortune in not having Beveridge, his team, the operating fees and the accommodation at St.Mary's." Then reverting to Jane he commented, "She's such a slip of a thing. How she managed to expel even one child naturally is a mystery, and I can't imagine why you wanted to experience that."

"Admittedly I didn't expect it to be quite so gruelling, but to see your child born is amazing."

His father harrumphed. "Margaret did it three times without need of me. Ah here she is. I'll put her on."

The conversation of David with his mother was much the same as that with Jane's, except Joyce was so anxious to see her daughter he'd agreed to let her know when Jane was well enough for a visit.

With nothing more urgent to take his attention he took up Bob's offer to join them at church and lunch at Beatty's. Jill was so at home with Paul's family and friends he wondered if they might move back to the house Paul owned in Kent. On hearing Jill speak his name he looked up from his meal. "David and William might have been the centre of attention after church, but Paul is the hero of several mothers when they heard how he'd overcome Sister Keenan's stringent rules.

David grimaced. "It was so embarrassing, all those women at church asking after Jane, and giving me gifts for the twins."

Jill giggled, "I expect your 'high wattage' smile sent many of them weak at the knees!"

As he glared at Jill, Beatty touched his arm. "I thought you handled it like a true gentleman, a good balance of reticence and graciousness. And there's nothing wrong with charm David as long as it is as sincere. Tomorrow Jill, Paul and William return to London I wondered if you'd keep me company and stay here."

Delighted, Beatty became the recipient of David's 'high-wattage' smile. "I'd love to, well if Bob and Lillian don't mind."

"Not at all." Bob grinned, "We're out at work all day so you'd certainly be better off with Gran, and her cooking!"

"I have to go to London to collect the things Jane and I are going to need, so 'thank you' on my return I'll come here. A glance at the clock had David saying, "Time now to visit Jane."

Eventually, he discovered Jane had been put in a side ward off the main post-natal ward. Overnight she seemed to have shrunk. Despite the blood transfusion she looked pale, and her usually animated face remained expressionless, her eyes dull and her hair greasy and lank. Cold lips met his kiss, her arms too weak to embrace him. Gently, he ran his knuckle down her cheek, "You feel cold, are you warm enough?" Jane's reply was a nod, her lower lip wobbled. And in the rather austere room he pulled up the only chair and took her hand.

In no more than a whisper she quavered, "It's like a nightmare."

Unable to respond, he lifted her hand and kissed her fingers, before reassuring her, "The worst is over. We have a son and daughter. We'll soon be home."

Marginally louder she said, "It's not over. My tummy feels it's been kicked by several horses." Her voice picked up with the momentum of her ills. "When I move the stitches pull and even breathing I can feel them tighten. I hate this needle in my hand, it the sight of blood makes me cringe. I feel weak, yet they urge me to sit up. When I lie down to sleep they awaken me to check my blood pressure. It's like a torture chamber and this room a prison cell." She waved the hand without the drip. "Even when that frosted glass window is open, there isn't a view. And the wall so near means the sun won't penetrate."

Obediently, he glanced around and mocked, "The green bedspread and chair matches the flooring!" For that he received a peeved look to which he responded, "My dear Jane I'm sure I can cheer it up." At her wide-eyed scepticism he bantered, "It may come as a surprise to you, young Jane, but it's a privilege to have this room." At her cynical expression he continued, "Oh granted it's not what we hoped for, but I can come in at any time to cheer you up."

Tears rolled down her cheeks. "I should be grateful, but I just want to go home."

Carefully he sat sit beside her on the bed, mopped her cheeks with his handkerchief, smiled tenderly into her eyes to encourage, "Each day you will feel better."

"But how many days?"

"I don't know, but it will pass." His voice filled with fatherly pride and excitement, "And we have our babies!" This 'nightmare' as you call it will soon be over, and you'll see it's been worthwhile." Jane didn't look convinced. To distract her he retrieved the carrier bags he'd brought in. "This bag contains presents from the people at Beatty's church, I thought we could open them together."

"How kind." But she showed no excitement or interest. When he opened one he'd so little response to the baby booties he suggested, "We'll open them when you feel better." Injecting brightness into his voice he tried to raise a smile by being like a magician flourishing the items from his other bag. "Flowers I picked from Beatty's garden, chocolates from Jill who had the forethought to purchase them yesterday, fruit from various members of the Stemmings family and bowl courtesy of Beatty. And she also promises to supplement the hospital diet with cake." He produced a small box. "The first being lemon drizzle because she'd heard it was your favourite."

"Thank her, so thoughtful," but her eyes barely focused on the things he put on the bedside table. Worried, he drew his chair closer to the bed, picked up her cold hand and confessed, "I don't know what to say or do to make it better, but could I tempt you with a chocolate, or one of those peaches?"

Despair was evident in her eyes as she spoke in short stiff phrases. "It hurts…to eat…move… lie or sit. I can't even have a cuddle."

Unable to do much else he lifted and kissed her fingers, stroked her hair and said sympathetically "I know." And then to take her mind off those things he spoke of the twins, how he was looking forward to seeing and feeding them, but was taken aback when she said miserably, "You'd better go then. You won't want to miss that."

Puzzled, he frowned, then realizing she probably thought he was scowling, he smiled and said soothingly, "I'll only leave when you need to rest." His mind went back to those tiny little lives. "They are so small, yet so wonderfully made, it's amazing, and to see them you know there has to be a God. Love just welled up out of me for them."

Tears brimmed in her eyes causing him to question, "What's wrong?"

"I'm frightened you'll love them more than me."

Without thinking he bit out, "That's ridiculous! They're babies! They will be children, but they aren't you." To clarify his remark and offset his irritation he forced a smile and deliberately injected amusement in his tone. "Come on Jane, you are the one who keeps me in order, runs the house, cooks me delicious meals, warms my bed at night and brings me intimacy and friendship. My love for you is completely different."

Slowly, between careful breaths she said, "But they will… take your attention…be in your thoughts…like now…it won't be you and me any more…will it?

Disturbed he countered, "Jane this isn't like you."

"I am trying… to be positive. With no-one here…just lying here…it plays on my mind…I've tried praying." She sniffed, tears rolled down her cheeks, "I can't even cry, it hurts."

"Oh Jane, my poor little Jane." In an attempt to cuddle her he saw her wince as he jogged the mattress. "I'm sorry." Gently he kissed her mouth, and tried to think of comforting words. "It's early days. We'll make time on our own." Then changing the subject told her of their parents and friend's interest and a few funny snippets of the day before. Bravely Jane forced a smile. What we need is something to take your mind off how you are feeling."

Wistfully she looked at him, "It is awful just lying here. I've tried to let praise songs go around in my head, to pray, but I'm so uncomfortable, I can't concentrate."

"Try listening to the radio. I can get you whatever you want. But once you begin to recover you'll be busy with two babies to feed and look after." He chuckled, "That'll keep you occupied day and night!"

In wide-eyed panic she pulled herself up, and then cried out with the pain.

Concerned he jumped up. "What is it, what's the matter? Shall I get the nurse?"

"No, no!" In a rush Jane spilled out her fears. "That horrible Sister Keenan said I'd have to stay here ten days to a fortnight. I don't know the first thing about babies. Your new job starts tomorrow. You'll go home, and leave me here."

"Whoa Jane! Stop!" Taking her shoulders he stared down into her panic stricken eyes. "Listen to me. You are my first concern. I have to go home to get things we need, but I'll come straight back." Her shoulders sagged, "Relax! This is a time for you to be looked after, adjust and learn about motherhood. The priority is your recovery, the stronger you feel the more you'll be able to cope. Your Mum is eager to visit ,so how she comes down on the train and stays overnight, while I go to London. I'll be back before you miss me. This week will quickly pass and in the following one you'll be fit enough to go home."

A nurse entered as Jane observed in a tired voice, "You're always good at problem solving."

"Oh hello Mr Reinhardt. I'm just going to check on Jane's blood pressure and give her a couple of painkillers." As she chatted, and bustled about, he moved to stand by the window that gave little light and no view. How could he brighten up the utilitarian room? Nurse Nichols drew him into her chatter by asking about his 'Sister Keenan episode' and when she turned to put the chart back at the end of the bed Jane had fallen asleep. With her assurance that Jane wouldn't awake for an hour or two he slipped out to the special baby unit.

Sister Giles in charge of the baby unit welcomed him, her look and broad smile conveying his reputation had gone before him. Sensing his anxiety as she placed Joshua in his arms and explained, "Babies aren't as fragile as they look." Delighted he watched Joshua greedily latch on to the bottle's teat, but later his little girl who he already thought of as Rebecca quickly tired, and like her mother fell asleep on him.

Jane was still asleep when he returned, so he rook the opportunity to stroll out of the barrack like hospital grounds, along a road of privately owned houses. In a window he spotted a bed and breakfast sign. Joyce didn't drive, but if she could stay this close to the hospital! Half an hour later, he strode back to Jane pleased at having accomplished so much in so short a time.

Propped up by pillows Jane was drinking a cup of tea. Pleased, he also observed the drip had gone from her hand, and flushed with success he boomed happily, "Have I got news for you?"

Jane winced. "Ssh you'll be thrown out."

"I've found a house five minutes from here doing bed and breakfast. The couple who run it let me use their telephone and so tomorrow I'm picking up your Mum at four o'clock from the local station." Delighted to see Jane perk up, he added "Joyce says, 'I'm a star for organising it'" Jane raised her eyebrows. "So your Mum will cover for me while I return to London to get the things we need. Let's make a list. And I'll get some straps to put in the car to hold the carry cot because that's the only way we can transport the twins home. Oh, and Sister Giles, at the baby unit, said that having met the handsome father of the twins in her incubators, she hoped tomorrow to meet their mother because she was sure she must be quite beautiful to have produced two such gorgeous babies."

That haughty expression he so adored came with the words "I suspect you exaggerate Mr Reinhardt."

"Do you, well the truth is their mother, and the babies she produced, are quite beautiful." Jane grunted as he continued, "I thought Jill, Paul and William would love to see them before they go home tomorrow, so perhaps we can combine that with their feeding times.

A shadow crossed Jane's face. "I'm not sure I'll be up to that."

"We'll see." He chortled, "I haven't told you but Freeman thought we named Joshua after him. I didn't like to disillusion him, but he asked if we'd like to use Francis, his second name for our little girl."

"How embarrassing!"

"I think it was a joke!" Anyway I'm already thinking of her

as Rebecca so what do you say? Jane looked thoughtful. So he continued, "I know we said we'd choose their names when we saw them, we can do that tomorrow."

Alarm was evident in Jane's instant reply. "There's no hurry."

Puzzled he queried, "Don't you want to see your babies?"

Weariness seemed to envelop her, and after she said, "Oh David, just let me rest" their conversation became desultory, and when her dinner arrived she suggested he leave and get an early night.

On his way back to Bob and Lillian's he called into Beatty's house. Paul opening the door put his finger to his mouth. "We're just getting William ready for bed. Come through to the kitchen." In accepting a cup of tea he found it came with a pile of cheese on toast. Paul grinned, "You're definitely going to like staying here my friend, Gran's mission in life is to feed the hungry!"

He laughed. "Beatty I appreciate your food, but also value your wisdom." Jill joined them, so he added, "Well collective wisdom" and between mouthfuls he updated the three of them on Jane's apparent disinterest in the twins, and his worry that she appeared jealous of his love for them.

Jill tutted, "Oh David, give her time! Those babies yesterday caused her hours of agony, she's still in discomfort and pain so it's hardly surprising she is finding it hard to accept them. Remember Jane has struggled throughout her pregnancy with the concept of being a mother and having a family, she will need time to adjust. Don't you agree, Paul?"

Paul's mouth twitched with a smile as he observed, "Who is the doctor here?" Jill cuddled into him and squeezed his arm as he answered. "Giving birth is a lot for a body to cope with, and it isn't unusual for a Mum to feel depressed for a few days, weeks even. But we aren't going to believe for that."

Beatty added, "And its good that Joyce is coming tomorrow. Mum's are usually good at making their daughter's see sense! Now, David, you shall have a piece of my lemon drizzle cake and go off for an early night. You'll see, things will pan out, its early days!"

Next morning his first priority was to ring ITP. Mavis, his new secretary, delighted at his news, assured him, "I'll let everyone know, and don't worry about anything, you stay as long as you need to." He explained that Rosemary might be under the illusion she was continuing to work for him, and asked Mavis not to contradict that, but ask her to stay with Robert until he returned. Next he spoke to his fellow directors, Maud and Chris, who congratulated and then commiserated at the inconvenience of being stuck in Kent, but they too gave their reassurance of being able to deal with any pressing problems.

But time was pressing on, and he guessed Jane would be anxiously awaiting him. Before he could visit her he needed to go shopping and that took longer than expected. Two hours later Nurse Nichols opened the ward door and giggled like a teenager when she saw him. "Your wife's room looks and smells like a florist shop. We've run out of vases and places to put them all. Have you got any brothers?" Puzzled he shook his head. "Pity, I'd like a husband like you." At her sideways coquettish look, he gave one of his booms of laughter causing her to shush him to be quiet.

On opening Jane's door he had to admit perhaps he'd overdone the flower purchases. Two large displays on wrought iron stands were in the corners of the room, and the window sill had four vases filled with tall bright chrysanthemums and lilies. Tears shimmered in Jane's eyes, her voice filled with emotion. "Oh David…all this…for me…oh thank you!"

Her bottom lip quivered as he bent forward to kiss her. Withdrawing he said, "I thought this would cheer you up."

"They made me have a bath." Jane closed her eyes as though to do so would block out the memory. Bewildered as to why a bath could cause such distress he pulled up the chair, took hold of her small hand and kissed it, while awaiting further information. There was an emotional catch in her voice as she reported, "Oh David when I came back in here after…to see the room transformed…all the nurses have come to see them and say how lucky I am to have a husband like you. And" she sobbed, "It's true I don't deserve you."

Embarrassed he grunted, then bantered, "That's right, most of the time, you certainly don't deserve having to put up with me. But I'm glad you do." He bent to kiss the tip of her nose, "Did you see the card? I wrote: 'You are a wonderful wife, the delight of my life, and there is no other better, to be the twins' mother.'"

She grinned, "Oh David, your little ditty's need some work,

but the flowers always make up for those". His mind reverted to four years earlier as she continued, "You've chosen well, the scent of the lilies overrides the hospital odour and the brightness of the displays cheers up this awful room."

Outwardly he acknowledged her praise. Inwardly he thanked the florist who, on hearing what he wanted, had obviously put some thought into how to spend his money. And whatever the problem with the bath, although pale, Jane with her hair washed did look better.

Curious, she eyed the bags he'd put down by the bed. "It looks to me that you've been on a spending spree."

"Patience, my dear Jane, patience" and he deliberately spun out the showing of his purchases. "First madam, open this." Inside was a very modest, but attractive mint green silk nighty that had her eyes glowing with pleasure. Next he produced a woman's magazine and a book by her favourite author. But at the music cassette tape Jane squealed, "How did you know I wanted that. I was going to buy it." Her face fell, "Except I haven't got anything to play it…"Like a magician he'd delved into the last bag, causing Jane's eyes to round as she gasped, "No you haven't, you've bought a portable tape recorder."

Delighted at her surprise he answered, "That's what it looks like to me. It plugs in, uses batteries and we can use it in the car." He lifted up a small bag, "In here are earphones so that you can listen without disturbing anyone."

With a painful grimace Jane lifted up her arms and said, "Come here, let me kiss you properly. Oh David, I do love you, you've thought of everything."

With a broad smile he agreed, "That was the general idea. I also visited a bakers shop and bought a couple of filled rolls so I could stay until I go and get your Mum at four o'clock." For a second her face clouded, but having sat on the bed so her arms could be around his neck, he moved forward to tantalise her lips with little butterfly kisses before moving to a gentle nuzzle.

From Jane came a soft hum as she relaxed back against the pillows drawing him with her. Slowly he retreated, but felt guilty for being so quickly filled with desire for more, oh so much more."

Eyes closed, Jane sighed wistfully before murmuring, "I love your kisses." Opening her eyes she inquired, "Do you think 'it' will be the same after this?"

It would seem Jane could read him better than he thought. Sitting back in the chair he steepled his fingers against his mouth, and pointing his forefingers towards her he said with an amused lift of his eyebrows, "If 'it' is our love making, be assured my desire for you hasn't lessened." His mouth curved into a sexy smile. "As to 'it' changing I don't see why. Paul is the one person I could ask, but as in the past I've been accused of being in cahoots with him, and constantly spouting his wisdom, you'll…"

His sentence was cut short at the entry of Joshua Freeman followed by Sister Knight. Freeman's eyes twinkled in merriment as he tweaked the ends of his moustache and commented, "Good morning Mrs Reinhardt, good to see that sparkle in your eye." Jane blushed, but Freeman had already turned to address and shake David's hand. "It's no surprise to see you here, Reinhardt. And I've no doubt the turning of one of our side wards into a florist shop is your doing?"

David shrugged, "I saw it as a simple way to cheer up a somewhat austere room."

Freeman looked around. "Umm, not quite your St Mary's private wing is it? But good man, you've certainly a way of making the best of situations." He gave him a wink, and turned to speak to Jane. "Now then little lady, how are you feeling?" Sister Knight handed him the charts to study. When Jane didn't answer he looked up and gaining Freeman's full attention she, in her own inimitable way, furnished him with a litany of her discomfort ending, "When can I go home?"

In the midst of that David caught Freeman's glances toward him, which conveyed something akin to sympathy, understanding and amusement, but Freeman's firm tone betrayed none of that as he spoke to Jane. "I think that will, to some extent, depend on you, and your response to us, trying to help you recover. I gather we've barely managed to persuade you to get out of bed. And that you didn't find the salt bath a pleasant experience, but it does help to heal wounds. I also believe you refused the offer of a wheelchair so you could visit your twins." From where David stood he saw Jane stiffen at Freeman's rebuke, and after saying, "And You are still having regular painkillers" Freeman's voice softened, "But I understand your discomfort and nervousness about your stitches. Trust me, no patient of mine has ever had reason to complain about the strength of my embroidery." He chuckled, "There's no fear of your insides bursting out." In seeing Jane didn't share his amusement he said firmly, "Now my dear, if you do a little exercise, follow instructions, Sister here could be taking out your stitches by Saturday." Freeman lent forward to pat her knee, "Enjoy the rest. The longer you recuperate here, the stronger you will be at home to give your full attention to the twins. In ten days you should have healed…"

Jane cut across his words to protest, "Paul…Dr Stemmings lives with us. He can look after me, and I've lots of offers of help with the babies."

"I'm pleased to hear it. You will need it." He handed the chart back to Sister Knight and said dismissively, "Thank you sister. I'll join you for my rounds in a few minutes." Eyes twinkling with mirth he glanced between them and commented, "Dr Stemmings, now there's a very competent man." As the Sister closed the door he let out a loud guffaw. "What a brilliant plot! Granted Peggy Keenan wasn't fooled for long, like her name she's a keen one alright!" In a conspiratorial voice he added, "Ten minutes into her shift she rang me to demand, 'What do you know about Hanson inviting his colleagues into my delivery room?' I noted the emphasis on 'my' and hedged by replying, 'He did mention to me about an old friend from med. school turning up, doing research I think.' At that she came right back to ask, 'His name wouldn't be Stemmings by any chance?' I think she caught the amusement in my voice when I asked, 'Why, is there a problem?' Her immediate response was to bark, 'Don't give me that Freeman, I wasn't born yesterday. This old friend of Hanson's has a colleague who, despite the mask over his face, bears a striking resemblance to my patient's husband'. At that I feigned innocence, but I fear she knows me too well, because she went on, 'I've got no time for games. My hands are full here with twins, and a possible forceps delivery, so get yourself down here, and rest assured by the time you arrive I will have challenged and exposed them. No-one gets the better of me!' With that she slammed down the telephone. I allowed myself to have a good belly laugh, for I was quite confident you and Dr Stemmings were up to any of her challenges. But despite her appearance of annoyance, you see she did take it in good part, because she gave Stemmings permission to do the delivery." Joyfully Freeman rubbed his hands together as he glanced between them, "So good of you to name him after me. And for allowing me the opportunity to be one up on Peggy."

Despite verbalising her previous frustrations, Jane replied sweetly, "Thank you for your support, to have David and Paul there was such a comfort. David tells me you offered us your middle name for our daughter, but I hope you'll understand if we choose another." A jovial boom of laughter caused Jane to comment, "Your laugh is as bad as David's."

Freeman patted Jane's shoulder and said firmly, "Take my advice, little lady, push through the discomfort, get used to your babies, this isn't a bad place and once home it will be tiring." Jane's expression wasn't wholly positive, but David stepped forward to shake Freeman's hand and thank him for intervening of their behalf. Freeman smiled, "Not at all, it's been a pleasure, and good to meet you Reinhardt." On opening the door he turned, "I don't suppose you are any relation to Professor Franz Reinhardt?"

Taken aback David confirmed, "He's my father."

"Really! Even more then of a privilege to have his grandson bearing my name, and to deliver his grand-daughter. I only know of him, but would be very interested to know why Inharts didn't produce, or sell, the Thalidomide drug under licence." Sister Knight was hovering down the corridor, so he stopped, lowered his voice to add, "I've delivered a child affected by it, a tragedy and terrible shock for the parents. Of course the courts will soon be deciding on paying damages, but nothing can compensate for a drug giving someone a life time disability."

The thought of a maimed baby caused a shudder down David's spine. "That must be heart breaking. I'm not involved in the business. I don't know my father's reasoning, but he was horrified that any drug would produce such devastating results. I'll tell him of your interest. By the way, he's also going to despatch to you a case of vintage champagne to go with that finest malt whisky!"

Freeman rubbing his hands together smiled broadly. "I shall look forward to drinking it. Give my regards to Stemmings. Now, I'd best away, patients to attend to."

An hour later, Jane having had her lunch, and he his rolls, Freeman's voice was heard again in the corridor as he boomed, "Ah Stemmings, good to see you. And this is your wife and boy, well pleased to meet you. Very capable husband you have Mrs

Stemmings." As David opened the door Freeman was crouching down to talk to William. "Hello there, you're handsome little fellow." William though had seen him, and skittering straight past Freeman he came to hug his legs with a desire to be picked up. Paul apologised said, "Don't be offended, William adores David."

As David whisked William off his feet to zoom him up and down through the air he asked, "Do you want to see Auntie Jane and the twins?" William gurgling in pleasure clapped happily so he concluded that was a 'yes' and much to his giggling delight flew him into the room. "You can sit at the bottom of the bed, but very still, Auntie Jane's got a sore tummy." William, head on one side looked puzzled, but as Jill entered, he smiled happily.

Behind Jill, pushing a wheelchair, came Paul to proclaim, "Here we are Jane, let's go and see these babies of yours." David's quick glance at Paul was enough to receive and translate his silent message to chat and distract while helping Jane out of bed. From the locker David pulled out the oversized quilted dressing gown Rosemary had made for Jane, as Paul continued, "We must be on the road before the traffic builds up through London. And David I'm sure you won't be far behind."

He looked at his watch. "I've first to collect Joyce from the station. I'll take her to the guest house before bringing her back here to be with Jane." While talking he was struggling to help Jane put on her dressing gown. Suddenly she snatched it from him, and shaking her head, held it tightly against her.

Jill didn't notice as she was talking of Paul delivering the twins, and added, "I am so looking forward to meeting them. Paul says that Joshua is dark haired like David, and your daughter is blonde. It's hard to tell about the features at this stage who they take after."

Quietly he whispered into Jane's ear while ostensibly helping her, "What's the matter? Surely you want to be there when they meet the twins?"

Between clenched teeth Jane retorted, "I'm not going."

Unaware of the undercurrent Jill was still chatting away. "I liked your comment about each twin being no heavier than two bags of sugar." Equally firmly David quietly reiterated Freeman, "Your stitches will be fine. You've got to make an effort."

Jill moved to speak directly to Jane, "Are you going to call her Rebecca?"

Seeing the stubborn resistance on Jane's face brought Jill to silence. Paul stepped in to suggest, "David and I can stand on either side of you to take your weight and help you into the chair."

Jane, her hands still clasping the dressing gown to her chest, said defiantly, "I don't feel up to it. And I don't care Paul what you think, or what Freeman says, it hurts to get out of bed, and I'm not doing it unless absolutely necessary."

Puzzled, Jill asked kindly, "Don't you want to see your babies?"

Irritably Jane retorted, "If you'd been hours in labour then cut in one place to get the baby out, and then cut again across your stomach to get the other out, with stitches in both places I doubt you'd want to get out bed either."

Taken aback Jill folded her arms and gave a heavy frown.

David said sharply, "Jane!" and then noticed William's bright blue eyes observing them and saw him bend forward to pat Jane's foot. Surprised Jane's head swung round to look at the little boy where, with head on one side, he gave what could only be termed as a loving and sympathetic look. That melted even Jane's grumpiness to send him a small smile.

Once William realized he was the centre of attention he clapped his hands. Jill's lips twisted into a quirky smile. "Oh my, with that kind of bedside manner we could have a doctor in the making."

Paul gathered William up and hugged him. "Hardly surprising as that was Ben's career choice. And with a doctor in loco parenthesis I suspect he'll develop a empathetic nature. Children don't just take on your looks and character, but replicate your traits and personality. So if this young man could speak he'd persuade you, Jane to be with us when we meet the twins."

Somewhat sadly Jane agreed, "Maybe he would, but I don't feel up to it. And Paul thank you for all you did. I was rather out of it when you delivered Joshua, but I've heard tales from a variety of people here, and by all accounts you are highly acclaimed!" William struggled in Paul's arms, he put him down as Jane continued, "I'm sorry Jill, I didn't mean to be rude. It's just…" Jane shook her head as though unable to put her feelings into words.

Paul took up the conversation. "I was delighted to be part of what Joshua Freeman called our 'skulduggery'. Now if you won't change your mind we need to press on."

Stubbornly, Jane shook her head.

Paul nodded. "David is so proud of you producing such beautiful babies I hope you won't mind if he comes to show them off to us." Tears brimmed in Jane's eyes, but she stuck with her decision. On a sad smile Paul put William in the wheelchair and instructed, "Wave goodbye to Auntie Jane."

Obediently Jane waved back. Jill gently hugged her. "Each day you will feel a bit better. You'll soon be home."

David gave her a rueful smile, "Do you mind me going with them?" The reply was the shake of her head. "In that case I'll stay to feed the twins, then collect your Mum." With that he dashed out the door to catch up with the others.

How proud he felt lifting each baby out of their incubator to show them off through the big viewing window. William's eyes rounded, and he got so excited, they had trouble holding him up to see in. That distraction allowed him to wipe his eyes at this first family viewing of his children.

CHAPTER 8

It was eight o'clock when he reached London, and the silence of the upper half of the house reminded him of his bachelor days. In three years of marriage he'd often been away, but Jane was always there to welcome him with delicious smells of cooking wafting in the air. Tonight he'd have to make do with one of her music tapes and the toasting of a couple of stale currant buns.

The knock on the dining room door caused him to turn and expecting to see Paul he was surprised to see Rosemary. From her pinched expression he guessed she wasn't visiting to congratulate him on his new family. In an attempt to neutralise the situation he welcomed her with a broad smile and said genially, "Hello Rosemary. I was intending to come down to see you, but now you are here can I offer you a cup of tea or coffee? I'm about to toast a couple of tea cakes, would you like one?"

The toss of her head causing the swing of her long dark hair, the pursing of her lips and the sharp refusal of 'Neither thank you' irritated him enough to shrug, and say, 'Please yourself" before busying himself cutting two buns in half.

"Thank you, I will."

A quick glance showed Rosemary wasn't making a decision change about a currant bun, but delivering a polite barb. Conscious of her standing in the archway to the kitchen watching him he realized she wasn't intending to speak until she had his full attention. As he dropped the four pieces of bun into the toaster he suggested with a touch of irony, "Please feel free to sit, these shouldn't take long." From the large hatchway, which before the kitchen extension had been the dining room window, he watched her take up that offer!

In an attempt to put her at her ease he used the same tactic as when cross examining a hostile witness by talking in a friendly manner. He spoke of Jane's delivery, how she was feeling and how Joyce was covering for him. Rosemary listened, but said nothing. But when he spoke of his feelings of overwhelming love for Joshua and Rebecca, Rosemary's stony expression almost crumbled into a smile. Pleased he was making progress he jumped as the toaster suddenly spat out his buns. Picking them up he asked, "Are you sure you won't have one of these?"

Rosemary shook her head. "What I have to say won't take

long."

That sounded ominous, but buttering his buns he hoped in continuing to talk of the twins he'd diffuse that. Picking up the plate and his mug of tea he moved through into the dining room, placed them on the table and pulled out a chair at right angles to her. In seeing her eyebrows arch at the sight of his plate he queried, "Is something wrong?"

"All that butter. It's bad for you."

Unable to resist he bent forward to tease, "Dear Rosemary, how good of you to care." Despite seeing those sculptured lips purse into a thin line he continued in a conspiratorial tone, "Just don't tell Jane." With that he picked up half and consumed it in two mouthfuls. Jane would have issued a retort, but in Rosemary he saw something akin to alarm lodge in her big, dark brown eyes. What had caused that? Would he ever understand the machinations of a woman's mind? Licking his fingers and desiring to keep the atmosphere friendly he announced, "That was delicious." And picking up the plate offered, "Go on Rosemary try one, there are times when it's good to indulge in the forbidden." Rosemary jerked back as if the plate was about to attack her. Surprised he boomed, "Good grief woman it's only a currant bun." Clearly embarrassed she appeared to be on the verge of leaving so he quickly apologised. "I'm sorry, I didn't mean to upset you."

Quietly, in a voice edged with anger, Rosemary retorted, "But you have. And I'd like to know when you intended to inform me about my role in ITP"

"Your role is as an excellent personal assistant, and I believe you will be invaluable to Robert Jones." At Rosemary's grim expression he hurried on. "To move with me would have wasted your abilities and capacity for responsibility. Mavis' job is secretarial, with barely any responsibility beyond serving me as she did Joseph Plaidon." With no visible response from Rosemary he pressed on. "Obviously Mavis' position pays considerably less than you earn, so with no sensible options it didn't occur to me to discuss this with you." Keen to eat the rest of his buns before they went cold, he consumed another half, but observed Rosemary's straight back and her fight to mask her feelings. "Are you worried or unhappy at being left to work with Robert?"

Disdain filled her voice, "Common courtesy would have

been to inform me rather than my discovering it by default."

Surprised at her censure he viewed her over his tea cup. Was it anger, or a disappointment in him that was motivating her confrontation? He took several mouthfuls of tea before making a considered reply. "I'm sorry Rosemary. I assumed you'd realise with the Exhibitions Director's widespread responsibility, and frequent absences from the office, he'd need you more than me. My role as Managing Director will have greater responsibility, but much is delegated to departments. There won't be the myriad of daily problems that come with Exhibitions and Exhibitors in different countries."

Despite the sourness of Rosemary's expression he smiled encouragingly, "And I'm hoping the Exhibitions Department will expand, and then your help will be invaluable."

Clearly unimpressed and not diverted by flattery he caught the sarcasm in the mimic of his favourite statement, "Is that so? If you feel I'm so valuable I'd have thought an explanation was in order before now, especially as Jill…"

"Yes, I know and I intended to, but…" at her derisive look he burbled on about all the interruptions and difficulties, but the contempt didn't leave Rosemary's eyes and her lips remained compressed.

Obviously exasperated she took a deep breath before saying fiercely, "David I live here! It surely wasn't that difficult, I thought you…oh never mind." Brows knit she shook her head as if unable to comprehend his behaviour. "And it would seem my role and remaining with Robert hasn't been explained to him either! Maybe we both resent being left with each other."

Wearily he ran his hand through his hair. "Rosemary, what can I say! I'm sorry for my lack of thought. But I'd really appreciate it if you would stay with him. Robert might not want help, but inevitably he will need it. He made it obvious he doesn't want me continually looking over his shoulder, so I trust you to keep things running smoothly. I might now be Managing Director of ITP and overall boss, but remember my door is always open to you." He gave her an encouraging smile, stood and picked up his empty plate and mug. Rosemary unsmiling, took that as her cue to stand. Jane's voice echoed in his head, 'Has anyone ever responded to your open door policy'? The truth was he called people into his office, but it was rare they came to him. Rosemary's confidence tonight wasn't from their working relationship, but her friendship with Jane and Jill knowing she'd their support. What would change the 'them and us' situation that prevailed in his business life?

Rosemary interrupted his chain of thought to say with studied politeness, "Thank you David. Give Jane my love. I'll look forward to meeting the twins. Good night."

"Goodnight Rosemary, sleep well." As she left, he closed the flat door behind her, and after tidying up made his way up to bed considering how he might become more thoughtful and considerate.

Next morning he rang the office to speak to Robert. With a smile he started by saying, "Robert, good morning. You've no doubt heard my twins were unexpectedly delivered on Saturday..." In expecting the usual congratulations he paused, but continued swiftly when Robert said nothing. "That meant I wasn't able to come in yesterday to clarify the changeover arrangements. I've asked Rosemary to stay with you, she is excellent at her job and will be a useful liaison for you settling in and getting to know the Exhibitors. Obviously it is up to you how you organise your workload and delegate, but as the travelling and exhibition arrangements build it is advisable to keep Rosemary in the frame enabling her to step in and make decisions when you aren't there."

There was what he could only term as a pregnant pause before Robert answered. "I see. Well David, I'll keep that in mind. I'm sure for both of us life is rather busy so I won't keep you. Thank you for letting me know." With that Robert terminated the call, causing him to stare at the receiver and mutter words his father would use, 'arrogant little whippersnapper'!

When Jill arrived upstairs with William he guessed she was curious about his conversation with Rosemary. But Mrs Perkins' constant chat, titbits of advice and her cleaning the flat around them, stopped any meaningful conversation. Jill having helped him pack the things Jane needed, finally returned downstairs to cook William's lunch. And in his need to be away as soon as possible he was thankful to Mrs Perkins when she presented him with a thermos and sandwiches. With the cases in the car, he slipped downstairs to say 'goodbye' to Jill and was touched by her thoughtfulness to give him a 'packed lunch', and felt it best not to tell her he already had one!

In high spirits and pleased with all he'd accomplished he arrived at Jane's room just after three o'clock. Jane didn't seem very responsive to his kiss, and her Mum jumped up as though keen to leave. "I hope you don't mind David, but I like to be on the platform in good time for the train. I need to collect my suitcase from the bed and breakfast." At that he concluded Jane and her mother had had a disagreement, and from experience he knew it was best to keep out of it. He responded with a smile, and stood by the door for immediate departure, as Joyce spoke to Jane, "Now when you get home, if you need any help you know where I am. You will adjust, you will manage, because it's part of life's learning curve, but remember God helps those who help themselves. You have to make an effort, and sometimes we have to push beyond the 'I can't, or the 'I won't' and believe that as we do, what seems hard, or impossible, becomes possible." Jane's face wore an obstinate expression, her Mum sighed. Jane's stubborn streak could be an asset, but also infuriating, and he heard her Mum's frustration as she said sharply, "Stop feeling sorry for yourself. Think of David and the twins, and determine to get through that dark cloud. That's life Jane. And believe me you've got it pretty easy. Granted you've had a difficult pregnancy and delivery, but despite your negativity you have survived and like it or not, you are now a mother. People who love you want to help, but they can't if you refuse to listen. Make the most of your time here to adjust to the babies, in doing so you will feel better." Joyce bent forward and kissed Jane's cheek, "Goodbye love. See you again soon." Jane pursued her lips and ignored her.

Sternly David pointed out, "Jane, your mother is saying 'goodbye'."

Petulant hazel eyes focussed on him giving insight to her as a strong willed child. At his austere look she capitulated, and muttered somewhat half-heartedly, "Goodbye Mum." He followed Joyce out the door and said to Jane, "I'll be back soon" and wondered how she would have turned out if her father hadn't believed in the Biblical edict of 'spare the rod, spoil the child.' If the twins had that same stubborn trait, or were full of mischief as his nephews had been, similar discipline would be necessary.

Once in the car he decided to ask Joyce, "What was all that about?"

The reply came with a heavy sigh. "David you are going to

have to be firm with Jane. She's not one to be depressed, quite the opposite as you well know, it's probably hormonal, but I don't understand her reluctance to see her babies. It's as if she's afraid to love them. And she's finding it difficult to cope with anything. The nurses insist she gets out of bed to the toilet, so she's not drinking much, at her bath you would have thought they'd tortured her by the state she was in when I arrived. When Dr Hanson examined her she cried out, but he couldn't feel anything to be concerned about. He said she was healing nicely, but could continue on the painkillers for another day. However, he did say she needed exercise, and seemed surprised she hadn't been to see the twins. She barely touched her lunch, she said she felt sick, and when they came with a wheelchair to take her to see the twins, she said she felt too ill to go." The conversation halted as he went into the guest house to collect her case. But Joyce resumed as he drove on to the station. "To be honest David I told Jane that she was behaving like a spoilt brat. She told me to mind my own business, and so on. In the end I went on my own to see the twins, and David they are delightful. The Sister on the Ward, and on the baby unit, wanted to know when you were returning. They are both anxious for Jane to begin feeding the twins, and feel you'll persuade her."

The more he heard, his earlier elation ebbed away. He reiterated the conversations he'd had with Paul, Jill and Beatty concluding as he stopped the car, "The consensus is she'll get over it, but as much as I hate the idea it seems as if I'm going to have to be cruel to be kind."

"You're a good man David, and good for Jane." She chuckled, "Your antics I gather have made quite an impression in the hospital, as has your interest and care of Jane and the twins." His response was to give a self-deprecating smile and say, "Is that so?" but inside he was pleased.

On the drive back to the hospital he considered how Jane had said about feeling under a dark cloud. Was it coincidence that in his recurring dream he was galloping from the light of dawn into darkness? Jane seemed to be losing her sense of purpose whereas he might not like it, but he felt on a mission. His arrival at the door of the side ward coincided with Sister Knight coming out with a wheel chair. "I was just trying to persuade your wife to see the twins."

Taking her to one side he asked quietly, "Does this happen

often?"

Motherly concern replaced her firm expression. "We've given your wife some slack because she's been through a normal delivery, a Caesarean section, and lost five pints of blood. Normally Mum's have their babies by their side during the day, but your wife hasn't had that opportunity, that can make adjustment harder. But she does need to get up and about."

Grimly he took hold of the wheelchair, "Okay Sister, let's do it."

The moment Jane saw the wheelchair her expression was one of alarm, followed by pleading as they both took a firm line against her arguments. Anxious to alleviate all her fears David explained, "To make it easy I'll lift you out of the bed into the wheelchair, and then you won't have to move unnecessarily." Sister Knight seemed about to speak, so before she could say it wasn't hospital policy for a visitor to lift a patient, he'd done it while saying, "I'm quite practised at this." A vivid memory of Jane several weeks earlier flashed into his mind. She'd been standing in the bathroom wrapped in a white bath towel complaining she couldn't see her feet, let alone bend to wipe them. He'd pointed out he couldn't help if she was standing on them and then swept her off her feet and carried her to the bedroom. Now he commented, "You aren't as heavy as last time I did this." His mouth twitched in a seductive smile knowing Jane's mind would follow his. Hazel eyes locked with his and her fear turned into love. Gently placing her in the wheelchair he said, "Just wait until you see our babies, you'll love them."

Together they peered at the two little people in the Perspex cribs on wheels. The babies were airing their lungs with bird like squawking while stretching their limbs, but Jane didn't seem eager to touch them. Sister Giles appeared with a couple of bottles. "I expect Mrs Reinhardt your milk is in, so as Joshua sucks greedily from the bottle we'll first try him at the breast. We'll wheel you into that room, so you can be more private.

With an expression of alarm Jane's hands clamped on to the wheels of the chair. "No. No, I can't do that."

Unsure what to say, or do, David looked at Jane and then Sister Giles who quickly reassured Jane that breast feeding was easy, and lifting Joshua from the crib said, "Let's start with a cuddle,"

Fear was evident in Jane's response as Joshua was held in

front of her. Her hands came up to push him away as she bewailed, "I might drop him. He's so small. I don't want to. My stomach's sore!" Despite knowing there was a need to be firm, David saw Jane was genuinely frightened. And in believing a slower, and more persuasive introduction would work, he stepped in to request, "Give me Joshua, and his bottle I'll show Jane how easy it is." As Joshua sucked hungrily, the bottle quickly emptied. Jane watched in silence as he chatted to her and the baby.

Sister Giles reappeared with a pillow and demonstrated how Jane could put it on her lap and rest the baby on it. "With this you've no fear of dropping your babies, or the weight pulling at your stitches. Obviously we think it's the best option for babies to have their mother's milk, but that choice is yours, we won't force you. Your husband has done a grand job bottle feeding, would you like to try?"

Jane looked nervous, she gave him a long look, but to his relief she responded to his encouraging smile and suggestion, "Try holding our little girl, she's lighter and you can be thinking about her name."

It had saddened him seeing her struggle not to shy away from the little bundle. She did what was required, but without enthusiasm, perhaps because she'd no experience of tiny babies. On the rare occasions she'd held William he remembered she looked uncomfortable. Once they were back in her room Jane said she was tired, would eat the sandwiches that had been left for her tea later, and when he suggested he go to Beatty's, she didn't try to persuade him to stay.

Beatty however, took one look at him and suggested, "Have a relaxing bath, get ready for bed, and I'll reheat some stew. After you've eaten that you can tell me about Jane and the twins, and then bed."

Grateful for her care, he bantered, "Yes Gran." But after a bath, being full from Beatty's food he only managed to tell her the bare facts because he couldn't keep awake.

Both being early risers, Beatty insisted and cooked him a full English breakfast 'to keep him going throughout the day'. And in talking to her about Jane's difficulties he hoped he'd gained wisdom.

When he arrived Jane, in her dressing gown, was walking slowly down the ward corridor, bent over and holding on to a nurse's arm. The young nurse saw him before Jane did and chirped, "Sister Knight says Mrs Reinhardt should sit up in the chair today." She giggled, "If you would like to borrow an easy chair from the Day Room we promise not to notice." He sent her a broad smile, and took over her supporting role, as he addressed Jane. "It's good to see you up and about." Inside her room he gently hugged and kissed her, she didn't pull away, but kept her distance to protect her sore stomach. Solicitously he helped her get comfortable in the chair. From the top of her locker he picked up a dog-eared newspaper several days out of date. "Anything interesting in the news?"

"Stella brought it in last night, but I haven't looked at it."

"That was kind of her." Jane nodded thoughtfully, as he handed it to her. "I brought The Times back with me to read, but haven't glanced at it. I'll get that chair and you can tell me what I've missed."

To his retreating figure she commented, "This is hardly the kind of newspaper you'd be interested in."

Carefully he backed out from the Day Room with one of the more comfortable chairs as a voice said amiably, "I see you're making yourself at home Mr Reinhardt."

Putting down the heavy chair he turned to reply. "Ah Sister Giles, we're going to be here a while so might as well be comfortable." In seeing the Perspex cots containing his infants he added, "I didn't realise the twins were ready to join us, we'll have to make adjustments if we are to all be in Jane's room!"

Sister Giles drew him to one side and talked of how breast feeding would help Jane bond with her babies. That caused him to ask, "Will Jane have enough milk for two babies?"

"The body usually supplies all that is needed, but if the baby is still hungry after a feed you might have to supplement that with a bottle."

"Bottle feeding then does have the advantage of telling us the babies are full, and of course enables me to share in the feeding process." At Sister Giles nod he continued, "In which case I think it best I tell Jane of the pros and cons and leave her to decide. Now I think I'd better install this chair before you bring in those cots."

Quietly she asked, "Do you always turn things to good, Mr Reinhardt?"

Surprised at her question, he turned to see her expression was one of curiosity, not criticism. He gave her a wry smile, "I try Sister Giles. I find it generally makes for an easier life." With that he picked up the chair and headed through the doorway of Jane's room.

A quick glance at Jane showed the newspaper open on her lap and an anxious frown creasing her brow. "I'm glad you're back because…" And then seeing Sister Giles in the doorway, she interrupted herself to say nervously, "Oh, the twins! Surely they aren't strong enough to be out of the baby unit?" As he placed the chair at a slight angle to hers he reassured her they'd learn together and received an approving smile from Sister Giles. And when he took up her suggestion to remove one of the flower displays and let others enjoy them in the Day Room, he caused much amusement as he wrestled the stand through the doorway and across the corridor.

Jane appeared distracted as Sister Giles pointed out the two made up bottles of milk for the twins next feed. And she barely listened about the classes where she could learn to sterilise bottles and teats, makeup the formula milk, and ask questions especially about breast feeding.

The instant they were alone Jane said, "David I need to talk to you, there's something…" she hesitated as the door opened. Nurse Nicols entered and Jane's frustration was evident. Puzzled he frowned at her. She shook her head, and although feeding, burping and changing nappies he could see her mind wasn't on it. Finally the twins were settled, the drinks trolley had issued them with cups of tea and Jane picking up the newspaper said, "Listen to this."

"Is this from the paper in which I'd find nothing of interest?"

Jane gave a derisive tut and he sat with an expression of feigned concentration. "The article is headed:

"Death by Misadventure.

"Police are investigating what first appeared to be an accident, at lunch time on Friday 26th June, when an ambulance was called to The Travellers' Rest public house on the outskirts of Maidstone, where one man died, and another was seriously injured"

Astonished he burst out, "Good grief! Andrew Carlton died?" At seeing Jane jump, and then wince in pain he mouthed 'sorry' as she glared at him, before continuing:

"What at first appeared to be a simple incident of a man

tripping and plunging through the window of a Public Bar door has now taken on a more sinister edge. The Police believe that when Mr Jake Charlton hit the glass, the force and angle would suggest he was lifted and rammed against it." Anxiously Jane looked up. "David I didn't push him. Andrew strode towards me and the force of his hand propelled me away, I stumbled, the barman caught me, but it says here: *His body went half way through the door bringing injuries to his head, face, neck, chest and stomach."*

He shivered, "Horrible! But seeing you no-one would believe you could pack that kind of punch! Tell me, did the barman come from the counter of the Snug or from the Public bar to catch you?"

"I don't know."

"So he could have run past, pushed Andrew hard, then turned and caught you?"

Jane focussed inwardly, "It's possible, He caught me as I heard glass breaking, but he did growl, 'What now!' before dashing off."

Thoughtfully he hummed. Was the barman covering his tracks? He spoke his suspicion aloud, "Henry would be my prime suspect."

Jane tutted, gave an upward glance, before saying. "David, there's more."

Still considering Henry he mused, "Andrew and Henry were known to be collaborators in crime, maybe they'd fallen out, and that's…"

"David, it wasn't Henry."

At that he grinned, "Who was it then, your guardian angel? He might protect, perhaps help us in a fight, but I can't remember any Biblical premise where angels take revenge."

Straightening the newspaper Jane said firmly, "Listen: *'The flying shards of shattered glass caused Mr Henry Nimbya who was standing on the other side of the door to take the full force. A large piece of glass struck him in the neck, severing the main artery, causing him to bleed to death before the ambulance arrived.'"* Jane ignored David's gasp and continued, *"'Three other people sustained minor injuries took the full force.'"*

"So Henry died, not Andrew! Now that really is a freak accident."

Jane added, "And if Andrew was pushed, then Henry

couldn't have done it. Let me finish: *'The Traveller's Rest is a popular tavern for the workers in the local industrial area. On a Friday lunch time the bar would have been crowded, but although many must have witnessed the incident, the place had emptied before the emergency services arrived. The Police are now making local enquiries in the hope of gaining more information. In the mean time the barman has been taken into custody for further questioning.'"*

Concerned he commented, "Which means they suspect him."

"And so the barman will tell the police we were in the Snug." Jane shrugged, "Except he doesn't know who we were."

Promptly he pointed out, "Until the police speak to Andrew."

"Surely Andrew won't want the police knowing his true identity. But if they do find out who he really is, it wouldn't surprise me David if he accuses you."

"Me! Oh that's ridiculous!"

"Is it? Andrew is trouble with a capital 'T'! We have a history with him. He was talking to us. He attacked you, you were afraid for me. After he hit you with that glass you could have leapt up, rushed into the back of him like a bull in a china shop, propelled him into that door and then stumbled back and fallen over that table." Aghast at the scenario she'd created David stared at her. "Now we know that isn't true because I saw you fall across that table when Andrew hit you. The barman heard me scream your name, he too saw what Andrew did. But last time, in a fit of jealous rage over me, Andrew cleverly twisted the facts to accuse you of attacking him. That wasn't true, but months later we became a couple, he could say we lied then, and I'm lying again to protect you."

Sudden fear gripped him, his recurring dream danced into his head. As a lawyer, and short career as a barrister, he knew about twisted facts! Here, his only witnesses were Jane and the barman. If the barman was a suspect, but didn't do it, wouldn't he be looking for an opportunity to point the finger at someone else to take the rap? "Look David I don't know what's going through you head, but in being forewarned we can be forearmed. And whoever pushed Andrew through that door didn't mean to kill Henry."

Not wanting to worry her unnecessarily he refrained from explaining about the 'vicarious liability' law that deemed whoever pushed Andrew would be responsible for the death of

Henry.

Jane waved the paper, before aiming it into the waste basket. "We'd be none the wiser if Stella hadn't left me the paper."

Still considering the angles he summed up, "Let's assume Andrew lives and gives the police our name. We know we're innocent, we knew there had been an accident, it wasn't our business, we left. But supposing Andrew dies and the barman, without our witness statement, is accused?"

Jane breathed deeply, and on her expelled breath she proposed, "Oh David, let's only worry about that if we have to. Believe me, if that happens, the newspaper report will be more than ten lines in a narrow column on page five of a local rag."

"I take your point, but I'm not sure it's the right thing to do."

"Oh David haven't we enough to cope with without complicating life further? I put it down to Andrew for my being stuck in this dump. Let's forget it, and him, and talk of something else."

Not completely convinced he gave a contemplative hum as he considered the black man he believed to be Henry. Had he been a figment of his imagination?

CHAPTER 9

Throughout the rest of the day David's mind re-ran the scene of a tall, well built black man whose working clothes seemed to have camouflaged him in the dark shadows just beyond the Snug door. At visiting time, perhaps because of his preoccupation, Jane took more of an interest when Beatty, and several members of the Stemmings family came in.

Still troubled he returned with Beatty for dinner and was glad to divert his thoughts when Bob and Lillian joined them. They talked of Paul's first wife, her death at Maria's birth and their joy in adopting her. Beatty told several amusing tales of Jill's stay with her two years previously, and gradually he relaxed and pushed Andrew to the back of his mind. Later he took Bob and Lillian to visit Jane, and at their obvious adoration of the twins, he felt their sadness at not being able to have children of their own. So when Lillian said if they wanted a weekend away they'd be happy to look after the twins he was quick to quip, "There Jane, the Lord's supplied you an escape route." Lillian crooning and rocking Rebecca looked up with such eagerness, David thought she'd have probably taken them there and then! And Jane with equal eagerness suggested they book them for next June to cover their wedding anniversary! At Lillian obvious disappointment he said cheerily, "I expect we could arrange something before that."

Jane brightened considerably. "Oh yes, that would be good. It doesn't have to be a special occasion or far away. We went to Windsor for our wedding anniversary this year. To an old coaching inn with low ceilings, a bit difficult for David's height in places, but the room had wood panelled walls, mullion windows, four poster bed and the view over the Thames. Jane's face went dreamy, "It was so romantic." Bob, with raised eyebrows directed him a smile as Jane exclaimed, "I can't believe that was only two weeks ago. The weather was glorious. We strolled into the quaint bits, saw a bit of the castle, and went to the theatre in the evening. I think I sat on every bench to and from the hotel" she chuckled, "To prove it David took my photo at each one!"

Afraid Jane might continue by telling of the en suite bathroom with its double bath, flickering candles and champagne he quickly interrupted. "Jane gave me a camera for my birthday so I clicked away, and after a boat trip on the Sunday, and lunch at a pub by the river ,I'd used my first reel of thirty-six film. I've sent it for developing and am interested to see how I did. That gives me a thought." He pulled the camera out Jane's locker, "Could one of you take our first family portrait?"

The next morning, with no hurry to get to the hospital because Jane had been persuaded to join the class on breast feeding, he and Beatty had a leisurely breakfast. Later he and Beatty walked around the garden and she spoke of her Bill, their happy years. Now, and then her voice caught, or her eyes misted over and he felt to admit, "I don't know how I could live without Jane."

"You could, and you would. I loved Bill and have wonderful memories, but I'm not going to get maudlin. He's enjoying heaven and one day I'll join him, but he'd want me to continue to take pleasure in this life as long as I have it. David dear, would you'd be kind enough to dig that area out for me to plant potatoes for next year." As he obeyed Beatty picked strawberries for him to take to Jane.

Mid-morning they sat in a sheltered, sun warmed spot and as he stretched his legs to enjoy the coffee and cake, he mused aloud. "I still can't really believe I'm a father."

Beatty chuckled, "You will, once those lovely babies are home." Leaning over to pat his knee she continued, "Jill told me you've no grandparents, so I adopted her. I'd be happy to adopt you and Jane too."

"I can definitely speak on behalf of Jane, we'd love that." Pleased he grinned and lent over to kiss her cheek, "Hello Gran."

Obviously delighted Beatty's hand went to where he'd kissed her. "Appearances David are deceptive, for beneath that tough exterior I see a heart of gold being revealed."

Embarrassed he grunted and said, "Jane's influence."

Beatty nodded knowingly. "Oh I think it's more than that."

Understanding she meant his growing relationship with Father, Son and Holy Spirit he asked if she'd thought more about his repeating and expanding dream. "The last time as I came into consciousness the words 'the gates of hell will not prevail' ran through my mind. That was followed by knowing the dawn will eventually overtake the darkness."

Beatty hummed, her eyes focussed with a faraway look. He waited expectantly. It was several minutes before she said quietly, "David, God is showing you that you are part of an army, it's His army, His light in your heart, and you aren't alone. You asked Jesus into your life. He is the light of the world. Throughout the ages God has used dreams to strengthen, promise and warn. Whatever the circumstances you find yourself in God promises to always be with you."

The words, 'whatever the circumstances' brought the incident with Andrew to mind. Beatty knew of their encounter so he told her about the newspaper article and their thoughts. "Jane might not want to get involved, but I wonder should we tell the police Jake's real identity? But if Andrew is then convicted for previous crimes would he, in retribution, accuse me of pushing him through that door and Henry's subsequent murder." Earlier reading his Bible he'd followed Jesus' instruction to give his burdens down to him, but speaking of the situation caused him to groan before burying his head in his hands.

Beatty put out her hand and tapped his knee, "David! I thought you were a level headed man!"

He looked up to say, "It fits the dream."

Beatty shrugged, "Maybe, but that should encourage you, for you know the light comes from within you. God's ways aren't always ours, but He does promise to never leave or forsake those who love Him. It was a dream that showed Joseph to take Mary and Jesus and flee to Egypt to safety."

Quickly he responded, "Do you think Jane and I are in danger?

Gently Beatty pointed out, "I think this is more about you wanting to go one way, but feeling pulled another." That had been true with his marriage and working for ITP. Would being a father bring a conflict of his loyalty and time? Beatty continued, "Abraham went where God took him, in waiting years for the promised son, he tried to help God out, never a good idea! Moses did much the same, having been rescued, adopted and brought up as a prince, he killed a man and escaped to live in the desert for forty years! Yet God didn't waste that time, for in using his knowledge of palace etiquette he had audiences with Pharaoh, and once the Jews were released, his forty years training guided and helped millions of people to live in the desert for another forty years. Nothing is wasted if we allow God to use and teach us. Remember Joseph sharing his dream? It put him on a path not of his making, yet that was God positioning him one day to provide food for the Jews in famine. Later he said to his brothers, 'that which you meant for evil, God meant for good'. Oh I could go on with people like David, anointed as King, who became an outcast before he could take up the role, and even Jesus, God's own Son, had to die before he could bring eternal life to those who believe in Him."

With a sigh he acknowledged, "I know, life even following the Lord isn't guaranteed to be easy. The pattern would appear to be, a time to wait, hope, believe even in difficult circumstances. Yet it's good to know when each of those people had the 'dawn' come into their lives they received more than they expected!"

Beatty nodded and added, "But each had to trust in God to provide, prepare and position them to outwork His plans and purposes. The Bible says for those who love the Lord all things work together for good. If Jane hadn't had that incident with Carlton, Jill wouldn't have met Paul. And later Paul recognised Jill when she needed help! After you have 'cast your burden on the Lord' just take each step as it comes."

He grinned, "God's perfect timing! I read that this morning. Thank you Beatty. You know I'm indebted to Paul for securing my place at the birth of Joshua."

"That's what friends are for. You are both good men seeking to do your best." Beatty sent him an indulgent smile. "Such different characters, but you will learn from each other. It is in our trials where we learn the most, but we have to choose to love the Lord above all else, and walk with the right attitude. Then comes the peace and knowledge that 'the gates of hell won't prevail'."

For a while they sat and contemplated that, before he felt to speak his thoughts. "Jane is a strong believer, her black cloud dispersed when you prayed, but now she feels it's trying to engulf her again. Perhaps I'm to ride into the darkness to rescue her?"

Beatty shook her head. "David, I don't know. Dreams, like prophecy, often are only in part, but if we can align them to Bible verses and speak out what God shows us it can be very powerful. Ask the Lord to flood the eyes of her heart with light."

"That's amazing I stumbled over that verse at the beginning of Ephesians yesterday. I prayed it for Jane and she did perk up enough to go to those 'baby' classes. And I forgot to tell you we've chosen their names: Joshua James and Rebecca Elizabeth."

"Excellent!" Beatty looked at her watch, "Now, having dug to put next year's potatoes in the ground, perhaps you would dig up a few from this year's crop! I'll get lunch and then we can go and visit her."

It was obvious the contact with other mums had helped Jane's confidence in handling the babies. He left Beatty to talk with her while he made phone calls to those he still had to tell his news, and who probably wouldn't have read the announcement his father insisted he put in The Times. After feeding the twins, he took Beatty shopping, and then returned home for a quick meal before returning to spend an hour with Jane who chatted about the people she'd met that day. When he mentioned having an early night she agreed. At his saying he would register the twins' births the following morning, she seemed pleased. And, didn't seem put out when he said he'd arranged to meet up with Paul's policeman friend, John Perrington, at lunch time the following day.

The pub where he met John had a warm and convivial atmosphere, so opposite to the one the week before! John was middle-aged and quite a character with lively tales to tell. Briefly he considered speaking to him of the Carlton incident then thought like Jane, 'why get involved if we don't have to'. Oiled with several drinks and being thoroughly entertained they decide to have lunch.

Afterwards, singing with happiness due to slight inebriation, he drove to the hospital with the idea of him and Jane having a short stroll in the grounds. Filled with the sheer joy of life he walked into Jane's room. "And how is my lovely...?" The words died in his throat, at the sight of the misery on her face. At the sight of him she practically threw herself into his arms to plead, "David, please, please take me home." His heart sank. "In the night I lay awake, I feel panicked, because I feel I'm never going to get home. Then I was fast asleep when the twins awoke and needed feeding. I went back to bed, but an hour or so later the nurse awoke me for breakfast. And when that was over, I tried to sleep, but there were constant interruptions before the twins wanted feeding again. I thought then I'd take a nap, but the doctor came because the Sister said I was constipated and they needed to treat that...so they...well...oh David, it was horrible.

I hate this place. I've been waiting for you. I was beginning to think you weren't coming."

Rocking her against his chest, he cuddled her gently, "Of course I was coming" but at a loss of how to comfort further he suggested, "It's a lovely day, get dressed and we'll get out of here and go for a walk." At the stiffening of her body he detected an argument so he quickly added, "And it will show me, and the staff, that you're recovering enough for them to consider you going home."

Jane pulled away from him, and brightened enough to announce, "Sister Knight says they'll take out my stitches tomorrow, so after that I could go home."

He drew her back in to hug her and replied slowly and thoughtfully. "I suppose it's possible, but I doubt recommended."

She drew back from him. "I've heard that tomorrow they might move me out of this little room into the main ward, that will mean only seeing you at visiting times. Surely that alone is reason enough to get me out of here?"

At that news he hummed, while Jane, preoccupied, continued her litany in an attempt to convince him to take her home until finally he broke in to say firmly, "Jane let's ask if the twins can go in the nursery so we can take that walk while discussing this."

Ten minutes later she was dressed for the first time in nearly a week. With her hand through his arm and resting slightly against him they strolled slowly along the perimeter of the hospital grounds. But Jane, as if realising all her positive reasons for being at home hadn't made any headway, turned to the negatives about staying!

"The hospital is like a prison with its regime and atrocious food. Even at night the noise is…" as she went on and on he tuned out. He tuned back in as she queried, "And what will you do all day with only a short visiting time? Her hazel eyes stared persuasively up into his. David, making the mistake of hesitating, was presented with fresh argument. "If London is considered too far to travel perhaps we could go and stay with Beatty, or even Lillian and Bob for a few days - they like babies."

Irritated he retorted, "Jane I've heard enough. And we aren't presuming further on the Stemmings' family." And seeing Jane about to speak he raised his hand. "And you've only fed the twins through two nights. You are already tired and that always makes things seem worse than they are. Granted at home you have good food, pleasant surroundings and a comfortable bed, but for the next months a decent night's sleep is predicted to become a thing of the past. Let me think about this."

Jane squeezed up against him reiterating the offers of help and ended with a winsome expression, "I sleep better when cuddled up to you. I've so missed you."

"And I you, but that won't solve any problems" but Jane seemed incapable of hearing his reservations.

Back in her room Sister Knight was cuddling Joshua and both babies were both making what he could only describe as a squawking noise. David, as did Sister Knight, caught Jane's grimace at the noise. The Sister admonished, "There's nothing wrong with babies airing their lungs, you will have to get used to it. Your babies need you. You said twenty minutes, but it's been an hour, they're hungry. Now you are both here you can have one each." Sister Knight addressed him as he took Joshua from her. "I've been trying to persuade Mrs Reinhardt now that her milk is fully in to try breast feeding, and perhaps you could encourage her."

Jane shook her head, picked up Rebecca and said, "My husband and I have been talking, and once my stitches are out tomorrow I'm going home."

Surprised, and cross, he retorted loudly over the wailing Joshua, "Jane I didn't agree to that! I'm not sure it's wise."

Jane glowered at him. Sister Knight commented, "Your husband is right. I know you don't believe it, but we are caring for you, and you will enjoy the company being on the Ward. We recommend a ten day stay to ensure your wound is nicely healing, and you are as fit as possible to cope when you reach home. For you there is a car journey of several hours which itself could be quite gruelling, and once home you'll have two demanding tiny babies to look after."

Jane's face wore that stubborn look which told him once her mind was made up it wasn't easy to change. Inwardly he groaned as she reiterated, "But once the stitches are out there is nothing to stop me going home?"

Sister Knight's brow furrowed. "No, but if you go against a doctor's advice, you'll have to sign forms to clear the hospital of their responsibility towards you."

Quickly he intervened. "Mrs Reinhardt won't be going anywhere unless I'm willing to take her." He heard Jane's sharp intake of breath and ignored it. To Sister Knight he said with a wide-eyed look, "But it would be good to have a doctor's assessment of Jane's fitness to travel."

With a nod, obviously understanding his position, Sister Knight said. "Fair enough, I'll organise that" and promptly left the room.

From under the cot he picked up a bottle, and said curtly, "If you aren't going to try breast feeding take this and feed Rebecca." Jane stared at him, tears filled her eyes, but she obeyed for no other reason than to stop the baby squealing. The hungry sucking of two babies became the only sound in the tense atmosphere of the room. Finally he broke it saying, "Jane you can be upset, but I'm not having you leave here unadvisedly. And, I don't appreciate being made party to a decision I haven't made."

Fiercely Jane retorted, "And I'll remind you that I am not a child, but an adult and can take responsibility for my own life."

Eyebrows raised, his voice stern, he counteracted, "That may be so, but I'd remind you that it isn't just your life that has to be considered." Jane made a face, but there was no rejoinder for that! Cross he continued, "You heard Sister Knight. You aren't fully fit, and as the twins' father I'm taking responsibility for them." In believing it might help to share his feelings he spluttered, "And if you must know I'm worried about my ability to cope with the journey."

Surprise registered on Jane's face, but she still tried to push the issue until he declared, "Jane, that's enough! We'll take medical advice." Exhausted he combed his hand through his hair and said wearily, "I need a break."

Furious Jane retorted, "You need a break! What about me? Look what I've been through? You've just been an onlooker. There's no break in all this for me."

Firmly he commanded, "That's enough!" Her eyes narrowed, her mouth resolute, and in hope of defraying further argument he stated, "We're both tired. The twins are nearly asleep, let's change their nappies, and then get some rest." Jane pouted and turned away to change Rebecca. He sighed and changed Joshua who once in his cot was instantly asleep. Turning to Jane he said, "Look I'll get going and we'll see what tomorrow brings."

Jane stepped back from his kiss. He shook his head and annoyed stated, "I thought you said you were an adult, but it seems not above childish pettiness" and with anger rising he walked out.

On the way to Beatty's his anger turned to fatigue. He'd never envisaged having a child, or children, would be so fraught with difficulties. Office problems he could detach from. In personal issues he learnt to keep his own counsel, and keep a tight rein on his emotions. But Jane always wanted to discuss feelings and was upset when he didn't. The truth was in being vulnerable he didn't like being open to others censure. Paul's friendship often brought wise counsel, but he wasn't there to ask, and past options of drowning his sorrows in alcohol, or burying his head in academia, wouldn't bring the answers he needed.

CHAPTER 10

Beatty's house always reminded him of a gingerbread cottage with its gabled roof and white picket fence. Before he left the car, her red front door had opened and Beatty with a bright smile welcomed him as he walked up her path. But with the same intuitiveness as her grandson she drew him in, hugged him and said, "You poor man, you look quite done in."

Suddenly, the years rolled back, he was no longer thirty-seven years old, but a small boy needing his mother. A sob broke in his throat, his voice cracked as he murmured, "Oh Beatty."

"David, you're safe here. Cry if you want to, it isn't weakness it's God provision to let out tension. You've probably been holding on to that for weeks, months, maybe even years!"

That simple permission felt as if the gas had run out of his air balloon. The gas being his own strength, abilities, academic achievements and career progression all of which kept his confidence fired up, and in this situation were totally irrelevant. The speed in which that revelation came was similar to plummeting to earth with the belief of certain death. His life flashed before his eyes, he felt sick and weak. Beatty, as if understanding, drew him to a nearby armchair where he collapsed to bend over and weep uncontrollably from what felt the depth of his being. Beatty perched on the arm of the chair, rubbed his shoulders and spoke comforting words, and as his own handkerchief became soggy, she gave him another. Embarrassed he fought to regain control, blew his nose and wiped his eyes, and without looking up stammered out, "I'm sorry Beatty."

From above Beatty said quietly. "No reason to be sorry. This is more than a build up of tension. You committed your life to Jesus, who loves you and promises eternal life, but that's just the start. As you desire to know Him, there comes a stage where He shows you the base of your trust, it's not a pleasant experience to see yourself as you are. It's like Jill and Jane having babies. You've conceived God's love, but there comes a time to labour to bring forth newness of life. For some it is short and sharp - for others longer and over time. But, by pushing into, and not from, this painful experience you discover what it is to be born again into the Kingdom of God. Take your time and let the Lord deliver you, and in the days ahead He will begin to show you a whole new perspective of who He is, and who you are in Him in order you can grow into a mature man of God." Like a loving Gran she ruffled his hair as she moved towards the kitchen, her words, and the gesture bringing fresh emotion, and it was some while before he felt coherent enough to join her.

On entering the kitchen Beatty handed him a mug of tea and continued preparing the vegetables for dinner. Grateful, he drank the hot liquid, the shaky feeling dispersed and peace flowed in. Feeling foolish he didn't know what to say when Beatty sat opposite him his only words, "Thank you". Her response was a small smile. After their meal, he explained how Jane, having constipation and the treatment for that had been the final straw of her discontent, and her badgering him to go home, had been his!

Beatty nodded. "You know David, the Lord doesn't take away our troubles, but He will help us through them. Bowels remove unwanted food. Emotions allow us to remove unwanted pain. Both are under our control, and if we deny their existence, or don't allow them to do their job, we can get ill. This latest onslaught of problems has finally burst your emotional blockage, and it would be good to find, and get rid of the root cause. Usually it is a painful incident where you either pushed down your feelings, or made an inner vow."

Puzzled he repeated, "A vow? What kind of vow?"

"The example that comes to mind would be, "I'm never going to cry again." A vow causes a blockage, which if unhealthy, stops what should be a natural progression of release in a constructive way. If you block a healthy emotion it will come out in an opposite form, for example anger, hatred, bitterness. As an adult to reveal those emotions is unacceptable, so people learn to live behind a mask. The deception can build to the extent that a person will believe that if people really knew them they wouldn't like them. So as I said, as much as our bodies need our bowels to function regularly to remain healthy, our emotions need to do the same. And, there are times when we have to let others help us."

Feeling vulnerable he questioned sharply, "So what are you saying? I should tell people what I think of them, or speak of how I feel in any given situation? I can see that causing untold upset and hurt!"

Undeterred Beatty held his gaze. "No David. That's what happens when people haven't learnt to use their emotions correctly. Like everything else in life we need to find balance, and as Christians we are fortunate that the Lord can teach us how we can have honesty, integrity, and walk in His peace and righteousness."

At that he lapsed into silence to consider her words while Beatty washed strawberries, put them in two dishes and added a scoop of ice cream. The dish in front of him caused him to refocus. "I'm sorry if I sounded rude, you are right. I've seen the mask I wear, its pride. I have my life under control and expect that of others. I've little patience with peoples' personal problems, am frustrated by their feelings and what I'd call their small talk, and have an aversion to gossip."

"I'd agree about gossip. But your frustration at peoples' feelings and small talk is because you don't understand it because of your own emotional blockage."

Even he could hear his underlying frustration as he asked, "So how do I change that?"

"Eat your strawberries before the ice cream melts and then we'll ask the Lord to show you the root cause of the problem."

Unsure whether he wanted to participate he slowly ate and realized Beatty was already silently praying, peace was invading his mind and his reticence faded. Head bent, he knew how he drove himself in a need to succeed. He wanted to be the best, he'd studied long and hard to get two degrees, one in law and the other accountancy. Basically, that was logical, yet in his mind's eye he was seeing himself in the kitchen of the farmhouse in Bristol. From that a memory triggered of the day he'd found his cat had been run over. Grief stricken he'd carried it in, placed it in its basket then wept in his mother's arms. Jill at six, hearing and seeing this, had run from the kitchen crying, 'Daddy, Daddy, come quickly'. On his father's arrival he'd snorted in derision at his mother's explanation, and catching hold of him pulled him away from her telling him, "Pull yourself together boy. Stop behaving like a baby. You're fourteen, too old to cry over cats, whatever next! Come on." Then he'd watched his father pick up the cat and its basket and open the back door. In desire for his father's approval he'd obeyed and wiped his eyes on the sleeve of his jacket. By the time he'd helped his father dig a hole to bury it, he'd put on a stiff upper lip and in true British fashion determined no-one would ever see him cry again. But that tough resilience had begun to melt way when he fell in love with Jane.

When he looked up Beatty smiled and asked, "Do you want to share what you saw?" Elbows on the table he buried his head in his hands and tears trickled down his face as he told her the story. The pain at the loss of the cat had long gone, but Beatty showed him how hurt he'd been by his father's attitude and his mother for not standing up for him.

"That emotional blockage has held you back in your relationship with others. First, you need to forgive yourself for making that vow, then ask God to forgive you. Then forgive your father, maybe your mother, and even Jill. Forgiveness is a big key in situations that need healing, physical, mental or spiritual."

In acting on Beatty's instructions deep sorrow stirred within him for times when he saw the affect that vow had had in his life. Head down, his elbows on the table, sobs wracked his being. Beatty moved to hold his head against her, and like a mother nursing a small child, she stroked, rocked and prayed for him, and with him. He didn't know how long they stayed like that, but it was like a balm, a release of a heavy burden. "Beatty how did you become so wise?"

She shrugged, "I just speak out what the Holy Spirit, the Comforter, gives me."

"I need wisdom." He explained about Jane's pleas to go home and finished, "If I take her and the twins out of hospital against everyone's recommendation I'd never forgive myself if something went wrong." Beatty gave him a wide-eyed look and he immediately understood, "Sorry Beatty. Wrong thing to say, I break that vow off my life." He sighed, "Do you know Beatty, I make decisions involving thousands of pounds, have control over the working environment of a hundred people, stand up to competitors, bring legal advice and counsel to companies, yet I feel so inept to handle this situation. If I say 'yes' to Jane, it'll involve and put pressure on others, if I say 'no' even with the best of reasons she'll see it as my lack of support."

"Ask the Lord for wisdom, believe, receive and use it. Go and ring Paul, get his medical advice, then go and put your feet up, watch the television, read a book, have an early night. You're exhausted, and that's no place to make a balanced assessment and decision."

Unexpectedly he slept well, awoke refreshed and with a peace that did pass understanding he arrived in Jane's room and seeing her feeding Rebecca said happily, "Now there is a picture

I want to snap, mother and baby, it's so beautiful."

Jane looked up, and greeted him with a small apologetic smile. "David I'm so sorry about last night. Please forgive me. I know, you always want the best for me."

With his hand on the arm of the chair he bent to kiss her upturned mouth and lingered a little longer than necessary. "Jane I forgive you, and I am so proud of you and the twins I feel I could burst with happiness."

Those hazel eyes held his as he looked into them. He saw love and hope as she inquired, "Have you decided? Can we go home?"

Straightening he answered, "That's something we need to discuss."

Her hopeful smile vanished, and she insisted, "I can manage, and we've got so much support…"

Not wanting to go through it again he interrupted, "I spoke to Paul last night. He's in favour of you staying here at least a couple more days." Something akin to apprehension filled her eyes. "And if we ignore Paul's advice we really can't expect him to take any responsibility for you."

"But has he categorically said he wouldn't be willing to keep an eye on me?"

To that he had to answer truthfully, "No. But he felt the travel would be exhausting, and with the twins' demands to consider, he thought it would over tax you."

"But would it do me harm?" To that he shrugged. "Have you contacted my Mum, Jill, Rosemary about helping us?

Puzzled he answered "I didn't think there was much point until we know when you are going home."

"I've been thinking about this. Rosemary will be keen to help, Paul and Jill will when they can, and if I was still here you wouldn't go back to work, so you'll be home to help so what's the difference?"

Not wanting her to know her arguments were making him waver, he frowned before saying, "The doctor here would have to feel the risk is minimal to you and the twins." Jane's eyes brightened so he warned, "But young lady I shall need some assurances from you."

Curious, yet obviously hopeful she said, "Go on?"

"First, if at any time, on the journey or at home you feel more than just uncomfortable, or have any worry about yourself

126

or the twins you'll tell me. And if Paul is willing to check you out you won't object, or if he feels you should return to hospital you will go?"

A rueful smile touched her lips, "After the birth of Joshua all embarrassment I felt with him has gone. And St Mary's will be a palace compared to this place."

He grinned, "That's my girl. Second, you will still need to rest, eat and exercise, in between getting used to managing the babies schedule. I understand that the District Nurse comes in to give advice. Whatever she tells you to do, or recommendations she, or those supporting you make, I want your word it will be done without argument."

That caused Jane to frown. "What if I don't think its right?"

"You can tell me, and I will have the final word and be accountable for the outcome. I am not taking you and the twins out of hospital on a whim. Paul recommends you stay. The staff here won't condone you leaving, so the responsibility for your welfare will lie squarely on my shoulders, so I need to cover all contingencies."

Jane's mouth had firmed into a thin line. "Excuse me! I might be your wife, but I haven't lost the ability to take responsibility for myself. I can sign myself out of here."

He matched her grim look, but despite striving to keep a pleasant tone it carried an equally grim edge. "Yes Jane you can. And you do have a point. In signing yourself out you will be responsible for your own well being and thus exonerate me. But I would remind you as the mother of two babies you have a responsibility for their well being too. And I would hope you would see that as their father I share that with you."

"Okay David, drop the magisterial tone. I get the point. Let's not argue about it. I suggest we let the hospital decide if it would be detrimental to the twins' or my health to make the journey." In knowing from Paul the answer to that he grunted. Jane, taking that as his acquiescence, continued, "So David, Sister Knight said she would take my stitches out about eleven o'clock, and the duty doctor has been informed that we might 'still be hell bent on leaving'. Once we have signed the forms you can return to Beatty's, pack and have lunch, while I do the same here. If the twins' are fed just before we leave they shouldn't need feeding again until we are home, and that should alleviate any problems on the journey."

Less than twelve hours later, Jane after an uncomfortable, if not painful journey, had arrived home exhausted, succumbed to a check up by Paul, and having been tucked up in bed, promptly fell asleep. Jill and Rosemary, thrilled to see the twins, told him to relax while they fed them and prepared him a meal. So he'd bathed, changed and with Handel's Water Music quietly playing in the lounge he sat legs stretched, ankles crossed and closed his eyes. It was good to be home with the support of his family. And he now had his own new family! His thoughts meandered to Jane's cooking and the international variety of meals she cooked. At lunch time he'd joked to Beatty, "Your meals have made a man of me."

Her response was immediate. "No, David, not my meals. The Lord has been 'making a man of you' part of the preparation for the next stage of your life. Listen to Jane, she's not a child, or a precious pet, but the mother of your children. Be open about your feelings, show your emotions. It's in sharing and caring of both ideas and problems that your relationship will develop, and bring the stability the twins will need as they grow up." Beatty was a wise woman and it was his intention to take her advice. He drifted in and out of consciousness considering how that might pan out.

A hand on his arm awakened him and he looked up into Paul's face. "We've let you sleep a bit. Jill says the spaghetti has stuck together and is looking a bit dried out, but I'm sure with a beer you won't notice that. I'll keep the champagne for when we can celebrate together."

Slowly he stretched and yawned. "Goodness it's almost dark. Thanks Paul. I'll slip upstairs, check on Jane, and join you."

When he bounced down the open staircase into the basement lounge three pairs of eyes looked up at him. Jill came forward to hand him Joshua. "Here cuddle your son while I heat up your dinner."

Rosemary cuddling Rebecca sent him one of her enigmatic looks.

"Here's your beer." Paul handed him a glass and clinked it against David's saying, "Here's to the twins long life and happiness." For a few moments they considered that before Paul spoke again. "I'm pleased to hear you and John had lunch together, did he tell you he's in line to become a chief superintendent? Before he could answer Paul continued, "In the circumstances that could…"

From the kitchen Jill interrupted, "Paul, let David eat his dinner first."

A wave of love for those around him filled him. Rosemary might barely converse with him outside of the working environment, but she was happily cuddling and crooning to his baby. Paul and Jill persuading Rosemary to stay living in the flat after they were married had worked out well, both in her help with William and when Paul spent several weeks, several times a year abroad. David drank deeply from his glass, handed Joshua to Jill before sitting at the table where a mound of spaghetti Bolognese awaited him. Filled, he pushed back the empty plate and looked across the room where Jill and Rosemary were feeding his babies. "That was excellent. Thank you Jill, it tasted just as Jane makes it."

"That's because it was her recipe, but Rosemary cooked it."

"In that case Rosemary thank you, it was delicious." He lifted his glass towards her and drained it. Rosemary's acknowledgement was an almost imperceptible nod before she stood with Rebecca and offered, "I expect now you'd like to cuddle Rebecca" and indicated the seat she'd just vacated.

In taking the proffered little bundle he gave her a broad smile, "Thank you. I can't tell you how good it is to be home." She gave a little smile and headed towards her bedroom. Quickly he invited, "Rosemary stay, you don't have to go." But at Paul clearing his throat he turned to see him giving Rosemary a dismissive nod. Puzzled he glanced at Jill. In seeing her worried expression a knot of tension began to form in his stomach, and he demanded, "What's the matter? Is something wrong with Jane? The twins?"

"No David, nothing medical, it's Andrew Carlton."

Instantly he sat up straight to retort, "That man! What have you heard? Has there been another newspaper report?"

Paul frowned, "I wasn't aware there had been one. But it appears he was seriously injured, and your name has come up?"

"Damn the man, he knows we weren't involved in his accident."

Paul shrugged, "Obviously the police have to go down all avenues of enquiry."

Frowning he asked, "How do you know about this?"

"Jill had a telephone call on Wednesday from woman from

the Kent police asking if she knew a David Reinhardt."

Jill took up the tale. "I said you were my brother, and the woman asked if I knew a Jake Charlton, I said 'no' but I knew an Andrew Carlton, and that you'd had a run in with him in Kent last week'. There was a brief pause, before she thanked me and said they'd call back. Before I'd a chance to say you were away she put the phone down. Do you remember Det. Inspector Jordan?" He nodded. "Yesterday he turned up on our doorstep. I told him I was your sister, and recognised him as I was ITP's receptionist when he came about Andrew Carlton's accusations. Happily, I added how I'd met Dr Stemmings then, and later married him. At my chattiness he looked disgruntled, and said in an officious tone, 'It's your brother I wish to speak to.' And he didn't look pleased when I asked was this to do with Andrew Carlton. So I told him how he'd tried to hit Jane, you'd restrained him, and he'd smashed you over the head with a glass. His reply was it was a pity you hadn't reported the assault. When I explained why you hadn't, and were still in Kent, he frowned deeply and asked for your contact details."

Distressed David ran his hand through his hair. "I knew it. I said to Jane that Andrew would use this as an opportunity to get revenge. If nothing else to discredit me in the way he said I discredited and ruined his life."

"I said much the same to Inspector Jordan, but I hated the way he said, 'Thank you Mrs Stemmings you've been most helpful'. I wondered if I'd said too much."

"Not at all. Thank you for sticking up for me, although I'm fairly certain four years ago Jordan was convinced of Andrew's guilt, and must be pleased he's been apprehended. But Andrew having been identified and knowing his next stop is prison is obviously determined to take me with him on a trumped up murder charge."

Jill gasped. Paul repeated in astonishment, "Murder charge?"

"Jane read about it in the local newspaper."

Bewildered Paul stated, "But Andrew isn't dead."

"No, but the local newspaper reported Andrew went with such force through that glass that Henry who was in the Public Bar at the time was killed by flying glass. It's a puzzle because I'm sure he was still in the Snug when Andrew hit me. Yet I told you, Jane didn't see him and we decided at best Henry was a guardian angel sent to assist, and at worse a figment of my imagination! But that aside, Henry's death is the responsibility of the person who pushed Andrew, and I suspect Andrew wants to accuse me of that."

Paul said abruptly, "Vicarious liability."

"Exactly! And I wouldn't put anything past that man. Once we'd read the story Jane and I didn't know what to do. Then decided why implicate ourselves when we weren't directly involved, and had nothing useful to add?" He gave a tired sigh, "It looks as if these two have fallen asleep. I hope you don't mind, but I think the wisest thing would be for me to sleep while I can, and we can discuss this with Jane tomorrow."

Jill gave him a small sympathetic smile, "I'm afraid the Kent police rang us just after you got home and weren't too pleased to have been taken on what they called, 'a wild goose chase'! I apologised, explained the circumstances and DI Gage said they'd take into account your situation, but they needed you in Maidstone to help with their enquiries."

"Surely he wants a statement from Jane too?"

Jill shrugged. Paul sensibly pointed out, "With the twins needing round the clock feeding I'd say by asking only that you go, they've cut you some slack. Now let's carry these two upstairs, Rosemary's made two more bottles for the twins next feed, and I'll check on Jane." Paul reassured him as he climbed the stairs behind him, "It's inconvenient and annoying, but don't worry about the police. Anything left in the pub hallway could have caused Andrew to trip and be propelled forward through that glass. And you've Jane and the barman as your witnesses."

He turned on the landing, "Paul, I just hope it will be that simple."

The twins stirred as they put them in their cots in the study. A tussle haired Jane slept so Paul quietly instructed, "Get some rest," patted his shoulder and left. All thoughts of Andrew faded as Jane snuggled back against him with a gentle murmur of pleasure. Love for her soared and he relaxed in her nearness and warmth.

A squealing two hours later brought him back to consciousness. It wasn't loud, but it seemed his brain had tuned quickly to his son's frequency. Silently he slipped from the bed. Joshua went quiet as he picked him up, but Rebecca was stirring. How could he feed both babies at once? He sat in his leather chair, put a pillow on his lap and cradling a child under each arm. Using the chair castors to slide to the desk he picked up their bottles. The moment he popped the teats into their little mouths they sucked hungrily.

Behind him came a giggle. Jane's breath fanned the back of his neck as she proclaimed over his shoulder, "Oh very inventive! Until they grow you've the right size lap, and length of arms to do that."

With a grimace he twirled the chair around, "I thought I'd left you asleep."

Careful not to disturb the twins she bent forward and kissed him. "Don't be cross. In hospital they'd expect me to feed them so I'm not doing anything I shouldn't. Let me have Rebecca, because it can't be very comfortable like that. Maybe we can get them into a routine where we fed one before the other because if we are both feeding them every three hours we're going to get exhausted. I wonder how other couples with twins manage."

At that he couldn't resist bantering, "If you'd stayed in the hospital long enough you might have found out."

Carefully lowering herself with Rebecca into the new rocking chair he'd bought, she frowned. "I don't know if it was just the physical pain I went through, but in that place there were times I felt I was fighting for my life."

Abruptly he retorted, "That's ridiculous!"

Cross, Jane snapped, "It maybe to you, but I wonder how you'd feel if you'd be through what I have?"

Contrite and seeing her eyes shining with tears he nodded, "You're right, even from my perspective you went through a terrible ordeal."

With a grimace Jane acknowledged, "One I don't wish to ever experience again. Please don't get angry, but..." She paused and looked at Rebecca who was sucking away.

Unable to see her expression, and with Beatty's words 'listen to Jane' echoing in his ears he quickly reassured her. "I won't be angry. If you can't share your innermost thoughts, fears and worries with me what kind of husband am I?"

A little smile flittered across Jane's features as she looked at him. "Do you want the truth?" He nodded, determined to be reasonable although unsure he'd like what he heard. "I know you love me, but at times you treat me as if I was a child because your response to me is either dismissive, or you just frown or scowl which indicates to me your annoyance or frustration." Was he like that? "You're scowling at me now!"

At that he protested, "Oh Jane, that isn't how it is! I'm thinking, but don't always feel the need to comment, but when I'm cross you surely know it! The truth is these last months have been the most difficult of my life. Paul has helped me to cope, but on Friday everything got too much for me and I wept all over Beatty."

Wide-eyed Jane questioned, "Really? At his serious nod her mouth twisted into a little smile. "Are you telling me Mr Reinhardt that the controlled problem solver, who studies everything in detail, is a mine of information and knowledge, actually came to a place where he couldn't find a way to help God out? And are you acknowledging you don't have all the answers?"

Aghast, he could only query, "Is that the way you see me?"

"Truthfully, yes. But it didn't, and doesn't, stop me loving you. But I do long to be more a part of your life, to know what you think and feel. And maybe I could add something worthwhile to your ideas and opinions."

At that he bantered with a broad smile, "Believe me Jane I've never been in any doubt about your intelligence or integrity."

"Is that so Mr Reinhardt?" Jane's pert expression told him there was more to come. "Do you need reminding that our relationship started with your manipulation of my life, and it's something you still do?"

"Only because I think it's in your best interests."

Jane lifted an eyebrow, "And who gives you the right to decide what my best interests are?" In considering that, he realized Jane did have a point. "But it's only because I love you. I bring you gifts and try to be thoughtful."

"Important as those things are in marriage there is more to it. To grow together we need to be free and happy to share how we feel, as you did with Beatty." She gave him a rueful look, "I've felt jealous of Paul because you tell him things you don't tell me."

She was right, Beatty was right, and he needed to address that. He reached out his hand, and moved the chair on its casters towards her. Catching hold of her hand he asked, "Forgive me. I don't mean to shut you out, I feel I'm changing, but it has been good to have a friend like a brother."

Her eyes locked on his. "David, I wouldn't want to deny you friendship with anyone, but we do need to support each other by being open and honest. I know it will make us stronger, and we'll need understanding and unity as these two grow up!" They both looked down at the baby they were cradling. "These two are falling asleep and time we went back to bed." Rising from the chair Jane put Rebecca in her cot and asked, "Can we talk tomorrow? I've things I'd like to share with you?"

Amused he said, "And I also with you." Hand in hand they returned to bed and within seconds snuggled up together. Did he keep things from her? Was that why he hadn't mentioned that the Kent police wanted to question him? Thinking of their talking tomorrow he drifted back into sleep.

The horses seemed greater in number, tighter in rank as they galloped in the darkness. The thundering in his ears was like a loud heartbeat. He thought of it as God's heartbeat, His will, His way. And the darker it became around him, the brighter the light glowed from each rider. Eyes fixed ahead he longed to stop, but knew to do so would mean being trampled to death from those behind. There was no going back, he'd been positioned in this place, it was God's plan, God would be his provision and strength.

Consciousness came gradually. The warm glow of his chest was Jane cuddled up against him. Joy replaced the apprehension of the dream. Eyes closed he basked in the enveloping warmth. A slight breeze from the open window behind him rustled the curtains making a sound of a whisper similar to the one he'd when Jane needed rescuing four years ago. It took him a second to comprehend the words. "Perfect love casts out fear." He opened his eyes to see a glow of light bathing the room. Was it a Holy Presence? In fear he shut his eyes remembering that the Bible said that no man could look upon God and live. Hardly daring to breathe he began to feel what he could only describe as a liquid gold of love filling him. Its felt as if every nook and cranny within him was being penetrated and anointed with a soothing, perfumed and healing balm reminding him of Mary pouring expensive ointment over Jesus' feet. The words of the psalmist came to him, "You anoint my head with oil, my cup overflows. Surely goodness and mercy will follow me all the days of my life and I will dwell in the house of the Lord forever." Was God anointing them? Tears coursed down his cheeks. What had he done to deserve such a visitation? Gradually the beautiful aroma, the all encompassing light and warmth began to fade. He wished he could keep that sense of well-being, but his heart knew that the love, peace and promise would remain with them long after the room returned to darkness.

For some while he didn't move, then slowly he turned over. Had he imagined, or dreamt it? Should he awake Jane, but what would he tell her? Was it God, or an angel visiting as Gabriel did to Mary, or Michael reporting to Daniel his prayers would be answered? Michael had still to fight battles in the heavenly places. Was the army of horses in his dream taking him to fight a battle? At least he'd the assurance that 'the gates of hell would not prevail'. Was this to do with Andrew Carlton's vendetta? In the morning he'd talk to Paul. No, he must first tell Jane. His mind meandered, he slept and when he awoke Jane was missing.

Barely audible he heard the fretful cries. The desire to sleep was strong, but he thrust it off and headed toward the twins. Jane wasn't there so he gathered one under each arm and gently rocked them. On her arrival she said pertly, "Oh you're awake. I could barely hear the twins crying because you were snoring so loudly."

Immediately he retorted, "I don't snore."

For that he received a wide-eyed look and a baby's bottle with the instruction to feed Joshua as she took Rebecca from him. Once the twins were sucking happily Jane asked, "David did you open, or spill some of that anointing oil your Dad brought back from Israel?"

Frowning he asked, "Why?"

"It's just the bedroom smells of it, didn't you notice?" Shaken, he sat up so abruptly the bottle slipped from Joshua's mouth causing him to give a little cry. "David! Are you alright?"

"Yes, yes fine. It's just that...I well...I thought I'd dreamt it..." Awkwardly he explained what he termed as a bizarre experience.

Dumbfounded, Jane didn't interrupt or speak until he finished, then she challenged, "Do you mean to say this very unusual, exceptional in fact, spiritual experience happened in our bedroom and you didn't wake me!" He opened his mouth to point out he was too terrified to move when she continued, "I'd have agreed you dreamt it, except for that beautiful smell. Why did I miss it?" For that he had no answers and Jane went into deep thought while he relived and considered the event until both babies were fed, burped and changed.

"Jane I think I'll stay up for a while and do the next feed. You sleep through now and we'll have a late breakfast and talk again."

Jane yawned, reached up to put her arms around his neck. "I'll admit that sounds a wonderful idea."

"I'm glad we are in agreement Mrs Reinhardt" he nuzzled her upturned mouth with his lips, lifted her into his arms and carried her back to bed. "Thank you for giving me the twins."

There was no doubt of the twinkle in Jane's eyes as she looked up at him, "Well I can't say the producing of our family was a pleasure Mr Reinhardt, but I will agree I thoroughly enjoyed the conception!"

Desire ran through him at the picture and pleasure she conjured up. He adored this petite, pert, provocative woman. As if knowing his thoughts she chuckled as he lowered her to the bed and kissed her soft, sensitive mouth. In need to deflect his rising passion he sat beside her to ask seriously, "Do you feel happier now about being a mother?"

"David just watching you with the twins helps me, they already recognise and seem to adore you, and I'm sure with your help I'll learn and adjust."

The answer wasn't quite what he'd hoped for, but in drawing the bedclothes around her he was thankful that her rejection of the twins was over.

CHAPTER 11

The clock tower chimed ten as the twin's completed their sixth feed since arriving home. How did people manage without the support of their family? A bacon and egg breakfast had been supplied by Jill, Paul was coming up to check on Jane, and Rosemary said she'd time the lunch between the twin's feeds.

Jane, stretched out on the settee with her back to the door remarked on hearing David enter the room, "Paul seems very serious about taking care of me. I don't think even at St Mary's I'd be seeing the doctor several times a day."

Before David could comment Paul's voice from behind him retorted, "I heard that. You forget I've Mr Reinhart to answer to."

Twisting her head to grin at Paul as he manoeuvred between the coffee table and the adjacent settees Jane bantered, "Would that be Reinhardt Junior or Senior?"

Paul perching beside Jane answered, "Both!" Then having satisfied himself that her temperature and pulse were normal he queried as he wrapped the blood pressure cuff around her arm, "Anything to report? I'm thinking constipation, feeling sick, breathlessness, extra bleeding, or pain anywhere? I can check your vital signs, but I'm not infallible and all seeing as God!" At the mention of God Jane turned her head towards David seated on the settee at right-angles to her, causing Paul to question, "Is there something you're not telling me?"

Jane urged, "Go on David tell him."

Unsure how to start, and aware of Paul's intense gaze, he cleared his throat to say in a matter-of-fact tone, "During the night we had a visitation of either the Lord or an angel?"

Jane chirped, "Except only David experienced it."

To which he retorted, "But that cloud of love also covered you and left a delightful aroma in the bedroom which you thought was that anointing oil Dad brought back from Israel."

Paul with puzzled expression refocused on Jane as she commented, "When Moses met with God he was surrounded by the cloud of God's glory." Amused she bantered, "In fact I'm quite jealous. I sing about hallowed ground, and David gets to experience it while I sleep through it!"

Paul shaking his head pumped the air into the blood pressure cuff and suggested, "Maybe David I should be checking your blood pressure. It sounds to me as if you've been having hallucinations!"

"I certainly have not!"

Paul's mouth twitched as he concentrated on Jane. He pulled the stethoscope from his ears to announce, "That's fine" then looked across at David to declare, "Your turn."

Crossly he retorted, "Don't be ridiculous, there's nothing wrong with me."

There was no mistaking the laughter in Paul's eyes, nor the sceptical mimic of David's favourite phrase, "Is that so!" Disappointed at his friend's response to what he felt a significant event he scowled. Unperturbed, Paul repacked his case while instructing Jane to rest as much as possible.

The telephone in the hall rang. David jumped up to answer it. Paul stood to leave. David's words, "What the…" were cut off as Paul's weight fell against him, losing his balance David fell back on the settee with Paul collapsing on top of him.

Jane gurgled in glee, "Oh if you could see yourselves!" Over her paroxysms of laugher he boomed at Paul, "Get off me!"

Against his chest Paul's retort was a muffled, "Give me a chance!" Tangled together he had to turn to allow Paul to roll sideways on to the seat beside him.

Peeved at Jane's mirth, David declared "It's not funny Jane! Paul's wretched case hit my leg." In the need to answer the telephone he stood, winced at a sharp, stabbing pain, and looked at Paul to accuse, "I think you've dislocated my kneecap."

Paul straightening his clothes retorted bluntly, "Just be grateful I decided to fall on you and not Jane." With a grin he added, "Trust you to decide to stand at the same time and in the same place as me."

Doubled up in laughter Jane burbled, "Oooh my poor sore tummy. It reminds me of that time in your office when Paul nearly head butted you because you were peering over his shoulder."

Cross, David snapped, "Yes, thank you, Jane!"

The telephone stopped ringing. Jane's infectious laughter was making Paul chuckle. Annoyed that they appeared to have forgotten about his knee injury David began rolling up his trouser leg saying tersely "You won't find it funny if I can't walk." Paul bent to feel his knee. Cross, he swatted away his hand wanting to be the first to see the damage. Voices in the downstairs hall caused Jane to warn, "Paul you'd better go. Jill hates being late for church."

As he picked up the offending case Paul advised, "I doubt

you'll need stitches, but should you need ointment and plasters they're in the First Aid box in the boiler room." Heading to the door he turned to remark, "Jane it's lovely to hear you laugh again" and as he missed the kiss she blew toward him, she called her thanks after him, and received a wave as he disappeared down the stairs. A second later they heard him asking, "Are Rosemary and William in the car? Then darling, there's no need to fret we won't be late."

The front door closed, the car engine started and Jane still giggling looked across at David's exposed knee where, despite the blow, there was only a small scratch and red mark. At her expression David felt to complain, "It might not look much, but it hurts enough to wonder if the bone's chipped."

"Shall I kiss it better?"

Churlishly he retorted, "I'm not a child" then realising he was behaving like one he rolled down his trouser leg and limped manfully towards the door saying, "I'll make a cup of tea. By the way, your Mum rang earlier, and said she'd call back about now, that might have been her. She's upset because the hospital told her you'd left, and because you haven't spoken to her since Tuesday she felt she couldn't go to church until she'd sorted the problem out."

Jane raised her eyebrows and followed him to the hall. By the time the kettle boiled the telephone conversation had changed to happy chatter reminding him of the bubbly girl he'd fallen in love with. His mind went to Andrew who'd draw his attention to Jane. He still had to tell her about the police wanting to question him. As he carried the tea tray into the lounge Jane wound up her conversation.

Feet up on the settee Jane smiled, and said fervently, "Oh it's so good to be home."

David handed her a cup of tea saying, "Until Paul commented about you laughing I don't think I'd realized just hard these last months have been for you." With a wry smile he added, "Beatty told me I should listen to you, so here I am, and I promise to do that more in the future."

"Did she, oh bless her. Paul is so lucky to have a Gran like her."

"I know. I really appreciated her especially when I cracked under the strain on Friday. I'm afraid I had a bit of a breakdown."

"You! You had a breakdown, surely not!" He sent her a self-deprecating smile. With a puzzled, but sympathetic expression she patted the settee next to her. "Come and sit beside me, and tell me all about it."

It wasn't as difficult as he'd thought to explain how Beatty had helped to release his emotional dam. Throughout Jane's eyes had revealed her love of him, tears had filled her eyes when telling her of the death of his cat. The shaking of her head revealed her disbelief that any father could be so hard-hearted, and her comfort expressed by hugging him. Snuggled together he added, "Beatty pointed out Dad came from an era when emotion in men was seen as weakness and not acceptable." Thoughtfully Jane nodded, and encouraged he continued, "I vowed then never to cry or show any negative emotion again. I studied hard so I, like my father would be seen as a tough and successful business man because I wanted him to be proud of me."

Jane drew away from him to exclaim, "He is proud of you!"

With a rueful expression David smiled down on her. "I'm not sure about that. But I now know that the root of my ambition came from a bitter experience, not a healthy desire. Beatty asked me to pray a simple prayer forgiving my Dad, and forgiving myself for making that inner vow. Her view was that it would change me, and often, in an inexplicable way, could change and soften him. He hugged Jane, "That's why I've always found it hard to be vulnerable, but I am a work in progress."

Jane's hand reached up and touched his face. "Oh David, we're all that. I know your heart is for me, even when your face is stern." Her hand dropped to her lap, and looking down she admitted, "And these past months I know I've been particularly difficult to live with."

"True, true!" he bantered, as his hands slipped around her heart-shaped face, lifting it toward him with the intention of kissing away her gloomy expression. A finger jabbed his chest, her words although said with seriousness had an underlying amusement, "Careful, Mr Reinhardt for you might get the truth of how difficult you are to live with."

Gazing into her eyes he challenged, "But, Mrs Reinhardt, you and I know I have some very notable good points!" Before she could protest he proved his point by kissing her until her eyes glazed, and he could declare, "An area, Mrs Reinhardt, where we're very compatible!" Cuddling her into his chest he confessed, "My perception from youth has been women are full of irrational emotion…" Jane drew back to look at him, "…that's because I didn't understand that feelings are important, and not a sign of weakness." Gently he lent forward to massage her neck and shoulders. There was no doubt of the physical pleasure they enjoyed and as Jane hummed her response he added, "I think we're agreed we experience a oneness of body, but still need to work on our minds. I can understand why the first time Adam saw Eve he exclaimed, 'whoa man' and that name has stuck to this day!"

Jane chortled, "You're not the first to think of that."

"I don't suppose I'm the first to experience what I'm going to call 'a glory cloud' either?"

"I've not heard anyone talk of such a thing. I wonder why you experienced it and I didn't? I think we'll have to be wise who we tell, Mum was more sceptical than excited."

Careful not to bring into question Jane's Mum's spirituality he said, "Beatty and Paul are probably more open to the activity of the Holy Spirit."

Thoughtfully Jane added, "I do feel more alive today than I have for months. You thought it ridiculous for me to feel death was stalking me, but in hospital there were several occasions when I thought it was!"

"I hated seeing you in such terrible agony, but Paul said it was normal."

"Oh David, it wasn't just the births, several times I had what I'd call a panic attack, I couldn't breathe, but putting on that tape you bought me helped me relax and it went away."

Concerned he frowned. "You should have told me."

"But your stock reaction is, or was, 'that's ridiculous!'"

"Oh Jane, I'm sorry." Pulling her against him he kissed the top of her shiny head of hair.

Promptly she replied, "Forgiven" and smiled up at him. "I wrote letters to Joshua and Rebecca so they'd have something from me if I shouldn't be here for them."

"That's ridiculous!" At Jane's wide-eyed gaze he gave another self deprecating smile. "Sorry! It's me who's ridiculous, a reaction of not wanting to contemplate such a thing." As if to demonstrate that, he hugged her tightly.

Snuggled against his chest he still heard the despondency in Jane's voice as she confessed, "I'm afraid I just haven't got that motherly instinct everyone talks about."

Unable to think of something comforting to say, he gently drew her back, and taking her hands, said cheerfully, "Don't worry about it, I think I've got an over developed fatherly one."

Lightness and love flowed into her upturned face. "Oh David, I do love you. And knowing more about your childhood makes me feel closer and more part of you. At least your glory cloud has wiped out my black one. Pass me your Bible." As he stretched to pick it up from the coffee table, she continued, ."This morning chatting to the Lord these verses in Isaiah caught my attention." Jane thumbed through and read: 'Behold, I am doing a new thing! Now it springs forth; do you not perceive and know it and will you not give heed to it? I will even make a way in the wilderness and rivers in the desert.' Oh David new life has sprung forth from us, whatever happens the Lord will make a way and provide." As Jane considered that, he thought of the verses relevance to his dream.

At a crying sound David glanced at his watch. "It's just over three hours since their last feed, where did that time go? But at least they'll be fed and settled before lunch."

Jane smiled up at him, "I am reminded of that Bible verse the Lord gave me after that incident with Jacques, 'Do not stir up, or awaken desire, until it please,' but as your wife I'd really like another of your very special kisses."

With a flourish of his hand he said, "My dear Jane, it will be my pleasure, and it's lovely to have you back to your chirpy little self. Let's believe that all you've been through won't spoil the enjoyment of that area of our marriage."

"It better not, but should you have objections to me taking the contraceptive pill..." Jane paused and giggled.

Immediately his mind focussed on a family dinner several months after their marriage. Gruffly he stated, "Dad nearly had apoplexy at you talking of our birth control arrangements and I felt the fool of all fools!

Grinning cheekily Jane responded, "But everyone else thought it was funny, and we need to be able to laugh at ourselves. Now kiss me, and then I'll make up the bottles. Let's bring the twins down here to give them a change of scenery."

Light in step and heart he took the stairs two at a time. Rebecca still slept despite Joshua's attention squalls, his little arms going up and down in the air. Gently rocking him he thought his heart would burst with love as his son's eyes seemed to focus on him and then quieten. For a few minutes he contemplated parenthood. In knowing Jane must be waiting with the bottles he gently scooped Rebecca up with his free arm. She blinked awake and although it wasn't possible, it seemed she smiled at him. Carefully negotiating the stairs with a baby in each arm he could feel Joshua was heavier than Rebecca. Once the hospital informed the District Nurse they were home he'd no doubt she'd visit and confirm that. It was as it should be, his son taking after him, his daughter petite after her mother.

David peered into the lounge, Jane wasn't there.   Passing the telephone he made a mental note to ring his parents to say they were home. They'd be keen to come and meet their new grandchildren, and he was equally keen to get some help with these three hourly feeds.

Joshua began crying again as he strode across the dining room so he boomed at Jane's back "Are the bottles ready? This little man is going to take after his Dad with the need to be constantly fed." Jane didn't respond. Joshua's crying must have drowned out even his loud voice. Two filled bottles were on the work surface, and about to pick one up he turned to speak to her. His words died in his throat for her eyes were rounded, her fist against her chest and she looked to be holding her breath. Urgently he demanded, "What's wrong?"

Struggling she gasped, "Pressure" and tapped her chest.

In three steps he'd laid the twins on the dining room carpet. In three seconds he'd picked her up, and carrying her through the dining room he instructed, "Take shallow breaths, don't panic." Grabbing the telephone from the table he sat on the floor cradling her head against his left arm, and dialled with his right. Gently he rocked, reassured and repeated his instructions to breathe slowly. He fought growing alarm at Jane's inability to do that, and frustration at the excruciatingly slow telephone dial as it returned each time from nine. Jane's lips were turning blue. Fear chased through him as her body began to sag against him. She was losing the battle. Sternly he cajoled, "Come on Jane, fight it, fight it." In asphyxiation the colour was draining from her face. Her eyes filled with love locked on to his as if to impart the words she couldn't speak. Desperate he cried, "Jane, breathe, come on breathe." Automatically his arm under her head shook her, but her eyes were losing their focus, he shouted frantically, "Don't give up. I love you. Don't leave me." With a gasp, her eyes refocused, in that second he felt a jolt of relief, but it was brief for her small smile moved beyond him as her body went limp.

The telephone receiver dropped from his hand. A sob rose up from the depths of his being bringing a choking pain as his throat tightened and closed against his scream. It couldn't be, he hugged her body against his chest, rocking back and forth. Into her hair he moaned her name. From within rose up the plea 'Jesus help, help me'. Tears rolled unchecked down his cheeks. Liquid love began to rise from within him, coating, protecting, comforting, bringing the knowledge that to surrender his anguish to the Lord it would lessen the blow. Jane appeared to be sleeping, her small smile as though she were having a wonderful dream. Her body was warm, yet flaccid and feeling oddly empty.

This was the darkness of his dream, he was galloping into the unknown, yet hadn't God said that the gates of hell wouldn't prevail? That light within him was his faith, he had to believe, he had to trust in God otherwise he would be dragged into depths of despair.

Through the turmoil of his thoughts an eerie voice permeated, "Caller answer me? Caller are you there? Which service to you require?"

He snatched up the telephone receiver. "Ambulance, send an ambulance."

There was a click on the line, before anyone spoke he exclaimed, "Hurry, my wife can't breathe" his sobs cut off further words.

A woman's voice urged, "Your address caller. Caller? I need your address. Caller are you still there?" His brain felt like mush, but from somewhere he heard himself blurt it out. "Hold the line I'm despatching an ambulance…"

The front door opened, voices sounded in the hall. Relieved he dropped the phone and boomed, "Paul, help me, help me." The instant Paul took the stairs two at a time he realised the futility of that request.

Paul ordered, "Lay her flat." On his knees beside him he asked, "How long has she been like this?"

"Two or three minutes. I've called an ambulance."

Rosemary having followed Paul whispered, "Oh no, Oh God no!" and sank to her knees just beyond the top stair.

In giving Paul space, David glimpsed Jill through the banister rail, her eyes wide and questioning as she cuddled William. He shook his head and moved away to pick up the telephone receiver. "I've a doctor here now, but it's too late." The truth of those words ripped him apart. Overwhelming grief poured into him. Vaguely he heard the telephone operator saying the ambulance was on its way. Mindlessly David put the receiver back in its cradle, and replaced the telephone back on to the hall table. It was obvious Paul was as desperate as he to see life return to Jane for despite his murmuring, "It's no good, she's gone" Paul seemed determined to continue to try and resuscitate her. Agony resonated through him. This couldn't be happening. Numb his mind could barely function. He closed his eyes and sank to his knees. A keening sound from Rosemary touched and matched his grief. Across Jane's body he saw Paul's eyes brimming with tears as he shook his head. David tried to stand, instead stumbled and bumped into Rosemary. Their eyes met, her misery so mirrored his that in a need for mutual comfort they clung together crying over their loss.

Bells were ringing, voices called out. Paul drew him up from Rosemary as two ambulance men raced up the stairs and knelt over Jane's prostrate body. He heard Paul say, "David, I'm so, so sorry" and saw Jill helping a dazed Rosemary down the stairs. It was if he was watching a heartbreaking film, he wanted to turn it off, but couldn't. How could this be happening? A few minutes ago Jane was alive and well and they were about to feed the twins.

Anxiety replaced grief. David boomed, "The twins, Paul, oh the twins! I left them on the floor in there." He asked himself, why they weren't they crying? Paul standing in the dining room doorway was already turning as he directed, "By the kitchen wall". Heart pounding he skirted around the men with Jane and prayed, 'Oh God, please let them be okay.' Paul rounded the dining room table first, and stopped so abruptly he nearly bumped into him, causing him to demand, "Oh no. What's happened?" Paul stepped aside. "They're okay, but David look, this is extraordinary." In his haste he'd dumped the twins between a dining room chair and kitchen wall. In the inches that separated them they appeared mesmerised by each other and had stretched their little arms so their hands could entwine. In an awed voice Paul commented, "I suppose after nine months sharing a womb, we shouldn't be surprised at such a bonding."

A male voice asked from the doorway, "Who was with the lady when she died?"

David turned, "I was. Jane is my wife."

Paul intervened, "You go, I'll take the twins downstairs."

He pointed to the bottles in the kitchen "Jane had just…" emotion welled up in his throat.

Paul patted his shoulder, "Go to Jane. Jill and Rosemary will feed them, and I'll come straight back."

The ambulance man talked to him about procedure, but all David could think of was Jane, his adorable little Jane. It couldn't true, it mustn't be. After all she'd been through, just as they thought... They'd so little time together.

Dazed, he watched as they laid Jane on a stretcher, placed her in the sitting room and indicated he should go in to 'say goodbye.' This was her home, she'd only just returned. What could he say? 'Don't go?' But she'd already gone.

Paul re-appeared. "Rosemary and Jill are feeding the twins. You need to do this, and remember although Jane's body has given up life on earth her spirit lives on. Tell her how you feel. It will help you come to terms with what has happened." He nodded knowing Paul had been through this with Beth his first wife.

Beside the baby grand piano Jane so loved to play was the stretcher on which she lay. The sight sent through him such a gut wrenching pain of anguish, he fell to his knees beside her and heartbroken, wept as the door closed behind him. When the initial emotion subsided, he thought how she looked asleep. Cautiously he reached out to touch her face. It was warm, she felt alive. He drew his knuckle down her cheek. Between sobs, wiping his face, blowing his nose, he haltingly found the words to express his feelings. "They tell me...I have to say 'goodbye'... I don't know how...I panic at the thought... of not seeing you again, not hearing your voice, the bubbling laughter, the cross tone when I've done something without telling you first." Grief welled up, he wept again, but his mind thanked God that earlier they had talked, and he'd listened. And her eyes in those last moments had spoken of her love. And that smile for him, and then beyond...was it Jesus she'd seen waiting for her. In transitioning from death to eternal life she'd smiled, she wasn't unhappy and neither should he be, but... his heart cried out, "I didn't want you to go." Lovingly he stroked the hair on her forehead, and found strength to speak as if she could hear. "Oh Jane! We've had our spats, but I've loved the fun, laughter, kissing, the pleasure of ..." Overcome with memories he drew her up, cuddled her, wishing life into her and tucking her head under his chin as he'd done so many times before. Fresh tears fell into her soft newly washed hair with its familiar aroma. After the tears abated he confessed, "I manipulated you to get pregnant. I didn't tell you of the risk of twins. I should have stopped you going to Kent, or leaving hospital early." In an impassioned plea he rocked her and asked, "Please forgive me?" In that moment the words came into his mind, "There's no condemnation for those in Christ Jesus" and that gave him the confidence to ask, "Lord how am I going to live

146

without her?" The words of Psalm 23 followed, 'You anoint my head with oil, my cup overflows, surely goodness and love will follow me all the days of my life...'" Had what he'd termed 'liquid love' from that glory cloud been anointing and preparing him for this? It had to be! The assurance came. God would help him overcome his fear of tomorrow and bring hope for the future.

The warmth of Jane's body permeated through his shirt. He wanted to believe she was still alive, but he knew her body was now an empty shell. Despite that he bent his head to whisper in her ear, "I know you are alive in spirit and with Jesus, and one day..." His voice caught, it tore him apart to think how long that might be. He cleared his throat to continue, "One day we will be together again. Pain twisted and screwed tightly in his stomach, he hugged her close. Soon he would have to let her go. If only this was a nightmare from which he'd awake. Carefully he lowered her back on the stretcher declaring, "I'll always love you." And looking down on her he struggled in knowing this would be the last time he'd look upon her face. Tears ran down his face. Her children would never know her! In words, broken with emotion he bent forward to tell her, "I promise...the twins...will know...all about you. And...I'll do all I can to ensure that they...one day... will join us in heaven. You will always be their mother. Your character and personality will live on through them." Those last words initiated a wry smile remembering Jane's less positive traits.

The knocking at the door told him it was time for him, and then Jane to leave. Dread gripped his heart. "Oh Jane, I can't bear to know I'll never hold you again, or see your cheeky face and smile..." In an heartfelt plea he called, "Lord be my strength!" and sat back on his heels. "The Bible says, 'You give and take away' but I never thought you would take Jane from me." Yet suddenly he remembered the day he'd proposed to her, and his words, 'I know now even if I had to live without you the Lord still has a plan for me and my life'. It came to him that nothing changed that belief! In his daily relationship and desire to serve the Lord his faith had grown, and the 'glory cloud' last night assured him God would be with him. And hadn't Jane, in agreeing to marry, said the strangest words? 'I believe God has brought us together, and for however long that is, I give you my love'. With tears in his eyes he looked down at her still form for at the time he'd questioned if she thought he might end up in an early grave. Had God been speaking through her then? So often Jane's close up and personal faith with the Lord had taught him much. Even in feeling death stalking her she'd claimed the Biblical verse, "the devil comes to maim, steal and destroy, but Jesus came to give abundant life." A knock came again, prompting him to pray, "Jesus I believe Jane has just stepped into that abundant life, and I ask you to please pour your love in, and through me for our children, and that one day as a family we will be reunited." He took one long, last loving look at the face of irrepressible girl who had won his heart. As he stood, his eyes felt drawn to the corner of the ceiling above the piano to declare, "Dearest Jane, so short a time together, but there's a place in my heart made for you alone. To be your husband has brought me the greatest of pleasure…" Different scenes of their ardent love making flashed before him, pain arose to choke him, but he swallowed hard and groaned, "Oh Lord". Instantly he saw, similar to a wedding photo, Jesus and Jane facing each other, hand in hand. Happiness radiated from their faces as they looked at each other. The picture became alive, similar to a film, he saw Jane say something to the Lord and they both turned towards him. With that cheeky, tantalising expression he so loved, she did as she would often do, bent slightly and blew him a kiss before turning back to Jesus. Unchecked tears coursed down David's cheeks and dripped off his chin as he watched them hand in hand walking into the light and fading as they entered the mist of eternity. Softly he said, "Goodbye my beloved, little Jane" and waved as if wiping a window clean.

Grief mixed with inner peace. The body on the floor no longer held any significance. After blowing his nose, he wiped his eyes and face and opened the door. Paul, waiting for him, placed a hand on his shoulder and said kindly, "A tough call my friend. Come downstairs." Silently they descended, passed the open front door, along the hall and down to the flat below.

CHAPTER 12

The smell of roast dinner assailed David's nostrils, but for once he wasn't hungry. In looking at his watch he realised it had only been an hour since Jane's death. As he and Paul took the final stairs into the garden flat memories flooded his mind of Jane living with Jill, and his racing down these to sample her cooking. Bright sun shone through the large wall of windows, the line of the hymn 'Amazing Grace' jumped into his head. 'When we've been there ten thousand years bright shining as the sun, we'll have no less days to sing His praise than when we first begun.'

In seeing William bouncing up and down between Rosemary and Jill and their each feeding one of his babies, he hesitated as new tears blurred his vision. The slight pressure of Paul's hand on his shoulder kept him going, but when Jill looked across at him her cheeks wet with tears, his overflowed and trickled down his face. He used his hand to wipe them away as Rosemary stood and aimed her words at his tie. "If you take Rebecca I'll check the dinner." For a brief moment their eyes met, again his pain mirrored in hers. Quickly she redirected his attention by transferring Rebecca into his arms.

Quietly David murmured, "Thank you." Then added, "And for earlier when you were there for me." Obviously embarrassed Rosemary sharply retorted "Jane was my friend," and then retreated into the kitchen. He and Jill exchanged a wide-eyed look before giving his attention to his little girl who was gazing so trustingly up at him. More tears flowed silently down his cheeks as he gently touched her little face. Would she grow to look like Jane? Would she have her fun loving, but cheeky nature? David sniffed and pulled the soggy handkerchief from his pocket before sinking down beside Jill on the settee to blow his nose and wipe his face. Paul had disappeared, he guessed to oversee Jane's body leaving. Had they orchestrated putting Rebecca into his arms to distract him? Slowly he rocked her. Jill put her hand on his arm and in struggling to speak she squeaked, "Oh David!" He swallowed hard, shook his head, and with no words to say, Jill in a cracked voice added, "I can't believe it. We all loved her."

Despair filled him, but through a tightened throat managed to say, "She was everything to me." William, wide-eyed and aware something was wrong, was curled up against Jill with his thumb in his mouth. Grief so new and so raw filled David. It was an all consuming pain, he'd no comfort to give. The only relief was to focus on Rebecca and ask the Lord to help him. William's worried gaze penetrated his mind. David sent a small smile to the one year old with such a sensitive spirit. That was the only invitation William needed to slip from Jill to the floor. He toddled around their knees and with outstretched arms asked to be pulled up so he could snuggle in beside him.

Paul returned looking as devastated as he felt. Sitting on the chair opposite he sat forward and pulling his beard apologised, "David, I don't know what to say. There was nothing to detect a problem with Jane this morning. I wish I could have saved her, I really tried, I didn't want to give up."

David nodded, but the bleak look in Paul's eyes broke through his own misery to say abruptly, "Of course you did. Jane wouldn't blame you. Neither do I."

"The truth is even if I'd been here, or Jane in hospital, I doubt it would have made any difference. Of course we won't know until after…well later, but my diagnosis is that a blood clot dislodged from a vein, travelled up her body blocking the blood flow through the pulmonary arteries which carry blood from the heart to the lungs and…" upset he didn't finish.

Barely listening David murmured, "But the Lord knew, that's why He sent that 'glory cloud' last night."

Jill wiping her tears with the back of her hand, queried, "Glory cloud? What's a glory cloud?"

To relive the event he focused inwardly to describe that awesome sense of the holiness of God and being filled with an overwhelming love. When he refocused Jill was gaping at him. "Jane slept through it, but she was happier today than she's been for months. We had a long chat, and she told me how silly she felt in thinking that the spirit of death had been stalking her!"

Jill glanced across at Paul and then commented, "Granted Jane lost her chirpiness during pregnancy, but did she really think that? Yet, with what's happened…" She paused, then asked, "Paul, what do you think?"

Thoughtfully he stroked his beard before saying slowly, "'Glory cloud', 'Presence of the Lord', I don't know, but there have been times I've experienced the unexpected, and felt an overwhelming love for suffering people in famine ridden, or war torn countries. My belief is that because you and Jane spend time each day doing as it says in Matthew, 'seeking first the Kingdom of God and His righteousness' the Lord in His plans and purposes wanted you to know He is with you in this."

They meditated on that thought and watched William who'd slid to the floor, play with his train. At Rebecca's tiny cry David lifted her against his shoulder and gently patted her back before commenting, "Jane told me today she'd had a couple of panic attacks, as in difficulty in breathing, while in hospital."

Paul, who'd slumped in the chair, sat up to exclaim, "What! Why didn't she tell someone?"

"She thought it a spiritual problem, but do you think…" he trailed off, not wanting to consider…if only she'd told him?

As if reading his mind Paul answered his question. "Do I think it was a warning that a blood clot was circulating? It's possible. But considering that unusual experience last night…" He shook his head, "God's ways are not our ways, and often beyond our understanding."

A movement caught David's eye and glancing up he saw Rosemary hovering in the kitchen doorway. In response to his enquiring look she took a few steps forward to say tentatively, "Lunch is ready."

"This young man needs to eat." Paul spoke as he stood and picked up William. Gran would say Jesus was always concerned that people ate." He moved to the table to sit William in his chair and continued, "After all Jesus fed the multitudes, instigated the Last Supper for His disciples and prepared breakfast of fish on the beach for them after His resurrection. On a full stomach Gran maintains we are strengthened to deal with whatever life throws at us. So Rosemary serve it up because this afternoon we're going to need all the strength we can get."

With the twins laid side by side in William's cot they gathered around the flat's small round table. But it was obvious no-one had an appetite by the polite, but small portions they put on their plates and the desultory way they ate. In the pensive silence, the only interruptions were in helping William's attempts to feed himself. When Paul finished he said quietly, "I think we'll forget the sweet course."

Rosemary leapt up to take away the plates and dishes suggesting, "I'll make the coffee."

Jill sent Paul a grimace, and then asked, "David, would you like me to tell our parents?"

David placed his elbows on the table, closed his eyes, steepled his fingers and then shook his head. There was silence, and taking a large breath he looked up to speak. "I appreciate the offer, but it's something I must do." Jill nodded, and a few seconds later he added, "I fear it will be far more difficult to break the news to Joyce as she has already lost Jane's father."

Over the clattering of dishes Rosemary, as if offering a crumb of comfort commented, "But at least she's now married to Ted."

Paul advised, "I think, as they only live ten miles away, it would be best for you to go and tell her." With a groan at the thought of imparting such dreadful news he buried his head between his hands. "Look David, we'll have that coffee, and I'll help clear up here while you ring your parents. I'm sure Jill, you won't mind if I go with David."

"Of course you must go. David we're here for you. We'll look after the twins while you do whatever you have to do."

He nodded his thanks. When the coffee arrived he drank it quickly, and determined to get the odious task done, he strode meaningfully up the stairs. But once in their flat, Jane's absence, his last sight of her, hit him with such anguish he could barely breathe. Against his mouth his hands balled into fists to stop an inner scream coming out. Bent over he collapsed on the settee, and fought the panic spiralling out of control. Prayer, he must pray, but his mind was so numbed he could only whisper, 'Jesus'. The cushions Jane had so recently laid against sent an aroma of her perfume around him. Desperate, he imbibed that with a need to connect to her, he so wanted to believe she was still alive.

After a few completely irrational minutes he felt calmer. This was a time to use his training as a lawyer, and exercise his ability to steal himself against emotion. How was he going to do that when this was personal and heartbreaking? He stood, braced himself and walked into the hall to pick up the telephone. It was here…the last time…resolutely he dialled his parent's number. The moment he said, "Hello Mum" she began chattering excitedly about the twins, when were they going to be home, and asking after Jane.

"We came home last night."

"Oh how lovely, I didn't know they allow Jane to come home so…"

Interrupting he said bluntly, "Mum stop. There's no easy way to tell you…" a sob caught in his throat, but he pushed past it to say, "Jane's dead." There was silence. He rushed on in a need to explain, "Paul thinks it was a blood clot blocking the arteries to her heart, it was…it was a couple of hours ago." The lack of response had him questioning, "Mum, Mum are you there?"

A quavering, high pitched voice replied, "Yes, oh David."

More calm than he felt he gave his account of events but it was hesitant, jerky and interspersed with, "Mum are you still there?"

In his mind's eye he could see her nodding and whispering, "Yes go on."

Finally he said, "Forgive me for not ringing earlier, but I've barely stopped weeping, so can understand if you feel the same."

At his permission she sobbed, "It's too awful...so young, why her?" Over the telephone he was at a loss as to how to comfort her as she lapsed into crying. He was about to suggest she tell his Dad when his voice came booming down the line. "Who is this? What have you said to upset my wife?"

"Dad, it's me, David."

"Good heavens boy what is the matter with you, upsetting your mother like this?"

"Dad I'm afraid I had no choice b..."

"Of course you had a choice boy! If you've got a problem you should have spoken to me first."

"I'm sorry, and you're right." Before his father could berate him further he plunged in, "Jane died two hours ago. I loved her and am too distraught to think straight." There was silence. Now he asked, "Dad, Dad, are you still there?"

Abruptly, his voice strained his father replied gruffly, "Yes."

At his brief synopsis of events his father grunted, then said curtly, "Well thank you for letting us know, we'll get back to you later" and then to David's consternation he cut the connection. When he tried to ring back, the tone told him the line was busy.

Concerned he slipped back down to the flat where Rosemary was doing the washing up. "Where are Jill and Paul?"

Without turning she replied, "In their bedroom. Jill's very upset. Paul insisted she lie down and rest."

"I'm not surprised, at three months pregnant she shouldn't be overly stressed." He rested back against the work surface by the sink. "Rosemary, I need advice. My Mum is obviously upset, my Dad put the phone down on me. I've tried ringing back but can't get through. What should I do?

Briefly she paused from scrubbing the meat pan to suggest, "Give them time. Ring a neighbour. Get a friend to check on them."

"I don't know their friends, or the surname of their neighbours."

After rinsing the pan under the tap she glanced at him, "Have you rung Paula? If all else fails ask the local police to pop in."

"If I did that Dad would be furious!"

Rosemary shrugged, and turned back to the sink.

He stared at her, but when she said nothing more, he wandered away to look at the twins lying at the opposite end to William in his cot, all peaceful and fast asleep. For a few minutes he leaned against the cot pondering their future and jumped when Rosemary entered. In seeing him she whispered, "Sorry, I didn't know you were here. William will soon awake, and your babies will want another feed. I'll make up their bottles?" As she turned to leave, he caught her arm. Pointedly she looked at his hand, and pursed her lips. Quickly he removed it. "I just wanted to say thank you, I really appreciate your help."

Even in his numbed state he didn't miss her dismissive expression and the underlying message in her words as she left the room. "Babies are so uncomplicated, vulnerable and sweet." He gave a grim smile. Rosemary need have no fear of his repeating the earlier incident, or entertaining any amorous thoughts about her.

It being a Sunday the traffic was light and they arrived at Joyce and Ted's in twenty minutes. Barely composed he dreaded facing Joyce's grief, and was glad of Paul's company. Ted opening the door looked surprised, said "Hello" and after calling "Joyce" glanced behind them to ask, "Isn't Jane with you?" David shook his head as Joyce emerged from the kitchen.

"David, this is a lovely surprise. Hello Paul." She frowned as Ted closed the front door. "Aren't Jane and the twins with you?"

Quietly he replied, "I'm afraid not."

Mystified she first looked at him, and then Paul, who suggested they go in the lounge. As comprehension dawned that something was wrong, her eyes widened in trepidation and her hand went to her throat. "What is it? Jane? The twins?" Ted took Joyce's arm to lead her into the lounge while he and Paul followed. And despite having determined to be strong, silent tears started to overflow down David's face. Joyce wrenching her arm from Ted's turned to face him and demanded, the panic evident in her voice, "David, tell me?"

All he could manage was, "Its Jane."

Her eyes searched his face, "Jane will be alright, won't she?"

As a lawyer trained to deal with difficult situations, he fought to overcome the words stuck in his throat, and to his horror blurted out, "She's dead." Joyce gasped, closed her eyes and swayed. Paul shot forward and with Ted they caught her and sat her on the settee. David's only words as he followed were, "I'm sorry, so sorry."

In disbelief Joyce started rambling. "It's not possible. It can't be. She has all her life before her. And those lovely babies…" Drained by the emotion of it all he sank wearily on to the nearest chair. Paul filled in the medical details, but the way Joyce stared ahead he doubted she'd heard him. And a few moments later that was borne out by her saying, "She was very chirpy when I spoke to her earlier. I'm so pleased she's home, she hated that hospital. I said I would see her tomorrow."

Having mopped his eyes he answered, "She was happier at home. We had a lovely morning together. I know she mentioned my experience during the night, I believe now the Lord was anointing us in preparation for Jane going to be with Jesus."

Joyce's voice rose to near hysteria. "Why would Jesus take my Jane? She was only twenty-six. She didn't feel like a mother, but she would have adjusted. Who will look after the twins? What am I going to do?"

David tried to explain what happened, but Joyce put her hand over her ears, "I don't want to hear."

In a voice choked with emotion Ted, sitting next to her, pulled away her hands. And in a firm voice said, "Joyce love, stop that! Jane is with the Lord. Remember God's ways aren't ours. Listen to what David has to say."

"It's easy for you, she wasn't your daughter?"

Shocked at Joyce's reaction David looked to Paul who, with a shake of his head, indicated not respond. Ted's reply was quiet, calm and one of love and understanding. "I loved Jane too. I regarded her as my daughter, just as Bruce is like a son to you. I love you Joyce, you have me, you have Bruce, you aren't alone. And David here is still your son-in-law and father to your two grandchildren." Ted's face crumpled, silent tears rolled down his face. Joyce, still dry eyed, remained stiff in his arms. "Come on love. Stop denying the truth, Jane has gone. You, we, have to face this, and it's not the end, one day we'll all be together again." Joyce, as if unable to comprehend that stared at each them and frowned at their blowing of noses and dabbing their eyes.

David tried again, his words in jerky sentences. "Joyce, three hours ago Jane was alive. In three minutes she'd died in my arms. I was trying to get help. I loved her so much. And like you I don't know how I'm going to live without her. It seems we had so little time together, but we all have to trust the Lord in this. The blessing is she's now reunited with her father."

Joyce let out a wail so loud they jumped. Her grief broke through in deep heart wrenching sobs and in his pain he struggled not to join her. Ted eyes closed as cradled and rocked Joyce in his arms.

As if knowing David couldn't bear Joyce's heartache as well as his own Paul said, "I think Ted it's best we go. Joyce needs to cry it out, give her plenty of hot sweet tea, and help her to talk. A good night's rest will help." Out of his pocket he took a small envelope and handing it to Ted said, "Give her two of these if she gets over exhausted, or hysterical." Ted sent him a grateful smile and mouthed his 'thank you'.

Emptied of energy, in need of a hot sweet cup of tea himself, David crossed the room, gulped hard and crouched down before Joyce whose pain filled hazel eyes stared into his. They so reminded him of Jane he faltered, he'd no comforting words to speak, but reassured her, "We'll get through this together." How David didn't know, but Ted acknowledge that with a thankful smile before Paul drew on his arm saying, "We'll let ourselves out."

The moment the front door was shut Paul demanded, "Give me your car keys, you're not in a fit state to drive home." Exhausted, unable to see clearly through sore, tear drenched eyes, he didn't object. Once home his bones seemed to have gone to jelly, his head ached, and almost staggering from the car he declared, "On top of this I think I've contracted that nasty strain of flu."

Paul's reply was a quiet hum before directing, "It may only be seven o'clock, but as you were up half the night feeding the twins you need a good nights sleep. We'll look after the twins, so go off to bed and I'll bring you up a cup of cocoa. No arguments."

Grabbing the stair banister he said wearily, "I've no strength to argue." Nor did he refuse the sleeping pills with the cocoa and was grateful for Paul's company until he drifted into oblivion.

Semi-conscious, David turned over in bed, his mind a pleasant euphoria until reality kicked in. Jane wasn't beside him. She'd never sleep in this bed again. The pit of his stomach tightened in anguish. He rolled on to Jane's pillow still smelling of her shampoo. Under her pillow the carefully folded nightie put there by her only twenty-four hours ago! He buried his face in it and wept.

A gentle tapping at the door caused him to turn over, wipe his eyes on the sheet before calling, "Come in."

Jill carrying a breakfast tray sent him a sad smile, and reported as she placed it on the bed, "Paul's sleeping so I've bought this up". Sympathetic eyes scanned his face, but her tone was normal. "Now don't think brother dear that you'll get room service every day, this is an exception and merely to keep up your strength. Now sit up." He obeyed as she continued, "The twins have been little angels, taking their feeds and quickly going back to sleep. Master William feels very grown up sleeping in a bed, but is willing to return to his cot because his great grandma Beatty is coming to stay."

"Oh good." The smell of bacon wafted by his nose, was it disloyal to Jane to feel hungry?

Had Jill read his mind when she encouraged, "Eat it before it gets cold." With that she headed out the door before he realized he hadn't thanked her for her thoughtfulness. Love welled up in him for his family. And now he was a father, with twins, but they'd never know their mother! He stopped the downward spiral of thinking by praying, "Please Lord give me your peace and strength to get through the days ahead" and then began to eat.

Recommendations, proposals, strategies and goal orientated tasks at ITP certainly wouldn't take priority over the twins. Retirement or ill health might have reduced six directors to three, in his absence they'd be down to two, but Maud Baker, Finance Director, fifteen years his senior, was intelligent and capable. Although in considering her stick thin body, chain smoking and constant coughing, he'd had occasion to wonder about her life expectancy! Jane had never abused her body with drink, smoking or drugs, it was so unfair. Deliberately he diverted his thoughts to the recently appointed director, Chris County. Now he was an excellent choice, younger than him, but with his experience of the Press Department he'd proved his ability to think clearly under pressure.

To his astonishment as he'd meditated on his work commitments he'd consumed his three course breakfast. Biting into the last piece of toast after a tap on the door Paul entered. Still chewing, David beckoned him in. Glancing at his empty tray and Paul declared "Good, you're eating" then sitting on the bed he scrutinised his face before asking, "How do you feel this morning?"

Even to his ears his voice was gruff. "Not good." To clear his throat he drank his coffee.

Paul grimaced, his expression one of empathy. "I wanted you to know I've talked to your father and…"

Anxious he swallowed quickly to interrupt. "You've talked to Dad, when? How is Mum?"

Paul sat on the bed, "I spoke to them last night. Obviously they adored Jane. Your Dad was gruff and matter-of-fact due to his finding emotional issues difficult and merely said Margaret was made of stern stuff and would get over it. David don't tut for until recently you would have said much the same."

The truth of that made him grunt. Paul's expression turned bashful, his beard stroking revealing he was considering something. To encourage him he boomed, "Out with it man, what's on your mind?"

"Your father has decreed I'm the best person to support you at this time! And he's decided my reporting on his pharmaceutical business in Ghana can wait until things settle down." With a chuckle, he added, "Which was fortunate because I'd already made up my mind, in the circumstances, I wasn't going anywhere!"

"Thank you. I appreciate that, and your friendship." David wiped his mouth and fingers on the serviette. "It's quite amazing how you and Jane managed to infiltrate Dad's personal radar."

"Oh it's always easier not being a direct family member, or an ordinary employee. Now what can I do to help?"

"I need first to ring Maud and Chris at ITP. They'll have to cope with board matters as long, and as long as no legal situation crops up I've thought to take three months leave. I need to bond with the twins now they're without a mother."

"Excellent! I can see you are thinking straight."

He took a deep breath and sighed, "No, just the Reinhardt stoic character trait breaking through!" Paul gave a sad smile. "However that will mean shelving ideas for ITP to incorporate a comprehensive service to British companies wishing to sell their wares overseas."

Thoughtfully Paul commented, "It's a good time for market expansion. Bonding with the twins doesn't mean stultifying your mind. You could do the research from home, and between us I'm sure we could cover you going into work for a few hours a week. Once you return full-time your plans will be ready to augment."

"Paul, that's worth considering. It would keep me sane

between feeds and nappy changes. It would take my mind off…" he realigned his thinking…"give me a goal to work towards."

"Exactly! It's good to be home with William, yet I enjoy keeping my medical skills up to date with locum shifts at the hospital, and stretching my brain when working for your father."

Tears rushed into his eyes and overflowed. "Oh Paul, it's so hard. Why did the Lord take my little Jane?" Paul lent forward to pat his arm. David used the back of his hand to wipe his face and admitted, "I'm trying not to fall into self-pity."

"David, it's not self-pity. It's grieving, coming to terms with the situation, and there's nothing wrong in thinking, or talking about Jane, to do so will lessen the pain. And crying is like releasing a pressure valve, far better than bottling it up. Now how can I help?"

"Obviously I've numerous telephone calls and letters…" he swallowed hard, "maybe Jill could help with those. Perhaps you could help me by juggling with the ad hoc necessities of twin babies and guide me through the legalities and funeral arrangements."

"Of course." Paul took up the tray from his lap. "Come downstairs when you are ready. The twins next feed is due about nine-thirty."

As Paul headed out the room he called, "Oh and thank Jill for the breakfast, no doubt just what the doctored ordered."

Paul turned, "It would have been, but Rosemary cooked it before I awoke. Jill was just the waitress."

"Is that so! How kind. Tell her it was much appreciated." Paul nodded and gave a rueful grimace knowing as David did that Rosemary didn't seem to appreciate being appreciated!

A few minutes later David heard the front door shut and he looked out of the window to see Rosemary walking briskly along the road. Surely she wasn't going to work today? Granted, yesterday she may have regretted her rare show of emotion, but was she tough enough not to breakdown when people talked to her about Jane?

While in the bathroom David realised, that despite his being unsure about Robert Jones' ability to run the Exhibitions Department, it was fortunate he'd handed it over, for that job wouldn't have allowed him to take three months off. Unfortunately Robert had been the only suitable candidate who spoke several languages and was willing to sometimes be away for several weeks at a time. Perhaps Robert, once over his initial arrogance, would value Rosemary's help and advice. If so, it was possible the job could lead Robert to being a director. Hot water gushed over his body as he considered his rapid rise to director, and now the Board's Chairman. Jane had been…his stomach tightened and coiled. Vigorously he rubbed himself dry to counteract the desire to bury his head in the towel and give rent to his grief. For the next few minutes he succeed, but arriving back in the bedroom, seeing the pretty perfume bottles, Jane's hairbrush with her red and golden hair stuck in its bristles, and the little ornamental dish where yesterday Paul had put her wedding and engagement ring, anguish gripped his throat. She'd so enjoyed designing that diamond diadem. He picked it up and the eight stones sparkled in the light. Jane had brought sparkle into his life. The first time she'd worn the ring had been as bridesmaid to his secretary, Grace who'd married Wilhelm and gone to live in Germany. Many people would need to know that her light in this world had gone out. Tears blurred the diamonds into rainbow colours and slowly he put that and Jane's wedding ring into her jewellery box, closed the lid and pulled a handkerchief from the drawer. Between dabbing his eyes and blowing his nose he dressed. When he felt composed he headed to the basement to lavish his love on the twins.

The upstairs doorbell rang as David reached the ground floor. He didn't want to answer it, he didn't want to speak to anyone. Through the glass door into the outer vestibule he could already see a pile of envelopes on the mat and concluded the postman must have a parcel. First he cleared the envelopes from the mat, most of which felt like cards, and then opened the front door.

"Ah, Mr Reinhardt! Good morning." Dread arose like bile in the mouth. David recognised the voice before he saw the burly middle-aged man who added irritably, "I've caught up with you, at last."

Polite, but terse he responded, "Detective Inspector Jordan! May I assure you I've not been avoiding you, but involved in matters beyond my control. I presume you are here because Andrew Carlton's whereabouts are now known and you have been reassigned the case."

Jordan's reply was equally curt. "This isn't about the past. I've been sent regarding an incident at The Traveller's Rest public house on …"

He interrupted, "Yes, yes, a chance meeting I wish we hadn't had."

The Inspector drew himself up to his full height several inches below David's to say officiously, "But one you failed to report to the police! Was that because you didn't want to be known to be part of an incident that resulted in a man's death?"

At that David frowned heavily before retorting, "Carlton was very much alive when we left."

"And still is, but Henry Nimbya was fatally hit by a piece of flying glass."

He shook his head. "Neither Jane nor I saw that. Carlton hit me over the head with a glass leaving me lying dazed over a table and pushed past Jane as he left."

"I'm not here to question you, but follow orders. I certainly have unresolved cases involving Carlton, and as you it seems are implicated in this present one, the Kent police deemed it sensible that I escort you to Maidstone to help with their enquiries. Just be thankful that on hearing of your present circumstances you were given a day's grace."

The words 'present circumstances' echoed in his head. Jill or Paul must have rung and told the Inspector of Jane's death. DI Jordan was still speaking. "… a few minutes to inform your family."

Taken aback by the formality he questioned, "Are you arresting me?"

With a hard stare the Inspector stated, "Only Sir if you make it necessary!"

How could he leave? Dazed his mind raced with the arrangements he needed to make along with the twins care. "I'm sorry Inspector, but I can't…"

Frustration and kindness vied in the Inspector's voice, "Yes, yes, I know it will be difficult for your wife so soon out of hospital, and with two newborn babies to care for. But I understand your sister and her husband, Dr Stemmings live here, they will surely help her. Mrs Reinhardt isn't implicated, but she will need to give a witness statement, one of my colleagues can do that. He waved his hand toward the unmarked police car, "Now please don't keep us waiting."

It was difficult not to keep his voice from cracking as he responded, "Inspector I can't…"

The Inspector's voice raised a decibel, "Don't be ridiculous Reinhardt. This isn't some piffling back street attack we're talking about here, but murder."

There wasn't any need for him to feign shock, because on top of the events of the last eighteen hours, hearing the reality of what he had feared might happen crippled his mind.

The Inspector continued brusquely, "Now Sir, please go and tell you wife you're coming with us."

To steady himself he lent on the door frame and inadvertently pressed the doorbell to Jill and Paul's flat. With furrowed brow the Inspector asked, "Are you alright Sir?" Unable to answer he stared idiotically into his face. The Inspector stepped forward as though to chivvy him. Instinctively he backed away.

Paul's voice penetrated his confusion. "Oh David, was that our…?" The sentence remained incomplete for Paul seeing his obvious distress was now looking beyond him to see who, or what had caused it. "Ah, Inspector Jordan, Howard, you'd better come in."

How could he leave his babies? They'd have no mother or father? Anguish filled his mind blocking out the Inspector's reply, but his insistent tone conveyed that he didn't want his plans delayed. A strange whimpering noise caused both men to look at him. At first puzzled, he was then embarrassed to realize it was coming from him. Paul drew on his arm. "Come David, Jill needs your help with feeding the twins." Barely functioning he allowed Paul to guide him along the hall. As Paul stood back, and indicated for him to go down the stairs, he heard him interrupt the Inspector's haranguing to say quietly, "David's wife died yesterday."

Jill feeding Joshua looked up as he came down into their lounge. "Ah there you are David, that's Rebecca crying. Paul was just…" Her eyes went from him, to Paul, and the Inspector behind him. Despite feeding Joshua she leapt up and headed toward him asking, "David are you alright? Words failed him, and an overwhelming fragility caused him to stagger. Paul steadied him and led him to the settee. Anxiously Jill queried, "What's going on?"

Taking charge Paul instructed, "Jill give Joshua to David then could you get Rebecca. I'll feed her while I talk to Howard here. And sweetheart a cup of tea would be appreciated."

The warmth of the little bundle, and Joshua's face looking so trustingly up at him, brought a fresh rush of tears when he thought he'd no more left.

"Do sit down Howard. We all need a cup of tea, and you must understand David isn't fit to go anywhere today."

Even through the mist of his unshed tears he saw the

policeman's shocked expression and heard the genuine sympathy in his voice as he leaned forward to address him. "Look Reinhardt I'm sorry about your wife. It's a tragedy to lose someone so young. Two new born babes is a great responsibility, but they will be a comfort to you in your loss, and you are fortunate to have family support." Unstoppable tears were running down his face. Clearing his throat with a little cough the Inspector continued, "But you must understand that we have a murder investigation on our hands and according to Carlton you are a prime suspect."

At being called 'a prime suspect' it felt like the gates of hell had just clanged. Despair filled him and he was glad Paul intervened. "That may be so, but I think there is a need to assess the priorities…" There was a pause as Jill put Rebecca into Paul's arms, and as he rocked her to stop her cries, he explained, "First, there are two babies who need at least one parent's constant care. Second, there are important arrangements and personal legal matters that need attending to at this time. I'm sure you will appreciate that. And, although I've no longer any jurisdiction as a police surgeon, I believe all these factors should be taken into account. I would suggest with David having so much on his mind any interview at this time wouldn't be very constructive."

In lifting Joshua to tap his back, David felt the Inspector's slow appraisal of him and thoughtful nod. Paul took Rebecca's bottle from Jill. Now torn between compassion and duty DI Jordan said kindly, "Look Reinhardt, it's not for me to judge, but the speed and angle of Carlton's accident would suggest he was pushed, and the flying glass caused the death of another man. You know, as a lawyer …" he grunted, "…and a short-lived career as a barrister, the term 'vicarious liability'. You may consider 'the law to be an ass' but Carlton's testimony puts you firmly in the frame, and there have already been delays in questioning you."

Wearily he shook his head, "It wasn't me."

The Inspector arose, "I'm in a difficult position, but will report back to my colleagues in Maidstone, but I know they are anxious to press on with this. I really am sorry about the death …"

'Death' he hated that word! He rocked Joshua. Jane was dead. Who would believe him? He could go to jail for years. The twins wouldn't have a father or mother? He didn't look up when the Inspector laid a comforting hand briefly on his shoulder. Inside he felt as though the darkness was closing in, he was being drawn in a direction he didn't wish to go. His dream was fast becoming a nightmare of reality.

CHAPTER 13

The rest of that day was something of a blur. Beatty arriving brought comfort with her inner strength and prayers. But the days since Jane's death had been gruelling. There were disciplined times of lucidity, but equally times he'd be rendered useless by a memory of Jane.

That first day, Mavis, his secretary had brought Rosemary home in a taxi because in speaking to others of Jane's death she'd been overcome with grief. Maud recommended she didn't return to work until after Jane's funeral. And Chris said je would promote someone temporarily to help Robert.

As the days passed David became aware of how Rosemary's large and doleful eyes lit up at every opportunity to hold the twins, and in the same way, they also helped to assuage his pain. In an unobtrusive way Rosemary brought order to the supply and demand of caring for two babies.

Tuesday morning Joyce, pale, shaky and silent arrived with Ted. Keith, the leader of their church who'd known Jane for years joined them along with Stuart, the Vicar of Holy Trinity, their present church. It didn't take long to decide on a 'family only' service at the crematorium followed by a memorial celebration at Holy Trinity.

'The parents' as Jill called them arrived Tuesday afternoon. Within a minute, his mother's words and the sight of her tears caused him to revert to the broken-hearted schoolboy who'd lost his favourite pet. This time as they cried in each others' arms, his father didn't make any derisive comments and surprisingly disappeared to make a pot of tea. Desirous to help, but not wanting to be in the way, they'd booked into the Royal Garden Hotel, an easy walk to the house. His father said how desperate his mother had been to see him and her new grandchildren, while his mum told him his father was keen to make amends for his unconscionable response and behaviour at the news of Jane's death!

Throughout the week Paul's friendship proved invaluable. In knowing how fears surfaced and grew in the middle of the night he'd insisted being with him at every 3.00 am feed. When he talked of regrets, or 'what if's' Paul talked of Beth, his first wife who died in childbirth, his fears at the time and belief he'd never get over it. After speaking of his regret at missing Maria's growing years, and being without a wife, Paul firmly advised, "Don't let that happen to you. Don't bury your sorrow in hard work. Find a balance of taking an active part in the twins' lives, but also take time out to enjoy yours. Women will be attracted to you. Don't ignore your feelings in some kind of guilt trip, as I did. Be open to God's plan. I didn't pursue Jill, but in the end God did! And He's done so much more than I could have hoped or imagined. I don't just have Jill's love, but the opportunity to bring up Ben's child just as Lilian and Bob brought up Maria for me. And I've another chance at fatherhood with Jill expecting our baby! No-one could replace Beth, no-one will replace Jane. Jill is different, but I love her for who she is and have no desire to compare them. You have two children, they'll need a mother's love, and you want a family life. Don't close your mind to that, it's not what Jane would want."

In listening he took his point, but couldn't imagine being married to anyone but Jane. Oh it hadn't been perfect, the way she stood up to him hadn't always amused him, and her naivety had embarrassed, thwarted, involved or instigated things that had caused him angst. Equally she'd say he often appeared annoyed, was uncommunicative and could be pedantic! But that was marriage, adjustments and compromise, but her bubbly and outgoing manner had brought fun, laughter and a depth of intimacy and fulfilment into his life that hadn't been there before. Paul may not have any qualms of being a father to William, but twins, what woman would want to take on that kind of responsibility?

Interwoven with his grief was the worry of Andrew Carlton's accusations. Would the police believe him? What if they arrested him? Was it possible he could be sent to jail for a crime he hadn't committed? Paul had contacted John Perrington, his police superintendent friend, for advice. Under Paul's advisement, and perhaps John's intervention, it had been agreed for DI Jordan and another officer to visit and take his statement on Thursday. And when they came the DI asked him to clarify several issues, but they didn't question him further.

Every day gave David an occasion to miss Jane's involvement in his life, right down to realising he was running out of clean underwear. Commenting on that to his father who was reading the newspaper in his lounge, he'd received the usual gruff, tough reply, "A fact for now my boy you have to accept. You'll need to find another wife, for those babies need a mother. In the interim you'll need a nanny!"

Emphatic, he'd retorted, "I don't want a nanny, or another wife. I can look after the twins." Instead of the expected impatient response his father's eyes filled with unshed tears. With a catch in his voice his father admitted, "We all loved Jane. It's tough, but you will need more than brain numbing baby care to get over this." About to protest his father lifted his hand and said curtly, "Think about it David. Children need stability and routine. In all fairness you must see that as a family we are happy to rally around, but this is only a short-term solution. Here in London the Norland College provides highly trained, live-in nannies..."

The thought of any woman, however highly trained living in his house filled him with alarm that uncharacteristically he burst out, "They wouldn't want to live with a man facing a murder charge?"

At his father's uncomprehending stare he explained. To his credit his father listened carefully before advising, "Keep this from you mother. She's already worried about how you will cope and planning to help by spending several days a week in London." Those words revealed his father's nanny suggestion hadn't been entirely altruistic, but he continued to admonish him. "It is ridiculous for you to consider, let alone voice, that you, an innocent man could be put on trial and convicted of murder. In every crisis there's a solution. And believe me justice will prevail."

Irritated he retorted, "Remember Ben?"

In a dismissive gesture his father waved his hand. "That was different!"

"But justice didn't prevail, did it?"

"Ben did wrong, even if it was for the right reasons. I know his being made a scapegoat tainted your opinion of the law. You lost faith in man's justice, while I find faith in God difficult to comprehend. Jane would say a Christian isn't prevented from difficulties, pain and suffering, but apparently God promises not to leave or forsake you in those times, so hold on to that."

Jane's 'discussions' with his father had often made him feel uncomfortable, but it appeared he'd listened. Was that simple act at Beatty's to forgive his father's attitude over a dead cat now revealing his misjudgement that his father neither listened or cared? At that rare moment of fatherly empathy, his eyes filled with tears and his heart with love. Paul was right. The tough gruff manner was his father's inadequacy in dealing with personal problems, and he saw how, on occasions, he'd emulated that. With a need to assure his father that he believed God was with him he spilled out his dream and sited several significant ones given to Biblical characters. At that his father shook his head, but strangely he didn't feel it was unbelief, more his trying to grasp the reality of God breaking into man's mind and life.

For a while they sat in a peaceful silence before his father carefully folded his newspaper, stood, and gently tapped him with it on the shoulder as he left the room. Although believing it foolish he felt to look up to the corner above the piano and murmur, "Jane thank you for sharing the Lord's love, with me and my family. You've left a priceless legacy. But that doesn't stop me wanting you here so badly that it hurts."

Regardless of saying he should trust in the Lord his father was keen to employ solicitors and barristers even before the police took his witness statement, which he, Jill and Paul felt would be counter productive. They also agreed with him that it was pointless to employ a nanny for the twins with so many willing hands to cover the day and when he was happy to do the night feeds.

Church on Sunday was an ordeal. Conversations vacillated between smiles and congratulations on the birth of the twins, to tears and sympathy for his loss. Despite her obvious distress, Rosemary listed the giver and content of each gift, the offers of help and later offered to organise 'thank you' cards bringing his father's praise of at her efficiency.

Throughout the week's tensions it was Joshua and Rebecca's needs that kept him sane. Love flowed from the depths of his being to those tiny bundles not much bigger than his hand. Fascinated and comforted by the bond between them he'd just watch them in their cot as they lay contently looking at each other.

Now, he was about to face the most difficult day of his life, his final farewell to Jane. Emotions hovered on the surface, yet deep within an indescribable peace strengthened him. The Lord, and his family would be there for him and each other.

Jill and he both responded to their doorbells and arrived at the front door together. He stepped back to let Jill go first and as she opened the door the postman held out a pile of different shaped and sized envelopes saying, "There's more." His stepping forward to relieve Jill of the growing pile caused the postman to give him a shy smile, and then blurt out, "Your neighbour told me about your wife. Lovely young lady she was, always a cheery smile, ready to pass the time of day." To that David hummed as the postman continued, "Good job she believed in that 'eternal life' stuff with her going like that. I hear she left you with twins." The postman shook his head. "Fancy going quick like that, it makes you think…! So sad, when's her funeral?"

Choked with emotion and unable to speak David let Jill give the memorial service details. Then finding his voice he added, "Please come, there's buffet lunch afterwards."

Obviously surprised, yet pleased the man said, "Thank's governor, I might just do that." He tipped his cap, "Better get on. See you later."

Jill shut the door to ask, "Is there no end to those Jane made an impression on? Look at all these cards. I didn't know you knew so many people."

After clearing the lump in his throat his voice sounded gruff like his father's. "They vary between congratulations or commiserations!" He shook his head, "The latter often write of Jane's helping, giving them a gift, praying or advising them!"

"Oh brother dear, I don't think you fully grasped Jane's vitality, she wasn't your regular 'sit at home' wife."

Ruefully he nodded, "So it would seem! It appears, until recently, every Wednesday afternoon she visited an old peoples' home in Kensington and played the piano for their sing-a-long. Afterwards she talked and prayed with many of the residents."

Jill frowned, "Oh David, you've heard her talk of Ivy and Alice who sang such entertaining duets."

"I recognise their names. I assumed they were in our church." Seeing Jill shaking her head, he frowned in bewilderment. "In that case maybe you know Harry Baines? I've a letter from him saying how sorely she'd been missed at the dancing classes. Apparently without Jane's help his business wouldn't be the success it is today."

Jill snorted in laughter, "Oh dear, Jane's sins are being found out!"

To that he questioned sharply, "What do you mean?"

"Do you remember Jane asking if you'd go dancing one evening a week?" A memory stirred. "I believe your answer was that after a days work you couldn't contemplate prancing around a dance floor." He scowled. "So Jane persuaded Henry to start tea dances. She helped with advertising, cooked him scones, and not only got to enjoy the dancing free, but he insisted on paying her a commission from his soaring profits!"

Completely bemused he asked, "But how did she fit that in between setting up the nursery, working in the church office and visiting old peoples' homes?"

"Home David, not homes! You weren't keen on her nursery scheme and that was around the same time 'T-Dance' started. With my having William, you seemed more open to the church nursery, but she handed that over and did more for T-dance. Wednesday was a busy day. She went to the church office, ate lunch at her desk, did an hour slot from two to three at 'The Oaks' and at three-thirty to five she was at 'T-Dance' which just gave her time to be back here and cook your tea for around six-thirty. Another reason for her to dislike pregnancy for it quickly curtailed those activities."

"Why didn't I know this?"

Jill shrugged, "She didn't make any secret of them, but maybe you just didn't listen, or what appeared to be your lack of interest caused her not to talk about it."

Appalled he ran his hand through his hair, "Oh God was I so wrapped up in my own life I didn't take an interest in hers?"

"Jane didn't seem to mind, she often said even if your mind was elsewhere, the important things were in the right place. " Jill giggled, he glowered catching her inference, and she added, "David, your heart, just like Jane's has always been in the right place. She so enjoyed buying or giving people things without their knowing from where they came. Remember Phil, his story of opening his guitar case to find his cheap guitar replaced by a brand, new top of the range one. That came from the money she earned at 'T-Dance'." Oh we had such a giggle writing that card. I'd have loved to see his face when he read, 'The music you compose so glorifies Me that I'm sending you this instrument to play it on. Your loving friend, Jesus!'

"You and Jane cooked that up! Why didn't she tell me?"

Jill looked serious, "I've no idea, but there were times when you appeared to disapprove of her philanthropic ways, and why in earning money, she felt she could give it away."

Thoughtfully, sorting the last envelopes, he agreed. "I did tell her the money I gave her was for to spend on clothes, make-up, etcetera, and not meant to be given away. I felt as a couple we were more than generous in our giving from my salary."

"Maybe Jane's verve for life was such because it would be so short." In Jill's voice he heard the catch of emotion.

"Today was meant to be the twins' birth date...instead...." He broke eye contact, but not before he saw his grief reflected in Jill's face. In a few hours the body that had housed Jane's spirit would be no more. Gone would be the adorable face with its haughty look, or cheeky smile, the expressive hazel eyes fired with anger or filled with teasing laughter. Whatever Jane's mood often desire would spark in anticipation of so much more than a fulfilling kiss.

Hesitantly Jill said, "It'll take us all time to get over this. I'm trying not to dwell on what can't be, but what is. Today is going to be hard enough as it is." And then in true stiff upper lip British fashion she went on, "Now brother dear, I have two letters, and you about two hundred, evidence that Jane loved people and they loved her. Take those upstairs and then come and get your breakfast. Rosemary's just finished the twins' feed, she's coping with the loss of her best friend in much the same way as you, by being besotted with the twins."

With a nod, David picked up the pile of envelopes and slowly ascended the stairs knowing Jill's concerned eyes were watching him. Despite the gambit of emotions that constantly assailed him, inexplicably he knew God's everlasting arms were holding him up as he walked through this valley of the shadow of death. The reality of his pain was deepened by the knowledge he hadn't listened, hadn't shared Jane's life, any more than he'd shared his.

Two hours later, the funeral service at the Crematorium was about to begin. Despite Beatty's fortifying breakfast his stomach was churning. Beatty's words, "Remember 'big boys do cry' echoed in his head at the sight of the coffin being drawn from the hearse and carried in. In stomach clenching anguish he repeated in his head the comforting scriptures Stuart was speaking. "Jesus said, 'I am the resurrection and the life, anyone who believes in me will not perish but have eternal life." Joyce turned to frown at him bringing him to realize his grip had tightened on her elbow.

Despite this time being for close friends and relatives, as the two families walked in procession behind the coffin behind the reserved few rows every seat was taken. Desperate to keep calm he told himself it was only Jane's carcass in that wooden box, her spirit was with the Lord, but that didn't stop the tears rolling down his face. A few people turned, but most stared ahead gripped as he was in grief at a young, bubbly life so quickly extinguished.

Settled in the front pew, he took out his handkerchief to blow his nose, wipe his face and compose himself. The words of Stuart and Keith barely registered, and understandably the singing was half-hearted. All he could see was the coffin. His tribute in saying 'goodbye' the same as his 'hello' four years previously – four dozen long stemmed red roses in amongst white frothy gypsophila making it a huge bouquet. If only he'd been home more in the three years of their married life. If only he hadn't been so self-absorbed he'd have known more of Jane's zest, and how it had touched the lives of others. He struggled against the finality of never kissing again that sensitive mouth, or hugging and enjoying that little, but beautifully proportioned body. Never again would he receive that cheeky smile, the 'come and get me' expression, or blown a kiss in anticipation of seeing him later. In a few minutes that body was going to be consigned to the flames, 'ashes to ashes', 'dust to dust'.

A funeral was to bring closure, he thought he was adjusting to those facts, but instead there was a deep gut-wrenching hollowness of pain as if his insides were being ripped out. Only his years of self-discipline stopped him screaming out in the sheer agony of it and running from this place. Joyce next to him was suffering much the same by the sound of heartbreaking sobs, but she had Ted to hold her close. Silently he called, 'Oh God where are you in all this?' Behind him he could hear coughs, sniffs and sobs and was grateful they'd decided on a pre-recorded tape of the hymn 'Blessed Assurance' for he doubted anyone could have sung it.

The sound of his father blowing his nose gave him to understand that Jane's demise had touched his often hard heart, and it was that which broke his pent-up emotion. Tears spilled almost as soundlessly from his eyes as did the curtains closing on the body that had been Jane's. He groaned, and would have doubled over in pain if Jill's arm hadn't slipped through his. Time seemed to stand still and he was surprised when Paul lent over to urge, "We have to leave. David you and Jill go together, I'll chivvy the others." Automatically they stood, holding each other up in their walk to the exit. Behind him he heard Paul cajole Ted and Joyce in the same way.

Stunned at the finality they mingled wordlessly and briefly among the few flowers and wreaths for it was agreed Jane would prefer money spent on helping and blessing others. Even before the funeral a tidy sum had come in which they would give to Christian Aid. Keen to get away from that place which highlighted separation and death he headed to the funeral car, and left Paul to hustle everyone out.

Half an hour later they waited at one side of the church porch so the two families could enter together. From inside came a quiet buzz of voices that spoke to him of life, not death. Here they would celebrate Jane's life, not mourn her death. They would see her as promoted to heaven, not reduced to an urn of ash. And he knew for Jane that the gates of hell had not prevailed, and the Lord had the very keys of love, hope, purpose and eternal life ready to unlock the hearts of those gathered today.

Not wanting to process down the aisle, they entered as a small crowd. To David's astonishment the large church was filled, it was standing room only, causing Jill to comment, "Rather more than the two hundred people you expected." With the turn of her head she encouraged him to look around. "Our postman's come. And just along the pew I recognise our milkman. It looks as if they've brought their wives. Jane would be pleased. Oh look over there David, there's Mrs P you'd better give her a nod."

By her ear he murmured, "I'm not sure it's etiquette at a funeral to look around and acknowledge people?"

"This isn't a funeral, it's a celebration of Jane's life and she'd love it. I wonder who those two beefy-looking men are seated either side of Mrs P?"

With a raised eyebrow he queried, "Our dustmen?" Jill gave him a quizzical look, he shrugged, "With Jane there seems no end to the lives she influenced."

Following Jill's example David's eyes roved over the people as they continued to down the long aisle to the two front row pews reserved for their families. The majority of faces he recognised. On his right was a large group of ITP staff. Beyond them in the side pews sat a group of elderly people he guessed from 'The Oaks'. And the middle-aged, red-faced man behind them who was talking to three rows of couples could be Harry Baines of 'T-Dance'. Their families separated on either side of the aisle, and while everyone took their seats he slipped over to speak to Maria who had kindly looked after the twins and William while they were at the crematorium. With a few minutes to spare he cuddled the twins aware of people's eyes on him. It had seemed so right that they be present and part of honouring their mother's life and with everyone wanting to be here, to bring them had been the easiest solution. Should they, or William, get restless and cry it was arranged the two ladies who now ran the church nursery would take them out.

Chairs were placed down the central aisle for those standing, and were quickly filled. David glanced at his watch. It was time

172

to take his seat beside Jill, and he did he inclined his head towards her to comment. "There must be at least four hundred people here, we've only catered for two hundred and fifty?"

"Don't worry, brother dear, I'd an inkling you'd no idea of Jane's popularity and influence. I told Dad to order the catering for four hundred. He didn't believe me, but I told him if I'd got it wrong, the food left over could go to the 'down and outs' when the church had its soup run tonight, that way he'd have no fear of it being wasted."

"Jane's obviously left a lasting impression on you!" Jill gave him a puzzled look. He gave a small smile, "Jane's 'waste not, want not' attitude."

Jill might have replied except the choir stood bringing the congregation to follow. There was no lack of enthusiasm in the singing of the hymn often associated with Billy Graham rallies, "Oh happy day that fixed my choice, On thee my Saviour and My God..."

Despite the deep grief inside, the music, the familiarity of praise and worship, sparked a joy within him, and he, with Paul and Jill had no difficulty singing and clapping along. He notice Joyce and Ted across the aisle with their friends and family had also moved from death into life mode, albeit perhaps not quite so exuberantly.

And when the last line of the chorus finished, "And live rejoicing every day" Keith began to speak. "I think anyone who knew Jane would agree that was the way she lived her life. It was ten years ago when Jane asked Jesus into her life, and I had the privilege of seeing her grow in loving and knowing God. The apostle John wrote, 'For God so loved the world that He gave His only Son, that whoever believes in Him should not perish, but have eternal life'. Today we rejoice because Jane has moved into that eternal life. Jane would be the first to admit she wasn't a saint, but human, with human failings. But she was quick to see and learn from her mistakes and ask forgiveness from both man and God."

At that his mind jumped to several instances to fit Keith's observations. My fondest memories are those of her quick wit, inspirational piano playing and freedom from intimidation."

Keith was right about Jane not knowing the meaning of 'intimidation'. That was why his stern façade, legalistic way of speaking and need to be circumspect in behaviour completely passed her by. Keith in sharing several of Jane's antics brought

173

laughter, and David wasn't sure if it was the laughter in church, or it being at his dead daughter-in-law's expense that caused his father to look grim, but Jane he knew would have enjoyed it.

As they stood to sing "It is well with my soul" it brought a reminder of Bill's funeral service less than three weeks before. Next Stuart spoke of Jane's time at Holy Trinity, how she touched and changed people's lives, and the projects she instigated. "Jane read God's Word and lived by it. Those knowing her couldn't call her 'religious' or 'fanatical'. She was a woman who knew what it was to be loved by God, and that filled her with fun, zest and zeal for others to experience the peace and joy of the Lord."

Had Jane's zest rubbed off on him? Was he less pompous and pedantic? Stuart went on to speak of Jane's love of music and his mind wandered to the times at home when Jane would play and worship the Lord, sometimes he listened, sometimes he'd sing with her.

He tuned back into what Stuart was saying. "…last night both church music groups met to prepare the music for today. However, since then a song and its rendition has come to our attention." Stuart waved his hand expansively across the band and choir, "And we have taken an executive decision to use this rather than that which we prepared, for this truly could be called, Jane's song."

There was silence, then an audible gasp as Jane's unaccompanied voice sang out, *"Pausing, listening, hear the voice of Jesus, Resting in the presence of the Lord…"* It sent shivers down his spine, and tears ran down his cheeks, it was if she was singing to them from heaven. And just as the Lord's Presence had almost been tangible at Bill's funeral, it was now, but with an added poignancy. When the sound his voice on the tape joined Jane's he felt it spoilt that ethereal sound. Jane was now experiencing that which she had so often imagined. *"Gazing upward, into the face of Jesus, Basking in the presence of the Lord. Shekinah, glory, shining brighter than the sunlight, Chasing shadows from every corner of our lives"*. Mixed emotions vied in his heart, but the promise was there…their duet at the end spoke of how they would sing together again at the end of the age. *"We take our place at the Father's feet, Ready for the marriage feast, Join with all creation in heaven's praise. For this is hallowed ground where we stand, Let us rise before His throne…"* Jane's life wasn't over, it was just beginning, and she would be waiting for him, the cheeky smile, her blown kiss in his mind's eye that day she'd died had been saying, 'See you soon'. Stuart had made the right decision because as his and Jane's voices faded singing the name of Jesus, it felt as if the very fabric of heaven with its awesome peace had opened over them. After a minute he moved quietly to the microphone and looked out over the congregation. Squashed into the pews, every chair filled and with people standing three deep at the back no-one stirred, the silence seemed to hold time and space. It felt as if a connection had pierced through the veil separating earth from heaven bringing an insight of the holiness and love of God for the people created in His image.

Not wanting to break the atmosphere he waited for people to stir then closing his eyes he prayed, "*Father God, creator of heaven and earth, thank you that in believing Jesus is your Son, we can ask Him to enter our lives, enjoy your Presence on earth, and know that is but a shadow of the days of eternity we shall know with you. I believe Jane is experiencing that right now, that you have given us a small taste of what that feels like and I pray for everyone here that the eyes of their hearts' be flooded with your light, the knowledge of your love, and just as Jane did, they will commit their hearts, souls and all that is within them to you. In Jesus name Amen.*"

After a mumbled 'amen' from the congregation he suggested, "If you would like to experience the Lord as Jane did, the way is open, and the instructions on the back of your service sheet. And the truth is Jesus is the answer in every situation. After the group has sung a favourite of song of Jane's entitled, '*Joy springs up when you least expect the light*', you will all be welcome to join in the feast laid out in the church hall.

Ten minutes later throngs of people mingled together to accept that invitation, their comments along the lines of 'we've never experienced anything quite like it'. He saw Mrs P. dabbing her eyes and heard her declare to the men with her, "I prayed that prayer, and I 'ope you did too."

In the group surrounding Jane's parents, he smiled at Bruce who'd been Jane's boyfriend for several years before becoming her step-brother when Ted married Joyce. "Hello Bruce. A difficult time, but even in death Jane is larger than life."

Bruce, now rather Bohemian with long curly hair gathered and tied at the nape of his neck, pushed the bridge of his John Lennon style glasses back on his nose before replying. "I said to Joyce, and believe she appreciated it, that in twenty-six years Jane accomplished more than most of us in a life time." He looked around, "Such a diversity of people and backgrounds. Frankly Jane's idea of touching heaven and changing earth were quite beyond me."

It was hard to imagine Jane with Bruce, but he felt to reassure him. "I'm sure by identifying with the culture around you, the Lord uses you too. I doubt Jane knew of her influence, and sudden death does bring people to think about life!"

Bruce didn't look convinced, and he was pleased to hear someone say, "Mr Reinhardt."

He turned, smiled and acknowledged, "Ian, Sam and Mrs Bennett. Thank you for coming."

Sam, his voice cracked in emotion, said, "Coming, we couldn't not be 'ere. Loved 'er we did, made us feel..." He broke off as tears filled his eyes, and Mrs B red-eyed finished, "special". In comfort he briefly rested his hand on Sam's shoulder before asking Ian. "How's your job?"

Proudly Ian reported, "I'm now floor manager of the printing works. I wanted to say...well you know. Jane was such fun, her chatter entertained us in the canteen, the challenge of table tennis, and our err...dancing." Embarrassed Ian rushed on, "Religion and fun don't usually go together, but they did with Jane. I felt to pray that prayer, and have picked up these booklets to help me get to know Jesus."

Pleased he clapped Ian on the back. "Jane would be thrilled to hear that."

Rosemary spoke from behind him, "Hello Sam, Mrs Bennett, Ian, good to see you. Excuse me David, I'm sorry to drag you away, but there are a group of people from 'T-Dance' wanting to speak with you."

He thanked her, she moved away and seeing Ian's expression he chuckled, "Yes, T-dance, what a name. It appears having enjoyed your extraordinary dancing routines, and again unbeknown to me, Jane found other dancing frivolities, apparently this time at a local dance group. Although I believe T-Dance's routines are far less dramatic than yours!"

Ian blushed. "I wondered if you'd heard through the ITP grapevine about our last dancing escapade. I hope you weren't too cross with her. She loved dancing so I'm not surprised she found another outlet for her talent." With a small smile he confessed, "I was keen on Jane, but I was no match against you."

With a friendly grimace David patted Ian's shoulder. "Jane

was very loveable because she loved people. She'd be thrilled to hear you've made a commitment to the Lord. Find yourself a young and lively church, and enjoy the Lord's abundant life as she did." Ian nodded. "Now you'll have to excuse me I see the twins are about to the taken home and I need to give last minute instructions to their grandparents."

"Oh yes, sorry congratulations. That makes Jane's death even more tragic." Then looking uncomfortable he added, "I can't imagine how Jane, such a little person could have been pregnant with twins."

At that he chuckled. "Believe me Ian towards the end she looked like a barrel with two legs, two arms and head sticking out. Now I'm sorry, I must go. All the best for the future, and if you need help locating a church, come here and they'll sort something out for you."

Minutes later he approached Harry who seemed to bounce as he pumped his hand. "David it's so good to meet you, we so loved Jane." Others crowded eagerly around wanting to speak of Jane. In finding that difficult, he excused himself with the need to mingle, but Harry caught his arm. "Before you go, Jane suggested we use T-dance to help others. She suggested a yearly charity ball, where the profit could be used to hire halls in poor neighbourhoods and T-Dance couples could teach the locals to dance."

David nodded. "That sounds like Jane." Anxious to talk to a group of ITP people who appeared to be leaving, he smiled and made to move away.

"Jane thought to draw people in, and as an incentive, it would be good to have a yearly competition with a money prize…"

Coldly he interrupted, "And you want a contribution towards…"

Taken aback Harry exclaimed, "No, No! Well, if you wanted to give one, but that isn't it. I'd like to call it 'The Jane Reinhardt Dancing Award'. Would you have any objection to that?"

A frown puckered his brow as he tried to comprehend that, as Harry chattered on, "I understand now isn't the right time to discuss this. Here's my card, think about it and get back to me."

With a nod he put the card in his pocket, Harry moved away and he strode over to Chris County to express his delight at the number of people he'd seen from ITP.

Chris, looking slightly awkward, ran his black tie through his hand and admitted, "It appeared the majority of staff knew Jane, so Maud and I took an executive decision and closed the office for the afternoon. Although it was amusing to discover that several people seemed surprise to know the 'Jane' we drafted in as your temporary assistant two years ago was your wife." Eyebrows raised he looked questioningly at Chris who added boldly, "I think it's safe to say Jane's light-hearted, friendly manner, was seen as something of a contrast to your rather stern, austere approach to life."

David gave a rueful smile, "Yes, Chris that's fairly safe to say!" And changing the subject he asked after Chris' wife Patsy and son Peter, a few months younger than William. While chatting he realised the rawness of the earlier pain had been soothed by what he could only describe as God's presence, and despite the reason for the gathering, he was enjoying the sociability of the occasion. Jane, he knew, would have been delighted to see so many celebrating her life and that any leftover food would feed the homeless!

CHAPTER 14

Changed from his black pinstriped suit into light grey slacks and a short sleeved shirt David headed down to his lounge where Joyce and Ted were enjoying a 'nice cup of tea' while his parents sipped sherry. They had slipped away an hour after the memorial service to feed and look after the twins who were now asleep in their cots. But he'd wanted to stay until the last guest left and help with the clearing and packing up of the remaining food.

The smell of roast dinner permeated the house and although both Rosemary and Jill had put plates of food in his hand during the buffet it had been difficult to talk and eat, so he was ready for a meal.

Jill, hot and red faced emerged from his dining room, "Ah there you are David. Rosemary and I need to serve up before the joint becomes pork crackling."

"I'm ready." He glanced into the lounge at the two sets of grandparents, and then asked, "Where are Paula, Jim and the boys?"

"Downstairs in the garden, the boys needed to run off their energy. They've been so good all day. Paul and William are with them. William is too excited to go to bed so we're letting him stay up, but I might have to take him to bed during dinner."

"Right I'll get the grandparents seated at the far side of the table then the kids can sit nearest the door." Jill looked about to say something, hesitated, but before he could ask if there was a problem, she'd gone. And he knew well enough that she wouldn't appreciate his help in the kitchen!

Four pairs of eyes turned in his direction as he announced it was time for dinner. His petite and beautifully smart Mum smiled, her eyes filled with love and pride. Joyce, without the aid of what Jane termed 'merry sherry' looked pained, her eyes red and puffy from weeping. His father standing by the window talking to Ted turned and gave a brief approving nod, but Ted's sympathetic glance toward David changed to worry as he headed toward Joyce to take her hand and lead her in. He could understand Joyce's discomfort at being at a Reinhardt family meal without Jane especially as Jane had always insisted they sit at her right hand. Standing in the hall to usher everyone in he bent to say quietly to Ted, "Are you happy to stay in you usual seats?"

Ted nodded as Joyce hesitated in the doorway. With a hand on her back he urged, "Go on love, Jane would have wanted it." As they moved forward his Mum gave him a poignant smile before she and Franz followed them to the far side of the table. He swallowed hard for when hosting family gatherings Jane would sit at one end of the long table to serve the food from the kitchen behind her, while he presided over the other. It was impossible not to miss the girl who'd stolen their hearts and filled their lives, but she wouldn't have wanted them sad and subdued.

The strident voices of his two nephews came up from below. They'd certainly enliven the meal with their questions and antics. Paula's bulky and breathless figure appeared behind them. Four years ago Jane had described her as 'fat, fun and forty'. Fat was true, he watched as she squeezed her huge body between the sideboard and table to take her seat next to their father. Fun, yes she had a real sense of that. Although older than him, she'd initiated and involved him in all kinds of antics during their childhood, and now often ignited and ignored her boys' naughty behaviour. But forty, that birthday was still two months away. Had a smoking habit started with a farm hand behind the cow sheds stunted her growth, and made her look older than she was? Her penchant for sweet things, and inability to lose weight after the birth of the boys, had made her very lumpy and frumpy in her over-sized, and often creased clothes. But she'd smartened up for the funeral and today her hair bun with frequently adrift pins had been sculptured and lacquered to defy any collapse. What had been Paula's attraction to Jim? He was tall, thin and bald, a serious and meticulous accountant and who always wore a pristine suit, shirt and tie. Now, as always, his glasses were halfway down his long thin nose. Quietly he admonished his noisy boys to stand back for Paul to pass before they were seated. Until recently Jim had been ineffectual in everything connected to family life, but learning the ABC of discipline: authority, boundaries and care was changing him and his boys.

Richard was bombarding Paul with questions about pigs, and Philip, not yet eight, suddenly pulled on David's hand. One glance at his imploring gaze had him crouch to hear the problem whispered in his ear. "Uncle David, I don't want to eat a pig. I'll be sick."

He gave the boy a hug. "Don't worry, sit by me. Try it. If you feel ill I'll run you upstairs to the toilet."

Sulkily above him Richard retorted, "He's only saying that because I wanted to sit by you."

Paul having secured William in his chair next to Jill intervened. "If you sit by me I'll tell you all about pig dissection."

Pleased, and without further ado, Richard sat beside Paul as Philip putting his hands over his ears wailed, "I don't want to hear, I don't want to hear."

From across the table his father retorted gruffly, "And Paul, neither do we" then focussing on Richard he said, "Tell me, are you still in the school Chess Club?" Enthused by his grandfather's interest Richard regaled a set of complicated moves. After indicating to Philip to take the seat next to Richard, David shut the door, and braced himself to sit and face Jane's empty chair at the other end. But it wasn't empty! And he realised no-one but Beatty could, or would have wanted, to sit there. Immediately he sent Beatty his approval with a high-wattage smile, which he turned on Jill as she brought from the kitchen the huge pork joint. As the dish was passed down to him to carve Beatty looked around fondly at those gathered. "There's nothing like the love of a family, and David, Jill, thank you for the privilege to be included and made so welcome into yours." Her face creased, she pulled out a handkerchief from her sleeve, "Oh dear, silly me, I'm getting maudlin."

With carving knife and fork in hand he assured her, "Beatty, believe me, it's our privilege to have you here. You, and your advice has been invaluable. Even the District Nurse was impressed at your way of folding nappies to fit all sizes."

Paul held up an empty plate to indicate he was supposed to be carving the meat and advised, "And David, when Gran leaves tomorrow, you will need to meet and listen to the District Nurses' advice, no more escaping her visits."

David groaned for the plain featured, rotund woman in her mid-thirties with her jovial, friendly familiarity, irritated him. He was sure Mary Brown was either out to impress, or had designs on him. To Jill he pleaded, "Could you be there, I don't want to be left alone with her."

Whatever comment Jill opened her mouth to make his father cut across by saying impatiently, "For goodness sake David stop being so ridiculous. Carve the meat - we're waiting for our dinner."

Obediently he sliced away, as Jill fetched the bowls of vegetables. Once they were circulating she addressed the subject of Mary Brown. "David, she chatters because you make her nervous. Her hooded looks towards you are because she's shy. I know things are difficult, but your scowl and abrupt manner are intimidating."

Paul pouring the wine observed, "I can understand that. You have to be a very self-confident person to break through the hard, bossy Reinhardt exterior."

David jumped as his father boomed across the table, "Hard, bossy! What brings you to make that judgement?

Jill sent Paul a wicked grin. "Be careful darling how you answer that. You might loose wife, family, and job if you get it wrong."

Untroubled, Paul smiled, and while filling Franz wine glass said, "My dear father-in-law, I'm sure it is your sheer tenacity, work ethic, and clear vision that set your path and ability to achieve your goals. Your offspring here have inherited those same traits, and it takes someone who is equally persistent and stubborn to run with them, and love them, enough to curb their extremes. Would you agree Margaret, as one married to a Reinhardt?"

Franz turned his frown to his petite little wife. Her mouth twisted in a quirky smile before answering. "Oh Paul, I am very fond of you and of Jane. I believe she was good for David, as you are for Jill, and I am for Franz. Marriage needs a basis of love and loyalty, but often it is a partnership of two very different individuals, which only works where there is honour and respect and where both parties desire to listen and resolve problems without blame or accusation.

"Not a direct answer mother-in-law, but I like the sentiment."

Margaret saluted her glass towards Paul, then sipped on the wine.

Beatty murmured, "Here here." His father having begun eating said nothing, and with the exception of Joyce, who seemed too upset to eat, everyone else followed suit. Beatty broke the relative silence. "Families often have 'interesting discussions' around the meal table."

His father muttered, "Interesting discussions" in a derogative tone. David glanced at his father then saw Ted's speculative gaze and sent him a grin. It was as though that encouraged him to speak. "Neither Joyce, nor I, had siblings and we each only had one child." Joyce gave a sob, he paused to pat her hand before continuing. "With little experience of family life, I have to say we enjoy being here because you Reinhardts' are a prize act."

Franz choked on the food in his mouth. Paula next to him leapt up. Her chair crashed against the wall as she reached to slap his back. To David, Margaret seemed intent on sipping her wine, while Paul and Jill revealed that like him, they were finding it hard to conceal their mirth.

Rosemary thoughtfully poured a glass of water and lent across the table to instruct, "Drink this, it will help." Somewhat glassy eyed Franz obeyed. Ted undeterred, and with unexpected wit, began to recall several interesting 'discussions' where Jane had been the catalyst which opened up comments and laughter.

Franz ate steadily appearing to ignore Ted's stories. But on clearing his plate, he looked up to proclaim in a grim tone, "I'd say Ted, Jane was this family's 'prize act'!" In being unsure how to react to that statement there was a pregnant pause before he went on, "A more genuine and honest young woman would be hard to find. Her fault was perhaps in speaking her mind without thinking first. I'd like to find a way to honour her life and all she brought into this family."

Joyce who'd been fighting tears throughout, broke down. Ted put his arm around her and drew her to him. Jill after glancing at Joyce asked, "What have you got in mind Dad? There's no grave, by which to erect a tombstone, but if there was what would we put on it? She spoke slowly, "Jane, in her short life was… irrepressibly, indescribably, irrecusably irreverently, irresistibly, irrefutably, irrevocably unforgettable…."

As she paused, Franz clicked his tongue, then declared, "I was being serious" then delved into his pocket for his handkerchief and blew his nose. Jill countered that by saying, "Yes, Dad so was I." Around the table there was silence as each of them seemed caught up in the emotion of the moment. That was broken as his father in a tight and gruff voice said, "Jane touched many lives. She was a good match for David. She gave us two beautiful grandchildren and if nothing else we need to keep her memory alive for them." David's heart felt wrenched in two by his father's sincere words. "We need a tribute to Jane's life that is lasting. As much as I was disgusted by that Felicity woman asking for money I would have given Jane all she wanted." A derisive grunt from Jill drew all eyes to her. Gruffly Franz retorted, "It's true, each of you had money when you needed it."

Jill's face took on a belligerent expression. "Except until recently we thought it was our grandfather's money, not yours. Was that because you were afraid if we knew that, we'd ask for more? Oh do tell him David, what Jane said when, only two weeks ago, she found out about Dad's money!"

Quietly David cautioned, "I'm not sure Jill this is the right time."

Sharply she rejoined, "I don't see why, we're all family here."

From Jill he looked across at Ted, and saw although Joyce was still dabbing her eyes, the conversation had perked their interest. But it appeared his father felt as he did because he changed the subject by asking, "What's for dessert?"

As Rosemary jumped up, Beatty suggested, "One way to remember Jane would be to make a record of her life. Joyce, you must have photos of her as a child growing up. David, you have photos of your wedding and holidays. And there are in the cards and letters stories of how Jane helped people." Beatty glanced around the table, "Each of you could write of something she said, or did, what made her unique that would reveal her character and personality. I loved Rosemary's idea to have a book of remembrance for people to sign at the funeral. I wish I'd done that for Bill."

Rosemary returning from the kitchen and seeing everyone's eyes on her blushed at being the centre of attention. Jill deflected that by commenting, "Most people signed it and wrote a comment, I suspect that will make interesting reading!"

David passing down the dishes agreed, "Jane still proves to be a woman of surprises."

Beatty sent him an amused smile. "David, you'll find it cathartic to write about how she made you laugh, and made you cross." To him, right now, that felt too raw to consider. "If you do that, one day you'll have memories to share with the twins. It'll help them to know the woman who gave them life."

With tears close to brimming over David nodded, then seeing the desserts on the table, like his father he changed the subject by saying, "I can recommend Rosemary's apricot crumble. I'll start with that."

At Richard's "Me too" Rosemary filled a dish and sent it down the table to him with a small smile. A second later Richard piped up, "Auntie Rosemary" he paused until he had her attention, "I know you aren't as young, or funny as Auntie Jane, but as you already live here and love the twins, and with Uncle David liking your cooking perhaps you…"

Concurrent with Paula's sharply spoken "Richard!" there was an eruption of conversation across the table. Jim peering over his gold rimmed spectacles wore an expression as perplexed as his son's. Richard mumbled into his dish, "I was only going to suggest she could marry..." Paul interrupted in a voice of quiet authority, "Eat your pudding."

Fortunately only he, Paul and Philip heard that although Philip nodding thoughtfully added in a bright little voice, "Auntie Jane told us once she wasn't going to marry you, then she did." Worried at what either of them might say next, he responded by putting his forefinger to his lips. With a frown Philip continued in a stage whisper. "So even if Rosemary didn't want to, you could change her mind."

A glance towards Paul revealed his struggle not to laugh, and seeing Richard about to speak he lent forward and in a whisper advised, "Talk to Jesus about it He knows best." Richard nodded wisely, and Philip, as if given an important commission, looked so serious that he and Paul had to concentrate hard on eating to avoid erupting with mirth.

It wasn't until Paula put her hand on his arm David realised Beatty wanted his attention. "You could use that tape recorder you bought Jane to tell the twins about their mother." Mouth full he nodded. "The tape could go with other personal things you'll want to keep."

Having noted Rosemary's abhorrent expression as she had begun to comprehend where Richard's comment was heading David was surprised when she offered, "If I could borrow a Dictaphone and typewriter from work, I'd type them up for you." Richard sent him a knowing look. Under the table he patted his knee.

Joyce looking between Beatty and Rosemary said crossly, "David is going to have enough to do without considering that. He'll have to cope with feeding two babies during the night."

Gently, David responded, "Joyce, I'll just have to manage the best I can. I'll certainly need to take up your offer to come in three days a week. I'll catch up on sleep then, and as Rosemary has volunteered to do the eleven o'clock feed every evening I can go to bed early, and sleep until they awake around three o'clock." Joyce pursed her lips in much the same way as Jane did when she wasn't happy. To reassure her he explained, "Before I married Jane I was a compulsive studier and rarely slept for more than six hours a night, it's just a case of routine." Addressing his Mum he added, "And if you come up for a few days at a time, and with Paul and Jill's help I think we'll manage, after all it's only for the first few months." Looking down the table he said to Beatty, "I'm a task oriented person so it's a good idea to fill the night hours between feeds. But for now everything is a case of trial and error."

The word 'trial' reminded him that tomorrow the police were sending a car to take him to Maidstone for questioning. Up until now he'd pushed that to the back of his mind. His worry was, that without Jane's testimony, he might not be able to refute Andrew's Carlton's accusations, then how would they cope?

As though catching his thoughts Jill sent him a long look before jumping up to say, "Whatever happens we'll manage. William needs to go to bed, and perhaps David the boys could play cards in the other room while we have coffee? 'The boys' whooped with joy at being allowed down from the table and once settled playing 'Beat Your Neighbour' David returned to the table.

Immediately his father, stirring his coffee, boomed, "So David, what was Jill referring to when she spoke of Jane and my money?"

David knew without a glance at Ted and Joyce that their attention would be riveted on his answer. "Recently, a man I sacked several years ago blurted out in front of Jane that I was an heir to the Inhart fortunes. Later Jane asked me about it. I explained I rarely thought about it, and was grateful to you Dad, that you haven't expected, or encumbered me, with your business." His father nodded. David cleared his throat to continue. "I told Jane that from my perspective the magnitude of responsibility in having, and needing to invest, vast sums of money had become such it had distracted you from your family, and your desire to do research." His father's face wore that forbidding expression that as a child had quickly silenced him. Ignoring it David pressed on. "Jane agreed with your principle that children shouldn't be spoilt, and should have a healthy respect for money believing as you do, that too much easily diverts and corrupts lives."

The loud booming response of "That's my girl" made them all jump.

Beatty timidly inquired, "Am I allowed to ask what is a 'vast sum'?" Joyce's wide-eyed stare, and Ted's rapt interest, showed they'd like the answer to a question no-one in their family had ever dared ask. And with a hand gesture he side-lined the query to his father.

Straightening, his expression grim, his voice authoritative, his father said, "Gathered here tonight are those I consider family. I expect all you hear to remain in confidence. Do I make myself clear?" Sharp raven eyes bored into each person present until they'd each nodded their agreement. Satisfied he continued, "For the very reasons David spoke of I don't disclose the amount of monies Inharts Pharmaceuticals has amassed over the years, a sum that continues to grow and astonishes me. Since the war the pharmaceutical industry has become colossal, and runs into billions each year, of which Inharts has a huge share." Paul re-entering the room caused his father to point out, "Your grandson Beatty has been a Godsend." Paul gave a nod and sat as he continued, "In the last eighteen months the charitable work of the company has extended beyond supplying drugs to third world countries into permanent clinics where we can introduce preventive health care like inoculations for children. My aim is to also manufacture our drugs in those countries to bring employment to the indigenous population."

Beatty eyes had filled with love and pride as her grandson added, "For me it's an enormous privilege to be part of the expanding vision of 'In Our Hearts' for their ethos is close to my heart."

David allowed time for Paul's words time to sink in before he continued. "Obviously Dad, Jane knew of your work in underprivileged countries, but she pointed out there were many Christian organisations that needed funds. I explained that giving money away could be more of a headache than making it! It was then Jane asked about your personal fortune, the extent of which I don't know, but believe it runs to several millions." Around the table he heard several sharp intakes of breath. "In realising that one day I'll inherit a third of both that, and the company, Jane suggested it would be wise to discuss with you now how we could tackle the accumulation, assets and disposal before it became as she described it, a 'million-stone' around our necks!"

At that his father grunted, "Did she indeed!"

Ted and Joyce were clearly astounded, the Reinhardt family were certainly entertaining them! Beatty looked thoughtful, Rosemary was fidgeting a sure sign she was either desperate to wash up, or leave! And the three of them knowing they would inherit this 'million-stone' nodded as though in agreement, but Jim surprised them to pipe up and say, "If the money is to be divided up now, Paula and I could do the things we wish to do, but can't afford, after all charity should begin at home."

Paula's embarrassment was evident and to divert attention David addressed his father. "Jane asked if you considered the business as a family concern. And suggested if you did then perhaps it was time we as a family became involved by taking some responsibility now. She pointed out then when the time came we'd be prepared, and able to make an informed judgement, to either run or sell Inharts." Was his father's scowl because of Jane's audacity, or the thought of their selling what he had worked so hard to build?

Incredulous his father burst out, "Basically Jane wanted to dispose of not only my personal fortune, but take over the Company!"

Jill sniggered at his father's outrage, and he was quick to clarify. "Jane's suggestion was that as a family we take an interest in the Company, to assist, and learn from you. But she did suggest you might begin to dispose of your personal fortune now. I'm sure you'll agree there is sense in that, because inheritance tax would take a large slice in the event of your death. Jane wasn't suggesting we keep and spend it, but desired to use it in a philanthropic way. We briefly talked of this while she was recuperating. There are several organisations, projects and missions that don't attract government funding, but nevertheless are genuine and do good work." Not daring to look at either Jill or Paul, David gave a nonchalant shrug before finishing with what he considered a punch line. "It occurs to me, Dad, as a memorial to Jane, you could embrace her suggestion by starting to transfer money into a charitable fund that we could name after her."

David sat back, steepled his fingers against his mouth and awaited the explosion. In his mind's eye he could see Jane's cheeky grin and knew she would have spun it out far better than he.

There was a pregnant pause before his father deflated their anticipation by booming, "Well Jill do we have to wait all night for the coffee?"

CHAPTER 15

Dressed in his dark business suit, David looked more the smart city lawyer than the man 'helping police with their enquiries'. When the doorbell rang at 9.00 o'clock, he was ready and determined not to dwell on the outcome of the day. After a cheery "Good morning" to DI Jordan, he shut the front door and walked with him towards the unmarked police car.

"I must say, Sir, you look a great deal better than when I last saw you." Seated in the back of the car, as the driver edged away from the kerb, DI Jordan seated beside him quietly commented, "I probably shouldn't tell you this, but your tragic loss holding up our enquiries has revealed Carlton's single-mindedness to put you in the dock for the murder of his friend."

Stoutly David retorted, "That's no surprise to me! Let's believe justice will prevail because I can assure you I'm innocent. Whatever Carlton's been up to for the past four years, I've no doubt he's made many enemies. But in believing I ruined his life, he's going to take full advantage of this chance for vengeance."

"Yet Carlton is keeping clear of the press, despite wanting to tarnish your name and reputation."

"Probably due to the past he wishes to hide?"

The Inspector hummed thoughtfully, and it was several miles before he spoke again. "Have you seen any of the press coverage?"

"No, I've not watched the TV since…it was three weeks today that Jane and I met Andrew, yet it feels like a life time ago."

The DI briefly touched his arm in a gesture of sympathy before saying, "The press have certainly enjoyed speculating about our mystery witness, and why 'he or she' haven't been called in for questioning. They are virtually camping outside Maidstone police station so as not to miss a scoop. News at Ten last night made quite a point of the police secrecy, so after today I'm afraid your connection with this case will be known."

Closing his eyes, David groaned. Perhaps he should have told the rest of the family last night? He voiced his thoughts, "Surely a murder in a sleazy pub isn't the stuff of headline news? I'm a business man, not a celebrity."

DI Jordan shrugged. "You can never tell! The sad slant could bring a sympathetic press, or a determination to prove no-one is above the law."

"Well I've nothing to hide, but hate the thought of the press intrusion into my family and life." He thought of Joyce and Ted. When they read the newspaper reports they'd be hurt that he hadn't told them of his involvement.

DI Jordan gave him a wide-eyed look. "In that alone Carlton will have extracted a vengeance of sorts. Your name and legal career might not be widely known, but I suspect, somewhere, a reporter will unearth the story of you commenting at Ben Fletcher's trial, 'If that's justice, the law's an ass'. There's no need to tell you how unrelated incidents can be made to seem something they're not."

"You mean, for example, two years later, unbeknown to me, Ben Fletcher was employed by ITP!"

DI Jordan nodded, "To some that possibility would seem unlikely."

Annoyed David stated, "Well, let me tell you, when I found out, no-one could have been more pleased than I to give him a new start."

The DI nodded. "I felt it was a shame that Fletcher lost his life after he and your sister, inadvertently, brought down that drug cartel. The ripples of that are still expanding across several nations. I'm afraid that too makes for great story and newspaper sales!"

"Oh God!" Head bent, David massaged his temples, his worry about proving his innocence was now negated by the damage the press could cause by stirring up those stories.

"Carlton is playing the poor innocent victim. All we have on him is a four year old warrant for his arrest, and statements from people I'm finding hard to trace. You know in court that can't be divulged, but if the information should leak out…"

David shook his head. "That's not my way. It would only prove I was as vengeful as he is. Jane isn't here to testify, but the barman can verify the truth."

DI Jordan didn't comment. In the silence David thought how grateful he was to Paul, that having delivered him a cooked breakfast at 7.00 am, they'd prayed for the Lord's peace and wisdom. And that last night, before his father left, he'd assured him of his readiness to engage Daniel Kemp, a barrister renown for his astuteness. He'd gone on to say he'd spare no expense to ensure the innocent remained free. He'd done that for Ben, so it proved again, when necessary his father could be generous. He closed his eyes to pray. Whatever happened the press mustn't unearth Ben's story.

Someone was shaking his shoulder. David grunted, and in struggling to remember where he was, the Inspector's voice broke into his semi-conscious state. "Wake-up, we're nearly there." As David opened his eyes Jordan continued, "I guess you needed that. You'll have plenty more sleepless nights in the days ahead." Groggily he nodded, and hoped the inference was about the twins, and not being in jail for a crime he didn't commit. "Jack will drive us into the police car compound, but to avoid photographs I suggest you sit with your back towards the window."

They executed the transition from the police car park to the interview room so smoothly he guessed it had been done a hundred times before. And he was grateful for DI Jordan and Jack who deliberately blocked the view of reporters.

On arrival, he was taken to a room rather like Jane's at the hospital, except this one contained a battered oblong table with two chairs on either side. And, although he was grateful for the cup of tea and bacon butty delivered just after noon, it was very frustrating waiting around for those who had so urgently wanted to interview him! The hope of being home by tea time was fading fast.

Finally the door opened and two men entered. David, pocketing the small Bible he'd been trying to read, stood as Detective Inspector Gage introduced himself and Detective Chief Inspector Bridges. Gage was probably in his thirties, wiry in build, but despite his gaunt features, his eyes held an amused glint as he shook David's hand and said politely, "Thank you for coming." Having had no option David responded with a nod. DCI Bridges looked in his late fifties, balding, pot-bellied, with a tough 'seen it all' exterior, who merely grunted in his direction, before sinking heavily on to a wooden chair. Taking out a packet of cigarettes, he lit one up and headed a thin line of smoke in David's direction as DI Gage added, "Sorry to hear about your wife. Sad business that."

Bridges ignoring that, took from a file in front of him the signed statement David had given last week. Tapping it he pointed out, "We need to corroborate this with other statements and evidence."

Gage chipped in, "We'll try and not keep you too long, I know you have twin…"

Bridges interrupted, "Yes, well let's get on with it then, read him his rights."

Puzzled David queried, "Am I under arrest?"

The DCI gave a sour smile, "Let's just say as we have no other suspects and you are 'helping us with our enquiries'! Now let's get on with it."

After the preliminaries, Bridges sat forward to demand, "We have your statement, but tell us what happened in The Travellers' Rest on 26th June between you and Jake Charlton, the man known to you, as Andrew Carlton?"

Bridges, it appeared was addicted to tobacco, evidenced by his nicotine fingers and the blue mist he was creating. Throughout David's description of events, he coughed several times, and finally he had to request they open a window.

As Gage jumped up, Bridges scowled and asked, "You said Carlton pointed across the bar to Henry Nimbya. How would you describe him?"

"Then I saw only his back view. A tall, broad and well built black man. When he entered the Snug I saw how large he was. I wondered how I'd fair if he muscled in. I couldn't see his features because he blended into the shadows by the Snug door."

Gage took a photograph from his folder and handed it to him. "Is this the man?"

It wasn't a pleasant photo, but he'd seen worse during his time as a barrister. The black man's dead eyes had bulged in shock, he was lying on a carpet in a dark pool of blood, and in his neck was a fair-sized triangular shaped piece of glass. "Well I can't be absolutely sure, but I'd say it looks like him." He handed the photo back.

Gage continued, "Yet Pearce, the barman, doesn't recall him leaving the Public Bar."

"That's not surprising, it was lunch time and the bar packed with people. All of whom left before we did."

Bridges intervened. "Let's get back to what happened before Carlton hit you. Was Nimbya still in the room?"

He closed his eyes to relive the moment. "Jane screamed my name. I thought Henry had grabbed her. I started to turn and felt a blow to my head. I didn't know if it was Henry or Andrew who'd hit me, because only seconds before, Andrew appeared too stunned to move."

"I suggest Nimbya left the room before Carlton hit you. And he was in the Public Bar seconds before Carlton ran out and went through the glass?"

David nodded at Bridges. "That would explain his being there, but flying glass hitting the jugular seems rather far fetched to me. That picture shows it was a fair sized piece, are you sure someone didn't use the opportunity to murder him?"

Gage looked thoughtful and addressed Bridges. "It might be worth checking for fingerprints." Bridges gave a loud derisive grunt before viciously grinding out his cigarette to add another stub to the rapidly filling metal ashtray.

Ignoring Bridges obvious angst David warned, "In that place I'd say anything was possible, but the general grubbiness probably means there were layers of finger prints on the glass of that door!"

Bridges leant forward to say sullenly. "We don't need your assumptions. The facts tell us only you, your wife or the barman had the opportunity to speed Carlton's delivery through that door."

With a sad grimace David sat back. "You can rule out Jane. You see she was a petite woman, just over five feet tall and eight months pregnant with twins. And the barman…" He paused, "I'm sure Jane said the glass smashed as the barman caught and sat her down."

With obvious delight Bridges declared, "Exactly, so that just leaves you." He lit another cigarette.

Despite reassurances from Paul, and his father, that no-one would suspect him, this was going exactly as he'd envisaged. "True, and Jane can't tell you I was laid out across a table, but the barman can because he helped me up."

Inhaling and releasing another blue trail of smoke, Bridges took a typed sheet of paper from the file and waved it. "This is Pearce's statement. "I saw the man staggering from Jake's blow. No. I didn't see him collapse on the table. I told you, I jumped the counter and caught the man's wife. I was just sitting her down when the glass crashed. I rushed from her to see what damage those bastards had caused. I suppose I was gone at least a minute, if not two. It was a bloody mess with Jake's body stuck halfway through the door. It's a miracle he survived and was conscious. I recognised Bernie's voice as he shouted at me, 'Don't touch the door.' He went on to warn me that Jake appeared to be impaled by a piece of glass in his stomach, and there was a danger the glass above his head would slip down."

Sickened at the description David closed his eyes, bent forward, put his elbow on the table and hand across his mouth. He shook his head at the picture it portrayed, and at Bridges' underlying relish in relaying such gory details.

"Pearce goes on to recount, 'Because I couldn't see, I bent to look through a small hole in the glass. The men were horror struck, staring at Jake, but beyond I saw several men gathered around a body on the floor. I shouted to Bernie, "What's happened over there?" At that, those around parted to reveal Henry lying on the floor with a lump of glass in his neck, his blood pumping out over the carpet."

David lifted his hand from his mouth and rested his knuckles under his chin, before saying with feeling, "Poor Pearce, fancy having to face that. No wonder he felt it would be best if we were out of it. I wouldn't wish that on my worst enemy."

Bridges stubbing out his cigarette with slow deliberation looked up to question, "Wouldn't you?"

David sat up, frowned in querying grimly, "What are you inferring?"

The DCI shrugged, "Pearce said in tending your wife his back was to you and the doorway. When asked if he thought it was possible you could have run past him he shrugged and said, "Anything is possible."

Immediately he protested, "Why would I…"

Bridges cut him off. "Your wife had been attacked. Anger fuels retaliation. You'd easily felled Carlton twice that day. So with a run, head butting the tops of his legs you could have simply lifted, carried and propelled him through a door like a human cannon ball?" David shaking his head went to dispute that, but Bridges held up his hand. "I think you then stepped out into the street until Pearce became absorbed in what was happening in the Public Bar, and then you slipped back in to appear stunned over a table."

Incensed by Bridges' supposition David boomed, "Oh that's ridiculous!"

Bridges retorted, "But we've only your word that you fell from the blow across the table."

David gave a heavy sigh. It then occurred to him to ask, "With everyone leaving by the back door surely someone saw me lying across that table?"

The men looked at each other. Gage answered. "Pearce either doesn't know, or is reticent to give names. Our enquiries have only produced three people who were there besides Bernie and his friends. None have been very co-operative, and said they didn't see anyone in the Snug Bar before, or after the accident.

To digest and address that David steepled his fingers against his mouth as DI Gage took the barman's statement in front of

Bridges. DCI Bridges' stare at him as he flicked off the ash from yet another cigarette bordered on mockery. Gage reading the notes offered, "Pearce did say that in the rush to leave no-one would have spotted Reinhardt's wife by the door, or Reinhardt over the table. Pearce points out that the table was so close to the bar you'd have to look directly over it to see him. He turned to Bridges, "There's note here saying that's been verified."

Inwardly David thanked the barman and Gage for his support before setting his eyes firmly on Bridges. "It is, of course, your job to come up with a plausible scenario as to how this incident occurred. And as I appear to be the only suspect, I understand why you have worked out how I might have done it. But I put it to you to consider that as Andrew rushed through the Pub's entrance hall, someone could have come in off the street and taken the opportunity of heading him through the glass." Bridges gave a derisive snort. David continued, "The barman told us, and I am sure you are aware, that Andrew alias Jake, was known to be a nasty piece of work. To which I'd agree, as would DI Jordan from the Met!" He paused and gave Bridges a meaningful stare. "Pearce wouldn't have seen anyone coming in or out, for as you suggested, they could have slipped back into the street while he was dealing with the carnage, and then just walked away!"

The thunderous expression on Bridges face was such that Gage announced, "I think we'd better take a break". At that Bridges pushed back his chair and stormed into the hall. A man in the corridor questioned, "Got a confession yet?" to which they heard Bridges reply, "Huh! Typical lawyer, full of himself and his own …ideas! It'll take a while to get him to admit to anything."

Gage gave him a wide-eyed look and asked, "Can I get you a cuppa, perhaps something to eat?"

It was over an hour before they reconvened, and he was anxious to return to the twins. And inwardly he kept repeating the promise of the Lord, "I will never leave you, or forsake you" but it was a battle to keep a positive attitude in the reality of living his nightmare. As Bridges' thin trail of smoke headed towards him again, he realized he used his chain smoking habit to antagonise suspects. After asking several past question, as though to catch him out, Bridges finished accusingly, "And you are no better than those who didn't want to get involved, for you and your wife left by the back door as the police arrived at the front."

Coldly David countered, "Nothing quite so cut and dried! I dealt with Andrew's confrontation as best I could. He'd gone, we heard breaking glass, but saw nothing. We weren't involved, and with a time constraint, Jane eight month's pregnancy with twins, and the risk of her going into labour, we both felt the quicker we were with friends and family the better."

At Bridges' negative grunt Gage gave him a fleeting, but troubled glance, then commented, "And I gather that's what happened. Within a couple of hours your wife went into labour and was admitted to 'The General' that evening, your twins delivered twenty-four hours later."

With a grimace David added, "And why with that, and Jane's ensuing problems, our meeting with Andrew faded into insignificance."

DI Gage encouraged him to elaborate which clearly irritated Bridges who snapped, "This is not an enquiry into the National Health Service! I want to know why, when the murder was reported in the newspapers and TV news why you didn't come forward?

Tiredly he explained, "I was so tied up with Jane and the twins I didn't do much more than eat and sleep. And it wasn't until we returned on Saturday evening my sister told me of the call from the Kent police, and DI Jordan's visit."

Bridges' sneered, "Your sister hasn't just had twins? Doesn't she read a paper or watch the TV?"

He sighed, "Jill, even if she read, or heard anything about the incident, probably didn't make the connection with our meeting with Andrew Carlton. I presume reports would have named him as Jake Charlton. When DI Jordan called round she told him where to contact me.

"Are you expecting me to believe, that despite Pearce telling you that Jake Charlton had got what he deserved, you didn't ask him, or later discuss with your Missus what that might have been?"

"DCI Bridges, Jane was heavily pregnant, we had a funeral to take part in during which she went into labour and had our twins. Believe me, in that week far more important things overshadowed the incident with Carlton. And before I had chance to tell her on Sunday morning of the police's interest in our connection with Andrew…" he hesitated, swallowed hard and finished, "she'd died in my arms." A deep anguish stirred within him. For once he was grateful for Bridges' belligerent attitude for it overcame his rising grief. "All I can think of is that if Andrew had exacted his vengeance on us, we could have been the ones lying in a pool of blood and needing an ambulance. However, I am surprised Andrew has revealed his true identity in the hope I'd be convicted of the murder of his friend."

Gage gave a small smile. "That only came later after Charlton, or Carlton with life threatening injuries was in surgery for hours. His face is unrecognisable from the one on our file from four years ago. The constable waiting for him to recover heard him muttering and caught your name. You could have been relative, friend or foe, so we traced you, not hard with only two listed Reinhardt's in a forty mile radius of London, yourself and your sister." He chuckled, "When we had no answer from your telephone we tried hers, and bingo, she not only knew you, but told us Jake Charlton's real name. You're definitely Charlton's 'foe', and he's hell bent to put you in the frame for his injuries, and Nimbya's murder."

It appeared that DCI Bridges was equally hell bent on finding a way to convict him, for he scoffed, "So, having established a motive, we now have a cause. And as you well know, in going down for Charlton's GBH, you will go down for Nimbya's murder. Unless you have any other bright ideas where this investigation might lead to, we'll continue?"

Weary, he sighed, "Bridges' you can go through it a hundred times, but it won't change anything. I assume you questioned the people in nearby houses. Did any of them see anyone go in, or out, of the Pub during that time?

At that Bridges snapped, "Are you telling us how to do our job?"

Before he could respond Gage replied, "Yes we did. Most people in the street were working, but the little old lady living opposite gave us a statement."

As Gage shuffled through the papers in the file Bridges said, "I took her statement, there's nothing useful in it."

"Ah, here it is?" Gage scanned down the page. "She knew of the 'big black man' because every Friday he, and the rowdy factory crowd, always drew her attention to the window. Not long after they arrived she saw 'a big car draw up, a smart man and pregnant woman get out and enter the pub'. It being 'not a nice place' she was curious when they went in and didn't come straight out. She says, 'I was watching when that 'big black man' walked by. I thought he'd already gone into the pub. I've not seen him on this side of the road before because Denton's factory is behind the pub. He stopped outside my window, and I was afraid he might see me through the net curtains. Then having crossed the road he went into the pub. I went to make a cup of tea. The next thing I knew the ambulance was there, then police and fire brigade. That place is always trouble. I was worried for that couple, but saw their car had gone'." Gage looked up, "When asked she'd no idea of make or number plate."

Bridges jeered, "As I said, nothing worth noting."

David felt to point out, "It tells us Henry arrived late. Have you asked Carlton why?"

Bridges sighed heavily, "Why? Nimbya was there, and he was killed."

"But perhaps he wasn't well. It would explain why he decided not to muscle in and defend Andrew."

"Irrelevant! Now let's get back to your story."

Two hours later, despite Gage's attempts to curb Bridges' mounting animosity, David was loosing patience, and desperate to get home. He rubbed his temples and addressed Bridges, "Look I can't help you any further. Your smoking has given me a headache. And you have insufficient evidence to charge me, so its time I went home to my babies."

Bridges snarled, "This is a murder enquiry. We can keep you as long as we please."

"In which case its time to call my solicitor."

After a brief tap at the door, a constable beckoned Bridges' outside and was heard to say, "Superintendant John Perrington is here. He wants an update on the case." Before the door banged shut, Bridges irritated voice asked, "What's he doing here?"

At that David curbed a smile because he wasn't about to inform Bridges of Paul's friendship with Perrington. Or, after the twins were born, his very pleasant lunch with him, which, no doubt was the cause of his interest, and he hoped, support.

From that moment everything moved swiftly. Daniel Kemp, already briefed by his father, had subsequently engaged a local solicitor Martin Beresford. Much to the annoyance of DCI Bridges, he'd arrived within ten minutes of his telephone call.

An hour later, the press, like vultures, swooped on Superintendant John Perrington as he stepped outside. That acted as an excellent opportunity for two smartly dressed lawyers to start down the steps, but as they skirted around the crowd, two of the reporters turned to ask, "Do you represent this mystery man? Have you seen him? Is he under arrest? Has he been charged for murder?" David shrugged, and Martin nodding towards John said,

"He's making the press announcement." And with that they walked rapidly to Martin's E-type Jaguar parked around the corner, and were roaring away up the street before any suspicion was aroused. Settling back in the leather seat, he stretched his legs and rested his head back with a long sigh of relief. He'd come through the day, he'd kept calm, gained a little information, escaped custody and the press, and all he wanted now was home, his babies, bath and bed.

Martin said little beyond warning that once the press knew his name they'd find pictures of him, report both truth and fiction, and could decide he was interesting enough to camp outside his house for a few days. At David's groan Martin advised, "If you say nothing, stay out of sight you will find, news like everything else, grows quickly stale. Known one day and forgotten the next." Outside the house he thanked Martin who grinned, "My pleasure. I've been told no expense spared, so I'll be staying in a suite in the Royal Garden Hotel tonight."

"Then enjoy it. You're worth it, after my speedy and efficient extraction from DCI Bridges' clutches!"

Martin grinned, "Don't worry, Daniel Kemp and I will sort this out."

The initial flurry of journalists wanting a juicy story had only lasted a few days, although he had noticed a car constantly parked across the road. The twins slept peacefully in the enclosed back garden, and he'd no desire or incentive to leave the house, his life revolved around the twins needs and sleeping. He only made the headlines in the Evening Standard, the dailies relegated the story to either their second, third and fourth pages. Several ITP staff were interviewed, each commented it would be out of character for David Reinhardt to cause grievous bodily harm to anyone. And someone told the press about Andrew Carlton's dismissal for attacking one secretary, and beating up another who was carrying his baby. The Times and Guardian gave half a column to the case and quoted his remark about the law being an ass. The Daily Telegraph also used that to provoke letters from their readers, but fortunately neither named the trial in his short career that had caused that remark. The Daily Express and Mail dug up a picture of him, their articles read as a human interest story. The meeting with Andrew deemed the cause of the twins' early delivery and Jane's tragic death. David supposed it was inevitable, that the newly emerging Sun newspaper, becoming known for it's facetious by-lines and page three pin-ups, used that page to report the story alongside one of Felicity's modelling photos. But what really infuriated him was their innuendo that Jane had been the cause of his broken engagement to Felicity. Felicity was such an opportunist he wondered if she'd sent in the photo and report to gain free publicity.

Joyce and Ted were understandably upset. First, because they'd not known about Jane's first brush with Andrew four years earlier, and second, he'd kept from them the police questioning him as a murder suspect. Combined with the shock of Jane's death, Ted decided Joyce wasn't up to helping with the twins. There was relief in that, for there were times when David couldn't cope with his own grief, let alone hers. With an uncertain future, he spent as much time with the twins as possible, but sensed Jill, Paul and Rosemary were watching him. Admittedly he did keep drifting off, into either contemplation of the murder, or Jane's death, and hours would go by.

The saying, 'no publicity is bad publicity' proved right for ITP as they were bombarded by enquiries about their services to the trade, and his father found a long lost cousin whom he'd presumed dead. Letters also arrived from people long forgotten offering testimonials in their belief of his innocence. Ten days later, the only advance was the police finding of a set of fingerprints on the piece of glass taken from Henry's neck. Their formation, and the shape of the piece of glass, had given rise to the suspicion someone had taken the opportunity of an accident to commit a murder. A later a report said the factory workers fingerprints were to be taken, but if this had proved anything neither he, nor the press had been told.

Throughout those days their friends from church visited either late afternoon or evening, often bringing a cake and offering their help. The only other constant visitor was Nurse Mary Brown checking on the twin's growth. At his plea, Jill stayed around as he gritted his teeth in a parody of a smile at Mary's constant chatter, but he'd nearly had apoplexy at her joy in 'being allowed behind the scenes of an unfolding drama'!

Tired, frustrated by life and the police's lack of keeping him informed, self pity expressed itself in anger and tears. Yesterday, Jill suggested she clear out Jane's things, the thought had brought such anguish he'd boomed, "Leave me and her things alone," before collapsing on the settee to sob, "That's all I have left of her."

In true Jill fashion she'd stood her ground, folded her arms and retorted, "Untrue, you have the twins. And it was an offer of help, not an assignment to remove Jane from your life. Anyway how is the scrapbook of Jane's life coming along?"

Still upset he'd bitten back, "How do you think? I can barely concentrate on anything. I spend most of my time feeding first Joshua, then Rebecca. Everything reminds me of Jane. To divert my mind I'm constantly going over this wretched case. I feel I'm missing a vital clue."

Eyebrows raised Jill had countered, "Then count your blessings, because we do all your shopping, cooking, washing and childcare in order you can get six hours rest somewhere in twenty-four!"

At that, he felt bad, his temper diminished and he apologised for his thoughtlessness. In loving the twins, he didn't begrudge his life revolving around their constant needs, but inevitably there were times when Jane's loss so gripped him he found himself weighing up their lives against hers, which then sent him spiralling into a guilt trip. He knew the support of his family was vital to his sanity, and each day to have the opportunity to sit down to dinner with those who loved and cared for him, and be 'normal', felt like a lifeline to a dying man!

With a baby in each arm David went downstairs to lay the twins side-by-side in the big Silver Cross pram his Mum had used when they were children. Gently he wheeled it along the hall, past Jill and Paul's bedroom, and left it at the top of the stairs where he'd hear them if they cried. On arrival in the basement lounge, William in his high chair grinned and banged his spoon. As if on cue Jill appeared carrying plates and warning William the food was hot. David smiled as fourteen month old William understood enough to blow at his plate.

When Jill returned with her plate, he commented, "That boy of yours is so cute. And for someone who could barely boil an egg two years ago, your cooking has improved. Where are Paul and Rosemary? With a weary smile Jill sat beside William. Paul's been called into the hospital. They were desperate for a doctor in Casualty. Rosemary is visiting a friend."

Wide-eyed he questioned, "Rosemary has a friend?"

Crossly Jill retorted, "Don't be horrible."

Palms uplifted up he exclaimed, "It was a question, not a criticism."

"Glad to hear it. I'm sure she does have friends, and she's like a sister to me. Anyway, she told that reporter she was the twin's night nanny. And she's not missed an eleven o'clock feed, so rest assured she'll be home by then. This has been a difficult time for all of us, but I've sensed under Rosemary's calm exterior there's something troubling her beyond our problems. But there's no point in asking, for she's worked for you, and lived here for two years, and we still know nothing of her life or family before she came to ITP." They ate and considered that until Jill snapped, "William, that's naughty, food goes in your mouth, not on the floor." As his face puckered it was clear a scream of discontent was on the way. Jill pushed her plate away, rested an elbow on the table and rubbed her forehead. "Oh dear, I'm not sure, I can deal with this."

Over the noise he boomed, "I think we're all running on low, but how about you go and make a cup of tea. I'll look after him." Jill nodded, but her leaving the table caused William's yell to raise a few decibels higher. At his very firm, "That will do William" and heading a spoon of food towards his mouth it clamped shut. In the silence he suggested, "Now why don't we eat together?" Putting down William's spoon he loaded his own fork and said, Ready, "One, two, three, in our mouths." The little boy first watched with curiosity, then interest, and by the time he was on his fourth mouthful, William picked up his spoon, followed the count, and then cleared his plate. William grinned as he suggested, "Shall we now call 'Mummy'?" Together they shouted, to which Jill responded carrying a tray.

"I see David you haven't lost your talent for making little boys obey you, remember Richard and Philip?"

"I do indeed! Children don't like being chastised, but it's essential. I'd say with Paula and Jim exercising the ABC of discipline it's certainly working!" He gave a wry smile, "But you can't stop children speaking their minds."

Jill grinned, "We tried to cover it up, but poor Rosemary looked so embarrassed."

Embarrassed wasn't what he'd have called her expression, more horrified. In tickling William, bringing the expected giggles, he asked, "Do you want help to bath and put this little rascal to bed?"

"Thank you, but that might excite him too much. What a pity Jane isn't here to see what a great father you are."

Tears sprung into his eyes, he clenched his jaw and looked away. Jill's hand rested on his arm. "Oh David…I'm sorry. It's impossible not to talk about her. She was so much a part of all our lives." After a brief pause she said cheerfully, "At least the police have now matched the prints from that piece of glass to those of a factory worker?"

Astonished he straightened to ask, "What! When did this happen?"

"It was on the midday news. I assumed you'd know. The barman has confirmed, and identified the man. He is one of the three factory workers who were standing over the body when the barman looked through the broken window. The police must believe it was a deliberate stabbing because all three men have been charged with murder, but they've yet to establish a motive."

"From what I've heard, he and Andrew terrorised people, so that shouldn't be difficult, but that doesn't clear me from the GBH charge."

"But, it's a start. The police should be thanking you. It's your help with their enquiries that's bringing results."

Grimly he retorted, "But not the one Bridges wants!" Punching one hand into the other David declared, I knew it was too bizarre to be an accident." They sipped on their hot tea until William gained their attention by throwing his plastic drinking cup on the floor bringing Jill to announce, "William time for bed. And David, I haven't seen anyone looking like a reporter hanging around, so with the twins in the pram, why don't you take a stroll around the park?"

"Is that, sister, your way of saying I'm putting on weight?"

Jill laughed, "Would I be so bold? But with cakes and my cooking, it is possible."

CHAPTER 16

At the sense of freedom David's footsteps quickened along the empty High Street. A couple he passed smiled, perhaps at his being a man alone pushing a pram. In Kensington Gardens he breathed in the smell of freshly cut grass and relaxed into a steady pace. Jane's words echoed in his head. 'David, your stroll is more like a route march' and seeing two little heads rocking against the pram's thick padding, he slowed.

It was one of those glorious evenings where the sun, in the bluest of skies, was an hour away from setting, but still warm. It made you glad to be alive. A shaft of pain went through him. He wanted his Jane alive, and beside him. Forlornly he watched an elderly couple throwing a stick for their dog to retrieve. In the distance a group of youths were shouting and kicking a ball around. As he passed he caught sight of a couple under a tree, laughing, romping and kissing seemingly unperturbed, that he and others, might see them. His jaw tightened, he steeled his emotions, and quickened his step to the gate in Bayswater Road.

Life had to go on! But it had been hard this morning when the last photos of Jane arrived, showing them smiling with the twins in their arms, the only family photos he'd ever have! The remainder were of the weekend celebrating their third wedding anniversary where Jane in Windsor was showing off her huge bump, with funny faces and poses. Jane was resting on benches in front of an historic scene, lying like a beached whale on the river bank, standing precariously on the boat deck and raising a wine glass while eating lunch in a pub garden.

A voice, calling his name, broke into those memories. Swooping down, blonde hair flying around her face, and almost throwing herself across the pram to cut off his stride, Felicity's breathless, but jingly voice spoke by his ear. "David, I thought it was you." That sound caused him to shudder, she was so false, and to think he might have married her! "I didn't expect to see you pushing a pram. Mum said you and Jane were expecting twins." She peered into the pram, "Gosh they look like little dolls. How sweet. Where's Jane, at home putting her feet up? It must be tiring having two of them to look after." Before he could speak Felicity launched into having been on a film shoot in Hollywood for the past three months and her meeting of the rich and famous. "I only arrived back this afternoon. We're staying at the Royal

Garden. I thought of looking you up, but Conran, you know the producer, Conran Taylor, he and I…well, we're good friends, but it's not really the thing is it to visit an old boyfriend with a new one?" She giggled.

The high pitch sound reminded him of a horse's whiney, he cringed. The woman was as insensitive as ever for he'd not yet spoken, and she hadn't noticed!

"Did you know that I and the parents had a frightful row before I left? They don't like my lifestyle, and think I should settle down like you and dear Jane." David scowled at the derogatory inference, but Felicity in output mode didn't notice. "I haven't kept in touch with them. They always go on about how stupid I was to give you up just because your Dad's parsimonious ways." She scoffed, "Still, as someone once said, there aren't any pockets in shrouds! Amused she added, "Conrad is rich in his own right." I'm taking him down to the West Country to surprise the parents who probably think I'm dead!"

Incensed by her words, and the shallow, self-seeking character of the woman, he bit out, "Just like Jane?" And with the intention of marching off, pushed the pram forward.

But Felicity, not easily shoved aside, grabbed his arm. "What's just like Jane?" But before he could answer she was again full flow. "Oh, she's now found out how tight your Dad keeps his purse strings. It must be difficult, on your measly salary, to afford to keep her, and the twins."

An inner rage rose within him. With an expression of disgust, which was reflected by the snarl in his voice, he demanded, "Move out of my way."

"My, my, your cage is rattled. What's Jane done this time? At least pregnant with twins it won't have been disco dancing with that lanky lad!" Felicity gave one of her false laughs. In wanting to throttle her David tightened his grip on the pram handle. "I knew that Christmas she'd be an embarrassment to you. Not your age or class!"

Afraid that his symbolic throttling might become reality he fiercely pushed the pram down the path causing Felicity to jump back, and at the jolt a cry from Joshua. Not easily put off, she fell into step beside him, "You always were good at keeping your anger in control. What is it, many a true word spoken in jest? You may have wanted to be a father, but I doubt a man like you, expected you'd be pushing a pram around the park on your own."

That was it, enough was enough! He stopped abruptly.

Ignoring Joshua's whimpering he stared at Felicity, surprised the molten anger wasn't transmitting from his eyes into her mocking blue ones. All the pent-up emotion, and his need of release, overcame what Felicity described as 'good at keeping in control'. Swear words he hadn't used since a boy, punctuated his words. "You've no comprehension of love. You treat your parents, who love and care for you, in the most despicable way. You are such a nasty and stupid bitch. You don't care a damn about anyone., but yourself." There was such gratification in seeing how Felicity's sardonic smile had turned into astonishment, he continued to let rip. "So...full of yourself, aren't you? It's all about you! What you want, think, need, everything else completely passes you by."

As a couple, they'd had their arguments, but he'd banked his anger behind an icy façade. And, always made a point of directing his comments at a person's actions, rather than annihilate their personality, or character, but not today! "I can only thank God Jane came into my life, and saved me from marrying such a conniving bitch." That really hit home. Felicity stiffened, her eyes widening, her lips pursing, "Go and enjoy your Conran, and his money. It certainly won't make you happy. And for your information Jane wasn't interested in Dad's money. We could easily live on my salary, and unlike you she wasn't a selfish, self-centred, extravagant woman, but a lovely girl who gave money away out of what she saw as abundance. So if my cage is rattled it's because you don't get it. Jane was the epitome of everything you're not, except you're alive and she's dead. Do you get that Felicity, dead, stone cold dead?" With that he stalked off at top speed along the path and felt callous pleasure at first having stunned her by his vehemence, then at seeing her appalled expression before she clamped her hand across her mouth at his news. That would teach her!

Joshua, probably frightened by the venom in his booming voice, was now red-faced and screaming. But he couldn't stop to comfort him. He had to get away, and out of sight of that woman. The pram rocked at his pace as he headed towards the distant trees and sheltered gardens. Joshua's crying awoke Rebecca, bringing her to wail also. At the turn, he quickly glanced back. In the distance Felicity was where he'd left her, in the middle of the path staring after him.

Inside, although still enraged, he felt shocked by his unbridled outburst, and the emotion of speaking the truth, Jane was dead, ashes to ashes, dust to dust! Faster and faster he walked. His

lovely, generous, beloved Jane, with a heart for others while…
Tears blinding his eyes, he pushed on.

A hand touched his arm. Furious, he whipped round to brush
it off while booming in a cracked, broken voice, "Go away, I
never want to…!" The words died in his throat. It wasn't Felicity,
but a tall, slim woman whose face, framed with a curtain of long
dark hair, was looking at him with big, dark, and troubled eyes.

Despite stepping back, probably due to the grim expression of
his face, she said quietly, "David - your babies!" Those words cut
through his anger, frustration and the unexpected bitterness that
had welled up from within. He stopped abruptly, stared at
Rosemary, and then became aware of the two lives he was
responsible for. Tears were dripping off his chin, to cover his
embarrassment he delved into the pram to pick up Joshua who was
now hysterical. Nodding to Rosemary, at her unspoken question,
she responded to pick up and cuddle Rebecca.

Murmuring words of comfort David rocked and gently patted
Joshua against his shoulder, while he surreptitiously wiped his
own face. Above the din of crying by his ear he heard Rosemary
direct, "There's a seat over there." With that she moved to sit on
it with Rebecca who had quickly quieted.

Carefully, he negotiated the pram towards Rosemary with one
hand, while nestling the tiny baby against his shoulder. At that
moment he had a rare opportunity to see her smile, and with eyes
filled with love, she cooed tenderly at the little mite as she held
her out before her. Although impossible, Rebecca seemed to smile
back. "Oh my goodness Rosemary, I see a smile." Rosemary
looked up, pursed her lips and nestled Rebecca against her. Now
what had he said to upset her? Carefully he put the brake on the
pram, sat beside her and touching her arm thanked her for her
intervention. Pointedly, she looked at his hand, quickly he
removed it and patted Joshua's back while meditating on the years
Rosemary had worked at ITP.

He'd barely known of her existence until he heard her nasty,
judgemental gossiping about Jane with whom she shared an office.
First he'd reprimanded her, next the fiasco of the Christmas kiss,
and her near dismissal after he and Jane became engaged. Jane's
intervention had opened up Rosemary to tell her tragic tale, but
he'd only been privy to know that she had been badly hurt and,
couldn't have children. From that day, Rosemary went from
Jane's foe to friend, bridesmaid and later, flatmate with Jill. Since
he'd noticed how she shied away from men, down played her

attractive face, and covered her curvaceous figure with expensive, smart, but unobtrusive clothes. On Jane's recommendation, and for the past two years, she'd been his efficient, if somewhat silent, personal assistant. Their relationship had been confined to business until the twins arrival had built a bridge between work and home. Outwardly she gave him her calm and unemotional support, inwardly he sensed she disciplined herself to say little, knowing, as he'd once experienced, that there were raw areas that if touched ignited her wrath.

Joshua's crying finally subsided allowing him to hear Rosemary murmuring soothingly to Rebecca. There was no hesitation, or boundaries, to her pouring out love on William, and the twins. Words, Jill had spoken some while ago, echoed through his mind, "It's going to take a very special man to break through what troubles Rosemary." Ben, the charmer, although in love with Jill had had a good crack at it. His teasing, cajoling, kind and caring ways had begun to draw Rosemary out of her shell. And Paul with his gentleness had made inroads in friendship, perhaps due to the confidential nature of his work.

There wasn't a need to explain to Rosemary why he'd been upset, but he felt he should. "It was fortunate you came along when you did. I was so beside myself, I didn't know what I was doing." Rosemary nodded, but didn't question, so he volunteered the information. "Felicity, my ex-fiancé accosted me. In not knowing about Jane, she made assumptions I couldn't handle." He arose to place Joshua in the pram, and continued to rock it as he sat back down. With his eyes glued to his shoes, he confessed, "I'm afraid I lost my temper, I swore at her. I was very rude, it was quite unforgiveable." When he looked up Rosemary's compassionate expression had turned to a rueful grimace. Encouraged he added, "If I'm honest, I'd probably do it again. She was obviously shocked at my outburst, but maybe it was time the wretched woman heard the truth."

Rosemary didn't comment, as she put the almost asleep Rebecca in the pram beside Joshua. But then she turned to quietly question, "But what sadness is locked inside her to make her that way?"

He gulped. The words were so similar to Jane's when he'd judged her.. Running his hand through his hair, he admitted, "You're right. Who am I to judge? I don't know what causes people to act the way they do."

Rosemary straightening, gave him a thoughtful look, before

her eyes focused beyond him. "I've only seen Felicity once, but I think she's coming this way." She made to turn, "I'll leave you to it."

Sternly he commanded, "Don't go!" At her tight-lipped expression he pleaded quietly, "Sorry Rosemary, please don't leave me with her." For a moment she stared him, then just as he thought she'd walk away, she moved to the pram, and was rearranging the twins bedding when, from behind him, Felicity spoke.

"David, there you are. I've never known you be so rude. But I suppose in the circumstances it's understandable. I wasn't to know, having been out of the country, about Jane's...." It wasn't compassion reflected in Felicity's blue eyes, but a renewed interest in him. If nothing else, he was right about her being an opportunist. Long, brightly painted nails rested on his arm as she murmured, "Oh you poor thing! It must be so difficult for a man, like you, to be left to care for two such small babies."

Cross, he snapped, "What do you mean by 'a man, like me'?"

Felicity slipped her arm into his, "Oh, good heavens David, you are tetchy." Looking into his face she gave her jingly laugh. "Lack of sleep I suppose. Let's face it you are all 'man' and looking after babies is not a 'man' thing, is it? And you've got two?" Giggling, she lent into his ear to say quietly, "Still I see Daddy has parted with his money to hire you a nursemaid."

Angry, he stepped back to shrug off her arm as Felicity addressed Rosemary waiting by the pram. "I'm an old friend of David's. We've a lot to catch up on, so perhaps you could take them home while we stroll around the park."

Rosemary raised her eyebrows, and without looking at him, replied, "I, too am a friend of David's, not his hired servant."

Felicity frowned. "Have I seen you before?"

With a toss of the dark curtain of hair, Rosemary stated, "I've worked at ITP a number of years."

Anxious not to get into another confrontation, he stepped in to say curtly. "Rosemary and I have to go. The twins will soon need feeding."

Revelation dawned on Felicity's face. "Rosemary, oh yes, Rosemary, that's it. You were Jane's bridesmaid, people were shocked because you... "

"Felicity!" At the cold, stern, sharp annunciation of her name she turned towards him. In seeing David's forbidding expression that had intimidated, or quelled mightier foes than she, Felicity finished lamely, "shared an office Jane." But a second later she tinkled happily, "But I suspect Rosemary, you knew Jane had set her sights on David. And how she'd charmed her way to promotion, first, as his secretary, then to his bed!"

Enraged, he bit out, "Untrue! Jane went from secretary to wife, before she shared my bed!"

With a sexy smile, Felicity twittered, "If you say so darling, for we certainly had our romps! Anyway Rosemary are you still at ITP?"

Was Rosemary's pink tinted face due to the reminder of her gossiping about Jane, or Felicity's sexual overtones? But she answered firmly, "I am."

Felicity's eyes narrowed, but she sounded amused, as she said, "Oh I remember now, you were promoted to David's personal secretary." He flinched at her false laugh, "So, you're now inveigling yourself into David's life, in the hope of following in Jane's footsteps?"

The obvious alarm in Rosemary's eyes caused him step between her and Felicity. "Felicity, that's quite enough! Rosemary has become a 'family' friend, and neither she, nor Jane inveigled themselves into my life. Don't judge others by the way you behave." It was rare he looked down his long nose in utter distaste at another human being, but as words seemingly didn't penetrate, he gave her a long contemptuous stare, at which Felicity looked more bewildered, than quelled. With an indication of his intent he turned, put his hand under Rosemary's elbow, and said in a voice far calmer than he felt, "Come Rosemary, let's head for home."

Rosemary, in stepping forward to push the pram, removed herself from his hand, as Felicity sneered, "Home?"

"Yes Felicity. Rosemary shares the basement flat with Jill and Paul." Sternly he continued, "I've no wish to talk further with you. And, the truth is, just as you chose to forget your family exists, I'd like you to do the same for me and mine! Goodbye Felicity!" With that he marched forward, caught Rosemary up, and as she eyed him with consternation, he apologised, "That woman is the bitter end. I'm sorry she was rude to you."

Worried, Rosemary stammered, "I didn't, I don't, I haven't inveigled …"

David jumped in to reassure her. "I know. Felicity certainly inveigled herself into my life and bed, but believe me, she won't again." At such a blatant confession a blush crept over

Rosemary's face.

They walked in silence until she spoke again. "I wish people didn't jump to conclusions. I love the twins, but..." she paused, looking self-conscious.

To save her further embarrassment, he teased gently, "But it is inconceivable that you could be interested in their father, and have absolutely no desire to follow in Jane's footsteps!"

"Exactly!" At her vehemence, he laughed, and in return received an enigmatic smile.

"Rosemary, you are welcome to enjoy the twins, and I'll do my best to assure everyone I meet, that you aren't on the list of 'want-to-be' wives!" His words extracted an appreciative glance in his direction, and pleased, he added, "It's a sad world if a man can't befriend a woman, or woman a man, without people putting sexual connotations on that friendship. I'm not going to bow to the small mindedness of people like Felicity, but I'll quite understand if you think being with me, might compromise you. However, I'd appreciate it if you stayed with me until we are out of Felicity's sight."

At her nod, he asked, "Would you like me to push the pram?"

With a little smile at the twins, she glanced toward him to reply, "Only if you want to."

"No you carry on. Talking of friends, Jill said you were visiting a friend, and I've kept you from her."

"I was on my way home."

"Well, I'd say our meeting was a divine encounter. I was so angry I was beyond rational thought." When Rosemary didn't comment, and with her steady pace, he wondered if she was anxious to get home, or wanting to avoid further conversation. To put her at ease he talked of documenting Jane's life, and finished, "She touched lives I knew nothing about. She could be so wise, and at other times so naïve."

Rosemary confessed, "She was easy to talk to." In a choked voice she added, "I miss her."

Without thinking, he laid a light hand on her arm, and immediately expected her to flinch or pull away. Instead she looked toward him with tear-filled eyes. He gave her arm a comforting pat, and fervently agreed, "I miss her too, Rosemary, oh so very much!" They walked on in silence, and then, curious about Rosemary's friend, he enquired, "Does your friend live near the park?"

Eyes fixed ahead, she replied succinctly, "Yes."

Inwardly he sighed, for personal conversation with Rosemary could be an uphill struggle. Then she offered in a worried voice, "But, she's never in."

"Does she know to expect you?"

"The phone's been cut off."

"What about contacting her friends?"

"I don't think she has any who care about her. I could ring her parents, but..." she trailed off in thought.

He digested that information before asking, "Do you think she's in with bad company?"

With a frown she stated sharply, "She's easily led."

Reminded of Jane saying, "David stop interrogating me, I'm not a witness on the stand" he injected into his voice quiet concern. "When did you last see her?"

"Several months ago!"

Ignoring the abrupt reply he pressed on. "So what made you visit now?"

"Her bank refused payment on her rent, for a second month."

Without thinking he cross questioned, "How do you know that?"

She hesitated slightly, and then confessed, "Her landlady is a friend."

The information flow might be stilted, but he was encouraged enough to point out, "If the rent hasn't been paid the landlady is entitled to enter the premises." Seeing Rosemary shudder he asked, "Do you feel something sinister might have happened?"

She shrugged, but looked worried as she murmured, "I don't know."

"If you've any cause to believe it might have, I'd suggest to your landlady friend she asks the police to accompany her."

"That sounds a bit drastic."

"Perhaps, but it may not be wise to go alone." From her look of apprehension he knew he'd conveyed the worse case scenario, and in order to be supportive he added, "I'm sure she's probably just upped, and left, but let me know if I can help in any way."

Rosemary gave him an unexpected smile, "Thank you, that's kind."

Warmed by her response he added, "That's what family and friends do. And we all appreciate the way you help us."

They walked in comfortable silence until they arrived at Church Road before he thought to ask, "You've been back at work two weeks, how is it working out with Robert?" Instantly

Rosemary's face tightened into a hard mask.

Disturbed he urged, "Tell me."

The intensity of her reply stunned him. "The man is despicable!" Before he was able to respond she'd reigned in her anger to state in a pinched voice, "His behaviour intolerable!" With that she shook her head, and pushed the pram ahead of him. In two strides he caught up, and having said quietly, 'Rosemary' in a questioning tone, she blurted out, "Susie Welch is doing my job."

"That's ridiculous! She can't do your job. She's not experienced enough. Her placement was to fill in while you were on bereavement leave?"

Rosemary retorted, "Tell Mr Jones that!" Stunned he grabbed the pram, halting her. In a weary tone, head down, she revealed, "I'm interfering in keeping the filing system tidy. My questioning infuriates him." Then, looking him in the eyes she said more stoutly, "In a supercilious voice Susie informed me her work for Robert was confidential! I was angry. I went to Chris County. He told me I was making something out of nothing. Later Robert accused me of undermining his authority."

David grimaced. For Robert had made it clear to him, he didn't want his interference, he'd assumed it would be different for Rosemary. But had the old acerbic Rosemary arisen to exacerbate the problem? It was possible Robert found her quiet, efficient ways, and only speaking when necessary, irritating. Carefully he replied, "He's only been there six weeks, it's early days." At that Rosemary pushed against the pram, and staring ahead, moved forward. To placate her he added, "I'm sure Robert will recognise how your quick mind can cut the workload by half. Last year, your systems were so efficient, we didn't have to work long hours, or draft in extra staff before the Brussels Exhibition. And your choice of Geraldine to join us was a good foil for your shyness. The support you both gave me was excellent."

Rosemary turned towards him. "That's because you constantly encouraged us, and showed your appreciation."

Delighted at the compliment he teased, "Thank you Rosemary. But remember there was a time when you felt the same way about me, as you do about Robert."

Her reply was an adamant "Never. You wouldn't…"

Amused he filled in, "Be rude. Oh Rosemary, I'll not forget your succinct words during that stressful time with Jill. Wasn't I ticked off by your polite, and to the point comment, 'Rudeness doesn't behove you Mr Reinhardt!'"

For that he was gratified to receive a small smile. Then she admitted, "I did say, 'I'm here to work Mr Jones, not entertain you', but at that he called me a 'miserable bitch' and told me to get out." At his sharp intake of breath, she continued, "I told Chris. He didn't believe me. But I'm sure Chris spoke to Robert for since Robert talks at me, not to me."

"Oh Rosemary, I'm sorry. The man's only excuse is his youth and inexperience. I will speak to Chris, for that behaviour, is not acceptable. Please stick with it. Be polite, but speak up, and stand up for what you know is right. I have every confidence in you doing the job to the best of your ability."

They were nearing the house and he felt to ask, "With Jane gone, will you still be happy living here?"

The deep worry, that had etched itself in her face, dissipated with the happiness of her next words. "Oh yes. Jill and I are good friends. I'm company for her when Paul's away. I have the garden to potter about in. And there's William." With eyes filled with love she added, "And now, of course, the twins."

Relieved, and encouraged, he also grasped how love could transform someone. As they manoeuvred the pram through the front door, he asked, "If you're free, would you like to help me bath Joshua and Rebecca before their feed?"

"Oh yes, please. I'd love to. Thank you."

"Don't thank me! It is I, who should be thanking you. And I was delighted tonight to hear you refer to me as a friend. I can't be there for you as Jane was, but if ever you need…"

Jill appearing from the basement flat interrupted. "David, I need to tell you DI Gage rang."

At Jill's glance towards Rosemary, he explained, "I met Rosemary in the park, she rescued me from Felicity."

Jill grunted, "Felicity! Did she thank you for the free publicity she had, as a page three pin-up girl in The Sun?"

"She only came back today from Hollywood, so doesn't know about it. I've volunteered Rosemary to help bath these two. If we use the basement bathroom I'll tell you all about it."

"And I need to tell you DI Gage rang me as he had no answer from you."

"So at last, he's decided to bring me up to date."

"I'm afraid it didn't sound as if it would be a friendly chat. He was quite abrupt. He said they wanted to question you further, and as DI Jordan is going to visit Carlton tomorrow at the convalescence home, they've arranged transport with him to Maidstone. He'll be here at nine o'clock."

In despair he raked his hair, "What am I going to do about the twins?"

"Brother dear, remember your sister's here! I rang Joyce, and asked if she felt well enough to come over. She sounded pleased, and said she could make it about ten o'clock. Paul is going to stay up until she arrives, then we'll use your flat, so he can get some sleep. I know he loves these locum opportunities to keep his skills up to date, but I'm glad it's only for three days!"

The following morning dressed in navy slacks, light blue shirt and navy blazer he hoped he wouldn't fuel DCI Bridges obvious animosity towards lawyers. DI Jordan was prompt, greeted him with a handshake, and in the back of the car talked of Andrew's previous crimes and the need to bring him to justice. But sadly his case was falling apart. The four women who'd made statement's about Andrew's abuse were no longer available to uphold them. Evie from ITP had married, and didn't want her husband to know about it. Anthea, who'd worked briefly for Andrew, had emigrated to Australia. And Jane, and the other girl, had both met premature deaths. Forlorn, Jordan stated, "All we have is your statement of Andrew manhandling Jane, and your rescue. With you later marrying Jane Carlton's claim, 'Reinhardt attacked me because he wanted Jane, and he couldn't bear the thought of anyone else having her' could now be seen as true."

David agreed. "Jane pointed that out to me after we left the pub, and briefly we wondered if we should report his whereabouts to the police."

Jordan continued, "There were, of course, the photos of Jane's bruises, they are still evidence."

"But I wouldn't put it past Carlton to twist the facts, and say I inflicted them, then accused him. That man is out to destroy me, one way or another."

Jordan lowered his voice, "Bridges was very put out when your suggestion that Henry's demise wasn't a bizarre accident, proved correct. But he is firm in his belief you pushed Carlton through that door."

"I can assure you I didn't, but I wish I could be equally astute in knowing who did. I would have sworn it was Henry, but can't see how he could have slipped back into the bar, before he got himself killed! Oddly, considering Henry's reputation, I felt strangely warmed to the man, and feel sad he died."

While contemplating the issues surrounding Carlton, David gradually began to fall asleep, and only awakened on arrival at the Police Station. But this time, he was shocked to find he was no longer a witness, but treated to the routines of a suspect, and led to wait in a cell. Immediately, he asked for Martin Beresford to be informed, and as the metal door clanged shut, he sat on the bench, put his head in his hands, and asked himself, how had it come to this? Overwhelmed, and to stifled his anguish, he reached for his pocket Bible, but couldn't concentrate and unshed tears merged the lines. Into his head came the Psalmist words, 'I lift up my eyes to the hills from whence comes help from the Lord'. He determined to do that, but it was an hour before he heard the unlocking of the door. He stood, but the policeman was only delivering a cup of tea and bacon butty. At his question, "How long are you going to keep me here?" he received a shrug. But, he'd barely finished eating when the door opened and a policeman announced, "Your solicitor's here" and indicated he should follow. It was a relief to see Martin, but his words tempered that. "Bridges feels he has new evidence. The word is he's out to get you."

They'd barely a minute before DCI Bridges and DI Gage appeared. Politely he stood to shake hands, but Bridges gave him a belligerent look, slapped a file on the table, and sat down. David glanced at Martin, and they sat to watch Bridges light up a cigarette, before deliberately blowing smoke at his face. He was grateful that Martin insisted on opening a window. Bridges bulldozed through the formalities, and said, "Right, with your solicitor here, the crime reduced to GBH, we're ready to hear your full confession."

David closed his eyes, took a deep breath, and stated, "DCI Bridges it is immaterial to me if the crime is murder, or GBH, because the only confession I have to make is, I didn't push Andrew through that door."

"Ah, but he is equally sure you did. Let me read from his statement. 'In an unprovoked attack, Reinhardt caught my arm, and wrestled me to the ground. I called Henry for help, but he didn't come. Reinhardt told his wife to leave and that gave me opportunity to get free and run. But Reinhardt caught my legs in a rugby tackle. I fell, catching my chin on the edge of a table, and tipping it up. He's much bigger and stronger than me. Afraid of what he'd do to me when I saw him picking up his wallet, in self-defence I picked up his beer mug and hit him over the head with

216

it. I ran past his wife, and had just reached the small lobby by the front door, when Reinhardt ran into me, head butting the top half of my legs. I was carried forward with such force, that I catapulted, through the window of the bar door. I knew it was him. Neither Pearce, nor Reinhardt's wife, had the strength to do that." Bridges looked up with a satisfied smile.

David shook his head in wonder at Andrew's ability to twist the facts. "I grant you it's an interesting perspective, but he's assumed it was me, and I assure you it wasn't, because I was concussed, from the blow to my head."

Bridges said scornfully, "But you'd head butted him earlier."

"True, but remember I didn't attack Andrew – I only restrained him from punching Jane. He says Henry didn't come in, but he did. I can only suppose Andrew didn't see Henry because his black skin, and his dark clothes, blended into the shadows by the door."

Gage drew the file towards him, and began delving through it, as Bridges sneered, "What are you, some kind of clairvoyant? Do you believe, see, and know, things others don't?" Witness statements from those in the Public Bar say Nimbya was with them, so you'll have to conjuror up someone else to take the rap for you. And, you can forget your wonderful theory of someone stepping in, doing the deed, and stepping out again. Stop your mind games, and just admit you did it."

Exercising his mind was precisely what he was doing! For if Henry Nimbya was a figment of his imagination, or an angel sent to assist him, that wasn't going to be helpful in this situation. Martin leant forward to verify, "Witness statements may put Henry in the Public Bar, but that doesn't prove Reinhardt's guilt. I would remind you my client is innocent, until proved guilty. You'll have to produce more concrete evidence than that."

Bridges stubbed out his cigarette, and looked up at Martin to say with satisfaction, "We have measured the distances between the Snug, the front door and the Public Bar. A mathematical expert has worked out exactly where Carlton would have been standing in order to be uplifted, and propelled at enough speed, to break the glass, and go halfway through. That same specialist was able to include information based on Carlton's weight, and of the approximate weight of a man needed to execute that. Will that do?"

The triumph on Bridges face sent a spiral of fear through him. Gage intent on reading something in the file didn't even look up as

217

Martin exclaimed, "No that won't do! It isn't proof it was Reinhardt. There are hundreds of thousands men of his height, build and weight."

Bridges shuffled in his pocket and took out a fresh cigarette packet while saying confidently, "But he's the only one known to be in the vicinity at the time." David didn't need second sight to see Bridges wanted to put him firmly in the frame. A new line of thin blue smoke irritated his nostrils. A nervous spasm in his stomach made him feel sick, dear Lord he couldn't take much more of this. What he needed was a miracle. Bridges sent him a supercilious smile before asking, "It seems you're out of …"

"Good grief!" DI Gage's loud and excited exclamation cut across Bridges' words, and with three pairs of eyes on him Gage declared, "I don't know how we missed it?"

As an infuriated Bridges barked, "Missed what?" David's eyes were already looking at the paperwork Gage had spread in front of him. In the upside down photo of Henry's demise he saw that which his eyes had seen, but his mind hadn't comprehended! It was the vital clue that would prove his innocence. Elated he proclaimed, "That's it. Oh my God, that's it!"

Bridges muttered under his breath. Gage sent David a satirical grimace before warning, "It will need looking into, and checking, but you were on the right track, and we weren't listening." The air wasn't just blue with cigarette smoke as Bridges demanded to know what they were talking about. Pointing to the file, Gage stated, "There is evidence in these statements to reveal there was another man in the Snug that day."

Bridges obviously rattled by Gages statement stood "We'll take break here."

Martin and David glanced at each other. David shook his head to indicate he didn't want a break. Martin stood to face Bridges over the table to protest. "I see no reason for a break so soon into this interview."

Bridges blustered, "If fresh evidence has come to light we need to assess it." Gage didn't move, but asked, "Mr Reinhardt, perhaps you would like to explain." At that Bridges looked fit to explode. Martin stood his ground, and Gage said wearily, "Oh Bridges, do sit down, Mr Reinhardt, if you please…"

Bridges sat heavily in the chair as David reached across the table and drew the photo into its centre to state, "It's very simple."

Those few words drew an enraged growl from Bridges before he retorted with sarcasm, "Oh, what's this, another of your clever suppositions? Let me tell you, it wasn't the fingerprint formation, shape or size of the glass that proved Nimbya was murdered. It was our investigations that proved he was too far away from the door for a piece of glass to imbed itself in his jugular!"

David gave a small smile, and acknowledged, "I'm pleased to hear it" as he leant across the table to put his finger on the photo. Gage sat back in his seat with an amused expression, while the others followed the line of David's finger. "Here you can see the top of Henry's white sleeveless vest."

Bridges argued, "So what?"

"The Henry I saw wore a short sleeved black T-shirt, with navy overalls."

"Oh yes! The imaginary Henry!" Bridges gave a cynical laugh.

Gage put his hand on Bridges' arm. "Sorry Bridges, but Reinhardt is right." Annoyed Bridges thrust off his hand as Gage said, "I'll read again from the statement you took from Mrs Harris, who lives opposite the pub. She reported Henry entered the pub after the 'smart man and pregnant woman'. You asked about their car make or number plate, it's noted here she replied, 'I don't know anything about cars, my hubby did, he was a car mechanic, he always wore black overalls, the same as the 'big black man'."

Bridges shrugged, "So what?"

"Pearce's statement says, 'Henry came in with the usual crowd'." Gage elaborated, "So Mrs Harris sees a black man entering the pub in dark clothes, and in this photo he's wearing a white vest."

Bridges scowled, "Okay you don't have to spell it out to me. So what are you saying?"

He and Martin looked at each other, their eyes conveying that even if the law wasn't an ass, Bridges was."

Patiently Gage explained, "I'm suggesting Mrs Harris saw a black man, but it wasn't Henry. From what we know of Henry, it's uncharacteristic for him not to muscle into a fight. And even stranger, is his helping Reinhardt's wife by picking up the car keys, so she can leave." Bridges cool, slow smoking changed to frequent puffs as Gage continued, "Therefore, it is feasible, that the black man Mrs Harris saw follow the couple in, is the one Reinhardt saw. As Andrew pushed Reinhardt's wife, the black man could have slipped unseen around the door frame. That would put him in the very place our experts said the attacker would have been to produce the speed and trajectory, necessary to propel

Carlton through that glass!" Bridges gave a derisive snort. "And I'm forced to conclude that as Mrs Harris thought she saw Henry, this second black man would be of similar build to him. And Bridges, you have to admit, going on Reinhardt's height and weight it was borderline that he could be a suspect. Also Reinhardt pointed out that what was to stop a man, doing the deed, then slipping out of the main door, and walking away."

Bridges thumped the table to declare, "Speculation, mere speculation." But as Bridges continued to refute Gage's conclusions David's mind drifted to his height and weight being borderline, he'd always thought of himself as a man of muscle and fitness, was he getting fat? David's attention returned to Bridges' aggression. "Oh that's absurd, Gage. You're saying a man comes in, doesn't enter a fight, but decides to sends a stranger through a glass door."

Steepling his fingers David asked, "But was this black man a stranger to Carlton?"

Bridges snarled, "We ask the questions, Reinhardt, not you."

"Is that so? Then let's consider the fact that a factory worker took an opportune moment to get rid of Henry. And, two witnesses were willing to conceal the truth. It is then, quite possible, the man I saw took advantage of a situation, to take revenge on Carlton. We all know Carlton is the suspect of previous crimes, with a four year warrant for his arrest."

Bridges' face reddened in near apoplexy. Gage forestalled his outburst by agreeing, "Reinhardt is right and we need to investigate this before we can go further." Inside David felt a burst of joy, God had answered his prayer, and it felt like a miracle.

Martin spoke. "In the light of this, and the helpfulness of my client to your enquiries, I now suggest he is released to return home to his family." And as if expecting compliance Martin stood, and outstretched his arm to shake Bridges' hand. Bridges kicked back his chair, and stalked out of the room, slamming the door behind him, leaving Gage to finish the formalities and announce, "You are free to go". Pleased, believing it was only a matter of time before they got the real culprit, David shook Martin's hand, rang home and went off to enquire when DI Jordan might be returning to London. To which he discovered Jordan was just leaving, having been informed, 'Reinhardt is being detained indefinitely.'

Joyously, he jumped in the back of the police car, and began regaling his victory. Jordan's lack of enthusiasm led him to ask about his day, and David's jubilation diminished on hearing that the four year old cases against Andrew would probably be dropped due to lack of witnesses and insufficient evidence.

CHAPTER 17

The church bell struck six times as he entered the house. Excited to tell Joyce and Ted his news, David ran up the stairs, entered his lounge, and for a split second, saw Jane standing by the piano, holding Rebecca. Then as he realised it was Joyce, Ted was saying eagerly, "The TV news says new evidence has come to light, but they aren't saying what it is."

Before he could tell them, having heard him come in, Jill and Paul arrived with William and Rosemary in tow, impatient for his report. Playing with Joshua, David explained about the need for confidentiality. Their delight was obvious at hearing of the breakthrough, and Joshua falling asleep in his arms brought him to declare, "I need to settle the twins. I'm hungry, does anyone else want to eat?"

Joyce looked at Ted, "We ought to go."

Jill intervened, "Don't rush off. I've made enough stew for us all, I'll bring it up. Rosemary, could you set David's table?"

David reiterated Jill's invitation. "Yes do stay. And perhaps, as Rebecca is asleep on you, you'd bring her upstairs." Joyce nodded, and followed him. Having laid Rebecca in her cot, Joyce stood back to look at her grandchildren, giving him another surreal picture of Jane standing there, twenty-three years older! Why hadn't he noticed the likeness before?

The meal was simple, the conversation flowed naturally. And he was delighted when Joyce, who'd told Jane she often felt 'intimidated' by him, addressed him, albeit somewhat tentatively. "David, I hope you don't mind me mentioning it. I've…I've been thinking about your father's idea of a memorial to Jane." At his nod and encouragingly smile she continued. "I know your father has charitable ventures abroad, but I feel there is something in, 'charity begins at home'." Unkindly, David thought of Jim's words, and wondered if Joyce was about to ask for a hand-out. "Jane involved herself in unknown people and organisations, in her memory, perhaps…perhaps we could do the same, and…and call it, 'The Jane Reinhardt Trust?'"

"Jane liked to have fun. She loved music and dancing." All eyes went to Rosemary.

Jill giggled. "Oh yes! We remember her dancing exploits with Ian!" For Joyce's benefit Jill regaled, with great delight, Jane's dancing antics.

Disbelief reflected in Ted and Joyce's expressions. David grinned, "It's all true. Jane was an excellent dancer, and with Jane, everything was entirely innocent." Remembering T-Dance, he reached into his wallet for their card, and passed it to Joyce. "Unbeknown to me, Jane became involved in this dancing class. Harry who runs it came to the funeral. He asked if they could use Jane's name on a project she'd initiated." Between them, he and Jill spoke what they knew about T-Dance, and Jill added several other stories of Jane's philanthropic enterprises!

Enraptured, Joyce's eyes had filled with tears. "Why didn't I know about these things? It makes me wonder if what appeared miraculous provision to people in our church, came through her." Thoughtfully she hummed, "So my memorial fund suggestion is something Jane would approve of, and appreciate."

"In principle Joyce I agree." David smiled around at the enthusiasm on every face. "I can put the proposal to Dad. Perhaps T-Dance could be first to receive a donation, but I can't see Dad wanting the Reinhardt name associated with a charitable, but 'fun' philanthropy!"

Ted, who'd so far only listened, put forward, "In marrying Joyce, her name changed from Mackenzie. Perhaps to honour Jane, and her father's name, we could use that."

Joyce's eyes watered, and, as she said, "Ted you are such a good man", David was already up, and slapping the astonished Ted, on the back.

"That's it! That's brilliant! The Jane Mackenzie Trust! I like it! It reminds me of the slip of a girl who won my heart. Now all we have to do is convince Dad that charity begins at home."

As David returned to his seat, Rosemary said quietly, "Jane believed in lifting people out from their problems. And that, even briefly, it could open them up to new ideas. She'd say, 'Show people a goal to attain, and it brings a new lease of life.'

For several minutes they contemplated her words. Jill was the first to speak. "I was thinking of the people who came to the funeral. The postman, milkman," she laughed, "And it was the dustman Mrs P brought along! Jane's friendliness touched lives. She wasn't shy at sharing her faith, and I don't think we should be either."

Paul rubbed his beard. "I agree. It should be seen as a Christian charity. Donations needn't be confined to Christians, or their organisations, but there would need to be stipulations on how money given, was spent."

David boomed over the table. "Excellent! Joyce, thank you, for instigating this discussion. I suppose, Jill, it will be left to me, to convince Dad? At her nod, he addressed Paul. "In that case Paul, as Dad holds you in high esteem, I'd appreciate you being there. But now I'll admit to feeling drained and needing sleep, and have to get up in the middle of the night to feed the twins." At that everyone arose to clear up, but it was apparent the prospect of the Trust Fund was stimulating thoughts for the future, rather than dwelling on the past.

Several days later, the reporters who had wanted a story had given up the hope of his appearing, and despite a dull and overcast sky, he decided to venture out. An energetic walk to the park with the twins might help tone up his body. It wasn't that Gage had said he was fat, but he didn't want to be heading into middle-age spread.

At a steady pace, his thoughts drifted to his recurring dream. There was a sense that the horses racing to battle were slowing, but perhaps, as it was all in his imagination, it only signified that in life, the worst was over. Encouraged, his pace quickened, until outside the Royal Garden Hotel, he became aware that, although the twins were asleep, their bodies were rocking and rolling into each other. In stopping to tuck them in at opposite ends of the pram, he'd the odd feeling of someone watching him, and glanced up at the windows of the hotel. Was it Felicity, or as she pointed out, were people just surprised to see a lone man pushing a pram? Yet there were few people around, perhaps a reporter was following him. It could be the police keeping an eye on him? It being the beginning of August and, the Bank Holiday weekend, hopefully she, like Rosemary, had taken the opportunity of going home. But in case Felicity should appear from the hotel, he set up a pace to stop her catching up with him.

As he walked, he considered his conversation the previous day, with Chris at ITP. He'd used the opportunity to voice his displeasure that a staff member had been called, 'a miserable bitch'. Chris had been horrified, and determined to deal with it, until he revealed Robert had said the words to Rosemary. Chris obviously empathised with Robert with his sighting as Robert's excuse, his inexperienced to deal with a woman who has, 'a cold, aloof attitude, acts as if she is in charge, and talks to me as if I'm an errant schoolboy'. About to comment Chris had fervently added, "David, I know exactly what Robert means! I felt the same when Rosemary complained to me about Robert. And, she inferred she'd a directive from you to keep an eye on him." Taken aback, he realised in telling Rosemary to stand up for what was right, he'd probably exacerbated the problem. In thinking that through now he sighed, he'd told Chris he'd talk to Rosemary, but when and how he didn't know.

In the park, he made the turn into the tree-lined avenue. Suddenly his peripheral vision caught a flicker of something causing several birds to fly up, and away. He looked around, and saw no-one. Was someone watching him? Already speeding along, he quickened his pace, enjoying the momentum it brought. But by the time he reached home, his body was beginning to feel the strain, and after feeding and settling the twins, he was glad of a hot bath and bed.

After church on Sunday, having ate a substantial lunch, and in the belief to walk with the twins in the pram was a brilliant combination of physical, mental and spiritual exercise, he took a second 'stroll'. On his return, he wanted to aim at that being a daily constitutional, and named the exercise his "perambulations". That amused Jill, who scoffed, "Brother dear, we've all had our moments at wanting to loose weight, but the truth is we like our food, and eat too much. I'll lessen the size of the meals I serve you."

To which he exclaimed, "No, don't do that! That's my point - if I keep walking it will offset the calorie intake!" And now, on his third outing, the twins safely cocooned in their shawls, David was keeping up a very steady pace along the empty, shop shuttered, High Street. Passing the street, from where he'd rescued Jane from Andrew's clutches, he gave a derisive grunt. It appeared, Andrew would again escape justice. But perhaps, a disfigured face, and the damage to his body seriously curtailing his lifestyle, and future, was in itself punishment. No-one was beyond receiving the Lord's love, perhaps one day he'd feel able to visit Andrew, and tell him that. Once he reached the smooth tarmac path in the park he speeded up. Eyes focussed ahead, his momentum grew, the pram wheels went faster and faster, as did his mind.

Over the years, David had learnt his father was more benign after a good Sunday lunch, and several glasses of wine. So, when chatting on the telephone to him yesterday, he'd broached the idea of a philanthropic memorial to Jane. To his surprise, he'd agreed in principle, but true to his philosophy, he'd concluded 'people only appreciate money when they have to work for it'. And had gone on to recommend that rather than give grants, or donations to organisations, it would be more sensible to 'match fund' what others raised. It seemed then, more appropriate to call it a 'fund', rather than 'trust'.

Meditating on that he turned into the tree lined avenue to find his thoughts penetrated by an uncanny sense of being observed. There wasn't anyone around, but he supposed, racing a pram up and down the paths of the park was probably an odd sight, he grinned, he'd soon have to put on new tyres!

Like a blur, someone stepped across his path. Skidding to a halt, he smelt burnt rubber from the pram tyres, as he boomed, "Watch out!" And in the next second, he knew either his vanishing angel had appeared, or Henry had risen from the dead! But his prime concern was for the twins who, thanks to the robust chassis of the pram, slept on.

The black giant before him spoke with a twang of Caribbean mingled with a London accent, "Mister I's a need to speak with you." David glanced up and down the empty avenue, as the man before him said, "Man, I mean you no harm."

His first thought was, 'that's a relief', and recovering from the shock, he burst out, "Why are you here? What do you want?"

"I's a read your name the papers. Gotcha address from the telephone book, but I's a too scared to ring, or come to your house. With a sad apologetic smile, the big man went on, "I's a wait around. I's sees you out with your babbies, and follow you." The man, bent and peered into the pram, "Beautiful, a boy and a girl eh?" A big black hand outstretched to take his. "I's a Walter Nimbya, Henry's twin." Bemused, David shook his hand, and sensed a quiet gentleness, exuding from the big man. Despite that he began to push the pram forward. Walter, keeping in step, informed him with genuine sympathy, "I's a sorry about your wife. I's a lost mine, the week before you. I know's you're a good man. It's a not right, if you're punished..." Walter's voice cracked, "Henry wasn't meant to die. I's just wanted to talk to him. He's the only family, I'd left." David halted, and as Walter did too, he saw tears forming in the big man's eyes. Not knowing how to respond, David moved slowly forward. After a few seconds, Walter, controlling his emotion, explained, "I's a come to the pub to find Henry, and hear Jake's voice, and he's a threatening someone. So, when he calls Henry, I stepped inside. Jake is a spiteful man, and with Henry's bull-headedness, they can turn a simple situation into hatred, and violence."

"You knew Jake?" Seeing Walter's nod, David clarified, "Jake was Andrew Carlton to us. I rescued Jane from him, but there were others, not so fortunate." Walter gave a sad grimace. "But, I am sorry Walter, for the evidence leads me to believe, your brother wasn't much better."

Miserably Walter stated, "Henry and I are identical twins, but only in build and facial features. I's the brains, he the brawn, different as chalk and cheese my Mama would say, like Cain and Abel'. Anyways, I's a mightily glad, I's didn't murder my brother while taking out my revenge on Jake."

Abruptly, David halted the pram, and turned to Walter to exclaim, "You drove him through the glass?"

"Yes, and that will leave a fine man like yourself, charged with his injuries. I needed to show you Walter Nimbya exists. Through Jake, I's a lost my car repair business, our only child, and my beloved wife. She died of a broken heart, 'cept the certificate said 'cancer'." Walter pulled a brown envelope from his pocket. "I's written a confession, it explains everything. I've few possessions, a little money, and a passport to take me where no-one will find me. But I's a couldn't leave, knowing you'd go to prison, for what I did, in a moment of rage."

"Thank you Walter. I appreciate that." David sighed, "I'm afraid Andrew, alias Jake, is going to get away with his past crimes due to lack of evidence and witnesses. However, you've inflicted a kind of justice that will curtail his activities!" Inexplicable compassion for this big black man arose from within. David, put out his hand to receive the envelope and threw out caution by saying, "I shouldn't be telling you this, but I'm no longer a suspect. The police have deduced you exist, and by now, may have worked out who you are. It may be too late for you to leave."

Walter, shaking his head slid the envelope back into the inside pocket of his jacket. Tears filled his eyes, as he proclaimed, "Let me tell you, man, justice will be done!" Puzzled, David frowned, and retracted his hand. Walter patted his chest, "I'll put this in the post. You'll understand. I was a good, upright, and honest man, until fate decreed otherwise."

"Walter, I should report this meeting to the police."

Walter shrugged, and looked him in the eye, "Of course. Don't have any regrets, at what you might have done, or what might have been. Move on, and live life for these dear ones." Benevolently, he smiled down at the sleeping twins, and declared, "And you little ones, know you have a good Daddy, whose love will protect you."

David decided he liked this man, and pleaded, "Walter, don't run, give yourself up. If you plead extenuating circumstances, the conviction of GBH will be reduced to a few years. My father is a rich man who can provide you with the best lawyers."

Unstoppable tears flowed down Walter's cheeks, dripping from his face, as in wonder, he said, "So kind, so very kind! Such a good, and generous man. But this is for the best. I can't face prison, not with the likes of Jake, and what would I do with my life when I got out?"

Overwhelmed with sympathy, David stepped forward, and hugged the big black giant, whose shoulder he could barely see over. In return, he himself, was hugged. In the distance, David saw a couple entering the avenue, he pulled back from Walter to urge, "Best you go." Their eyes met. Seeing the sadness in them, David added, "And may God be with you."

Walter patted his shoulder, and with a rueful grimace, stated, "God with me, doubtful, but thank you." With that, he strode back through the trees, and disappeared from view.

Thoughtful, his constitutional forgotten, David wandered out of the Bayswater Gate to the main road. Would it do any harm to wait until the letter arrived? On the last stretch both babies awoke and, by the time he reached home they'd gone from grizzling to screaming.

Paul appeared, and was quick to pick up Joshua who was making the most noise, and informed him in a concerned voice as he mounted the stairs, "Jill's been overdoing it, she's in bed."

David snuffled Rebecca's cries against his chest, followed him and shut his flat door. "I hope we haven't woken her. Can you stay for a cup of tea? At Paul's nod, David retrieved the twins play mats from the lounge, and put them on the table in the dining room. As he laid Rebecca down, on her green padded mat of flowers and animals, Paul put Joshua on the one with blue waves, and a boat of animals. David chuckled, "Rosemary certainly adores the children. So much love went into making these mats with their patchwork shapes, colours and animals. The whole thing is sheer genius, with it's hanging rainbow of stuffed shapes, the little mirror and the plastic balls to entertain them."

Paul smiled, "Jill's old Singer hand machine is certainly being put to good use. Rosemary spends hours making things." Paul, sitting by the twins with their eyes fixed on shiny stars, circles and spirals above them, had to speak loudly, over the noise of the kettle, "John Perrington rang me this evening. He'd won a round of golf with Freeman, and had been given a bottle of the finest malt he'd ever tasted." David moved to stand in the archway, as amused Paul he added, "And we both know where that came from! But his main news was, Henry had a twin brother." His name was Walter, and apparently his wife died recently, her funeral the same day as Bill's. They rented a furnished flat in Battersea, but Walter's not been seen since that day. The neighbours reported that Walter spent his time nursing his dying wife, he was polite, but very reserved. They all felt he was a good, honest man."

"Yes I felt that too."

Paul's eyes widened, but before he asked, David answered, "I've just met him in the park. I'll make the tea and tell you about it.

After he'd outlined his encounter, Paul, having been thoughtful throughout, commented. "If Walter decided he couldn't face prison, why didn't he go when he could, and then write, and post his confession?"

"He said he wanted to meet me." David shrugged and thought about that as they drank their tea. "I confess that I told Walter the police knew about him, but he didn't seem to think escape was a problem. I said I ought to ring the police, and basically, he said I must do, what I must do."

"And, are you going to ring the police?"

"I don't know, I'll admit I liked him, and wouldn't be upset, if he escaped."

Paul grimaced, "Well that's honest, but not wise. I wonder why he wanted to meet you. And having done so, how odd to show you the letter, and then decide to post it."

They focussed their attention on the twins as they pondered that. Baffled, David reiterated Walter's words, "He said, I understood justice. I guess he read about that quote of mine, 'the law is an ass' in the newspaper." With a frown he continued, "And he told me I should move on from what couldn't be, and live for the twins. Walter is obviously intending to do that."

Paul rubbed his beard. "But why take the risk of talking to you?"

Rattling the little balls on Rebecca's mat, David chuckled, "Oh Paul, I don't know. "I'm the lawyer who cross-questions people. You're the doctor who gives the diagnosis."

Amused Paul retorted, "Impossible, if you haven't detected all the symptoms. And I have a sense there's more to this. You may have liked the man, but I think you should ring the police."

"What would I tell them? Walter was long gone, before I left the park, and to be honest I think he deserves a break."

At a tapping on the flat door he guessed it was Rosemary back from the long weekend. On opening it, she asked tentatively, "Can I come in?" At his, 'of course and beckoning her in, he saw her eyes light up at the twins enjoying her creations. Bent over to play with them she informed him, "Just to say I'm back and happy to do the twins' late feed." At his fervent, 'yes please' she gave a little smile, but when nothing else was forthcoming David invited her to have a cup of tea, and in asking if she'd had a nice weekend, the answer to both was a succinct "Yes, thank you." Paul took up the conversation to tell her Jill wasn't feeling well, and David filled her in on the latest developments, after which they'd drunk the tea, giving an excuse for Rosemary to excused herself. Paul rose to leave too. "I must check on Jill and William. And David before you turn in, I'd make that call, just to cover your back."

In the hall, David dialled the number of Maidstone police station. The front desk informed him, neither DI Gage, nor DCI Bridges was available, and asked if it were urgent. At that he decided to let God decree the outcome. "My name is David Reinhardt, please give DCI Bridges a message." Slowly, so it could be written down, he said, "Henry Nimbya's brother, Walter, spoke to me in the park this evening. He confessed to the GBH to Jake Charlton, and his written confession will be in the post." That done, he went up to bed, and slept until the twins cried at 3.00 am.

When the twins were back in their cots, David sat at his desk to peruse again the photo albums of Jane's growing up, her school photos, music and dance certificates, family holidays at a chalet camp on the Isle of Wight. So much he'd not known about her. Jill had purchased several big box files for all the letters and cards he'd received. And, there were enough photographs, of their three year marriage, for several albums. It wasn't so hard now to look at photos, perhaps the constant challenges of the past weeks was helping his anguish diminish, but if he allowed himself to miss Jane, there was still that yawning ache. Another of Beatty's cathartic ideas was to write a letter to Jane as if she would receive it. That brought him to consider Walter, and his written his confession.

The next morning there wasn't a letter, he was disappointed, then realised even if Walter had posted it yesterday, there wasn't a collection on a Bank Holiday Monday. He expected Bridges to ring, and demand details of his meeting with Walter, but he didn't, and when nothing happened by Wednesday he was unsure what to do next.

By then Paul had diagnosis that Jill had Asian flu, and a growing concern for her and the children, became upper most in their minds. During its pandemic stage in January, it had killed over 2,000 very young and very elderly, so they took every precaution. William's cot was brought up into his spare room away from the air borne virus. Rosemary remained downstairs. Paul was sleeping in William's room. But all other activity now centred in his flat.

William might be cute and funny, but like Jill he'd a stubborn streak, and with the twin's almost continual demands, and despite Mrs P's help, he was growing tired and loosing patience. Paul, worried about Jill's constant coughing, her needing more fluids, and the effect on their unborn child, was seriously considering admitting her into hospital. Before David could voice his concern as to how they were to going to continue to manage, Paul had thought it through. Not wanting to expose Beatty to the flu because of her age, he'd organised for David's parents to stay, because, being in the pharmaceutical business, they'd had their flu injections. It meant they'd sleep in his twin-bedded room, and William's cot would be moved into his, but in the circumstances he'd no objection. And, perhaps understanding how ill Jill was, his father had left his business commitments to come. Mrs P prepared several meals in advance, but with Jill going into hospital on Thursday, by dinner on Friday evening his Mum was so anxious she was almost useless, and his Dad's determination to hire a nurse on Jill's return, developed into an full-blown argument. For the first time, he witnessed Paul's iron will to do what he felt best for his wife, and with the tension palpable, his parents retired early to their bedroom.

With the twins fed and asleep, Paul putting William to bed, David stepped in to help Rosemary wash up the items that wouldn't stack in the dishwasher. Embarrassed that she'd witnessed a family row, he apologised for it and to make conversation he asked if she'd heard from her friend. Concern etched her face as she shook her head, but when she didn't elaborate he left it at that. Used to working together, they did the job with maximum efficiency, but Rosemary, as if noticing his weariness, advised that once William was asleep, he might as well go, and get six hours himself. In taking up her offer, he slipped in to whisper 'goodnight' to the twins, and exhausted wondered if he too was getting the flu.

It was very odd, not having either Jill, or Jane around. And even stranger to leave the twins with his parents the following morning and drive Rosemary to the large Tesco supermarket in order to replace the depleted stocks in both kitchens. Rosemary disappeared after lunch, and he guessed she'd had enough of his banal remarks. However she left a message with his mother to say she'd return in time to do the twin's late feed.

It felt most odd, walking into his kitchen the next morning, to see Rosemary preparing the Sunday lunch. Feeling awkward he asked,, "Have you had breakfast?" At her, 'yes, thank you, he continued, "I'll get mine, and try not to get in your way." When he saw she was in the midst of making a crumble mix, he got a dish from the cupboard above her head and said, "Apricot I hope?"

The reply was brief, "Summer fruits."

"Well I'm sure that will be equally delicious." There was silence as she continued to work. Collecting his breakfast he ate in the dining room, and in considering her dedication and dependability, but thought too how irritating her lack of response could be. When she started to peel the potatoes he offered to help, and in working together it occurred to him this was a logical time to tell her about his conversation with Chris. "I spoke to Chris the other day, and feel I have been unfair to you." Rosemary turned to stare at him, "I had no right to ask you to teach, or show Robert our ways of working, it is after all his job now, not mine."

As David put a peeled potato into the saucepan, she said hesitantly, "But what about the way he treats me?"

"I'm sure he'll be more reasonable, if you let him do things his way." And seeing her almost wilt before him, he added, "Just be your quiet efficient self, and do what he asks of you. If he makes a mess, or things go badly wrong, he'll have no-one to blame but himself."

"But the exhibitors, the exhibition, Brussels?"

To reassure he said briskly, "The Brussels Exhibition won't need attention until October. I'll be back in the office by then." Glancing across at her, as he delivered another peeled potato into the water, he added, "I know this isn't the best solution, but do nothing in haste, and please, if the difficulties persist let me know." They continued in silence, but having peeled the final potato, he asked, "Is there anything else I can do?" For a brief second her eyes locked with his, her look unfathomable, and then with a cursory shake of her head, she gave her attention to putting the meat and potatoes into the oven. He hoped she realised, he was trying to be considerate and understanding.

In church, David was taken aback to see Mary Brown, the District Nurse, and irritated when she bowled over to see the twins, introduced herself to his parents, and gave the impression Jill was a near, and dear, friend. As the service started, she indicated he move up, and sat next to him. Over her head his father sent him a quizzical look. One he returned, and was relieved, when despite Mary talking about Sunday lunch, no-one took the hint, and invited her!

The day was full of tension. Paul's concern being for Jill coming home, his Mum insisting Jill's hacking cough was something Jill often had as a child, and his Dad tight-lipped in anger at not having convinced Paul to hire a nurse. Rosemary only spoke when necessary, her attention and smiles kept for William. And, to David it seemed everything he said caused his father to be argumentative, and disagreeable.

The strain was definitely getting to him for unusually he had a thumping headache. For on top of missing Jane, Jill being ill, the hospital visiting, looking after the children, who were picking up on the tension in the house, he'd not received Walter's letter, and heard nothing from the police. Rosemary caught him in the kitchen taking painkillers, she said nothing to him, but perhaps to his Mum because as he retreated upstairs to get in six hours sleep before the twins feed 3.00 am feed, she offered that she and his father do it for him, to which he gratefully agreed.

CHAPTER 18

The horses' hooves were galloping over a desert and rocky surface, the pounding echoed in his head, on the horse his body felt heavy, and his limbs weak. Despite the blackness of the sky sweat dripped off his face and permeated through his clothing. For the burning dryness in his throat, he was desperate for a drink. Eyes set on the invisible goal, there was no slowing in the ranks of horses and soldiers. He felt he could barely cling on, and if he fell he'd be trampled to death. Noises of battle, hammering, shouting, penetrated into his dream. Were they nearing their destiny? But as the battle sounds drew nearer he knew he'd no strength to fight. Strident voices pierced through the darkness into his conscious mind. Someone shook him, a male voice commanded, "Wake up". A child was screaming. Whose child, where was it? Over that the demanding voice saying, "Get up" seemed louder.

Paul's loud and angry voice penetrated his dream. The screaming became muffled. Although the dream was dissipating the horses' hooves were still pounding in his head. Over-riding that was Paul's voice was declaring, "I don't care if you do have a warrant. What is the matter with a reasonable hour, and ringing the doorbell? My wife is seriously ill, my child scared out of its wits, our family disturbed."

The tough, gruff voice of his father joined in to boom, "What the hell is going on here? Do you know what time it is? Why were you banging on the door ? What's all the shouting about?" In the confusion of voices, David struggled to open his eyes that felt glued shut. For a brief moment he saw an unknown man leaning over him, he could barely lift his head from the pillow, but it was enough to see Paul holding William and talking to another man standing at his bedroom door. From his dry and burning throat, he managed a weak rasp, to ask, "What's happening?"

Immediately the words came, "Police! Get up! David Reinhardt we are arresting you for the murder of Andrew Carlton, anything you say will be taken down and maybe used in evidence."

Both his father and Paul's objected. He closed his eyes and tried to fathom why the police didn't know it was Henry who was murdered, not Andrew. The bedclothes being pulled from him, along with another demand for him to 'get up' forced him to open his eyes. To oblige, he turned slowly with the intention of putting his feet over the side of the bed, only to be hoisted to his feet. Disorientated he wobbled, as a curt voice said, "Get dressed, you're coming with us." In lifting and turning his head, the hammering pain was so great he closed his eyes, groaned, and would have collapsed, if an arm hadn't been supporting him. The dream swirled through his mind, had he fallen from his horse? His body ached as though pummelled by hooves. Paul's voice broke through, sounding distant, he heard the words, 'Asian flu'. The man supporting him spoke an expletive by his ear, let him go, and he sagged down onto the bed, his head falling between his knees. Fingers encircled his wrist, for a second he opened his eyes and saw Paul's slippers, and light blue pyjamas. When Paul instructed him to look up his neck felt stiff, his head had an inbuilt painful drumbeat, but slowly he complied to see Paul crouched before him, his eyes full of concern. Desperate to rest his head, and hearing more voices coming up the stairs, he squeezed his eyes tightly shut.

Instantly he forced them open again, as his father boomed, "You can't go in there, the twins…" At that he gritted his teeth against the pain, and turned his head. Paul put a restraining on his shoulder. Two policemen were in his bedroom. His father stood in the hallway fully dressed in his pin-strip suit. William was peeking out from behind him, as he boomed angrily, "Leave those things alone." Over the sudden, shrill crying of the twins, he saw a policeman put a baby in his father's arms, as he continued to claim, "Those things are private. Why are you taking a box containing cards and letters from friends and well-wishers? This is absurd! That's David's scrapbook, he's putting it together in remembrance of his late wife. What are you doing with those photos?"

His crying babies, his precious scrapbook, photos. Motivated, David found inner strength and leapt forward, the pain in his head so intensified that he closed his eyes against it, and felt himself falling headlong on the carpet.

The force of the cough rising from his chest had David briefly open his eyes. A pleasant, smiling woman in nurse's uniform bent towards him with a drinking cup. He tried to lift his arm, but it felt like a lead weight. As he rested against the pile of pillows, she gently tipped a feeder cup up into his mouth. "Drink this it will help." From the recesses of his mind came snapshots of brief lucidity. Strident voices, carried to the bed, odd dreams, words, cold flannels on his head. As he let the cool liquid slip down his throat the nurse said, "I'm Lorna. You've had a nasty dose of flu, with a high fever." Back came the knowledge of his body rolled across the bed, being washed, pyjamas changed and the smell of fresh sheets. Embarrassed, feeling weary and vulnerable, he closed his eyes as Lorna said cheerily, "But you're a healthy and fit man. You're over the worst, although it'll take a few days to regain your strength."

Despite the cool refreshing liquid his voice came out as a raspy whisper. "The children?"

"Fine and in safe hands. Your wife, and her mother, had this flu in the 1957 outbreak, so your father felt to protect your twins they should stay at your mother-in-laws house. And he's hired them a live-in nanny, from that exclusive Norlands College. David grimaced, typical of his father to have his way when he couldn't object! Lorna continued, "William has gone to Bath to stay with your mother, and she has a local woman's help. I'm also looking after your sister, she's home and recovering, but it'll take her longer because of the baby. She, like you doesn't seem happy about Paul agreeing to your father's arrangements, although in the circumstances, I don't know what else he could have done. Now rest, you need to regain your strength.

Memories began to return of policemen in his bedroom. Lorna was leaving the room, he took a deep breath and called, "Lorna, the police…" but a tickle in his chest cut off his words, and his body shuddered at the force of the cough.

Unable to speak, his mind grappled with echoing words, 'arrest, murder, evidence' along with the stirring of unease as Lorna returning to the bed, to inform him, "Your father is staying here, and dealing with everything." She smiled broadly and added, "But remember, ultimately the Lord is in control." In reading the surprise in his eyes, she continued, "Yes, I'm a Christian. I've just started coming to your church. I know Paul through being on the bank staff at the hospital. He asked the nursing agency for me, so here I am to nurse you, and your sister back to health. And that rather quiet lady who lives in the basement, Rosemary, says when you are up to it, she will cook nourishing meals for you both to restore your strength."

The bout of coughing over, he gave a small smile, his eyelids felt heavy and he drifted off to sleep.

During the next two days of his 'enforced' rest he slept, coughed, drank delicious soups and slept again. Occasionally he was aware of raised voices, and when he asked, the answer was always, "Nothing for you to worry about." On the third morning of his recovery, and no longer needing help to the bathroom, he skirted the bed to look out at a torrential storm. Along the street a gaggle of men were taking shelter under a tree, and a car was parked on the double yellow lines opposite. He clicked his tongue, if he did that the police would be towing it away! Along with regaining his strength was a growing realisation that he wasn't getting direct answers to any of his questions. When he asked for a newspaper he got a magazine. When he suggested having a radio, he was given tapes, and the tape recorder. In asking if Jill could visit Paul declared she wasn't well enough to climb the three flights of stairs.

Frustrated, he tried to read his Bible and pray, when he couldn't concentre he listened to Jane's music tapes, but today in hearing raised voices as the front door shut, he slid out of bed to look out of the window. Below Paul was speaking to several men, but as he drove away, they, in a desultory fashion, wandered off to congregate further down the road. He suspected they were reporters. Why were they here?

The sun had finally come out, he'd watched his father leave earlier in his pin-stripped suit obviously going somewhere on business, and so who, or what, would stop him visiting Jill? He was sure he could manage three flights of stairs. However, on reaching the basement he'd cause to wonder if he'd make it back up again. But when Lorna, surprised to see him, enquired if he was alright, he said, "Of course," but he knew he wasn't fooling her.

It had been worth the effort to bask in the sun with Jill, who was pale, but recovering. Between their coughing and resting back on the sun loungers, heaped with cushions, he asked, "Do you know what happened on Monday morning?"

"Paul told me it was unnecessary and ridiculous. The police were banging on the front door at 5.30 am, the commotion was quite frightening. Paul opened the door, the police burst in and rushed upstairs with no explanation. He's made a formal complaint to John Perrington. But, I know little more than you, brother dear, because it seems 'mum' is the word!" Jill giggled. "Jane's Mum had the twins later that day, and our Mum went home with William on the train! I did overhear Dad say grimly, 'I'm staying until this mess is sorted out', but my impression was that had nothing to do with us being ill."

Speaking slowly, he began to recollect what happened. "My

recurring dream and reality, seems muddled. I thought someone said I was under arrest for Andrew's murder. That isn't true. Andrew survived his injuries, and they were no longer life…" The tickling that arose in his chest manifested itself in a bout of wracking coughs.

Jill groaned, "The coughing is awful."

David agreed, but what he felt more 'awful' was being incapacitated and no-one telling him what was going on. When he could speak again, he declared fiercely, "Jane's gone. The twins were keeping me sane. This police business is driving me mad. They've taken all my files, including household bills, bank statements, legal notebooks, even my private journal. Heaven knows what they'll make of that. I've recorded, my dream, the glory cloud, God highlighting biblical verses? But what I want to know is, why?" Jill frowned and shook her head, as he raved on. "It doesn't make any sense, and when I ask, I'm told not to worry!" His voice cracked, "How can I not worry? It's far harder to struggle against depression when you've time on your hands."

Jill leant across to pat his arm. "If it's any consolation, Paul told me Ted, Joyce and nanny are coping admirably and both he, and Ted feel the twins are helping Joyce come to terms with Jane's death."

"Of course, I'm glad about that, but I feel bereft. There are no cots in my study…the scrapbooks, photos of Jane…" he swallowed hard, "the police have taken…" he tried to finish, but as the tears rolled down his cheeks, his voice petered out.

Firmly Jill admonished, "Now don't upset yourself, brother dear, they will return them."

Brokenly he stated, "It was bad enough when my life went public, and the twisted newspaper reports, now this…" After wiping his eyes he said more strongly, "But my journal. It's an infringement of my thoughts, a violation of my privacy. What evidence do they think they will find in those?"

Staunchly Jill replied, "That you are a good, upright and trustworthy citizen. You pay your bills on time, you give ten percent of your earnings to the church, and very generously donate another ten percent to a variety of other charities. You work hard, loved your wife, adore your children and provide a home for your extended family."

David retorted as he struggled not to cough, "Of that home, you own ten percent, and pay your way with all the bills!"

Jill smiled, and then appeared to be waiting, until his coughing fit passed, to speak. "You know David, if I'd been through all you have, I'd feel a bomb had dropped, buried me in the rubble, and I'd never see the light of day again. But believe me, you have the best rescuers to dig you out, of whatever this mess is. Two years ago I felt I'd never come through it all, but I've Paul and William, and this new baby coming. You're a man of tenacity, you will battle through."

Wearily he stated, "What use are my diplomatic, detection or defensive skills when I don't even know what mess I'm in? I thought my innocence was settled?"

Jill sighed, and then pointed out, "Lorna's beckoning us, it must be time to take our tablets, drink our cough mixture and have our lunch. Dad always reads The Times, see if you can find a copy, that may shed some light on the case. Now, cheer up, brother dear, there is one consolation in all this...." At her chuckle, David raised a quizzical eyebrow. "...you have been losing weight, and need have no guilt in consuming another of Rosemary's delicious nutritious soups, her home made bread and covering it with lashings of butter!" Jill's amusement turned to a cough, her hand went on her rather large four month baby bump, but when it was over she declared "I've every excuse to eat for two."

At her mention of his weight, he couldn't resist an amused retort, "Are you sure it's not three?"

Unperturbed, Jill grinned, "Not what my doctor says, but if it was twins, brother dear, we'd have to succumb to Dad's persistence, and hire that Norland nanny. Five children in under two, in one house, would definitely be beyond our capabilities."

On Lorna's insistence, he have an 'afternoon rest', David determined to do the stairs alone. She watched his steady progress up the first flight, but out of sight, in the hall and breathless, he recuperated by sitting on the stairs up to his flat. Believing he heard Lorna's voice, he bent low, and using his hands and feet he scurried to the top. Grabbing the banister he pulled himself upright, entered his flat, slumped on the piano stool, and gave into a bout of gut wrenching coughing.

Grateful that the police hadn't taken the family photos from the piano, he looked across at Jane's smiling face. How she would have laughed seeing his out of character, ridiculous behaviour to outwit his nurse! He picked up the large silver framed photo taken on their honeymoon in the Caribbean. The camera angle had caught Jane's eyes filled with love and adoration, as she looked up at him. Jane had filled his house with warmth, laughter, singing, and making melody on this piano, but a glance around showed his lounge now devoid of clutter, it felt, cold, unlived in. To the ceiling, the corner of the room where he'd said, 'goodbye', he murmured, "How I miss you, my little bundle of fun." He waited, in the hope of another glimpse of her, then hugging the picture, he slowly climbed the remaining stairs, and exhausted, lay on the bed, pulled the eiderdown over him, and slept.

Awakening just before six, he determined to watch the TV news. Halfway down the first flight to his lounge he heard Paul coming up the other. "I hear you came to visit earlier. I wondered if you felt well enough to join us downstairs for dinner?"

David growled, "I'm not an invalid" and added for good measure, thinking of the news being kept from him, "Nor a child."

Paul hummed, "You are better. You sound like your father."

At that David grunted, but then proved he was an invalid by not being able to do his customary bounding down the stairs. And worse, had to take hold of the banister, and go slowly down, like a frail, old man. At his, and Paul's appearance on the basement staircase, his father jumped up, to add a place setting, and get a glass. The wine poured, Jill raised her glass, and tapped his. "Here's back to health and happiness" and promptly went into a fit of coughing. His father's derisive grunt was similar to the one he'd made a few minutes earlier.

Rosemary, out for the evening, had prepared a lasagne and his father, usually not liking what he termed 'foreign muck', commented in a grim tone, "Good cook that Rosemary." The atmosphere was sober, the conversation desultory. His father pushed forward his empty plate. Gruffly he commented, "What a strange, and difficult time, this is for all of us." To that, David couldn't have agreed more. "Tomorrow we will dispense with Nurse Bramwell's services. Paul thinks Jill will be fit to travel by Sunday. I don't know why David, you don't get rid of that old boneshaker of a Morris Minor, but I know Paul and Jill find it handy. However, I'm sure David you won't mind lending them your car, so Jill can be driven in comfort to Bath."

Although puzzled as to why his father wasn't taking them, David's response was "Of course!" But irritated by his father's high handedness, he asked, "Dad, surely it's time you went home to Mum."

Steely eyes focussed on his. "Obviously, David, you have no recollection that on Monday, the police came to arrest you for the murder of Andrew Carlton."

Jill gasped. David frowned as he queried, "I thought that I'd dreamt that. Carlton, murdered, by whom?"

Grimly his father retorted, "As far as the police are concerned, by you!" At David's aghast, 'What?' he explained, "Last Saturday, Carlton's landlord went to collect the rent on Andrew's bedsit and found he'd been battered to death." David went to speak, but his father's raised his hand. "Let me finish. Carlton had been tied up in a heavy linen sack, hung from the ceiling, and used as a punch bag." Behind her hand, Jill squealed in horror. "There was no sign of forced entry, the police believe his attacker had been waiting for him to return from convalescence. From his injuries, it's thought it was a unhurried, systematic beating, causing an excruciatingly painful and slow death, two or three days earlier."

Although sickened, David felt to comment, "Andrew punched Evie in the stomach, damaging her internally, in order to destroy his unborn child."

"Is that so?" His father looked thoughtful, "The police need to talk to that woman."

"Jordan told me she's married, her husband doesn't know about Andrew and his attack on her."

Instantly, his father retorted, "He will now, because no-one can be ruled out, for someone did it, and we know it wasn't you."

Distressed, David ran his hand through his hair. "Oh God, even after death, that man ruins lives."

His father grunted. "From the size of the contusions, each punch came from a large fist, the weight behind it causing internal damage and bleeding. Your physique fits that description. On record from four years ago you told the police, and Jane confirmed it, that you punched Carlton and knocked him out."

"Yes, but a previous case can't be brought into the equation."

"The police evidently feel they have enough to arrest you."

"I suspect, Evie wasn't the only girl Carlton meted out that punishment. A father, husband, or boyfriend reading the newspaper would know he'd resurfaced. It wouldn't be difficult to discover where he lived, and beat him to death?"

"True, but we have to refute Bridges' suspicions about you."

"He just dislikes my being a lawyer, and having a brain."

That remark drew a grim smile from his father. "I'm told Bridges has noted that you are too clever for your own good! And Paul, also tells me that you met with the black man now identified as Walter Nimbya, the twin brother of Henry. I've no doubt he's a big man with large fists!"

"Yes, but he's a 'gentle' giant, I liked him."

"Yet, I understand he admitted to blaming Carlton for loosing everything. And his temper being aroused by Carlton threatening you and Jane was enough for him to pick Andrew up, and head him through a glass door."

David blanched. "True Dad, but cold bloodied murder, I don't think so."

"But the police assure Daniel Kemp that they are in possession of evidence to prove that even if you didn't do it, you were party to it."

"How ridiculous! If I had knowledge, or suspected anyone, I would have told the police. What can they possibly have to prove something that hasn't happened?"

Wide-eyed his father countered, "That's as maybe, but they have questions only you can answer. We've done all we can on your behalf. Reporters are outside, hoping for a scoop, and the police are keeping watch to ensure they stay out, and you stay in. Kemp informs me the police, despite sifting through your personal papers, have found nothing to incriminate you, and the things you've written about Ben…"

"Oh God, No!" David's hand flew to his mouth. My personal journal…"

"Don't worry, my boy, we've salvaged the damage by involving Pauls' friend, Perrington. We've retrieved the journal, and no-one will be able to delve further, but I believe there have been 'interesting' conversations, between Daniel and team, about your faith!" David caught a glimmer of amusement in his father's eyes.

With a sad smile he responded, "Proof then that I'm either mad, or have experiences in a supernatural God."

Jill giggled, his father raised his eyebrows, and Paul who'd been silent throughout, advised, "I don't think its wise David that we delay the police longer. They are anxious to solve the case, and if you are seen to be co-operating, despite being unfit, that will go in your favour."

"He's right, my boy. For believe me, if Bridges hadn't returned last Saturday from his holiday, and within a day developed this ghastly flu, he'd have done his utmost to have you incarcerated in a police cell, or even prison. Due to his excessive smoking he's been extremely poorly, but Daniel reported today he's now out of hospital, very weak, but determined to prove his case against you." Underlying amusement crept into his father's voice. "So I suppose we should all be praising the Lord for Asian flu. It's kept you out of a cell, enabled the police to see from your papers the quality of the man accused, and given time for us to refute any wrong assumptions. And I am sure, this 'incriminating evidence' can quickly be disproved, leaving you with no case to answer."

"Amen to that, Dad."

"It only then leaves me to tell you, that in the light of you being arrested, and your illness, Kemp thought it judicious to ask the court to bail you, pending further enquiries. Rest assured, you won't be carted off to either a cell, or prison overnight."

David had barely comprehended that, when Paul said, "So David, under my advisement, we've agreed DI Gage and Daniel Kemp come here tomorrow to present their evidence, and for you to answer their questions."

Tears of thankfulness overflowed. He wiped his eyes with the sleeve of his dressing gown. "It's hard to take in, being under arrest for conspiring to murder someone, and to be on bail. Even dead, Andrew's vendetta continues. But thank you, Paul, Dad, for believing in me, and supporting me." Feeling cheered that Bridges wouldn't be part of the meeting, he gave a small smile. "I've just had a thought if Bridges was on holiday, then sick, I wonder if he received the message I left telling him I'd met with Walter?"

"You rang the police!" The relief in Paul's voice was evident. "I told your Dad you'd met Walter, but said not to tell the police. I didn't want them jumping to any wrong conclusions."

"But surely, you've given them Walter's letter, his confession it must have arrived by now?"

"I'm sorry David," Paul grimaced, "It hasn't come."

"What! But it was his confession! Without that…"

As he tailed off Paul suggested, "It may still come, he's not been apprehended, but that doesn't mean to say he's left the country."

Worried, David shook his head, "I don't understand it. Walter said he'd send it."

His father informed him, "Kemp says there's been an 'all points of exit' detention notice posted."

Paul added, "Escape wouldn't be that difficult, there are plenty of foreign tankers in the docks with captains that wouldn't ask questions."

"Has Daniel looked into Walter's life? Walter blamed Carlton for the loss of his business and his only child, so if we aren't going to get his confession, perhaps delving into those things might help."

Immediately his father said, "It shall be done."

In considering that Jill interrupted their thoughts. "This is so horrible, but if it can be cleared up tomorrow, David could have the twins back, and we could all go to Bath for a few days.

Firmly, his father retorted, "Paul and I have decided you need to rest a few weeks, not days. And, I afraid, to expect this to be cut, dried and over tomorrow, is too much to hope for." And then turning to him added, "David, I think you'll agree, its best the twins stay with Joyce and Ted until you are fully fit. Without the support of Jill and Paul, you must realise you won't be able to manage the twins on your own. I've arranged for their present nanny to come with them." About to protest, his father said sternly, "They'll be no argument. She can share the basement flat with Rosemary, and sleep in William's room."

David tried to weigh his father's high handiness, against a desire to be helpful. "I know Dad, over the past days, you've had to make decisions on my behalf, but I'd prefer to make my own arrangements for the twins. Joyce, originally was willing to help during the day, and Rosemary loves helping in the evenings, we'll manage."

Without answering his father, tight-lipped, pushed back his chair and headed for the stairs, saying "The world doesn't sleep, I've calls to make. I'll use your telephone David, I'll be undisturbed in your lounge?"

That tactic of his father's to decree, ignore argument, then change the subject was so annoying that he retorted, "Help yourself, the cable will just stretch inside the door, do as you wish Dad, you always do."

It wasn't clear whether he received the underlying sarcasm, but he turned to comment, "When the next bill comes in let me know. I'll reimburse you."

That wasn't his intention, so David boomed after him. "What's a telephone bill against all you have invested in me?"

Booming a reply, down the stairs as he disappeared around the corner, came words tinged with amusement, "You won't say that, when you see it!"

Next morning, eating his breakfast, the silence of the house made David feel like the condemned man, awaiting execution.

Three hours later, he was again alone at his dining room table as Paul and his father were accompanying DI Gage and DCI Manning from Maidstone, DI Jordan from the Met., and Daniel Kemp and Martin Beresford to the front door. He heard it open, the reporters shouting questions, and wearily he put his head in his hands and groaned. Maudlin thoughts prevailed. He was trapped, in his own house, in a situation not of his making. His wife was dead, his twins sent away. When would he see them again? He coughed, his body shook. Continual coughing had punctuated almost every sentence throughout the interview. A court appearance, and jail, could be next.

The meeting had started well. No-one smoked, they drank tea, ate biscuits and the three men were polite, and although wincing over his every cough, had been patience and kind. But the continual questions he'd found exhausting, and he sensed they were trying to trap him. Finally, they came to the evidence of his involvement in Carlton's killing. Even he had to admit it was pretty damning! Out of a folder, Gage produced a series of photos, taken by the detective keeping him under observation. The first was of him, looking intent and speeding along Kensington High Street with the pram as though he'd a goal in mind. The next, heading across the park, he was blurred, his speed too fast for camera, the assumption he was late for an appointment. Following those were Walter looking into the pram, his smiling, their shaking hands. Further pictures showed a friendly conversation, David's outstretched hand, and Walter pocketing a brown envelope. The inference was, and it looked like a pay-off. But the most damning of all was the hugging of Walter. It had been long enough for the photographer to get two shots of him smiling ruefully over Walter's shoulder, and the other of the bear hug Walter gave him in response.

In revealing these, and laying them on the table, one after the other, Gage's expression was one of wide-eyed curiosity, Jordan looked perplexed, and Manning's gaze was challenging. The expressions of his father, Daniel and Martin, were classically non-committal, as they heard what appeared to be damning evidence. If he'd been them, he'd have doubted his innocence. Fortunately, when asked why he'd not reported the meeting to the police, he had been able to reassure them he'd left DCI Bridges a message.

Downstairs the front door closed, the outside voices silenced. A few seconds later his father entered the dining room, his manner cheerful. "Well, David that went well. I'll put the kettle on for a cup of tea, and make us a sandwich."

Astonished he looked up on three counts, his father's 'went well', unaccustomed joviality, and the offer to make tea and a sandwich. Weakly he repeated, "went well?".

Behind him in the kitchen, his father boomed through the hatch, "Of course my boy! You were marvellous. You could have been a top-notch barrister, a QC no less, if you hadn't thrown it all up after that fellow Ben's case."

David moved his head to rest on one hand, closed his eyes and rubbed his forehead, and as his father came to perch on a chair at an angle to him David murmured, "Your perspective isn't the same as mine."

"Rubbish my boy! You fielded every question with a calm ease, brought a little humour into the proceedings, revealed how well you could bowl a ball, caught one batsman unawares, and another, believing he could make a hit, found himself stumped out, and when you caught their winning ball with such panache, it was over and out."

Scowling, he sat up to retort, "Dad this wasn't one of your village cricket matches."

The smile, on the usually dour face caused him to blink. His father's words caused him to frown. "No my boy, it was far more exhilarating and exciting. Now do you want ham or cheese, I think I'll have both, shall I do the same for you?"

Still sunk in despair, he waved his hand, "Whatever you're having." And then, to his utmost surprise, his father started whistling, but more incredible, it was a hymn tune! He wondered if his father knew the words were, "Oh happy day when Jesus took my sins away!" What had caused such a metamorphic change from the serious, grim man he thought he knew? David steepled his fingers was pondering on that, when so clearly the answer came, bringing tears to his eyes. Over the past few weeks, his life had been open to public scrutiny, the police, his father and lawyers, and through reading his private journal had invaded his precious and most personal thoughts. But as Jill had pointed out, those things had served to confirm he was a man of love, faith, honour and integrity. His father was revealing his pride and joy in his son! And with that revelation he saw without Bridges' belligerent attitude toward him, the men today had looked at him with respect. Not because of the exclusive neighbourhood in which he lived, the upmarket house he owned, or the top shot lawyer his father had hired, but for who he was, and represented.

Despite the damning photographic evidence, and his feeble explanation, they'd believed him! His short talk with Walter gave the police more to investigate, they'd believed him! And despite the message Bridges had never received, they'd believed him! For a brief moment he felt pleased, but despondency returned with a wracking cough. This wasn't over, their believing him didn't mean case closed, and they'd made it clear, until they'd investigated further, he was still under arrest. His father might feel jubilant, but he still felt a condemned man.

The promised mug of tea, and an oddly shaped sandwich, overflowing with cheese and ham was put before him when, from the doorway, Paul proclaimed, "David, you should be rejoicing, not sitting there looking as if you've lost a shilling and found sixpence."

Gloomily he replied, "It's not over is it? He pushed the plate away, "I'm not hungry."

Appearing with his own tea and sandwich, his father boomed at Paul, "Wasn't David incredible? I never made one of his court cases, but under questioning he's got a quick brain, his thinking and words, so clear and concise."

Wearily David murmured, "Only because I'd said it all, several times!"

Still upbeat, his father encouraged. "That's as maybe, but don't be so discouraged. I'll agree, my heart sank seeing those photos, but from your explanation the police saw that 'the camera can lie'! It's just a case of waiting for the police to make their enquiries, and conclude you had nothing to do with it." Unconvinced, David grunted.

Amused, and with sarcasm, Paul commented, "Nice sandwiches, Franz!" To which Franz's grunt wasn't dissimilar to his son! "Now, David, as your doctor, if you really don't want to eat, drink up that tea, and off to bed with you. You're too exhausted to think straight. After you've slept you'll see everything in a more positive light."

When David next came downstairs, on the dining room table were the household bills, his bank statements, and more importantly the scrapbooks he'd started of Jane's life. His journal was still missing, but maybe his lawyers thought it would shed more light on his explanation. Restless, and unable to concentrate, he wandered around, read a couple of the newspaper reports his father had collated, and was grateful those incriminating photos hadn't circulated further than the police files. The telephone was still off the hook, he returned the receiver to its cradle, but after receiving two calls from reporters, he once again let the receiver dangle to the floor. Family and friends knew to ring the downstairs flat.

CHAPTER 19

David looked out of the window. It was Sunday, the street was empty, but for two reporters sitting in a car opposite. With so few left, he wondered if they'd wind of another story brewing. Physically, he was recovering. Mentally, he felt more stable. Spiritually, he was at peace. On Friday, Paul had prayed into his life the promises of God, declaring the Lord would be his strength, and that He was a refuge in times of trouble. And, David felt he was now living in reality of that.

Yesterday, his father had unexpectedly decided to go home, his explanation, that he'd a business to run and, if needed urgently, the journey to London was only two and half hours by train. And five minutes ago, he'd driven away, with Paul and Jill, in his Jaguar. Below, he heard the front door close. Rosemary came into view, no doubt on her way to catch the bus to church. What was stopping him going? On bail he couldn't leave the country, but he could go out! He'd no responsibilities, and only two reporters between him and freedom! Gathering up all he needed, he went downstairs, opened the garage doors, backed the car out, and was just pulling the doors back together as one reporter started shouting questions, while the other adjusted his camera angle. Head down, he ducked around the car, jumped in, backed around them, and drove away knowing the camera hadn't taken a decent picture of him. The thrill of outwitting them lifted his spirits. And his arrival at church, the warm welcome he received, gave him to realise no-one here believed he was a murderer. It was strange to be alone, and having ten minutes before the service began, he sat down to talk his friends, Alan and Janet. At Nurse Mary Brown sidling up to join their conversation, he sent her an unsmiling nod, but she seemed insensitive to his monosyllabic replies to her irritating chatter. And, as the organ started to play, Mary hurriedly squashed herself between him and the end of the pew, causing those in the row to move along to make room. Spotting Rosemary walking down the aisle, he made her his excuse to move. Mary frowned, as she stepped out to let him pass, as did Rosemary, when she saw him following her into the pew. By Rosemary's ear he said, "I hope you don't mind, but Mary Brown sat by me, and I'd rather not get involved." Rosemary's response was to pick up her hymn book and begin singing, making him consider if she felt the same way about him, as he did Mary!

Janet and Alan had invited him for lunch, but afterwards Alan, looking concerned, drew him aside. "Janet thought I'd better tell you, Rosemary is already coming for lunch. She's so good with the children. Is that alright with you? You, being single now, well, I know it must be awkward, we don't want you to think we're match-making."

David grinned, "I've no objections" But remembering Rosemary's earlier frown, he went on, "But ask Rosemary. And if you think she's at all reticent, let me know, I'll happily come another time." Alan looked relieved, and later told him Rosemary had commented that it would be good for him to have a change of scenery, and that with no-one to home to cook for him she'd remarked, 'I don't want him to miss out on my account'.

Rosemary although quiet throughout the meal was a big hit with Adam, five and Fiona, three. And the afternoon was such a pleasurable experience he forgot his troubles. When at five o'clock he felt he should take his leave, Rosemary stood too, and despite the children's cries for her to stay, they left together. As they drove away he teased, "Janet's crumble isn't up to your standard." At the tiny smile of response, he felt confident to ask, "How's your friend, I assume she's returned to her flat?"

"I don't know what to do?" Plainly disturbed Rosemary admitted, "I have a key, but I'm afraid at what I might find."

"Would you like me to come with you?" He turned towards her, "We could go now."

The expected refusal, turned into being a fervent, "Yes please."

Five minutes later, having expected to be directed to a squalid flat, he found himself in an upmarket cobbled mews, with quaint old fashioned street lights. Window boxes, filled with a variety of flowers and colours, fronted a diversity of old stable conversions. Parking where he could, Rosemary led him to a whitewashed narrow building at the far end. Opening the door, she stood back, so he could enter the very attractive looking, two up, two down, cottage.

Rosemary, behind him, with a finger under her nose, said, "It's that horrible smell…" Throughout, the open plan living area, were strewn magazines, newspapers, dirty glasses and plates, wine and beer bottles. Beyond, the long narrow kitchen looked equally disgusting. "Keep the front door open. I'll get the window open. Is there a back door?"

Still in the doorway, Rosemary nodded. "The key is in the top drawer of the sink unit." As he made his way across the debris towards the kitchen the vile smell got stronger. He called back to her, "Stay out there" and prayed he wasn't in the midst of another crime scene, and the smell was nothing more than putrid food!

The back yard had a small washing line, and room for a small table and chairs, hopefully there'd be enough breeze to run through the house. Mouldy plates, with rotting food were stacked randomly by, and in the washing up bowl filled with dank smelling water. But, on opening the fridge door, it was almost impossible not to gag at the pungent smell! He shut it quickly, took several deep breaths at the back door, and then called to Rosemary to stay where she was, but take the lid off the dustbin that he'd seen by the front door. Picking up several scattered carrier bags, he took a deep breath, delved back into the fridge and without examining the contents swept them into the bags. Rushing across the living area, he shouted, "Stand back Rosemary" as he dropped them into the open bin, he grabbed the lid from her to slam it on saying, "That's your horrible smell." Gagging, he took several deep breaths, that brought on a deep wrenching cough, through which he managed to say, to the very obviously relieved, yet sickened Rosemary, "The fridge will need a good clean." As he rested back against the window box of dead flowers, he pointed out, "I'd say your friend hadn't been around for awhile." Rosemary looking pale didn't speak, so he asked, "Would you like to go and sit in the car?" When she shook her head, he suggested, "I've several carrier bags in the car boot, if you get those, I'll get started clearing the kitchen."

Looking relieved Rosemary nodded, and on her return, she cautiously entered the living area, and began collecting up the beer and wine bottles. Four further smelly bags from the kitchen were loaded into the bin, before he'd boiled enough hot water to put the mouldy crockery and cutlery in soak. Collecting up glasses David commented, "I don't know how anyone could live like this. Your friend certainly didn't appreciate this cosy love nest." Rosemary blanched, and he shrugged, "It looks to me as if she made the place into a beer swilling squat, then just upped and left. I'm surprised you'd have a friend like that."

Amidst the clanging of beer bottles, in the two carrier bags Rosemary was carrying to the front door, she remarked, "How very judgmental."

Aggravated, he disputed that. "The evidence speaks for itself."

To which Rosemary retorted, "You, of all people, should

know the evidence isn't always what it seems!" And by the bang of bottles landing into a galvanised dustbin he knew he'd upset her.

"Sorry Rosemary. I'm here to help, not criticise. Shall I check there's nothing untoward upstairs? Rosemary shuddered and nodded. A few moments later he was able to report, "Both bedrooms, much like down here, but nothing obviously gruesome to find. The bathroom, like the kitchen is filthy. Wardrobes and drawers are empty, so I'd say she did a runner! Now shall I carry on down here and you clear upstairs?"

He began washing off the dirty cutlery and crockery. Stuck between two bowls was a torn envelope, when he pulled it off he discovered the name of Rosemary's friend. For a moment he stared at it, then taking the stairs two at a time he demanded, "Why didn't you tell me Helen's been living here?" Rosemary gave him one of her unfathomable looks. "Oh come on, I might not have known her well, and she might not have liked me, but she did live in my house, okay the downstairs flat, with Jane, and with Jill for three years. And I'm sure, Jill must have told you how Dad, feeling sorry for her losing the hope of husband, home, and family gave her a large cheque to help her through that."

Suddenly, as though he'd touched a raw nerve, Rosemary's eyes flashed with anger. And at the torrent of words tumbling from her mouth he knew that underneath that cool, calm, aloof façade, there was still the woman who had caused Jane angst by her bitterness and sarcasm. "That's typical of the rich, isn't it? There's a problem, oh give them a fat cheque, that'll keep them quiet. You think you can just pay someone off, and forget about them? Oh don't look so shocked, because that's what your family did!"

Palms raised, he stepped towards her, "Whoa there lady, that's a very warped view."

She backed away from him. The bed hindered her. She stiffened, giving him a hard glare, her hands clenched. "Is it, I don't think so? Have you, or your family, thought about Helen, or even inquired about her in the last eighteen months?"

"Jane and Jill visited her in hospital several times."

"But when she came here neither of them visited her."

"I didn't know that."

Rosemary, having opened the sluice gate of emotion seemed unable to stop the flow. Her voice sneered, "Do you know what they did? Jill, appalled at Helen's attitude dumped her. But, believe me that was just bravado, for an agony of heart and mind, after the pain of her physical injuries left her. In that fiasco, Jill got off lightly, but Helen's mental anguish affected the way she thought, and when I tried to visit regularly, she saw it as interference. You push away friends because you are afraid they will reject you. And, of course eventually they do, so you counter balance that rejection with whatever comfort, or escape you can find. For Helen she found it with drink, drugs and friends who only saw her as a meal ticket. I talked to Jane about it, she wanted to come, but Helen didn't want religion spouted at her. So Jane prayed, and said she'd speak to Jill. I like Jill, she's been a good friend to me, so I don't want to blame her for Helen's downward spiral, but the bottom line is Jill did ruin Helen's life."

Embroiled in the Brussels' Exhibition, he'd not had much sympathy for Jill, or Helen. But he saw it had shaken his father, and upset his mother. And it was out of sympathy for Helen, his father had told him he'd sent her a cheque, generous enough to buy a small property outside of central London. Not wanting to challenge, but with a need to contest her assumptions, he said gently, "You've got it wrong. That money wasn't a pay-off from my father. He made it clear to Helen he was giving it to her on behalf of Ben, who wanted to ensure she was looked after." About to speak Rosemary stopped, and while processing the information, glared at him. Was her strong reaction due to an underlying, perhaps similar personal issue? However, as disagreeable as it was to hear, there was some truth in Jill spoiling Helen's life. "Look Rosemary, I understand you are incensed by what happened to Helen. I agree that Jill made some wrong character judgements, which had consequences that touched all our lives. But she didn't do it deliberately." Seeing Rosemary about to challenge that, he held up his hand and quickly added, "I can see the truth of what you are saying. Difficult too, to see Jill blessed with Paul and William, while Helen struggles on. My father had no reason to give Helen anything, but in seeing the injustice of the situation he did what he felt best."

Rosemary's scorn didn't abate. "Say what you will, and it wasn't money she needed, but people's support, acceptance, and tender, loving care."

"If she'd chosen to go back to the flat she would have had that."

Frustrated Rosemary pushed past him. "Oh use your head. How could she? It was the place of memories and nightmares.

And Jill didn't like her 'pot' smoking friends."

"But she had her parents."

Fists balled by her side, Rosemary countered, "Who told you that? Was it Jill thinking Helen's Dad was upset because of her injuries? Untrue! But no-one took the trouble to find out. By the time she left hospital they'd rejected her. She told me in the taxi here, her Mum said that sleeping with an ex-jail bird made her a slut. It was no surprise to hear that 'a man like that' having found out she was pregnant, had conveniently disappeared, before marrying her." Seeing David's incredulous expression, Rosemary gave him a look of disdain. "And if that wasn't enough, her Mum added, that having been beaten up, it had, at least, solved the problem of her having the jail-bird's brat." Aghast, at cruelty Helen's mother, who obviously knew nothing about the 'jail-bird', he'd no words to speak. Rosemary seeing that said more calmly, "It was their perspective. Helen had got herself into bad company, and they didn't want a part of it, or her. The bad company, of course, was the Reinhardts, no less. But, the Reinhardts' abandoned her too." Put like that, he sank on the end of the bed, and put his head in his hands.

In the doorway Rosemary gave a derisive laugh, "Getting through to you is it, at last? You see it's the old, old story. Here have some money. Buy yourself some new clothes, you'll feel better. But you don't. You feel battered, degraded, you can't face people, and their judgements, or even their stupid advice, like 'pull yourself together' and 'get over it'. The situation you're in plays havoc with the mind, bringing confusion, a struggle to live, listlessness, loss of confidence and self worth. You can't work in that state, so eventually you lose your job. Helen had friends, but they were unreliable at best, and siphoning her money at worst."

David looked up at the tall girl, with her beautiful figure, and attractive face surrounded by a curtain of shiny, dark brown hair, and a deep sadness filled him, which reflected in his words. "I'd guess Rosemary to know it, you've experienced it, and for that, I can only feel sorrow for the deep pain still in you, and for Helen wherever she is. I don't know what else to say except I'm sorry. And Jill, hearing about this, will be sorry too. She sees you like a sister, and I think of you as part of our family." With a rueful grimace he stood, "But after your outburst tonight, that news might not be a blessing to you."

David saw the tears filling Rosemary's eyes before she turned, and ran down the stairs.

To give her time, he cleared up the bathroom, and meditated on Helen frittering away all that money, rejecting those who offered friendship, and how different people reacted in adversity and crisis. Jane had pushed into friendship with Rosemary, maybe she should have with Helen?

He sighed, it was too late now, but he could ensure Rosemary felt she supported. He ambled down to find her on her knees, making a pile of papers for the dustbin. With a small smile he gently inquired, "Are you alright?"

Wide doleful eyes looked up at him. "I'm sorry, I shouldn't have said all that. And…well, thank you for saying what you did, about Jill seeing me as a sister, and my being part of your family."

He placed a comforting hand on her shoulder, "Please, don't let things fester, speak to Jill, clear up any misconceptions. I don't think Helen will come back, and guess she doesn't want you to find her. Have a chat with the landlady. If she's owed money I'll pay it, but she'll have no trouble renting this out again, it's so compact and bijou." With eyes brimming with tears Rosemary mouthed 'thank you', and feeling uncomfortable, he suggested, "I'll finish the washing up, and clean the fridge. There doesn't seem much here of any value, but we could store in the loft anything you think Helen might want if she comes back."

Later getting ready for bed he reflected on the situation and considered how quickly Rosemary's anger had flared. Had she been the same with Chris County and Robert Jones? One thing he knew now was that in the past Rosemary had suffered similarly to Helen.

He couldn't remember the last time he'd awoken on a Monday morning with no specific reason, or purpose, for getting up. But his habit, like his father wasn't to hang about in pyjamas, but he did have a leisurely bath, before dressing and going down to get his breakfast. He felt he'd regressed five years, when he'd lived alone in the house, before its renovation. The words, the day he'd proposed to Jane, came to mind. It was harder to live with out her, than he could have ever imagined.

Upstairs, he sat at his desk in the study, and tried not to dwell on the space where the twins' cots had so recently been. He pulled out a new notebook and opened his Bible at Psalm 37, where God promises to give His people the desires of his heart. But it said more than that, and he felt to pray and declare those words over his life. "Lord, I have committed my way to you. I trust you to act on my behalf. And your word says, 'if we do that, then you will 'bring forth vindication as the light, and your righteousness, as the noonday'. When will that noonday come for me, Lord? When will these trials be over?" He tapped the Bible with his finger, "I know this tells me to be still, and wait patiently for you, not to fret over those who carry out wicked devices, but being an action man I find that hard. I can't have Jane back, but I want my babies back, my life back, when will that happen, Lord?" Yet, he knew God was building his trust, to believe in His promises, even when there was another hurdle to jump, or barrier to face. He didn't always get answers to his prayers, but grief, stress, struggle, tension, worry did dissipate when he spent time reading God's Word and talking to him.

Deeply engrossed in doing that, and writing to the Lord, as Jane used to do, several hours passed as he poured out his heart. God hadn't left, or forsaken him, He had good plans and purposes to be worked in, and through, his life. Resting in the knowledge of God's love, he jerked up at his doorbell ringing. With no further thought, filled with fresh energy, he bounded down the stairs, opened the door, and said, cheerily, "DI Jordan, what are you doing here?" A reporter was hovering at the end of the path, he stood back to indicate Jordan should enter."

Once inside Jordan answered. "I've come with news." David indicated to go upstairs as Jordan continued, "We've been trying to ring you, but all we get is the unobtainable signal, and your sister's telephone just rings and rings."

"That's because Jill and Paul have gone to stay with my parents," he pointed to his telephone, "Nuisance phone calls, so I've left it off the hook. Come into the dining room. I could do with a cup of tea."

"Daniel Kemp is on his way, he's contacted your father who expects to get here soon."

"My father?" Dread began to fill him, but David had to ask, "Is this good, or bad news?"

"If you don't mind, I'll wait until the others get here to save repeating myself."

Standing in the archway to the kitchen he fought panic, and made casual conversation. "Daniel obviously hasn't far to come from Lincoln's Inn, but my father coming from Bath will take a while." Moving into the kitchen, he put the kettle on, his hand shaking as he took out the cups and saucers.

As he stepped back into the dining room, Jordan nodded toward the large clock on mantelpiece, "Kemp said the train your father was on was due into Paddington at 11.20 am. He should be here in about five minutes." As he raised his eyebrows in surprise, Jordan informed him. "Kemp spoke to him several hours ago, and we planned to convene here at 11.45. The doorbell rang as if on cue. In summoning his lawyer and father, this had to be important. On his way to the front door he tried to assess the situation from Jordan's manner.

They'd not even convened around the table, before his father was demanding, "So Jordan, what's happened that's so significant, that you needed us here?"

Jordan, having taken it upon himself to make the pot of tea, waved them to sit down. "First, DI Gage and DCI Manning, sent their apologies for not being present, but felt it would be a waste of police time for them to attend, when I could pass on the relevant information." At that David glanced around at the faces, and was then surprised as Jordan said, "DI Gage, in particular asked me to thank you, Mr Reinhardt, for the input you had in their enquiries." As he nodded his acknowledgement, his father and Daniel sat forward, with an air of expectancy. "The information you obtained from Walter Nimbya confirmed what we knew, and helped us locate Walter's car repair business, which closed down two years ago. The 'For Sale' notice is still stuck across its doors." He paused to look at his notebook. "Bear with me, I've only notes made from my conversation with DI Gage this morning. An ex-employee told the police, Henry worked for Walter until two years ago when there was a row. Henry stormed out shouting, 'I've only taken what was rightfully mine'. Later Walter told the staff Henry had cleaned him out and there was no money for wages. Apparently, loyal to Walter, they finished the work they had, and Walter, having asked the customers to pay in cash, gave it to them. Walter was respected, whereas his brother was not."

Unable to wait, David asked, "Is there a connection between Walter's bankruptcy, and Carlton?"

DI Jordan smiled across at him. "Yes! Two years before Walter's bankruptcy, he'd moved his accountants to Jeffrey Charlston and Associates. It would appear Carlton had changed his name to evade detection, and then set about embezzling the Nimbya's out of their money. There's no registration of that company at Companies House, no record of Charlston paying tax, or national insurance, but Charlston did have a bank account, which closed the week after Walter's business failed. It's my guess, Carlton lived off small businesses, his accountancy expertise gained their confidence, while he stole their money. Yet Henry, and Carlton's greed for Walter's money, opened up the opportunity for Carlton to take all, rather than skim off the top. The ex-employee interviewed told the police Jeffrey Charlston was always around the garage in his sports car and flashing his money about. Henry was Charlston's close friend. Walter didn't like him, or his enticing his very attractive 17 year old daughter to go up West with him."

The vehemence of David's "Oh no!" had Daniel, and his father staring at him. DI Jordan nodded. "Carlton's previous proclivity with young woman, did bring consternation that he could be linked with her death."

Before David could ask, Daniel queried, "How did she die?"

"At the time, the police reported finding her in an alley where it was thought thugs had viciously attacked and robbed her. The extensiveness of her injuries for the little she had, and her subsequent death, gave rise to the suspicion there was more to it, but with no witnesses, and no suspects, the case fell by the wayside."

"And was she pregnant at the time?"

Jordan sent him a rueful grimace, "I knew you'd asked that. Yes, the post mortem report said about eighteen weeks."

David groaned, and wrung his hands in distress, as he asked, "Do you think Walter believing it was Carlton decided he'd nothing to lose and avenged his daughter's death?"

Jordan looked up from his notes, "I'm coming to that."

On a heavy sigh, David sat back, steepled his forefingers against his mouth. How devastating that news must have been to Walter, and his wife.

"The initial visit to Walter's garage showed it boarded up, the doors padlocked, and clearly not opened recently. However enquiries revealed that the premises had a small yard, and an outside toilet, and, on the suspicion that Walter could be inside, officers' broke in just before six this morning. They found Walter in the driver's seat of an old car."

Puzzled David sat forward. "I don't understand! Why, when Walter said he couldn't face prison, did he stay…?"

Jordan butted in, "He won't be going to prison."

"No! Why? What did he say? "

"I'm afraid he was dead." As grief arose for a man he barely knew, David slumped forward, put his elbows on the table and his head between his hands. Jordan explained, "It was suicide, by inhalation of fumes from a hose connected to the exhaust. He'd fed into the car with enough fuel to do the job, and run out. Carefully planned, and thought to have happened about four days ago. Beside Walter, on the seat, was a brown envelope, addressed to you, Reinhardt." At that news he sat up as Jordan went on, "It had a stamp, looked as if it had been sealed, and re-opened to add a final piece of paper."

Daniel sighed, "Hopefully that was the promised confession."

"Yes Mr Kemp, Nimbya was true to his word. He has provided an irrefutable confession. He gave the reasons why he pushed Carlton through that glass, and subsequently, beat him to death. You are once again a free man Mr Reinhardt."

Relief, mingled with sorrow, as the church clock chimed twelve in unison with the one on the mantelpiece. Instantly David recalled the Psalmist words he'd read a few hours earlier. 'The Lord brings forth your vindication as the light, and your righteousness as the noonday." His heavenly Father had been true to His word, 'the gates of hell had not prevailed' against him. If only, he'd had opportunity to share the Lord's love with Walter.

Daniel queried, "If the letter is written to my client, when can he expect to receive it?

"Hard to say, being its evidence. The envelope also included Walter's Will written on a Post Office form dated two weeks ago. Police have visited the witnesses who he asked to confirm his signature, but they didn't know anything about him. His Will states that the monies in his account should be used to pay for his, and his brother's funeral, and the remainder to be share between his faithful employees. He attached a list."

His father spoke. "Walter sounds like a good man, but in grief lost his way."

Jordan nodded. "I'm told it's a three page confession. I've written down the main facts. It includes the demise of his business, the belief Carlton went off with his daughter, and subsequently murdered her. Recently he'd discovered Henry lived and worked only twenty miles away, and in wanting to be reconciled to him after his wife's death he went to The Travellers' Rest after the funeral on 26th June. He responded to Carlton's call for Henry, watched you restrain him and saw Carlton hit you and push your wife. Enraged, he slid around the door to head-but and propelled Carlton through the glass door. He speaks of his anguish at believing he'd unintentionally murdered his brother, but felt greater pain on hearing others had taken the opportunity to do so."

Tears filled David's eyes, "I liked Walter. What a sad end."

Jordan hummed. "Walter and his brother, knew all about where and where not to punch, they were both heavy-weight boxers. And as we haven't told the press how Carlton died, Walter's confession is conclusive evidence. His letter to you says, he hoped to meet you. He wanted to say sorry, for the untold suffering, and expense to you and your family, because he wasn't brave enough to come forward. He'd signed that, the same signature as the Will. He'd added a PS of how he was pleased to talk with you." Jordan read from his notes, "He wrote, 'I've nothing to lose, I want to ensure justice is done, and that's why I decided to hold back the letter, so it's receipt, would be too late to change the outcome'.

The extra page is a list of the women Carlton had used and abused, including his daughter, and we can only assume that confession came forth, under what we would politely call 'extreme duress'! Not much use to us now, but nevertheless might clear up some unsolved crimes. At the bottom of that page, before Walter's signature were the words, "This kind of justice only prevails, because the law fails."

Stunned David thought of their conversation. Walter had read the papers and quoted, 'you're a man of justice', and in knowing his faith did he think God's justice was still a life for a life? It was obvious now, that Walter's passport to escape prison was to commit suicide. Why hadn't he understood that? If he had he could have saved two men's lives. Walter's words, in his strange mixed accent, came clearly to mind, 'Don't have regrets at what you might have done, or what might have been, move on from here, and live life for these dear ones'. It also made sense why Walter didn't think God would be with him, but even at this late juncture, David intended to ask the Lord to have mercy on his soul.

CHAPTER 20

Several days after the case was closed, Rosemary announced she was taking two weeks annual leave from ITP. And so after the challenges of the past two months, this last two weeks of August had brought David mind-numbing boredom, and at night, desperation in his loneliness. His parents had suggested he bring the twins and join Paul, William and Jill until her birthday on 6th September, but staying a few days with his parents was one thing, a few weeks another! He was genuinely grateful that his father took over when he was ill, but it had been a battle to stop the Norland nanny returning with the twins'. The victory only came when Lorna offered to help on the days Joyce couldn't, but neither stayed over a night.

As a bachelor he'd managed basic living of cooking sausages and mash, and Mrs P, the ITP canteen and business lunches had filled the gaps! Loving the twins was one thing, but it was mindless responsibility with endless washing, feeding and sleeping. And what a trial to take the twins around Tesco, and after his first attempt he took Joyce with him. Together they stocked up so either she, Mrs P or Lorna could cook a meal, and leave it in the fridge for him, when he got up. His day started at 4.00 pm, and ended when either Joyce, or Lorna, appeared the following morning.

Alan and Janet organised for several couples to visit in the evenings, some brought a meal with them to share, so food, and company! The first weekend they looked after the twins' both on Saturday and Sunday so he could get six hours sleep, and Adam and Fiona so loving them had asked Janet if she too could have twins!

Last weekend, Bob and Lillian asked to stay, ostensibly to visit the London sites, but it soon became clear the twins were the attraction. Grateful to have a break, he wanted to do something 'normal', but he felt aimless without Jane.

However, this coming weekend with what was almost now a Reinhardt tradition they wanted to gather together for Jill's birthday in Bath. To him, it would be foolish, on his own, to attempt a drive of five hours with the twins, to Bath. They were small for nine weeks, their feeds still three hourly, but being more aware of their surroundings they needed more stimulus, and had certainly learnt how to air their lungs! Paul volunteered to come by train, and drive back with him, but a day later Maria, able to take a few days holiday, suggested she accompany him, going on Thursday and coming back on Monday.

Despite the fact Maria was only nineteen, several people at the pub where they ate lunch, mistook her for his wife and the twins' mother. Maria told him about being out with Paul two years earlier. "I was returning from the toilet and this rather drunk young man started to talk to me. Dad, seeing that walked over, and very politely said, 'Excuse me, the young lady is with me'. The guy belligerently stuck his face into Dad's to reply, "You mate, that's absurd, you're old enough to be her father." To which Dad looked him in the eye to retort, "That young man is because I am her father!" Maria giggled, "The poor chap backed away muttering 'Sorry, sorry.' Dad said that was a relief because he didn't know what he'd have done if the guy had challenged him further, because 'hello, I'm a doctor', wouldn't have helped in that situation!"

That had made him laugh, and he'd felt better for it. Maria's chatter reminded him of Jane's light hearted banter. As the journey progressed, he began to unwind and tell a few stories of his own, enjoying Maria's interest in why Jane had called him her guardian angel!

By the time they arrived, unpacked and fed the twins, he realised the change was already becoming a rest. And although cross his father hadn't consulted, or told him, he found at ten o'clock he was welcoming the first of the two nannies hired for the weekend, one for night duty, the other doing midday to seven. Too tired to protest he'd gone to bed, but having met the capable and qualified Jenny, who'd a family of her own, and did the odd overnight shift to boost her income, he felt quite confident to leave them in her hands.

The next morning, with a hollow nervous rush to his stomach, he wondered why he hadn't awoken during the night to the twins' cries. Then realising he wasn't at home, and a nanny was doing his job, like a contented cat he stretched in pleasure, at having his longest sleep in nine weeks.

Shaved, washed and dressed, he arrived downstairs to eat his breakfast, while his Mum and Maria got the twins ready to go shopping. And despite the dull day, he enjoyed traversing Bath's Georgian thoroughfares and enjoying the quaintness of little shops down cobbled streets, but had trouble stopping his Mum buying everything from cot mobiles to twin push chairs.

On their return Nanny Partridge had arrived, curtly introduced herself, and moved forward to take over. The large, matriarchal woman eyed him sternly, and firmly stated babies should be fed in the 'nursery'. The only 'nursery' he knew was the spare bedroom on the second floor which, with the arrival of William, his Mum had had redecorated with Winnie the Pooh wallpaper. With a small smile his Mum picked up Rebecca, and led Nanny Partridge carrying Joshua up the stairs, while suggesting he make, and bring up the bottles.

Maria, with a picnic lunch, had gone off on Jill's old bike to get some exercise and explore, and as 'usual' his Dad was at work. He couldn't remember the last time he'd been alone with his Mum to enjoy a late and leisurely lunch. And in her new, and brightly refurbished kitchen, they sat in the bay window and looked out at the magnificent view across the valley, to the hills beyond. After a couple of glasses of very fine red wine with French bread and cheeses, he began to pour out his heart and thoughts about the future without Jane.

Some of the questions his Mum asked he'd considered in the long nights of looking after the twins, but as yet, had no clear answers. Did he want to return to ITP? Was London the right place to bring up children? Should he employ a nanny, or stay at home and look after the twins himself? With a loving smile his Mum suggested, "There are options you might not have considered. I'd love it if you moved nearer, I could help, and perhaps Jenny would come on a regular basis. And maybe I shouldn't say this, but it would give you an opportunity to work with your father, perhaps in preparation for his retirement."

In astonishment he gasped, "Dad retire? I know he'll be sixty-five in January, but he's made no mention about it to me. Even after we had that discussion about a memorial to Jane, and relieving him of some of his wealth, there's never been an inkling of that. I've been pleased, and relieved that he's never pressured me to follow in his footsteps, and suspect he'll still be working at 80."

Eyebrows raised his Mum, with a sad grimace, said, "You know that's always been a problem, he's responsible for the Company, loves the research and has poured his life into that, often to the detriment of his home and family." Tears filled her eyes, "I've often felt unloved, and alone without his support."

At her unexpected confession tears filled his. That same trait of being involved in work had caused him to miss much of Jane's

263

chatter, and the life she led when he wasn't there. Yet Jane, like his Mum, for his Dad, had always been there for him. Had Jane felt alone and unsupported? Fresh grief welled up within him, inwardly he prayed, 'Sorry Lord, sorry Jane, forgive me for my thoughtlessness, and he determined if he should ever marry again, he would spend time listening, discussing and supporting his wife.

Carefully wiping her eyes his Mum apologised. "I'm sorry David, this is about you, not me. I don't know how you envisaged family life, or what your future holds. Jane coming into our lives, and leaving so abruptly has changed us all, even your Dad."

"Was it just Jane? I know after God's intervention in Jill's life you both started to go to church. Dad has mellowed, but is it just a Sunday thing to him?"

Putting her hand over his, she answered, "Your Jane's openness, and willingness to share her faith, at first, irritated your Dad. But when he saw it wasn't just talk, that she lived what she believed, it made him think. He liked the way she rose to his challenges, was open to learn, quick to apologise, never blamed others for her mistakes, and exuded happiness and love. That was when your Dad realised the difference between fanatical religion, and genuine relationship with the Father, Son and Holy Spirit. He's interested, and studying it."

At that he smiled. "That was my first reaction, until I realised Christianity wasn't academic theory, but 'taste and see that the Lord is good'."

"I know dear. Jane, Joyce and Ted all stirred childhood memories of church, school assemblies, and my friend Angela Trentham who loved Jesus, and often invited me into her home. I've always believed, prayed even, but until Jane came along I hadn't heard about being 'born again' and committing your life to the Lord, it was something only nuns did! But Jane's faith stepped up my daily seeking the Lord for my life. Your Dad's not spoken of commitment, but I believe during that time over Jill, it so rocked his controlled, enclosed little world it was like the words of 'Amazing Grace', 'I once was blind, but now I see'!" Your father realized, despite his research, philanthropy to poor nations, he'd been blind to the love of God, and the love in his heart for his own family. But like you he's a man who does nothing lightly, he wants to find God on his terms, and in his time. But since Jane's gone, his grief has been evident to me, even if not to others."

David wanted to ask what had made her fall in love with an introverted, stern, intimidating man. And, as if she read his mind, her eyes twinkled as with a wide smile, she said, "There are similarities between you and your father!" You both have a gruff exterior, but within is a caring heart. You know he's very protective of me. In the early days before his research built into a multi-million business…" For a moment she trailed off, but curious he kept his eyes on her, and she continued, "I met your father when I was nineteen while skiing in Switzerland." Thoughtfully she added, "He's always been better at expressing himself in writing than speech! Anyway, a year later he spent a summer holiday at our farm. My parents liked his serious manner, and I liked his looks, for at twenty-four he was big, bronzed with dark brooding eyes and thick raven hair. My friends were so jealous of my gorgeous hunk and…" Briefly she looked embarrassed, "Well let's just say when he kissed me my toes curled…" At his wry smile, his mum responded, "And I rather think the Reinhardt chemistry worked for Jane, as it did for me!" After a brief pause, she continued, "As soon as I reached twenty-one I left home to live in Germany. Not with him, that would have never have done, but at first with his parents while I learnt German, then I worked and flat shared, we got engaged and married a year later."

Still thinking of Jane, and their chemistry, he said in a hoarse whisper, "Jane was my soul mate."

Leaning across the table she patted his hand, "I know, but you will love again, it won't be the same, but Paul thought he couldn't love after losing Beth, yet he and Jill are so happy together… and talking of which I think I hear a car?"

Paul, Jill and William arrived back from a three day trip to Wales in a flurry of noise bringing Nanny Partridge to stand at the top of the winding staircase to say, "Quiet please. The twins are sleeping!"

As they all looked up, Jill, wide-eyed in astonishment questioned in a stage whisper, "Who is that?"

To answer David drew her out of sight through the kitchen door. "That sister dear, is our father's provision so we can have a relaxing weekend. Nanny Partridge is one of two nannies hired to look after the twins and William."

Incensed Jill demanded, "What! After I told Dad when we arrived here we were quite capable of looking after our own son. Did you know about this?" Arms folded, Jill stared at him for an answer.

"Not until I got here yesterday." And to placate her, he added,

"I think Dad's done it more for me than you, so while here I get a good night's sleep." Jill hummed, and he continued, "This woman is a bit of a dragon, but Jenny who is 'sleeping in' during the night, is very different."

An hour later, it was agreed by all that Nanny Partridge's time in the house would be short-lived, the strict discipline and regime she wanted to impose on the twins and William was from Victorian times. That might suit his father whose attitude had always been, 'children should be seen and not heard', but that wasn't their idea of family life. However, his Mum persuaded them to keep Nanny Partridge for the weekend so he could have a break, without worrying about the twins' needs.

During dinner, around the table there was the usual lively discussion and banter, and Jill, amused looked at Paul and commented, "Paul, tell everyone about your run-in with Nanny Partridge."

As all eyes went to focus on Paul, David caught his father's scowl, probably at what he perceived criticism of his 'nanny' provision for them over the weekend. Jill also seeing that remarked, "Oh Dad, she's a tyrant! You should have heard her lecturing us on the importance of having balanced diets and daily eating fresh fruit and vegetables. I had to stifle a smile at the way Paul listened, nodded attentively, and he rebuked her."

Stroking his beard, Paul shrugged. "I merely agreed with her by saying, 'Nanny Partridge, I'm constantly trying to instil that in my patients'."

Amused Jill reported, "You should have seen the horrified look on her face. Her hand flew to her throat, she turned beetroot red, and admitted, 'Oh my, oh dear! I didn't know you were a doctor. I'm so sorry. Forgive my presumption."

In a serious tone, Paul, stated, "Which Jill goes to show some people, still have respect for my profession." He gave her a wide-eyed, quelling look.

Undeterred Jill continued, "But you did rebuke her, albeit kindly."

"I only suggested that, in future, it might be wise to consider if it was more prudent to wait to be asked for her views before giving them."

Jill looked around, "I know it's unkind, but after she'd been so dictatorial, I couldn't help being pleased that flustered she grabbed on the twins' bottles said, 'Yes, yes, of course, you're right doctor', and scurried upstairs. Perhaps tomorrow she'll have a different attitude, but Dad don't employ her again!" Jenny arriving at ten o'clock prompted an opposite response with her friendly, helpful, and respectful manner.

David, after a second unbroken night's sleep could feel the sadness, loneliness, self pity was dissipating, helped by his family's bond of love which had strengthened through grief. And, the unexpected heart to heart with his mother yesterday, he knew was part of that. And at peace, as the family gathered around the breakfast table, and his father poured the champagne to celebrate Jill's birthday, he toasted her saying, "Sister dear, may this be the best year yet."

Quietly she said, "Paul says I have to wait until later for my present from him, I can't imagine what it will be." She giggled, "I've seen no evidence of it, even though I've tried to search his pockets, but that ended in…" Laughing she added, "Well moving on… I need my breakfast, before the alcohol goes to my head!"

Maria helping William into his high chair commented, "William and I have had breakfast, we were up before Jenny left. She told me, 'Your Dad was up early, he kindly fed one baby as I fed the other.' Puzzled, because I knew Dad was still in bed, I realised Franz it was you. Jill, you should have seen Jenny's face when I explained you weren't my sister, but my step-mother!"

David and his mother exchanged a surprised looked at his father feeding a baby while Jill fretted, "Oh Maria, there's only ten years between us, please don't tell people that. I'd far rather people thought of us as sisters."

An hour later, with the Stemmings part of the family departing for the shops, he was even more amazed when his Dad suggested, "We can manage the twins until Nanny Partridge arrives at midday. Why don't you do something you enjoy? You used to like the river. I know your boat's gone, but perhaps a walk along the tow path?"

It was one of those idyllic days, blue sky, warm sunshine, and as he turned down the road leading to the river he hummed to himself, then stopped, his face grim. At the family gathering this time last year he'd been trying to persuade Jane to stop taking the contraceptive pill. When at the bottom of the hill the bus into Bath passed, he thought of Jane's first visit here, and grinned. They'd just got engaged and she, acting the tourist had enjoyed walking around the Roman Baths and afternoon tea in the Pump Rooms.

David stood on the bridge overlooking the river where boats

and barges nestled against the bank. Memories flooded in. When his grandparents decided to sell their farm in Bristol to move into a luxury residential home on the Bristol Downs, his parents had bought the house in Kelston. Jill was thirteen, and he'd just finished reading Law at Oxford with the hope of a place on the one year vocational course at the Inns of Court School of Law. Demand was such he missed out that year, so while waiting to reapply, he joined a London firm of solicitors. And with a discipline of study, he used the evenings to learn the rudiments' of accountancy. Time spent in Bath, was either a long weekend, or a week's holiday, it had never been his home. Eighteen months later, while flat sharing, he'd the opportunity of purchasing a semi-derelict house, and after making it secure and water-tight, he'd moved in. By then, he was on his law course, and the Bar Council had found him a pupilage to Anthony Chalfont, a leading Queen's Councillor.

It was in that summer he purchased a second hand rowing boat. Jill, then sixteen, constantly nagged him to take her with him. When he finally agreed, she appeared dressed like a lady going punting on the River Ox, and had been upset when he'd not provided cushions in the bow for her to lie on. To appease her he covered his canvas bag with his thick knit sweater, and the short rowing trip to Saltford had been pleasant enough, if not chilly for him in a thin shirt! But despite his explaining that for a barrister in training it would be sheer stupidity, to buy alcohol in a pub for an under aged teenager, she'd sulked when he had a beer and she a coca-cola. For sheer devilment, back at the boat house, he'd rocked the dinghy to scare her, but he hadn't bargained she'd fall in. Or, that the bedraggled heap he'd dragged out of the river, would continue to scream abuse at him as she walked dripping wet all the way back to the house! That was thirteen years ago, but he knew, not forgotten! Jill with a glint in her eyes, still used the expression, "David's rocking the boat" during family discussion times, and four years ago, alerted his family to his interest in Jane by cooing across the table that Christmas, "My friend Jane is rocking David's boat!"

Today, as he stood on the bridge only a lone canoeist broke the tranquillity of the water. Over the years Jill had continued to be his loveable, scatty, batty sister, yet since Paul's arrival she'd become quieter and more content. Yet, he knew, she'd love it when, after their family lunch, Paul whisked her away for forty-eight hours pampering, before she became too rotund with baby

Stemmings.

He crossed the road and looked at the view from the other side of the bridge where the river, with weeping willow branches nearly touching the water, wound its way towards Saltford between green fields and hills. After the overnight rain he decided against the tow path, his father wouldn't appreciate him arriving with muddied shoes and trousers. He glanced at his watch, at a reasonable stroll along the road it would take about forty-five minutes to the pub in Saltford, he'd have time for a beer before everyone arrived for lunch.

The fields alongside the road were ripening with a variety of crops, the valley stretched out before him. He looked back at his parents house nestled against the hill and considered if he wanted to move to Bath. He'd miss working with Exhibitions, but he'd not yet had time to work out his new role in ITP. His house was all he desired it to be, and very convenient with Paul and Jill in the basement flat. And generally despite their tiffs it was a happy situation.

The sun was bringing unexpected heat, he paused to remove his jumper and watched a train speeding through the valley going from Bath to Bristol. Trains had a track, its path and goal determined, with life you never knew what was around the next corner! After the train had long gone he remained thoughtful, gazing into the distance over the field of maize before him. Jane on numerous occasions in her enthusiasm for the Lord had embarrassed, intimidated, bored or tired him. Was that because she'd only a short time to complete her mission on earth? Once she told him crossly, "Oh David, do stop scowling. What kind of witness is that to a loving, caring God?" At that rebuke he stalked off and beyond being polite had barely spoken to her for several days. Yet she'd not admonished him further, and chattered away in her usual fashion ignoring what, after all, was very childish behaviour.

Yesterday his Mum had said, 'What will be, will be, you have to grieve, then accept and move on." Before him was the magnificence of God's creation and a desire grew to cry out his pain to the maker of heaven and earth. No-one was around so out over the fields he boomed, "Oh Father God, I am not going to ask you why, I believe your Word and your promises, but Lord I loved and I miss Jane. Forgive me Lord for not treating so precious a gift with more thought, care and love. If only she could be here, laughing up at me, teasing me, and enjoying this beautiful day."

A cool, light breeze from behind blew over him causing him to shiver despite the heat. A perfumed aroma he associated with Jane met his nostrils. He stared at the maize swaying in the wind's wake. The rattling of leaves sounding like an amused whisper, "I am His, He is mine."

Astonished he glared at the tall, tight stems in the field several yards away, then feeling ridiculous he shouted 'Jane' as a question, as if she were there.

In answer it seemed a gust of wind blew hard into his back, as though to propel him forward, drawing that aroma around him. Beyond over the small stone wall that separated him from the field slightly below, the wind's strength opened a path in the swaying maize. The clacking of maize stems and leaves seeming to echo, "Come, Come."

Was he going mad? Had he emptied his lungs in such a heartfelt cry that his brain was suffering from a lack of oxygen making him hallucinate? That thought had barely passed through his mind when an even stronger gust hit him with such force in the small of his back he had to counter balance in order not to fall over. Muttering, "This must be you God" he didn't hesitate.

With a hand on the wall, he jumped down into the field and followed the wind's path, pushing his way through into the midst of the maize. It was so tall it rose several feet above his head. When the gust of wind no longer opened the way, he asked, "Which way, which way, Lord?" And, as though by divine hand leaves fluttered. Excitement mounting, and losing all sense of direction, he pressed through, the thick stems hitting against him, and their clattering together sounded like clapping. And suddenly there was silence. All movement ceased. He halted and instinctively looked up. The sky remained bright blue, but the sun didn't penetrate the maize that surrounded him. In that moment he'd the sensation of merging with creation, becoming part of the crop. The words came to him, "I am, who I am. You are in Me, and I am in you." What was happening? He wasn't drugged, or drunk. Moses saw a burning bush, but it didn't burn! It was surreal, yet awesome. Words from what he now considered 'Jane's song' came to mind, '*Remove the shoes from your feet, Lift your eyes to the mercy seat, Can't you see that the veil is torn in two, For this is hallowed ground where we stand…*" David bent his head with that intention, but instead of seeing his feet, his eyes focussed on the top of a head with golden, reddish brown hair. He gulped, in a voice no more than a whisper, he queried, "Jane?" In her own inimitable way Jane lifted her head to grin cheekily up at him. The heart-shaped face with the bobbed hair seemed to glow with health, "Oh my God, you're alive, and you're here." He grabbed her to him, expecting it to be an illusion, but she was real. That perfume, that smell of her freshly washed hair assailed his nostrils as he held her close. He buried her into his chest, and rested his head on top of hers booming, "Oh thank you Lord. I love you, I love you."

Jane pulled back her eyes full of love, laughter and teasing. It seemed she was speaking into his mind. "Isn't it glorious? Heaven is only a breath away. But for you, there's treasure to find in earthen vessels, follow the clues, and enjoy the journey. And at the end, in the revelation of eternity, we'll meet with our children, and all those whom we loved. But now you can say 'goodbye', with a proper kiss." As if knowing he had things to say, or ask, she gave a rueful smile and shook her head. Obediently he lowered his head toward her mouth. The warmth of those lips, the melting into her was more than a physical kiss, it touched the depth of his being, it set his heart on fire, not with sexual desire, but with love. He wanted to hold on to every second, to remember it forever that love for Jane, Jesus, the creator God, and all that He'd created. Her lips left his. His eyes flashed open. She was gone. His heart sank at her departure. He looked around, but couldn't see her. He called, but she didn't answer. Gradually creation separated itself from him bringing the reality of a man standing between tall stems of maize in the middle of a field. The surrounding crop rustling gently under the blue sky. Dazed, he wondered if he'd dreamt it, but he was wide awake, and the very air around him seemed alive with static electricity. He didn't move, he wanted to hold on to that place, he wanted more, oh so much more. Jane had assured him, in eternity there would be more. Heaven was only a breath away, and that brought peace to his heart. He'd a new life to lead, a treasure to seek, clues to find, and one day he'd be able to report to her all that had happened since they met in the midst of the maize crop. But he couldn't stay in there, he needed to know which way was out. That thought had barely registered when the sound of a train broke the silence. He knew the maize crop grew right up to the raised railway bank. If he followed that it would take him towards Saltford, and he could then get back on to the main road. He looked at his watch, 11.40 he felt that was significant, but didn't know why.

In the euphoria of what had happened, he slowly made his way to, and along the railway embankment into a green field. On hearing a farmer shouting at him about trespassing he headed toward him to apologise, but before he was near enough, the farmer marched off, leaving him to stare after him. Finally back on the main road he began to wonder if it had been real, and would anyone believe him if he told them? By the time he'd turned down the road leading to the pub he began to be amused, stupidly amused, laughter bubbled inside of him, everything seemed so funny, and on the road leading down to the pub, he stepped behind a large tree and let himself have a real belly laugh.

"David, David, is that you?"

Grinning stupidly he came around the tree, "Oh hello Jill." At the furrowing of her brow, through new guffaws of laughter he managed to get out, "Jane's been rocking my boat."

"How many drinks have you had?"

Nonchalantly, he leant back against the tree, and retaliated joyfully, "Sister dear, not a drop has passed my lips."

Grimly she stated, "Well that's not the way it looks to me. And where on earth have you been? Have you seen the state of your clothes?"

He chuckled delightedly. "You'd never believe it if I told you. I'm not sure whether it was here on earth, whether I was in the body or out of it, but it all felt pretty real." At her raised eyebrows, the shaking of her head , he looked down. Both his short-sleeved, light-blue cotton shirt and beige trousers were covered in brown and green smudges where the branches and stems had slapped against him. Blood from scratches on his bare arms had added to the strange pattern. He muttered to himself, "So much for not wanting to get muddy". That sent him into another fit of laughter, gurgling through that, "Oh my, I really did, I must have, it's true, I've done battle with a maize crop. It was real."

Jill tutted. "Couldn't you have walked down the road like any sensible person?"

"That was my intention, but the Holy Spirit and Jane had other ideas!"

She gave him a worried look and pointed out, "You've a host of bits and pieces stuck in your hair."

"Have I? God and His ways are mysterious their wonders to perform."

"Did you booze on Dad's malt whiskey before you left?"

At Jill's assumption he chortled, then catching the two sides of his open neck shirt declared magisterially, "I assure you sister dear, it's not Dad's whiskey that's made me high, but the wind of the Holy Spirit, the seeing of a vision and experiencing the fire of God's love in my heart, but I'm in good company the disciples were accused of being drunk too."

"Right, if you say so. Mum and Dad aren't here yet, so I suggest you go to the men's toilet and clean up." The inference behind Jill's tone was 'humour him', her expression one of concern.

And he had to admit, minutes later when looking in the mirror, to understanding Jill's consternation, but her question of why couldn't he be sensible and use the road, tickled him and he creased up in laughter.

He was still attempting to use his hand as a comb to remove cobwebs and other rather unsavoury bits from his hair into the wash basin when Paul arrived. Instantly Paul suggested, "If you aren't up to the party, I can drop you back and say you aren't feeling well."

Turning sideways he looked up at him while making a final run of his hand through his thick black hair, then he straighten to declare, "Paul I may seem drunk, but not with alcohol." Jovially he slapped him on the back. "I have just had the most incredible experience, and been overcome by God's love. Laughter just keeps bubbling up from me. Do you know what Jill just said? In repeating it he shook with mirth, "Isn't that just the funniest thing?" Paul's responded with a smile, but he could see from his eyes he was assessing him. "Look Paul I'm fine. How about you run me back to the house for a quick shower and change? A half an hour delay won't upset the party, and I can tell you about it on the way."

Paul left to explain to Jill where he was going, while David sat in the car and wondered how to temper his ecstatic joy. On the five minute journey he joyfully gave Paul a brief outline, and noted the scepticism in his voice as he commented, "It's beyond me." And as the water coursed over him in the shower, he chortled wondering if Paul was checking the dustbin for empty bottles.

After a series of questions on the return journey, which he did his best to answer, Paul cautioned, as they parked next to his father's Jaguar, "It might be better not tell the others. Jill was undecided as to whether you had been drowning your sorrows, or going insane. I'm not sure what to believe, but telling people will bring some kind of judgement."

His father stood as they entered, "Ah good you're here at last.

Jill told us you took some kind of short cut to get here and then needed to go home to get cleaned up. I'd have thought by now, my boy, you knew the area well enough not to stray off the beaten track. Right Margaret, let's get to that lunch, I'm starving."

As the family flowed into the restaurant, he stood back to say hello to Paula, Jim and the boys. As he smiled down at the boys, Phillip looked puzzled and asked, "Where's Rosemary?"

Richard ticked him off, "Don't be silly, she's not part of the family."

Philip frowned. "But Uncle David she's going to be isn't she, because we're asking Jesus about it?"

Jim was already heading into the restaurant, and Paula turning lifted her eyebrows with an expression, 'boys will be boys'. He drew them to one side, "Now boys, listen. Jesus knows what's best for us, and it might not be Rosemary." Phillip looked so disappointed, he rested a hand on his shoulder, "You can pray about my finding a wife, but remember prayer should always be in secret."

Bewildered Philip stated, "But Uncle David we can tell you because you're in on the secret."

The joy bubbling in him threatened to come out as a guffaw of laugher, but he managed to say seriously, "Yes, that's true, but if it's to remain a secret it has to be kept between ourselves."

Both boys nodded gravely, as his father boomed, "David, my boy, come on, you've already kept us waiting once today." Entering the room with the two boys his father sent him a hard stare, but that didn't deter the ecstatic feeling of love for those around him. Several times throughout the meal he caught Jill, or Paul staring thoughtfully at him. In his formative years there were days when he adored Jill as the baby of the family, and others when he resented her, the years between them making their relationship strained. But Jill's assistance in drawing Jane into his life had changed that enmity into friendship and respect. And this last year he didn't know how he would have managed without her and Paul. Maria sent him a teasing smile in the midst of holding a conversation with her father and his. William banging his spoon drew his attention to his bright blue eyes that constantly danced with mischief. His gaze drifted to Paula. The closeness he'd had with her when young, had naturally been exchanged to Jim when they married. Would his family believe him that Jane had persuaded God to give him a glimpse of heaven and allowed her to impart a message to him?

Drawn from his revelry he smiled at his father as he said, "David, my boy, you questioned my wisdom at hiring a nanny, but a couple of good nights' sleep and a walk has made you positively glow this lunch time."

Happily he agreed, and then amused added, "It's incredible what you can discover about creation" before laughter overtook him.

Paul shot him a warning glance, his Mum sent him a questioning look, Jill shook her head in dismay and, Maria intuitive as her great grandmother, chirped "Sounds to me as if you had some kind of adventure."

The waitress arriving with the coffee distracted them, but once poured his father stood to make a speech about it being Jill's birthday and their family drawn together in grief. As he began to speak of a memorial fund for Jane his mother interrupted. "Franz dear, this is Jill's birthday party, let's not get into that now. I want to hear about David's adventure."

The expected grunt didn't materialise instead his father smiled to say cheerfully, "Of course, but if I may finish with an announcement. Up to date we've only given away a few hundred pounds, but I have now transferred into the 'Jane Mackenzie Fund' the first ten thousand pounds." Astonished no-one spoke. As though embarrassed his father added sharply, "Charity giving is a tax break! We'll need to discuss how its spent." Then more pleasantly he finished, "But as you wish Margaret, let's hear from David" then extending his hand he indicated he should speak.

"First, thank you Dad. Tax break it may be, but Jane would be delighted by your generosity. And perhaps, not a coincidence, that Jane was involved in my amazing adventure today." With that he'd everyone's rapt attention as they listened, and as he relived his escapade, it brought further small details to mind. "I'd say the episode was about fifteen minutes, it felt like seconds. The electrostatic charge after Jane disappeared was such, I was unable to move. When it diminished I felt disorientated, followed the train line, and dazed found myself in a farmer's field. He waved and shouted at me. but. I'd no idea of the mess I was in until Jill pointed it out, so he probably thought I was a crazy tramp."

Jill bantered, "Or shining with God's glory, like Moses when he came down the mountain."

"You thought I was drunk! But the experience was so surreal it became funny causing laughter to bubble out of me."

No-one spoke, each caught up in their thoughts until his father boomed, "Well my boy, that's some story. You've never had much of an imagination, so I don't believe you made it up."

Bemused Jill commented, "You said, you weren't sure if you were in the body, or out of the body, didn't someone in the Bible write something similar?"

"My namesake Paul in 1 Corinthians 12.1"

Maria smiled, "Trust my Dad to know that. And, I believe you, David because it's an answer to my prayer." All eyes turned on the vivacious young girl. "On the journey to Bath, David talked about Jane, and her likening him to her guardian angel because once, when Jane was in danger, God had whispered in his ear, 'Jane needs you'. So, if God did that then, I asked if David could be given an opportunity to say a proper 'goodbye' to Jane. And as our heavenly Father often does, He went one better, letting Jane put words in David's mind in the same way as He does when speaking to us."

Everyone around the table looked thoughtful before Jill piped up. "Not only an answer to prayer Maria, but I'd say, that the Lord is so delighted at the way David has come through these past months, it's like his reward. Our loving heavenly Father's way of conveying that neither He, nor Jane, want you unhappy, lonely and bringing up the children on your own."

Excited Maria added, "You said, Jane conveyed to you about clues and looking for earthen treasure. People are called 'earthen treasure,' the clues could lead to the woman who will become the twins' mother?"

"Maria, who knows but God, but in reliving the scene I realise it's something I'm not going to forget."

David looked across at his Mum, who sent him a gentle smile, before saying, "Another woman in your life might feel unthinkable now, but it is a Reinhardt trait to slip into self-sufficiency and feel you can manage. You'll need someone like Jane who isn't intimidated by your forcefulness. And unlike me, will be woman enough to challenge you, when impatience and discipline, should be replaced by sympathy and understanding."

His father challenged gruffly, "Margaret, are you inferring that I am without sympathy or understanding?"

His mother patted his father's arm. "You've got a good heart for the poor and needy, yet for those close to you, there's a certain lack. I should have stood up to you more, in the way Jane did to David, and the way Paul does to you. But that doesn't alter my love for you."

His father grunted, then burst out, "Make sure David you don't find someone like that dreadful Felicity woman, she certainly could persist and persuade. Still in realising she wouldn't get any of my money she soon upped and left." He gave a loud humph. "Called herself an actress, she was that alright. Knew how to turn on the charm, stun us with her looks, even had, still has, her parents fooled." David grimaced as his father glared at him, "You allowed her to wheedle herself into your life, but once engaged she showed her true colours."

Riled at his father's perspective, there was a steely tone to David's outwardly calm reply. "It was my understanding as the daughter of one of your friends you encouraged that relationship. Granted, she's stunningly attractive, but over the years our relationship was off and on, because I found her thinking rather shallow. Believing she had the right pedigree, she appeared the natural choice and I didn't hear any objections from you at the time! But Dad, it is to you I give my thanks." His father raised a quizzical eyebrow. "In telling Felicity you didn't intend supplementing what she considered my meagre income, it saved me the trouble of breaking off the engagement. After meeting Jane, I realised I didn't love Felicity."

David sent his father a questioning look. "Am I to conclude from your generosity into Jane's Fund that you believed she was a good woman?" The response of a sharp, 'of course' had David continue, "Then that is proof that I'm quite capable of discerning a good woman when I meet her."

With a grunt his father stood. "What I am discerning is it's time we left. Paul, transfer your cases into my Jaguar, and enjoy the drive to your hotel."

Mystified Jill exclaimed, "Hotel?"

Paul grinned, "Those diamond ear-rings weren't to wear at home. Lillian has altered that beautiful ball gown to fit your more rotund figure, and tonight we are going to Cardiff for a dinner/dance where you, my lady, are going to be belle of the ball."

Maria clapped her hands, "Oh Dad that is so romantic."

With a shrug, and a grin at Maria, Paul turned to receive the car keys. "I confess, Franz, my lady's carriage of a Morris Minor wouldn't have done her justice so thank you. Now we'll arrive in style."

"Paul, I need the Morris' keys otherwise everyone will have to walk home. And goodness knows what might happen next."

"Dad, if I thought Jane would be there I'd do it again, but I know it was her final 'goodbye'.

As though 'just married' they gathered to wave Paul and Jill 'goodbye'. Philip and Richard distracted William as he started to cry, and when they began to break up to go back to the house, David announced, "I hope you don't mind, but I'd like some time alone to disseminate all that has happened. I'll get a bus back."

Gruffly Franz assured him, "Forget the bus, I'll come for you at five o'clock.

Wandering along the road past the riverside houses he considered how alive, vibrant, happy and excited Jane had been, as if knowing his future. But oh that kiss, touching as it had the depths of his being, changing his mourning to joy. And was the treasure in earthen vessels a woman? He thought of the single women he knew.

Work relationships could be complicated, before Jane he'd not entertained them, and since Jane, he'd barely noticed ITP's array of young women.

Out of propriety, many women in the church wouldn't do more than smile or coo at the twins, but he guessed as time went by there were several who might show an interest in him. Did any of them interest him? That was an easy 'no', but then he'd only said 'goodbye' to Jane today.

Mary, the District Nurse, would like to be a contender for his affections! His mind went to the day when she'd been sitting on a bench in Kensington Gardens reading a book. It would have been rude to ignore her, and impossible to avoid her, so he'd rushed by calling 'hello' as he passed. Her feigned surprise needed more practice, as did his ability to brush off unwanted females who jumped up, and said they were going his way, and would walk with him! Afraid she might misconstrue conversation as interest, he said little, and let her chatter on about babies, her work, her life history, all he felt to impress him. When they turned into Church Road she'd pointed out a new restaurant, and asked if he'd eaten there. When he said he hadn't, she'd suggested, 'Perhaps we could try it one evening?' At that, he'd prayed for inspiration and answered, "To be honest Mary I've lost all interest in going out and about, and, with these two little ones to care for, I can't see that changing in the foreseeable future."

Disappointment had shown in her eyes, but with bravado, she'd given a rueful smile. "Well, I'll still be around at church when you feel able to do so." To that he said nothing, but she'd added, "The danger in your circumstances is to bury yourself in your children believing it's what you should do, but you deserve a life too. You need to give yourself a regular break of something adult and normal. The twins will cope if you're not there." That was true for they were happy with anyone who fed them, and he was appreciating this break.

Yesterday his mother had told him Felicity had returned to America. Her parents hadn't been impressed with Conran, or his drug habit. And after their expressing the wish, 'it would be lovely if she and David could get together again', his mother had pointed out that she couldn't see Felicity mothering twin babies. But he remembered the unmistakable gleam in Felicity's eye when she thought he was a free man, the very thought caused him to shudder. Yet his words telling her to get lost must have penetrated her thick skin for she'd pursued him no further.

At the end of the path he turned by the second public house to lean against the fence and watched the surfers ride over the weir. He smiled, Rosemary the closest single woman in his life, was the one who desired him least! He'd been pleased she trusted him to help her with the cottage, yet she'd made it obvious she didn't want his further involvement or intrusion, into her life. However, he'd discovered the only reason he'd been allowed to help was because she'd no-one else to turn to! But obviously appreciating his help, and wanting to return the favour, she'd tentatively offered to help pack up and dispose of Jane's clothes. Somewhat gruffly, he'd answered he wasn't ready, but he felt ready now. Rosemary would be back home this evening, he could ring and ask if she was still willing to pack up all Jane's things with the exception of the personal items that he could sort through later.

Behind him the Morris Minor's horn beeped. He walked to the car, "Good timing Dad, I'm ready." As he said that, he knew he was ready. This was God's timing for closure on his life with Jane, and the beginning of a new journey.

CHAPTER 21

On Monday afternoon returning from Bath David was saddened to see his bedroom bare of Jane's fripperies. He knew it was right, but it felt so wrong. Over the telephone he'd agreed with Rosemary that Jane's clothes, handbags and shoes go to the Oxfam Shop so others could benefit from them. The remaining personal items she'd packed into two medium-sized cardboard boxes. How little there was to represent a life that had been so alive and full.

Out the first box he picked up and hugged Jane's childhood teddy bear. A whiff of Jane's Madam Rochas perfume assailed his nostrils. The half empty bottle stood beside the scuffed shoes Jane danced in, the scarf she knitted, and her jewellery box. The only piece of jewellery, not in the box, was the gold bracelet with three entwined light chains locked with a heart. He'd given it to her as a wedding present, and he now retrieved it from his beside drawer. Each tiny charm held a memory. On one side of the heart was an exquisite golden key, a symbol of the unlocking of his heart, and on the other a gold ingot engraved with 'I love you' which turned over read 'All is yours'. The following Christmas he'd added an open book engraved with the words, 'Psalm 37:4'. On her birthday he added a 'J' and having whisked her away to Paris on their first wedding anniversary to Paris he'd purchased a miniature Eifel Tower. Jane pointed out that at the current rate she'd have thirty charms in ten years and suggested he stick to anniversaries. After a week's holiday celebrating their second anniversary he'd bought her a Maltese cross. This year he'd searched around London to find a castle, a reminder of their weekend in Windsor. But he had gone against Jane's wishes for he'd felt there was another significant event that deserved an addition to her bracelet. Putting forth his forefinger he lifted the charm specially commissioned to surprise her. Deep sorrow engulfed him as on his fingernail rested the image of two children holding hands standing on a small bar engraved in the tiniest writing 'The twins'. With the pretext of having the 'castle' charm soldered on to the bracelet he'd taken it to the jewellers, his intention to have that added too, and give it to her after their birth. But circumstances had decreed Jane had neither known, nor seen it. He determined not to ask, 'Why Lord?' Unable to confine the bracelet to storage along with her hairbrush, dressing table set and other personal items, which one day would be Rebecca's, he fingered it, and drifted in thought before putting it back in the drawer.

Inside the second box was the leather bound Bible he'd given Jane the first Christmas she worked for him,. Alongside was another translation from her Mum and Dad. Inside the dedication read: *'To Jane on your baptism, Together in Christ's family. Nothing can separate us from His love and eternal life. Romans 8:38. 5th July 1960.* The date, ten years to the day of her death! It was in that Bible she'd placed the two envelopes, one addressed to Rebecca, the other to Joshua. He put them, and the Bibles to one side. When the children were old enough he'd give them the letters and the Bibles. Underneath were daily Bible reading notes Jane used to spark off her prayer and questions to the Lord. She wrote letters to the Lord in shorthand notebooks, often finding she'd written the answers. These were stacked, the latest on the top.

In life these were private, in death...he questioned that. Could the notebooks contain the clues Jane had mention? Guiltily he flicked through pages of her neat handwriting. Each time he saw his name he stopped to read, often finding Jane asking for wisdom on a problem, or difficulty they faced, but also thanking the Lord for him. On 27th June the entry was short, probably because she was in labour, and written he guessed, while he was lunching with Paul. It included, *"David is being unusually patient considering it's my fault I am here."* 'Unusually patient' did she feel he was often impatient? The account of her hospital stay included her struggle to feel motherly, prayers for several girls, her desire to get home, a note about her panic attacks and her asking the Lord if she'd fulfilled her purpose in life. Why hadn't she told him about those attacks? Intrigued he read on, *'Lord, in years to come, I'll probably laugh about my need to write letters to the twins. David would feel my crying at something that may never happen was ridiculous...'* Tears filled his eyes, he swallowed hard, this notebook obviously had water damage, but he'd not suspected it was from Jane's tears! *'...but Lord what if it were true, I'd want to think he'd read of my love for him, for you and be comforted. What would you say to him?*

'My beloved son within you is My glory's glow, With Me, in your heart you'll always know, That even in life's bitterest blow

281

As did Peter hearing the cock crow, My Spirit is with you just allow it to flow, And let mutual respect and affection grow, For your children will show On whom your heart to bestow.'

It wasn't a literary work, but Jane, writing as the words came. She knew about his dream, the light in his heart, but he'd not experienced the glory cloud or the bitter blow when she wrote it. Had Jane recognised God's answer? With the back of his hand he wiped his wet face, and refocused on the page, '*I think Lord I'd want to say, 'Keep my memory, but not the pain. Lou's song comes to mind, for the Lord will lift us, and feed us, and bring us to life again.'*

Mindlessly, he stared at the page, then clasped it to his chest. Jane was happy, only a breath, her kiss had touched his innermost being. The pain was lessening, so often God's word had lifted him. Motivated by a need to hear Lou's song, he ran down the stairs into his lounge, found the LP and right track and sitting allowed the music and words to wash over him.

"*But precious to me is the death of my Saints, Don't you know you are on holy ground (And) when the lake of pain has been fully drained, I'll lift you and feed you and bring you to life again.* The song was about breaking up, yet those particular words were so right, tears flowed as he listened and the song ended, "*I love you, I'm near you, I'm here.*"

While allowing the truth of God's promises to soak into him the record continued to the last track. The words again felt as God speaking directly to him. "*Don't despair when you're conscious of the pain, Pain will fade but you'll find the joy has remained, And you'll have laughter in your soul when joy grows again.*"

These last months he'd had times of deep despair as he reeled under the blows of life and yearned for what he couldn't have. Yet unexpectedly laughter and joy had welled up on Saturday. The record on 'repeat' began again. When the last track came this time he knew he'd reached peace, and could find joy in which to embrace the future.

Light in step he headed down to feed the twins. About to round the corner to descend into the basement lounge he heard Jill say, "…David believes it." Rarely do eavesdroppers hear good of themselves, but still he hesitated and listened! "I thought he was either losing his mind or drunk, but like that song he's playing, 'joy' certainly bubbled up in him."

He strained forward to hear Rosemary's reply. "That's extraordinary!"

"I know! We didn't believe him at first. I wonder about the clues, the treasure in earthen vessels?"

Thoughtfully Rosemary said, "God made us from the earth. We're the vessels of His Holy Spirit. He sees those who love Him as His treasure. The Bible says, 'Your treasure is where the heart is. I'd say the treasure is the twins."

"What about a mother for the twins."

Rosemary snapped, "No-one could take Jane's place."

Fascinated, he didn't move as Jill continued, "True. But Jane would be the first to say she wasn't perfect. The Lord could bring someone even better into David's life. "

"I doubt he'd agree with that."

"But it's what Jane would have wanted. The Lord likes specific prayers, so I'd go for a committed Christian, aged 25-35, loves children and wouldn't be intimidated by David's stern manner. Amusement crept into Jill's voice, "A plus would be someone attractive, preferably had known Jane so she'd keep her memory alive for the children and ensure David didn't eulogise her! I believe, like the words of that song David's playing, his heart will open up again to love." About to confess he'd been eavesdropping, Jill giggled and said, "You know Rosemary you'd be a perfect match!"

Rosemary's retort was immediate. "What! Loving David's children is one thing, but …"

Jill's protest was equally swift. "Okay Rosemary, but there's no need to shudder, he's not that bad."

He'd heard enough! Not wanting to dwell on Rosemary shuddering, he bounced around the corner of the stairs announcing, "I've brought the twins bottles. Can I feed them here?" He was in time to catch Jill's glare toward Rosemary, before she looked up to send him a welcoming smile. Rosemary, with Joshua in her arms, gave him a sheepish glance as Jill said brightly, "Of course brother, dear, I'll make us a cup of tea. Did you find any clues burrowing in those boxes of Jane's things?" Before he could answer Rosemary was handing him Joshua. As his little face crumpled into wail he felt the challenge to overcome Rosemary's shuddering. Bestowing her with his high-wattage smile he exclaimed, "Joshua it seems prefers your arms to mine."

283

Lips pursed Rosemary retorted, "Nothing to do with me, hunger I suspect." And before he could thank her for packing up Jane's things she'd walked into her bedroom and shut the door.

He and Jill exchanged a glance. "What did I say, or do?"

"Nothing you'd understand brother dear, just Rosemary being over sensitive."

Once the twins were asleep he retired to bed, for whatever Rosemary thought about him, she could be relied on to feed the twins at 11.00 pm.

The 27th September heralded the twins being three months old. The day also brought closure to Andrew's demise in his receiving Walter's letter and last Will and Testament. Reading the details from the man's own hand made it more heart-rending and tragic. Another life Andrew had ruined, but justice would come, dealt out by His maker. And, as he closed the curtains to grab a few hours sleep, he questioned how a man could become so evil.

Through a gap in the curtains bright, hot sunshine touching his face awakened him. It was three-thirty! Hurriedly he washed, dressed and went downstairs where Mrs Perkins, in her old fashioned. fold-over overall, was on her knees cleaning his kitchen floor. At his jovial greeting she turned to grin up at him. "Just finishing up 'ere, Sir. Now you're awake I'll put the 'oover round."

"Where are Joyce and the twins?"

"In the garden." She stood, putting her hand to her waist. "You was tired today. Joyce said when she took the twins to the Clinic that Nurse Mary feels their ready for porridge. That'll 'elp them sleep during the night."

"That's good news for it is a strange life being up all night, and asleep most of the day."

Mrs Perkins shook her head, "I still can't believe that lovely Jane…"

Not wishing to be rude, but knowing how this conversation would continue, he interrupted, "I'm sorry you'll have to excuse me, I need to talk to Joyce before she leaves, and I'd better let you get on."

Both Joyce and Jill smiled up at him as he came down the stairs into the basement lounge. "Ah, brother dear, we've run out of bread and milk. Could you walk Joyce to the station so she could watch the twins while you go into the shop?"

"Fine by me. I'll go 'prambulating' from there, and be back in time for dinner."

Mrs Perkins was replacing the Hoover in the boiler room, and he and Joyce were negotiating the pram through the front door as the telephone began ringing. Not wanting to delay, he boomed, "Forget it, they can ring back later."

Strolling towards the High Street Joyce looked up at him. "Have you any thoughts about going back to work? I'm happy to still come twice a week to look after the twins, but need to leave around four to avoid the rush hour and be home to cook Ted's tea."

"Thank you, I appreciate that." Troubled he sighed. "I feel I should substitute the love and stability a mother gives. Fortunately, ITP is good at fitting in with child care arrangements, disabled spouses and aged mothers, but I can't think about that until they sleep through the night. And I don't want a Norland nanny however good they may be. David added with a rueful smile, "And when the twins are older they can go to the church nursery Jane started." Joyce's amused, but mocking expression, so reminded him of Jane it tore at his heart. Quickly he moved on. "Jill will need more rest the nearer she gets to her baby's delivery. Paul is intending to stay home so he'll be here to help, but they are considering moving to be nearer Beatty. And I don't know how I'd manage without them."

Joyce put her hand over his on the pram. "David, its early days, you'll meet someone else, and I'd expect you to marry again." Appreciation and happiness reflected in her voice as continued, "My love of Ted is different from that of Jane's father, but it's a happy companionship and he's been wonderful through all this."

Thoughtfully he nodded, "I know Jane wouldn't want me to be alone."

Looking serious Joyce commented, "I'll confess I had initial qualms, but you made Jane happy, and are a good father." Pleased, he responded with a high wattage smile. "In having the twins to stay it helped me come to terms with Jane's death. David, I need to tell you that they mean a great deal to me, and I hope you will continue to include us in their lives whatever the future holds."

Frowning, because Joyce felt the need to ask, he fervently declared, "Of course."

Joyce smiled up at him as they reached the food store. "I'm afraid your 'goodbye' visitation from Jane is too bizarre for me, but I can picture her enjoying eternal life." On Joyce's upturned face he saw the tears form, as she added, "The reality for me is she's with her Dad, one day we'll all meet again, and have much to share."

David nodded, and left to make his purchases. After seeing Joyce across the road to the station he headed for the park, and hoped today it wouldn't be a place of unexpected liaisons! Ten minutes as he entered the park in the distance was a woman with a resemblance to Rosemary, but a glance at his watch showed she'd still be at work. Speed walking he drew closer, and the woman diverted on to another pathway. He didn't follow for if it wasn't Rosemary it could be embarrassing. And, if it was Rosemary, it would appear she didn't want to speak to him. Maybe it was the thought of intimacy with any man made her shudder? Although hurt by overhearing that he'd rationalised Rosemary was often cold and aloof around men. It could be a fear issue, rather than personal dislike.

Far ahead he saw the same woman emerge from a side path and cross the road at the park gate. His eyes widened, the words "Oh God!" sprang from his mouth, his feet started to run, and the wheels of the pram started to spin as the woman hit by an incoming car collapsed against the bonnet, and slid to the ground. Fortunately because the car was moving slowly she'd not been thrown forward, but she was still lying motionless in the road. The driver having got out, looked at the woman, and then, as if at a loss, he watched David's approach.

Across the distance he boomed out, "Call an ambulance," but the man seemed transfixed, so he boomed again, "Telephone box on the main road." The man obeyed. On reaching the pavement parallel to the woman, his worst fears were realised, it was Rosemary! Ignoring the crying twins, he put the brake on the pram and ran across the road praying, 'Oh God, don't let her be hurt'? Crouching down beside her he drew back the curtain of hair from her face. Mascara streaked her face, he frowned, for she'd obviously been crying before the accident. From the pram he took his folded jumper and, speaking her name, he gently placed it under her head. She stirred, her eyes flickered open, she murmured, "David?"

"Yes, it's me. Shush. Relax, stay still." Worried, he gazed

into her dazed eyes and explained, "A car knocked you over. The driver is calling an ambulance." Her eyes closed. Pictures flashed before him of Jane dying in his arms, he fought panic to say firmly, "Rosemary, open your eyes. Talk to me."

Briefly they opened as she muttered, "The twins?"

"They're fine, in the pram over there, but you're more important right now." To his dismay tears squeezed out from under her eyelids. "Don't cry. I'm going to take hold of your hand and stay right here. The ambulance won't be long."

Rosemary's slender hand was ice cold, but at least she didn't snatch it from him. David wanted to question her, but people started to arrive to question him.

"What happened?" "Is she okay?" "Where's the driver?" "Has someone called an ambulance?" "Is she your wife?" "Are these your children?"

Aware of someone about to lift one of them out of the pram, he called sharply, "Please leave them. They have each other. They'll settle again, just rock the pram gently. Thank you." Rosemary moved as though to sit up, he cautioned, "Don't move, wait for the ambulance," but repositioned himself to keep his eyes on her, and the pram. The sound of an ambulance, a police siren, and the reappearance of the driver brought the relief that help was at hand.

After saying he'd stay with her, the ambulance men asked him to step away, but he did so assuring Rosemary he'd not go far. A crowd was gathering so he returned to the pram to cuddle and quieten each baby. In a need to move closer, despite his saying he knew the injured person, first a policeman thwarted him, and then the car driver pointed him out as a witness. While giving his account he tried to see what was happening to Rosemary. Suddenly the way cleared to reveal her being carried on a stretcher to the ambulance. A policeman holding up his jumper asking, "Who does this belong to?" diverted him yet again. But having claimed it David asked him to look after the pram, which initiated the question, "Do you know the woman?"

Without thinking he replied "Yes, she lives with me." That brought a murmuring of speculation from the crowd, and they parted to let him and the pram through. By the ambulance he spoke loud enough to the men inside so all could hear. "Rosemary shares a flat with my sister. How is she?"

Immediately came the reply, "Slight concussion, suspected

broken leg. Come with us, or have a quick word, because we must go."

Big doleful brown eyes out of a beautifully sculptured face looked up at him, one side, a mottled raspberry colour from scraping the road. Despite that, with her curtain of hair laid out on the pillow, she was still an attractive woman. Concerned, he wanted to comfort her and risked her wrath by taking her hand. With a small smile he said softly, "I'd come with you, but I can't with the twins." Tears filled her eyes. "Don't worry, Paul's working in Casualty, he'll look after you." More gruffly he declared, "You were upset before the accident, whoever or whatever caused this, I assure you, I will sort it out." With the ambulance man waiting to close the doors he gave her hand a gentle squeeze, bent forward and kissed her forehead. As he drew back her eyes had widened in surprise and tears were overflowing from them. Unexpectedly self-conscious he babbled, "You'll be alright" before he pulled out his handkerchief to add brusquely, "Here take this. Mop those tears." On the demand of the ambulance man he backed out as she whispered, "Thank you."

The doors of the ambulance closed, and with the incident over people began dispersing. Thanking the policeman for watching the twins, he exited out the park gate into the Bayswater Road where, at the telephone box, he rummaged through his pockets for enough change to ring Jill.

The moment Jill heard David's voice, hers, filled with urgency interrupted, "David, oh thank goodness. Chris County rang. He's anxious to…"

"Never mind that, Rosemary has just walked in front of a car." At Jill's gasp he rushed on, "She might have a broken leg, she's pretty dazed and on her way to hospital." Instantly Jill started to question, but aware of time he over-rode her. "No more change, alert Paul to look out for her…" Over the pips he heard her say 'yes' and the phone went dead.

Mercifully the twins nodded back off to sleep as he walked home. Jill, waiting in the hall, headed him to the basement as he described the incident and finished, "My guess is Rosemary was already upset, she saw me, and in hurrying to avoid me she crossed the road without due care."

Puzzled Jill shook her head, "I'm sure that's not true." And went on to instruct, "Sit down, you're dinner's ready." William in his high chair gave his four tooth grin and noisily banged his spoon.

As they ate, and with an ear to the twins left in the pram at the top of the stairs, David pursued his assumption. "I'd hoped with Rosemary accepting my help with Helen's things, and willingly sorting out Jane's, she considered me as a friend. I just don't understand why I cause her to shudder, or as today, run from me?"

Jill frowned. "We both felt when Rosemary talked about Helen she'd suffered a similar sense of hurt and abandonment. If she was already upset she probably wanted to be alone, there's no reason to take it personally. My guess is it's to do with ITP because Chris said he'd a problem he needed to speak to you about."

David sighed and was about to speak as Jill's telephone rang. Answering it she mouthed across at him "Paul" before repeating his words. "Rosemary has a minor concussion, bruises consistent from being hit by a car, she's awaiting an xray on her leg. It's badly bruised, but he doubts it's broken. If it is they'll keep her in." Jill refocused on the conversation, and said looking back at him, "Yes, I'm sure David could look after William." At his nod she went on, "I'll come at the end of your shift, hopefully Rosemary won't need them, but I'll put a few things in a bag for her just in case."

Two hours later, having tried several times, but had no reply from Chris' home, David paced back and forth across the basement lounge. How could he have been so insensitive to have Rosemary's unstinting help with the twins, yet not enquire as to how she was coping with Robert? Crying wasn't something he associated with Rosemary. Years ago when he and Jane had challenged her, he'd seen her as a hard woman full of anger and bitterness, her tears to gain sympathy. But Jane had reached out in love, changing Rosemary's ready sarcasm, negative attitude and tendency to gossip. Rarely did Rosemary's anger surface beyond cold sarcasm, but he guessed after he'd witnessed it burst forth under stress, it still simmered beneath the surface. Had that happened at ITP today? Was that why she appeared so distraught?

When she hobbled painfully, with Paul's assistance, down the stairs to head for her bedroom she appeared so ill at ease she barely acknowledged his welcome, sympathy and wish for a good night's sleep. Jill accompanied her into the bedroom, and Paul drew him into the kitchen and closed the door. "You need to investigate the situation at ITP. Apparently Robert sacked Rosemary this afternoon."

Furious, he boomed, "He's done what? How dare he make those kinds of decisions?"

Rubbing his beard, Paul observed, "Whatever caused Robert to do that has, I think, triggered in Rosemary a deeper, long held inner guilt and anguish. She believes she's let you down."

"But we so appreciate her. She's been a rock during this difficult time."

"I've told her that, but she wouldn't open up to me except in worrying about who would feed the twins at 11.00 o'clock. I told her I'd do it, but I'm exhausted, can you manage?"

Of course, he'd said, 'yes', and then spent the night either cat napping, or pacing the floor speculating on how to resolve the issue. Once the switchboard at ITP opened, he rang Chris, and without pleasantries asked "Was your call yesterday about Rosemary, because I witnessed her step in the road in front of a car?"

"What? Did she do it deliberately?"

Annoyed, David snapped, "Of course not!

After asking if she was badly hurt, Chris commented, "Well, that's a relief. Anyway, I'm afraid Rosemary's been up to her nasty, vindictive, undermining ways. Robert warned her on numerous occasions, and in the end told me he'd no option but to dismiss her."

Cross, he retorted, "And by whose authority did he make that decision? Dismissal isn't something ITP does lightly, unless he thought he had your approval?"

Nervously Chris stammered, "Well, I – we…I've talked to Robert and Rosemary on several occasions each complaining about the other. I know you think highly of Rosemary, but my experience of dealing with her is similar to Robert's, she's haughty and wants things done her way, not his."

David sighed, "But you can't fault her loyalty, commitment and work ethics. Robert might be more personable, but can you say the same for his character?"

Sounding uncomfortable Chris admitted, "Err…well…it's been difficult taking on a new job and putting up with Rosemary. And I did tell him to sort it out."

Impatiently, he boomed, "So it appears Robert has taken it upon himself to sack a woman who has served the company faithfully for the past seven years?"

Apologetically, Chris stated, "David, I was at Wainwrights' press luncheon and didn't know anything about it until my return at three o'clock. Several people then informed me of Robert's frogmarching Rosemary across the hall, asking Penny to ring for a taxi, and then announcing loudly that she was being dismissed for her constant manipulative behaviour."

Horrified he gasped, "That's public humiliation."

"Apparently Rosemary, with head held high, stalked out. Those in the hall heard Robert remark, 'That's just the kind of attitude I've had to put up with'."

Although burning with anger, David's voice was cold. "I hope you've told Robert that kind of behaviour is deplorable."

"Naturally I asked him to explain. He apologised for broadcasting his frustration, but said she deserved it. According to him, he lost patience when she confronted him about his decision that exhibitors should organise and pay for their stand's furniture and…"

Astonished at such news, David interrupted, "Rosemary had good reason to question him. Did you sanction that?"

"Robert talked of simplifying the job. My impression was you'd suggested it."

Sharply, he questioned, "And it didn't occur to you to talk to me about it?

Puzzled Chris replied, "I saw no reason to question Robert's ideas and changes."

Exasperated, he challenged, "Or consider that as our members pay a yearly contribution for our services, they'd see this as ITP eliciting more money from them?"

Chris sighed heavily, "No David I'm sorry, I didn't. I'm into marketing and press coverage of our members' products, not exhibitions, legal or financial agreements."

"Did you consult Maud as Financial Director?"

Somewhat sheepishly Chris replied, "I'm sure Robert knows what he is doing?"

Frustration at Chris' complacency had him saying brusquely, "Are you? Well like Rosemary, I don't share that confidence."

"Look David, I'm sure it will sort itself out. And you'll give Rosemary a good reference so she'll have no difficulty getting another job."

Incensed by Chris' attitude David could only say, "I'll ring you later. Transfer me to Penny."

Waiting for the connection to Penny, he drummed his fingers on the table. What was Robert Jones up to? How dare he make such decisions?

After wishing Penny 'good morning' David delved straight into asking, "I believe you were in Reception yesterday when Robert Jones ordered a taxi for Rosemary." At her confirmation, he asked, "In which case I'd like to know exactly what happened and what was said. Could you, as a matter of priority, please write it down as you remember it".

"Of course, Sir. Will you be coming in, or shall I post it to you?"

"I'll let you know. Thank you. Please transfer…"

Penny interrupted, "Mr Reinhardt, Rosemary is always polite, she doesn't say much, but she was obvious very upset yesterday. I wanted to go after her, but Mr Jones stopped me. Is she's alright?"

"My understanding is she'll be fine, and I appreciate your thoughtfulness. Now please transfer me back to the switchboard."

The moment Maud picked up the telephone she said, "David, I've been trying to reach you. I've just heard about Rosemary. Rumour has it that cocky upstart, who took your job, began berating her in front of those in the hall and she walked out. From the way he swaggers about you'd think he owned the place, and that Susie who filled in for Rosemary, runs behind him like an adoring dog constantly wagging her tail."

At Maud's forthright manner, he cautioned, "Let's not jump to any conclusions." But he knew, in the past, she'd been right about Andrew Carlton. After giving her a brief report of the car accident, he continued, "Chris tells me Robert has taken it upon himself to contract out our business, could you find out to whom, where and their charges. I'm going to get Mavis to check out his references. In our haste to employ him, we may have accepted them on face value. Between you and me, I feel Chris' friendship with Robert has caused him to mishandle the situation, so please keep this investigation to yourself."

"David, I should have told you that in the Ladies one day Rosemary was angry and upset. She confided in me that Robert was being difficult, but I dismissed it as gossip, as that was always Rosemary's way of stirring up trouble."

David sighed, "Maud that was four years ago, not now!"

"I know. In recognising his type, I felt sooner or later if Rosemary was right, Robert would overstep the mark and trip himself up."

"Maud, I rather think he's just done that. And we've probably more cause for his instant dismissal than Rosemary's. Now I'd better go and talk with her."

In replacing the telephone receiver he wandered into his lounge and prayed Rosemary would see him as friend, not foe, and thus trust and confide in him.

CHAPTER 22

With a twin under each arm David made his way down the stairs to the basement flat. It was just after ten o'clock, but Rosemary was still in her dressing gown just finishing her breakfast. When she glanced up he saw one side of her face was red and swollen, her eye puffy, and going black. Suspicion formed in her eyes as he said cheerily, "I, and the twins, have come to enquire how their favourite Auntie is after her collision yesterday with a car."

Her facial injuries muffled her voice. "Battered and bruised."

Sympathetic, he grimaced. "I'm so sorry."

In that strange voice she stated, "Jill's out with William. I saw you yesterday. I didn't want to speak to you."

It suddenly occurred to him that another apology was necessary. "Oh dear, forgive me. I've invaded your territory. Do you want to speak to me now?" She nodded. Relieved, he asked, "Would you like to cuddle one of these?" Pleasure filled Rosemary's eyes as she moved to take Rebecca, but at her startled jerk, he realised in the transfer his arm had brushed her breast. His apology this time was garbled, and sitting opposite her on the settee, and bouncing Joshua on his knee, he was unsure who felt the most embarrassed.

Nervously Rosemary looked across at him, gulped, and returned her attention to the gurgling baby in her arms. After an encouraging hum, he waited and observed how a baby could change a woman who people saw as snooty and superior, to a tender, loving one. Lifting her head, she remarked, "Your bullying…as Jill calls it…is nothing compared to Roberts."

At that he grimaced. "Thanks."

Oblivious to his sarcasm, Rosemary added, "But that's not important."

"It is, but we'll get to that later. Carry on."

Due to the immobility of her face her words came out slowly and painfully, and he didn't catch them all. "Robert…out of the office… Susie answers phone…writes messages. I explained… exhibitors…advise them…stood in for you…" She paused, and tried to speak more clearly. "I told…Robert I'd devised… efficient system. His reply...pity I hadn't devised to stick with you, because he'd no need of hoity, toity busybody…running the Department. The exercising of her mouth was steadily improving her diction. "And with my high salary...do as I was told, or get out." David scowled, the man was a tyrant, but before he could comment Rosemary continued, "I've tried to keep an eye on things." To that he gave a grim smile and nod. She swallowed hard, and commenced, "I updated and organised advertising and publicity information for Brussels. The Print Department ran it, the Membership Department despatched it to both our main and subsidiary members. As bookings arrived I began processing them. When I asked Susie to help, Robert wanted to know what I was doing. I explained, and he stalked out. I assume he told Chris because later he berated me for not consulting Robert." Her frustration was evident as she ploughed on. "I told Chris that Robert ignores me, and explained the situation as I have to you. That's when Chris suggested I take two weeks holiday and consider my future at ITP. I was angry. I'd done my job to the best of my ability. I challenged Chris on that. His reply, 'Do your job, but don't take any further initiatives without consulting me first.' By the Thursday I'd had enough of Robert and Susie's nastiness so took Chris' advice and told them I was off on holiday."

Running his hand through his hair he questioned, "Why didn't you tell me?"

Rosemary gave a heavy sigh. "You were recovering from the flu, and only just been proven innocent! I felt it could wait until my return."

"After my break, Robert and Susie have ignored me. The bookings were left for me to process. I've confirmed stand allocations, and noted equipment needs. I told Robert there were queries, and asked if he wanted me to discuss these with Exhibitors. Clearly annoyed he said, 'That's not your job.' I asked if he had the time and he shouted it wasn't up to me to query his workload, or tell him how to do his job. Quietly, I pointed out Exhibitors appreciated our personal service. At that he thumped the desk in rage, and as usual his invectives were in German. Then he declared he was sick of my interference, this was a final warning, and he would not stand my undermining his authority again."

Forgetting his need to have a gentle, soft approach David boomed, "What! That's ridiculous." Comforting Joshua who was frightened by his vehement tone, he added quietly, "I wish you'd told me."

Rosemary pursed her lips. "That's not all, the next day he announced from now on I'd be working for Susie, and muttered in German he hated the sight of me." Tears formed in Rosemary's eyes, "I tried talking to Chris, but he said, that I wouldn't have told you how to do your job, so why did I think I had a right to tell Robert."

Perturbed, he saw Chris although capable, had erred in judgement of Rosemary, and why hadn't he consulted him about the problem? Did Maud know about this? The board needed older, wiser, more experienced people. For now he could only apologise. He sat forward, "Rosemary I'm so sorry for the way you've been treated, and forgive me for not addressing this when you first explained Robert's attitude towards you."

Sad, doleful eyes looked across at him. "One lunch time I did interfere by burrowing in piles of papers and files on his office floor. He caught me, and despite my excuse to be there, in German he called me nasty names and now he keeps his office door locked when he or Susie aren't around. Yesterday he wasn't in when Jenny on the switchboard told me Jeremy Coates wanted to speak urgently with someone connected to the Brussels Exhibition. As he's the Company Director, not normally involved with Exhibition details, I said I'd take the call. Immediately Mr Coates demanded to know why his Company, who paid for full membership of ITP, was expected to pay a contractor for equipping their Exhibition stand. I could only reiterate that from my experience that wasn't the case, and finally said I would look into it and get back to him."

David frowned and exclaimed, "What contractor? What is going on?"

Rosemary shrugged, "I don't know. I told Robert about the conversation. To that he became very belligerent, shouting that I was interfering again! I'm afraid I lost my temper."

Her look of despair and guilt had him saying, "Rosemary I think you had good reason to, but carry on."

Rosemary's voice took on the tone, he suspected, she used then. "I said, 'Mr Jones, that's how I had to address him!'" She continued, I said, 'Mr Jones, I didn't contact the man, he rang us. You think you know everything, but in fact you know nothing. You are rude and arrogant and it's been my misfortune to be left to work with you'." A blush rose up Rosemary's throat. She paused, and then continued, "Robert replied that he hadn't wanted your rejected goods either." Faltering she added, "And, I no longer deserved my high salary because…" Rosemary gave her attention to Rebecca as clearly uncomfortable she finished, "because I well…he inferred… I…I slept with you."

David scowled. "Did he indeed? That judgement alone would make me decide to show him the door."

Encouraged Rosemary looked up, "I told him you wouldn't appreciate that remark. It was then he grabbed me, and despite my protests he dragged me through into the outer office. In front of Susie, he picked up my bag and thrust it at me saying, 'Believe me my dear, David Reinhardt's appreciation of you is lost on me, and you're out of here right now!' He manhandled me along the corridor into the lift. I told him he had no right to dismiss me, and he said, 'just watch me you frustrated and vindictive bitch.' In the lift I told him you wouldn't appreciate his insinuations and behaviour. At that he shrugged, 'You're word against mine, darling, and you're not going to get the opportunity to tell him'. From the lift he marched me across the hall telling those around he was dismissing me and escorting me from the premises before I caused further problems for ITP. Mortified I pulled my arm from his, walked out the door and just kept walking." David shook his head in disbelief as anger seethed through him. Rosemary sighed and added, "This last week was so awful I'd decided I must talk to you. Susie is now so bossy and obnoxious."

Four years earlier Jane had said much the same about working with Rosemary! He thought of the Biblical principle that we often reap what we sow. Rosemary was still speaking, "…I was so fed up with Susie sucking up to Robert I admit to saying, "Enjoy it while you can Susie for there's no future in it when there's a wife and two kids at home."

Surprised he countered, "I didn't know Robert was married."

Rosemary shrugged, "Probably isn't, I only said, 'when', but I confess I had pleasure at seeing her euphoria evaporate before she strode in to demand if it were true."

Amused he chuckled, but added seriously, "That could be construed as vindictive." She gave a resigned nod. Thoughtfully he hummed. Robert Jones was definitely out of order, but he also knew Rosemary had the ability to cause friction. He frowned for usually he was a good judge of character. When he refocused, silent tears were trickling down Rosemary's face. Puzzled he questioned, "What's the matter?"

"I'm sorry, I've let you down." The long curtain of hair blocked out her face as she bent over Rebecca's sleeping body.

"That's not true. I highly value your support here and at work. And you need to know, that if you weren't so shy, and Exhibitors so male dominated, I would have offered my job to you." Visibly overwhelmed, with tears streaking her face, she stared at him. "Believe me it's true."

Emotion cracked her voice as she whispered, "Thank you. After all that's happened that means a lot to me."

"Right well, wipe away those tears. I'll put the twins in the pram, make a cup of tea and then you must rest as I ascertain how best to limit the damage."

In the next four hours things moved swiftly bringing him to conclude he'd no option but to go into ITP. It was strange after three months to enter the building and find nothing had changed. Penny smiled, welcomed him and handed him an envelope. In striding across the hall he nodded to several people who looked surprised to see him, but he gave them no opportunity to waylay him. Sharon, Chris' secretary looked up, before jumping to her feet. "Mr Reinhardt, Good afternoon. I didn't know you were due back."

Not to cause ripples, he replied, "I thought to ease myself in gently."

At his appearance Chris looked nervous and fiddled with his tie. "David, it seems I've made some wrong judgements. I think it best I step down as a Director. I really don't have the experience to handle it."

That was an attitude he appreciated, so with a grim smile he assured Chris, "You have now! Sometimes we can learn more from our mistakes than from years of education or experience! As the Board of Directors responsible for this Company we need to quickly assess and redeem the situation. Cancel anything you have on this afternoon. We'll meet in my new office in half an hour. I'd appreciate it if you don't inform Robert I'm here. Neither tell him about the board meeting, nor his being the subject under discussion."

Mavis didn't leap up on his appearance, but sent him a motherly smile. "Your office is ready and waiting for you. Shall I get you a pot of tea and biscuits?"

"For four please. And I'd like you to join us at an emergency

Board Meeting. I know I've thanked you before, but I appreciate the efficiency with which you've dealt with things in my absence." He looked through the open double doors at the palatial room with its highly polished boardroom table at one end, the antique, leather-topped desk just behind the door and neatly plumped up cushions on two comfortable settees by the long French windows. "Who would have guessed that it would be three months before I would be here?"

Compassion filled Mavis eyes, "It's been a sad and very difficult time for you, but being catapulted back may help you to settle in quickly." With a gentle smile she asked, "How are the twins? I know people here would love to see them, and I'm up for cuddling and feeding them."

"Oh thank you Mavis, there might be times I'll take you up on that. They are thriving, but still wanting night feeds, so you might have to prod me awake some afternoons."

A little smile curled Mavis' mouth, "With nice comfortable sofas in there, let me know if you need to sleep. I'll make sure no-one disturbs you."

"Was that why Joseph was never available straight after lunch?" Mavis gave him a wide-eyed look before heading toward the door as Maud, grim faced walked in.

Together, he and Maud stood by one of three tall French windows overlooking the drive. "It is strange to be back, and this being my office. Shall we sit comfortably, or at the table?"

Maud's red-painted nails waved toward the table, "It's a Board Meeting."

Chris arrived, and seated himself next to Maud as she lit a cigarette. As Chairman David placed himself at the head of the table. Maud commenced, "Robert Jones is a charlatan with bogus University…"

Chris interrupted, "He speaks four languages."

Obviously Chris felt he should stand up for Robert so he agreed, "We're not denying that."

"His reference from the marketing company is genuine. I've met his ex-boss."

David sighed, "Well that's something. Despite Robert's youth, I felt this would be a career move for him, and with Rosemary experience and capabilities there was little risk of his messing it up. Under various pressures I made the mistake of not being firm with Robert, or making Rosemary's role clear."

Maud took a long drag on her cigarette. Chris fiddled nervously with his tie and then confessed, "I had sympathy for Robert because I've been on the receiving end of Rosemary's ire!" Then seeing Mavis arrive with the tea tray, Chris jumped up to take it from her. And as Mavis returned to the outer office for her notebook Maud leant forward to pour.

Once Mavis was in place David officially declared the board meeting open. After stating for the records why it had been convened and the information already disseminated, he asked, "Maud, I believe you had a conversation with Rosemary about Robert Jones?"

"Yes, David. You were in Kent when I met Rosemary in the Ladies, she was obviously upset. Her explanation was somewhat incoherent, but I gathered Robert didn't appreciate Rosemary's input into the work. I wasn't sure what to think so I didn't comment. I watched her gather up her bag and looking hurt she whispered, 'You don't believe me!' and rushed out before I could deny it. I decided she was probably just being over sensitive'."

Vehemently Chris agreed, "Exactly! That's been her problem all along. She's too sensitive, but equally insensitive to others."

A thoughtful Maud dragged on her cigarette and David noted Mavis' motherly features tighten. With her eyes on Chris, Maud said sternly, "Several people have spoken of Robert's negative attitude toward Rosemary. When I've tried to speak to her about it, she gives me a small enigmatic smile, and moves away. If you remember Chris, I mentioned it to you. Your opinion was that the problem lay with Rosemary, not Robert. But since I've heard snippets of unkind gossip, I suspect originated from Susie, and I intended to bring that to David's attention on his return." Maud, cigarette in hand, paused to remove a filament of tobacco from her tongue.

Pale and twitchy, Chris turned to Maud to condone himself. "If you'd experienced Rosemary's caustic tongue you'd believe the problem was with her. But, if you felt that strongly, why didn't you do something about it?"

Maud's retaliation was quick and sharp. "I trusted you to deal with it. Don't start hedging blame on to me. And if that's the way you treated Rosemary I'm not surprised her frustration boiled over."

While they argued, David scanned the statement from Penny,

and then waved it as a white flag! "This is an account of Robert's words and actions in the hall yesterday. But Chris, before we consider action on that, perhaps you'd like to explain why Robert is contracting out the arrangements for equipping Exhibitors' stands in Brussels." With that he sat back, steepled his hands against his mouth and awaited Chris' reply.

"I thought Robert's idea was forward thinking."

Clearly rattled Maud stated, "Except he didn't consult me as to the financing of it. David indicated Maud should continue. "David asked me to find out about the Company. Ledbury Events Ltd., was formed in August. I've not had time to ascertain if the two directors have any connection to Robert, but did ring their offices and found out the Company was set up to provide the business needs of conferences, training days and exhibitions. When I queried their experience the girl said she was new, she only answered the telephone and would get someone to ring me back. Whether or not Robert has anything financial to gain I don't know, but it certainly reduces his work load, and the responsibility for which he is well paid. And because our members pay for an inclusive service we'll have to foot the bill. It could the reason for wanting to dispense with Rosemary, but I wouldn't be surprised if Ledbury's charge is greater than her yearly salary. And I doubt they will work with the same efficiency and personal service our members have come to expect."

Chris, in what appeared an attempt to shore up the tide of damning evidence of his misjudging and mishandling the situation retorted, "Robert told me they gave a very good quote."

Maud snapped crossly, "I'm the Financial Director, if you knew about it why didn't you ask my advice?"

Not wanting a further argument David sat forward to address Chris. "Rosemary knows how ITP's finances work. Yesterday she tried to explain that to Robert, the consequence of which led to her being publicly humiliated. I've heard enough and we need to make a decision about Robert."

The forcefulness in which Maud stubbed out her cigarette portrayed her opinion, her blunt words confirming it, "Fire him."

Startled Chris complained, "That's a bit harsh!" We ought to hear his side of the story.

In response David requested, "Mavis please ask Robert to join us?" And while waiting he voiced his serious doubts about

Robert's integrity. Chris unable to grasp those, continued to stand up for Robert, causing Maud's indignation. To silence the argument, and in a desire for a majority vote, David suggested, "Let's see if Robert's attitude will redeem him."

But Robert's arrogant swagger into the room did little to endear him. His over confident manner, and unconcern at the discovery of his bogus qualifications began to stir his ire. But Robert's contemptuous manner towards Rosemary had him fighting for composure.

With a hard stare, David stated, "The lack of respect, the way you've spoken and treated Rosemary, has been deplorable." Robert made a face and shrugged. Incensed he continued grimly, "But your behaviour yesterday, for someone with a position of authority, was inexcusable."

With an insipid smile Robert said, "Point taken David. Bit of an over reaction, but she's gone so it won't happen again." He stood, "Now I'd better get back to work."

Anger overflowed causing David to boom, "Sit down!" Having startled the others, he asked in a quieter, but steely voice, "I need you to bring us up to speed on arrangements for the Brussels Exhibition?"

At Robert's nonchalant expression his jaw tightened, Maud puffed harder on a fresh cigarette and Chris looked as if his tie was strangling him. Sitting down again Robert stretched his arm out across the back of the chair next to him. "Not much to tell really. Nearly two hundred exhibitors have applied and they are making their needs known." Robert shrugged, smiled, looked around and added, "So things are ticking along nicely."

When Maud and Chris didn't comment, David questioned, "Is that so? And that 'ticking along nicely' I suppose is because you have contracted out the job you are paid to do?"

Full of confidence Robert addressed him. "No David, the job Rosemary felt she should do, at a salary she was no longer worthy of." Riled by the knowing smile Robert sent him, his answer was a grim stare. "In coming in fresh I saw Exhibitors would have a fairer deal if they each paid for what they wanted. Some need only a table and chairs, others ask for electricity, projectors, screens, cash tills, etcetera which causes extra work, cost and no end of problems."

"So part of your plan was getting rid of Rosemary to fund this?"

Unaware of the tension Robert concluded happily, "You must admit my scheme is much fairer, and with Rosemary gone ITP will be saving a considerable amount of money." At that Robert sent Maud a wide smile as if expecting her agreement. Her response was to glare at him, and blow a line of smoke in his direction. Puzzled he looked at Chris who had taken an unfounded interest in his empty tea cup. "I ran the idea past Chris. He liked it."

Chris looked up but didn't return Robert's confident smile, and before he could speak Maud commented, "Robert you don't seem to have grasped how ITP is funded. We aren't here to make or save money, but give good value and service for a yearly contribution matched to the company's overall needs.

There was no doubting the underlining sarcasm as Robert said, "Of course Maud I'm aware of that. But this is my job, and I'm doing as I think best. David had his way, I have mine. Ledbury Events will better serve our member companies by doing the donkey work while we liaise and network."

Maud retaliated, "But you've just said they would each pay for what they wanted."

Waving his hand Robert said somewhat wearily, "Yes, but you don't understand. They order from Ledbury, but they will pay indirectly. Next year we can adjust their membership fees according to their needs. But ITP will pay their bills. I'm afraid it's been Rosemary's aim to orchestrate difficulties and put my initiatives in a bad light."

David, glad he'd made his own enquiries glanced around at his colleagues before declaring, "As it appears Rosemary has no knowledge of your initiatives, how was it possible for her to bring them into a bad light?" Before Robert could make trump up further excuses, David challenged, "So Robert, perhaps you'd care to explain why Jeremy Coates, Roger Forrester and Gerald Oates tell me they've had letters telling them to contact Ledbury Events who will bill them accordingly."

Robert shook his head in disbelief. "I know, when I heard what Rosemary had done I was furious. She wouldn't listen, she constantly undermined me and I clearly told her not to contact the exhibitors, yet she seemed to think it was her job to do so. And why I removed her from the building yesterday." Robert lent across the table, "I didn't want to slur her character further, but I can only suppose that she sent out those letters to frame me.

It wouldn't be the first time her jealousy and spitefulness has caused problems." With a tight smile he sat back to observe them.

Without doubt Robert was an accomplished liar, for if he didn't know Rosemary he, like Chris, might have believed him. Chris was still dragging at his tie, Mavis looked up from taking notes with a frown, and Maud stared wide-eyed at him. It was hard to keep his loathing of this man from his voice. "Robert, in my opinion, the things you have just said are even more contemptible than your behaviour to date." David noted Robert's condescending expression as he repeated his conversation with Jeremy Coates, "He told me it was obvious Rosemary was as surprised as he about the supply of stand equipment being contracted out." To make himself clear David continued, "So I put it to you, as a consequence of her questioning, and informing you of ITP's financial arrangements, you realised your error and hoped by removing her under a volley of disparaging comments you'd cover yourself by blaming her."

Still casual, as if unable to comprehend the seriousness of the situation, Robert gave a sad, and derogatory smile, "I'm afraid, David your opinion of Rosemary is very flawed. She not only undermined, interfered with, and caused trouble over my contacting out idea, but is also a liar. Now, if you'll excuse me I've work to do."

Robert stood. David resisted the urge to thump the table, but did jump up. A glance at Maud's sour expression and confirming nod, he informed Robert, "Even before this conversation your career here was in already jeopardy. ITP does not tolerate employees being sworn at, or called names."

Clearly ruffled, Robert proclaimed, "I've already said Rosemary is a liar!"

"Is that so? Did you not know that Rosemary can speak fluent German?"

Robert paled, but still protested, "Oh come on David surely you aren't so obsessed by the woman you would believe her word against mine!"

For a second David closed his eyes and clenched his jaw. The man was beyond belief! With a steely glare, his tone glacial, he declared, "What Robert I'm 'obsessed' with is the truth, and would ask you what you think your word is worth? You've lied about your qualifications, and seemingly don't care.

Your arrogance is such you have taken no-one's advice. You have contracted out the work you're paid to do, and on top of that you have the audacity to blame Rosemary, and insinuate she is more than a colleague and friend to me."

The pitch of Robert's voice rose to demand, "Chris, tell him. I talked this contract over with you. You know what Rosemary's like. You told me to sort it out?" Chris gave him a dumbfounded look.

"Tell me Robert, in this 'talking things over with Chris', did you say to him that you were of the opinion that Rosemary's high salary was because she bestowed upon me sexual favours."

"Good grief, that woman's really got in for me! And I'll tell you why? I refused her sexual advances…"

Robert's words were drowned by Maud's loud cackle. Confused, Robert looked at her, and then at Chris who, groaning had put his head in hands. Maud's long red finger nail pointed at Robert. "That proves you're in fantasy land. You've sunk in the mire of your own lies. No-one who knows Rosemary would believe that."

The next two hours was enough to make his brain frazzle, and on the drive home he tried to clarify it in his mind. Robert, still full of bluster, had eventually packed up and gone. Chris wanted to resign his position on the board, but he and Maud persuaded him against it. Susie had collapsed in tears saying she was so sorry and begging for a second chance. He'd left her to the motherly Mavis to bring a resolution, the outcome that Susie would apologise and work with Rosemary to sort out the mess.

But the big question was how to get the Brussel's Exhibition back on track, and who would go for the fortnight in December? He was still considering that as he drew up outside the house. As he put his key in the lock, he was reminded of Jesus being the key, and the Bible verse 'cast your burdens upon the Lord'. He'd certainly do that, for he needed to make the right decisions, and as he headed up the stairs he felt peace roll in. Through the open door of his lounge he could see Rosemary feeding Rebecca and cheerfully boomed, "Rosemary you're reinstated, Robert has gone and …"

Entering the room he stopped mid-sentence for she wasn't alone. Unsure what to make of it he held out his hand, and politely declared to DCI Gerald Maysfield who'd stood to greet him, with Joshua in his arms, "It's been a while. You'll understand a visit from the police now causes me some apprehension! Have you news of Ben?"

Maysfield gave a small smile, and said euphemistically, "No, but safe in being presumed dead! And, I quite understand your disquiet after that business with Carlton. But, rest assured I'm only here to get Rosemary's statement about her accident." Maysfield glanced in Rosemary's direction, and to David's surprise, she sent him a shy smile.

Irritated by Maysfield's intrusion, David indicated he wished to hold his son, as Rosemary explained, "William was having a strop. Jill suggested we come up here, so we brought the twins with us."

To that he gave a curt nod, hoping Maysfield might get the hint and leave. But then in noticing Maysfield's unfinished cup of tea, he felt compelled to wave him to sit back down. Obeying, Maysfield informed him, "Rosemary's statement clearly shows the accident was her fault not the drivers. We'll not be prosecuting." As if reading David's mind, he continued, "I don't usually take statements about road incidents, but seeing the address I felt it an opportunity to express my sympathy over your wife." At his poignant grimace, Maysfield continued, "I can empathise because my wife died ten years ago in a car accident. When it's unexpected it's so much harder. Since then I've lived for my job, perhaps if we'd had children…well, it might have been different." Not knowing how to respond David gave a sad smile, and looked pointedly at Maysfield's tea, as he continued, "It would seem in recent years your family has had more than its fair share of troubles."

Tired, David said, "I'm sorry Maysfield, I don't wish to be rude, but it's been a rather fraught day, I've things to do and also have to grab my sleep when I can."

"Oh yes, yes, of course." As Maysfield stood, he smiled at Rosemary. "Thank you for the tea, I enjoyed our chat." In turning to him, he advised, "I gather Dr Stemmings married your sister, it would be wise to get him to keep an eye on Rosemary's bruises, and she should be resting." David's grim smile and impatience, finally communicated to Maysfield nd he strode towards the door saying, "I'll let myself out." Rosemary, catching the curiosity in his gaze, dipped her head over Rebecca, so to defray any awkwardness David launched into his news.

CHAPTER 23

Eight weeks later he tipped back his large leather chair, steepled his fingers against his mouth and surveyed the office he thought he'd left for good. Life seemed to have reverted to a time before Jane. And like the dream he'd awoken from this morning, Jane would have felt a figment of his imagination, if it wasn't for two babies who cooed, cried and burped at regular intervals. His recurring dream had been absent for several months, but last night he felt the horses of the army had slowed to a trot, and the dawn was catching them up. In itself, it was reassuring, but too he'd the knowledge that the battle they'd been engaged to fight had already been won.

Yet in the reality of life he was engaged in a minefield of legalities, situations and major decisions. In the past he'd have worked late, but that wasn't an option with two little people awaiting his return each evening. And with a demanding job, thrown into chaos by Robert, he needed enough uninterrupted sleep to ensure an active mind the next day.

Completely quashing Chris and Robert's accusations of being spiteful and vindictive, Rosemary had defended Susie's behaviour, saying, "She's young, taken in by an attractive man's charm. Don't add to Robert's misdeeds by making her a scapegoat of them. I'll work with her until the Exhibition is over. Let's see how things pan out." And 'pan out' they had. Through the open door to the outer office he could see Susie's animated face, brought on by Rosemary's kind and unflustered tutelage.

In those first days while Rosemary healed sufficiently to return to work Susie and Mavis had helped him to bring some order out of disorder. Unbeknown to him, while taking his place in caring for the twins, Rosemary was bringing order out of his need for child care. From both grandmothers she elicited promises that they'd cover the weekdays when she returned to work. Now, weeks later, his Mum was thoroughly enjoying her three mid-week days, and Joyce was happily covering Monday and Friday until 4.00 pm. Even more astonishing was how his father had stopped his constant haranguing that a live-in nanny would solve all the problems, and had accepted his wife's absence.

Each week ran with maximum efficiency, with only slight deviations. Each day at precisely 8.30 am he and Rosemary drove to work arriving at nine o'clock. Each evening, they returned to a meal prepared for the household, by either Jill or his mother and served around 6.00 pm to accommodate William. Each night, after News at Ten Rosemary would reappear to feed the twins, who, now on solids slept through until about 6.00 am. Each morning once he'd fed, changed and played with them, he still had time to read his Bible, and bring his prayer requests to the Lord. To ensure the smooth running of the house they each had tasks. One of his was to collect up the dirty washing from his flat, sort the colours from the whites, and put a load in the washing machine for someone else to hang up to dry. From that he benefitted from constantly replenished underclothes, and his shirts ironed. Grateful though he was for this regimented lifestyle, it was something of a treadmill, and Rosemary's quiet efficiency was making him feel dull and strangely inadequate. The only break from routine came at the weekend, and with the dark nights of November upon them, it was his only opportunity for his 'pramulations' in the park!

Without doubt Rosemary did far more than was required, but despite his thanks, encouragements, and friendliness she still only spoke when necessary. And he still wondered why he made her shudder? It wasn't as he'd hoped 'a man thing' for Gerald Maysfield's visits had started with the pretext of concern for Rosemary's injuries. The next visit to inform her that the car accident case was closed, and after his offering to fix a tap, that had escalated into his coming every Saturday morning, to do a number of small, simple jobs that neither he, nor Paul had the time or inclination to do. It was clear that Gerald enjoyed the family atmosphere, but it had begun to occur to David, that he was becoming more than just besotted by the twins! And with Rosemary inviting him to lunch these past few Saturdays she appeared to be reciprocating his interest. And he suspected that when Rosemary had declined her lift home on the last two Fridays she had been going out with Gerald. However, Rosemary so enjoyed giving the twins' their last feed she'd returned in time for that. He asked if she'd had a good evening and received the usual bland, 'yes, thank you,' but from the overall prickliness, he'd felt new buds of life were forming.

When this morning she'd arrived at the front door with a suitcase he'd commented, 'Going away for the weekend?' Her answer had been a nod. On the journey to work he asked, "Are you staying with your parents?" And then noted how cleverly she deflected the answer by saying, "They're away" and immediately asked, "Have you thought about being away in Brussels? Invaluable as Rosemary was in running his life, she certainly wasn't willing for him to encroach on hers.

On a deep sigh, he sat forward to put his mind on the paperwork in front of him. Staffing at Brussels was going to be a problem, and he could see no alternative to his having to go. Only he and Rosemary were fluent in several languages, but she wouldn't want to deal with the male Exhibitors without him. With three weeks to go he needed to draft someone in, and he sighed heavily as he considered again the names on the staff list before him.

Perhaps Rosemary might have some ideas, and as if feeling his eyes upon her she turned to give him a questioning look. He beckoned her in. On her way she picked up the book containing letters for him to sign and then sat opposite him.

"We need to make some decisions about Brussels." With a worried expression, Rosemary nodded. David ventured, "I know I have to go. It's usual for my PA to join me, and I'd really appreciate your support."

"As I said last year, I'd prefer not." At his wide-eyed look she expounded, "I managed to cope because I was with someone outgoing, and who isn't fazed by being a woman among hundreds of men. This year, those who tend to fit that bill are married, and don't want to leave their husbands. Others just don't want to be working long hours and miss the run up to Christmas. Susie is friendly, but too young and too easily led to let loose in Brussels. If Jill wasn't eight months pregnant we could have drafted her in."

"In that case, having looked at this list, we need to pray for inspiration." And before Rosemary could do more than gawk at him, he closed his eyes and simply asked, "Lord your Word says, 'Ask and it shall be given to you, so Lord we either need a suitable companion for Rosemary in Brussels, or find someone suitably experienced and has the ability to quickly grasp what is needed. Thank you. Amen'."

Automatically Rosemary added, "Amen" then tried to look as if to praying together was a common occurrence, but her relief was evident when she jumped up to answer her internal telephone.

309

As she went, he chortled, "Could be Lord answering our prayer!" Then opening the book of blotting paper pages containing his dictated letters he picked up his fountain pen to read the first one awaiting his signature.

Deep in concentration he heard nothing until the knock on the door between his and Rosemary's office. He looked up as the white-haired woman, of an attractive couple, said "Hello David, may we come in?" Jumping up, he rushed around his desk to greet Grace who'd been his PA for several years, before meeting Wilhelm at the Brussels Exhibition and had left to get married four years previously. "Come in, come in." Pumping their hands he questioned, "What are you doing here?" And before they could answer he laughingly added, "Do you two want a job?" Obviously taken aback they looked at each other, and he rushed on, "Sorry! Rosemary and I have just prayed about our staffing problem for the Brussels Exhibition, and then two people who know probably more about Exhibitions than I do walk into my office. Oh sit down, how lovely to see you both again."

Calling to Susie he asked, "Please rustle us up some tea and biscuits." And then to Rosemary, "Come and join us?"

Grace, looking younger than when she worked for him, perched on the edge of the seat of one of the leather chesterfield settees. Wilhelm commented, "We weren't sure if you were back at work. I thought you'd given up the Exhibitions."

"I did, but that's another story." He waved Wilhelm to sit next to Grace, then sitting in the far corner of the settee at right angles to them, he asked, "I assume from your last letter Grace you're visiting your Mum in the UK. Does she like her residential home?"

Grace smoothed her skirt with her hand, "Yes, but we are doing more than visiting. Mum's 89 and getting frail and well... we've come to live in England for a while."

Wilhelm took up the story. "A good opportunity to get out of my rut before it becomes so deep it's my grave!" He chortled, "So at nearly sixty, I've retired and here we are!"

Grace lent forward, "Oh David our hearts went out to you when we heard about Jane. I wish we could have been here for the funeral." Tears filled her eyes, "She was so special. Everyone at our wedding loved my radiant bridesmaid, as in love with you, as I, with Wilhelm."

Memories flooded in. The tightly tethered emotion of his love and loss stretched down into that void within curling and tightening to reach upwards to his throat. He nodded, swallowed, cleared his throat and changed the subject. "So how long have you been over here?"

Rosemary brought in the tray, poured out the tea as Wilhelm answered, "We flew in yesterday and staying temporarily at the Cromwell Hotel."

Grace added, "It's near Mum's residential home in Earls Court, and we still have her place in Fulham, but its let on a five year lease with two more to go, so we're looking for something small to rent."

He and Rosemary went to speak at the same time, she coloured slightly, and at his indication went first. Handing Wilhelm a cup she offered, "I have…know of a small mews cottage in Kensington…"

Surprised David interrupted "Is it still free?" Rosemary nodded, and distributed the cups and biscuits as he became her spokesman. "A friend of Rosemary's lived there. I've seen it. It's a delightful, cosy retreat. Basically two up and two down, but has everything you'd need, quite close to the shops, and probably on the right bus route."

Quietly, although pointedly, Rosemary said, "Thank you David" as she drew the upright chair from in front of his desk and sat on it. At her mild rebuke he caught the slight lift of Grace's eyebrows, was that in surprise, or interest? Intrigued he listened as Rosemary told of knowing the owner, that they'd be accepted on her recommendation, and having lived there she knew all the answers about rates, utility and the rental charges. "I'm away until Sunday, but you could probably move in on Monday evening."

Grace smiled at Wilhelm who nodded. "Rosemary it sounds ideal, but can you arrange it that quickly?

"It's vacant. She'll be very happy to let it to someone she knows."

"This is wonderful, isn't it Wilhelm. This morning as we were praying we felt the Lord prompted us to come and see you?" At Grace's bright-eyed enthusiasm Wilhelm smiled.

David smiled across at them, "Actually before Rosemary spoke I was going to suggest you might like to come and stay with me for the weekend."

Taken aback Grace repeated, "Stay with you?"

With a wry smile he said, "After all Grace, having my secretary living in my house is not unusual!"

Grace groaned, "Don't remind me! That Christmas I really did think you were going too far, but when I got back from Germany to find Jane was about to live in your basement flat I really didn't think it was right. Poor Jane hadn't a clue how you felt about her!"

Amused, he brought them up to date. "Jill, as you know, married Paul. Rosemary still shares the basement flat with them. I don't know how I'd cope without them and Rosemary organising life here, and at home." He smiled across at her and caught the look Grace gave Wilhelm. He'd put any wrong assumptions right over the weekend. "Anyway, this weekend it seems I'm alone with the twins, so the truth is I've an ulterior motive in the hope of having invited you, you'll help me out."

Grace made an amused moue, "David, you haven't changed! You were always quick to spot an opportunity, and use it to your advantage."

Pretending to be offended he teased, "Grace, how could you say such a thing? You were the one who told Jane how much you valued my integrity, my depth of thought, and…" He paused for effect, "My kindness and generosity."

By now Grace was giggling like a school girl, and Wilhelm was smiling broadly. "Are you sure we won't be imposing on you?"

"It could be said I'll be imposing on you! Do you know seeing you both has really cheered me up."

Wilhelm looked at Grace who gave a happy smile and nod, and accepting he added, "I'm not much of a cook, but have brought up four children, and we're grandparents to four boys and four girls all under seven."

Eagerly Grace added, "I'd hoped to see the twins and thought I'd ask if we could pop in sometime, but this is far better. Thank you David." Wilhelm emptied his cup, Rosemary offered him a refill, and Grace continued to enthuse how in so short a time they'd found somewhere to live, and stay over the weekend. In a pause Wilhelm asked, "David, when we arrived you asked, "Do you two want a job? What was that about?"

"I'll tell you the whole tale later, but basically the man who took over my job let us down. I've had to step back into running the Brussels Exhibition, which means my being away from home for two weeks in December. He smiled across at Rosemary, "Rosemary, although brilliant in all she does is shy, and needs someone outgoing to offset that. We'd prayed just before you arrived that the Lord would supply our need. It strikes me you could be the miracle of answered prayer?"

Wilhelm sat back, and placing his arm along the back of the settee smiled at Grace who nodded. "I like that idea, if this could be extended to my wife, you have your miracle."

For a moment he sat in stunned silence. Then enthusiastically he boomed, "Do you mean it? Grace, how marvellous it would be to have you back. We may do things a little different to Germany, but the basics are the same, and perhaps I won't need to spend more than a couple of days in Brussels, this is amazing, I can barely believe it."

Wilhelm asked, "Is this offer just for Brussels, or do you want someone to take the job over permanently?"

Immediately he responded, "How long can you both stay?"

With a deep rolling chortle Wilhelm countered, "Make it worth my while and I think we could commit to at least a couple of years, maybe longer."

Thrilled he'd looked at Rosemary and noted she didn't seem to be sharing his enthusiasm, but the provision was so incredible he felt quite delirious at the joy of it. "I have no doubt ITP will be able to pay you both a salary you'd be happy with, so my question is can you start on Monday?"

"Well it wasn't my intention to get straight back into work, but you have need, and it would seem God has brought us here to fill it."

The seriousness in Grace's voice earthed his delight. "Gentlemen, in your enthusiasm let's not rush into anything. There are other issues to consider." Both men stared at her as she stood, took their cups, put them on the tray and continued, "Wilhelm we should go and discuss this over lunch. And David, you owe it to Rosemary to hear her thoughts before any decisions are made." Grace's stern expression and wide-eyed look reminded him of the times she'd been upset with him, his broad smile turned to a frown.

In seeing them out, he arranged to collect them from their hotel that evening and transport them to the house. Still seated in his office Rosemary made it obvious she did have something to say. Relaxing on the settee he remarked, "Well who would have believed it, Grace and Wilhelm." The resigned look on Rosemary's face gave him to ask, "Have I missed something? What's the problem?"

With a pinched look she stated, "You've forgotten I work for you!" Puzzled he nodded. A frustrated sigh emerged from Rosemary before she elaborated, "David, I need to remind you that, with exception of November and part of December, this job needs only one full-time person! I currently have that job, but it appears you've just offered it to Grace?"

Rosemary was right! His pleasure in seeing old friends had over-run his usual careful deliberations and decision making. As Grace pointed out he was quick to spot an opportunity and use it to his advantage! Horrified he sent up an arrow prayer for wisdom, sat forward, and hoped she'd hear the sincerity of what he was about to say. "Please Rosemary don't be upset." In seeing her features tighten, he rushed on to reassure her. "I want you to know how highly I value you, both at work and home, and admit I've not thought this through." Large brown eyes that were portraying scepticism flashed with surprise at his confession. Encouraged, he continued, "Our prayer has reaped a far bigger answer than I could have imagined. Wilhelm's vast experience of Exhibitions all over the world is the opportunity ITP has been waiting for to help expand our trade promotions."

To continue to draw her interest he moved closer to her chair and lowered his voice. "This is confidential, but expansion was being mooted when I first met Jane. You may remember just before I was engaged, I was away for a month visiting the world's Exhibition Centres. That was to judge if we could expand our UK trade promotions to other centres across the world, and since I've been studying and monitoring the situation. Around the time Jane became pregnant, Arthur Tyler unexpectedly died, and I suspect Joseph Plaidon was spurred on to retire before he met the same fate. Both men shared the vision of an Overseas Department, where six men would each be responsible for a continent. Forget Antarctica, not a place we'd do much business. But world markets are opening up, it is a time of expansion. Manufacturers are more easily able to export their wares and exhibitions are a good place to promote them. We need men on board like Wilhelm to make it happen. I feel God's provision is for more than a few weeks. Obviously I haven't discussed it with Chris and Maud, but I'd like to bring Wilhelm in as a Director. We need a man of his calibre, age and maturity on the Board."

Rosemary although interested, her accentuated plumy accent portrayed she was still upset. "I appreciate that, but my question remains. On Monday Wilhelm takes over from you, and Grace from me, you've another job to go to I haven't?" The nuance in her tone, gave him to understand her expectation was, she'd be abandoned. Quickly he sought to reassure her. "Rosemary, at this point, we could do with all the help we can get. The Brussels Exhibition will also be an ideal time to introduce Wilhelm, and to talk through ideas with exhibitors. If they are interested they might have specific countries in which they'd wish to promote their merchandise, for example America or Australia. In which case we'd target those first and begin by appointing someone to oversee, and organise our involvement in exhibitions in those countries. I'm not talking of rapid expansion, but a careful foray into what works, and what doesn't."

"And so again I ask where does that leave me?"

"Rosemary you know ITP likes to make the job fit the person, not the person fit the job. I'm talking here about envisioning and experimenting, and you are a talented and intelligent woman, you will fit in. The possibility of moving this forward only happened in the last hour, and I assure you, you will not be abandoned, but very much involved."

Not entirely happy Rosemary nodded her acceptance, and he was quick to point out, "In the mean time there's plenty of work to do, but Grace and Wilhelm will ease the burden, and you'll have time to consider what you'd like to do in the future."

Into Rosemary's eyes came a far away look, as if she longed for something that he wasn't offering.

CHAPTER 24

The taxi drew up alongside the kerb. Excited to be home after Exhibition fever, the cut and thrust of negotiations and contracts for future expansion, he jumped out, hauled his suitcases on to the pavement, paid the driver and fished in his pocket for his house keys. Two weeks had felt a life time, despite daily contact with Rosemary and reassurances the twins were fine. How he was longing to see those little faces that were developing into little replica's of their parents.

The smell of roast dinner assailed his nostrils, but it was unlikely to be coming from his kitchen, which these days was only used to make snacks or fill bottles. The exception being during Grace and Wilhelm's stay, where Grace that weekend had stretched his stomach with her old fashioned English cooking. They'd been good company that weekend, loved the twins, and offered to babysit any time, but did admit to being tired by the Sunday night, and were pleased to move to the cottage on the Monday evening.

On hearing his mother's excited voice announcing "David's home" he left his cases in the hall and took the stairs two at a time. With a glass of sherry in hand, his Mum kissed him and said affectionately, "We thought we'd welcome you home with Sunday lunch. As you have a dining room and the largest table, we're cooking and eating it up here." She moved aside for him to enter the room as William shot forward to hug his legs, and grin up at him. Unable to move from the doorway he smiled around at his family, his eyes seeking out those two special faces that for the past two weeks he'd only seen in the now creased photo in his wallet! Surprised, he nodded at Gerald Maysfield standing by the piano talking to his father, then bent to pick up William. "Hi little fellow, you're getting heavy, tell me where are those twins of mine?" William bounced in his arms pointing upwards, "'osie, 'osie."

Jill seated on the settee looking like a beached whale called from across the room, "We've just fed the twins, 'osie is changing their nappies and settling them for a sleep."

At that his Dad boomed, "She's done that and back in the kitchen helping Margaret."

With William perched on his shoulders he headed across the room to grin down on Jill and observe, "I thought, by the time I

316

returned, you might be a bit slimmer!"

"Not yet brother dear, but you know me, huge one minute, delivered the next."

Paul tutted, "A worrying trait that will have me grounded here until this baby is born. Jill is having a planned home birth!"

Jill groaned her hands on her bump, "Baby Stemmings, you better not keep us waiting until Christmas. I can hardly move and there's much to do. However, with Rosemary taking her annual leave to look after the twins in your absence she's also been wonderful helping with William and the chores. A real Godsend, and it certainly wasn't a holiday for her, but she's been adamant it was preferable to being in Brussels."

Grabbing William, David dived him like a plane, and headed him into Paul. "Can you take him for I'm longing to see the twins?"

At six months the difference between the twins was becoming obvious. Rebecca was much smaller, her face heart shaped with fair-hair like her mother, while Joshua was solidly built, dark haired, and already had the Reinhardt features of a rather prominent nose, a squaring of his jaw and would probably develop a cleft in his chin. It was best to let sleeping babies lie, but he wished them awake, for these days at seeing him their eyes would light up, and their arms outstretched for hugs and kisses.

To show his appreciation for Rosemary giving up her time to look after the twins he bought her a gold and pearl necklace, but now he was home, he wondered if perhaps it wasn't too personal a gift, and she'd misunderstand his motives.

As he closed the door on the twins Gerald Maysfield's voice drifted up the stairs. "Are you sure it's alright for me to be here? This is a family party, I feel an intruder."

He strained to hear Rosemary's reply. "I'm not part of this family, but I'm included, and as my friend so are you. Now come, help me lay the table."

That was his answer! Rosemary saw herself as family, he'd wait until Christmas because as part of the family they'd exchange gifts, and her present could be from him and the twins. In previous years she'd received the customary chocolates and ITP's generous bonus, but this year was different for she'd been so much more involved in their lives. For a minute he remained on the landing considering how his family had pulled together.

Pride came in the way they'd drawn Rosemary in. Pleasure in knowing Rosemary felt included. And as a family they saw Rosemary in so many different ways. Appreciation of her love for William and the twins. Admiration, at the way she handled adversity. Gratitude for her approach to find a solution, not make a problem. Regard of her creativity and intelligence. His mouth formed a wry smile. Gerald Maysfield obviously considered she was an attractive woman! On a quiet hum, his brow furrowed. Gerald didn't share her faith, and didn't know that underlying her attributes were unseen scars and deep wounds, but David knew he'd no right to speak or interfere.

Lunch was the usual chaos of people talking at once, interruptions to pass food and wine, minor accidents, arguments and laughter. Rosemary was working with his mother to ensure everyone had what they needed, but David noticed when Gerald put his hand on Rosemary's arm, he didn't receive the customary cold stare, but she did withdraw from him. Had Rosemary asked him, because she too had gleaned Gerald was lonely in his three bedroom house, and an invite to a family roast dinner was a rare treat?

"You're very quiet dear, I expect you're tired after your trip?"

With a smile at his mother, he replied by extolling his trip and the positive response from exhibitors in wanting to promote their goods beyond Europe. "Grace and Wilhelm have accomplished so much in a short time." The babble of voices around the table ceased as they listened to him. "Early next year Wilhelm and I will need to go to the US to find someone suitable to head up the thrust into the North American continent."

Concerned his Mum pointed out, "What about the twins? You and Jane agreed that when you became a father you wouldn't gallivant about as you did before."

About to say he wasn't gallivanting, it was his job, when Jill, with a certain pique, piped up, "You are needed here. Mum and Joyce covered for you as the chaos was sorted out at ITP, but that can't continue indefinitely. And it would have been impossible to cope without Rosemary these last two weeks." Jill glared at him. "I hear Wilhelm and Grace are taking over the Department, so surely any gallivanting will be their responsibility? And that, I believe, pushes Rosemary out of her job."

"Jill, I didn't say that!" A blush began to defuse over Rosemary's face.

"But that's the nub of it. And frankly brother dear, I find it positively disgraceful that after Rosemary's been your unpaid, twenty-four hour skivvy this last six months, that's the way you repay her." Jill folded her arms over her massive bulge and gave him a grim, challenging stare.

All eyes focussed on him, but despite feeling indignant at Jill's bringing up a work situation at home, he responded calmly. "You've misjudged the situation. Rosemary is employed by ITP and there is no question of her not having a job."

Aggressively Jill challenged, "What job?"

"One that will be tailor made to fit Rosemary's abilities and talents, as was the one you had until you left because you were expecting William."

"But on Monday what happens, does she have a desk, an office, a role?"

"Look Jill, this is not the time or the place for this discussion. And don't look at me like that because I'm not fudging the issue. I have every intention of chatting to Rosemary about her future, and I know you mean well, but Rosemary is quite capable of speaking for herself."

Still belligerent Jill stared at him. Rosemary, without looking at anyone muttered, "I'll put the kettle on."

At that his father boomed, "Rosemary don't leave. David is right this isn't for public discussion, but I need to tell you that it has been obvious to us these past months that you have been invaluable in helping run this household. And, I feel, it was very commendable of you to take holiday leave to look after the twins in David's absence."

Quietly Rosemary said, "It was my pleasure."

"Good! Then if ITP doesn't specifically need you, I'd like to suggest we do."

All eyes focussed on his father. Mystified David questioned, "Who is 'we'? Inharts Pharmaceuticals?"

"No! No! my boy! Dear me, of all people I expect you to follow the logic of this situation. Your argument against a nanny was you didn't want a stranger living in your house." He nodded, and his father addressed Rosemary, "So young lady you live here, you aren't a stranger, so what would you say to us employing you in that role?" All eyes took in the stunned

319

expression on Rosemary's face, and watched as her eyes moved from his father's face, to David's.

Instantly, in the need she should know, David stated, "Rosemary I didn't instigate this, but Dad is right, you would be ideal, and I'd be very happy to entrust the twins to your care."

Unable to wait for her to recover his Dad demanded, "Well Rosemary, what have you to say?"

"Good grief Dad, give her a chance." Jill, palms on the table hoisted herself up from the chair. "Out of the blue you offer her a job, there's no mentioned of salary, conditions of employment, yet you demand she makes a decision. Is that the way you usually employ your staff?"

His father's features tightened his reply sharp. "Yes we do! And very successful it is too! People are employed because of their interest in the job, not the benefits they'll receive. Admittedly Inharts, as a company, are renowned for their high salaries, but new employees often start below average, but once they show commitment they are quickly rewarded."

Jill paused, arms akimbo as she rounded the far end of the table to retort, "Well this isn't Inharts! Rosemary has proved her commitment to our family and without financial...ohhh! Jill's eyes widened. Gerald sitting near leapt up, and backed away.

Paul jumped forward to proclaim, "Jill's water's have just broken" as Jill, with a deep groan began sinking towards the floor. Paul hoisting her upward declared, "You aren't having my baby on the carpet."

Gripped in agony she said between clenched teeth, "I shouldn't bet on it."

"You will pant, pant, not push! Gerald, David, get on either side of her because we're taking her downstairs. Rosemary, could you get the delivery kit from the boiler room and put it out ready in our bedroom." As Paul spoke, he and Gerald were moving chairs out of the way as Rosemary skirted around those, and the boggle-eyed children. Anxiously, David wondered how they were going to get sixteen stone Jill panting, and in pain, safely down the stairs.

Jill screamed, "I...can't...the baby is coming."

Paul instructed, "David, Gerald hold her up, lift her as best you can and move her towards the stairs."

Despair filled Jill's voice, as she panted out words as they hauled her along, "I can't walk. I can't stand. Put me down. The baby is coming."

"Keep going! Ignore her." Paul instructed, I'll go down the stairs first. Try and take as much of her weight as possible. Jill, don't even think about pushing. That's it now down one step at a time."

Richard and Phillip rushed around the group to watch their rotund Auntie Jill being trundled towards and then down the stairs in a very ungainly fashion. But it wasn't until William started crying, "Mummy, Mummy" that anyone thought to remove the children from the scene. Paula ushered her boys into the lounge, but William, screaming, pushed his plump little body between the wooden banister rails and would not budge. Jill couldn't see, and in pain couldn't talk. Paul trapped in front of Jill called up to calm him. Looking across Jill, and supporting her weight David tried as well, but William was becoming hysterical. Then to his utter amazement his father appeared, knelt down by the little boy said something, the screaming turned to sobs, and the little arms left the banisters to curl around his grandfather's neck.

"Last two stairs Jill. Hold on, nearly there. Keep panting. Ouch, who left those suitcases there?" Jill gritting her teeth gave Paul a 'serve you right' look as they rounded the stairs into the hallway.

From above his mother called, "When you've done that the custard is ready."

With Jill's weight David's voice came out in a higher pitch than normal. "The custard's ready, the baby's coming, life goes on, just another day in the Reinhardt household." Gerald's mouth twitch in amusement, and seeing the funny side they creased up in laughter, as Jill creased up in pain.

Anxious Paul urged, "I don't see what's funny. Hold Jill up. David, this is serious. I'm not having my baby born in the hall!"

"But if Jill's quick, the custard won't have gone cold!" Paul tutted at David's remark, Gerald guffawed.

A second later, Jill countermanded, "This baby's…ooh. Put…down. It's coming…Ohhh!"

David and Gerald looked at each. Gerald ordered, "Get your shoulder under her arm pit, grab a leg" and with surprising fluidity, which reminded him of a three-legged race, in step they ran her the remainder of the way. In manoeuvring her through the flat door and into the bedroom David narrowly missed cracking Jill's head against the door post, but by then she was screaming "The head's out." Unceremoniously they dumped her on the bed, and retreated. But as he closed the door he heard Paul declare, "She's right, the baby is here."

With a pat on Gerald's back he said, "Good team work. That was a close call, now to that custard." Sniggering like naughty schoolboys they entered the dining room where the rest of the family were eating their pudding as though nothing untoward had happened! The sight, and a glance at each caused laughter to overtake them, and they were still wiping tears from their eyes when Paul heralding his arrival was shouting "We've got a boy, we've got a boy!"

"Congratulations" resounded from around the table, and David bantered as and Paul went to leave, "Here, take Jill her pie and custard before it gets cold" and at Paul's bemused expression, he and Gerald howled again with laughter and couldn't understand the family's baffled expressions.

The camaraderie of the day opened up conversation with Gerald. After talking a little of his life he confided he was surprised when Rosemary had taken up his offer to go out for drink, and the following week to a meal, she's very restful..." Unkindly, David was just thinking that's probably because she says little, when it was their turn to visit Jill and Luke Jonathan Stemmings. The next distraction was the twins needing his attention, and although Gerald offered to help with their feed he didn't expect him to continue the conversation. But when Gerald asked questions about Rosemary he couldn't answer, his reply was rather gruff, "Rosemary and I tend to stick to impersonal matters, she seems to prefer it that way."

Gerald nodded. "Rosemary probably only told me she was born in India because I spent a year there. Her parents own a tea plantation out there. I asked questions, but she said she didn't remember much about those early years, but returning after the war her parents, particularly her father had never settled back here. And in the 50s it been impossible to go back, but when they did, they stayed, and had now retired there. I don't think she visits India, or they come back often, and she's not inclined to talk about it." David gave a sad grimace and nodded wisely. Oddly he felt hurt that Rosemary had privileged Gerald with such rare personal details, and although she hadn't lied, she'd given them reason to believe she went to stay with her parents.

Gerald chatting away went on, "I took Rosemary to see the 1958 film 'The Inn of the Sixth Happiness' and was surprised at her emotional response, have you seen it?"

Unexpected resentment that Gerald, and not his family, had broken into Rosemary's life brought David to say in a derogatory voice, "Sitting in the dark, with people you don't know, watching a huge screen has never appealed to me. And with the advent of colour television, and several TV channels, I suspect that form of entertainment will soon go out of fashion."

If Gerald caught his tone he didn't show it for he cheerily countered, "But with TV you are subject to what they are showing." To that David grunted, and further conversation was halted by Rosemary's arrival to ask if they'd like to go for a stroll in the park, or enjoy a family game. He chose the former, Gerald the latter.

It was well past eight o'clock before all their visitors had left, and the children finally settled. Tired, but knowing he needed to speak to Rosemary, David found her alone in the basement kitchen making hot chocolate. And having asked if he'd like one, he leant back against the work top to say, "I'm sorry Dad put you on the spot earlier."

Pushing the filled mug towards him she said, "You can stir it." To that he frowned, but quickly realised as Rosemary continued, "Jill shouldn't have spoken as she did" the stirring wasn't his making trouble, but connected to his hot chocolate! Pouring the remaining boiling milk into the mugs she added, "Jill was over compensating because of her guilt about abandoning Helen." In the brief moment her eyes met his he glimpsed the pain 'abandonment' would bring.

He stopped himself blurting out 'that's ridiculous' instead chose to tease, "I've a problem, I need two Rosemary's." At her questioning stare he smiled encouragingly. "The one who I trust to look after the twins, and the other needed to liaise with Wilhelm to combine ITP's old structures with the new." He laid his spoon on the work surface. "Thank you for this. But you need to know whatever your decision it won't affect this being your home, or us being your friends and family." He picked up his cup and before heading for the door assured her, "And there's no hurry, take time, think it over."

"David, I don't need time?"

Turning, he caught the rare sight of animation lighting up

Rosemary's face. Taken aback he knew he was staring, but it was as if he were seeing the original Rosemary before the face became dour, and the eyes doleful. "These last two weeks have been the best of my life. I've loved looking after the children, the feeling of family, and now there's a new baby to care for."

Understanding where she was going, and afraid she'd get hurt, or feel abandoned in the future, he warned, "If you decide to be nanny to all the children I must point out that as a job there are no long term career prospects."

A vulnerable, serious expression moved fleetingly across her face before she agreed, "I understand, but there are many jobs and few that give you the chance to be part of a family."

Thoughtfully he nodded, "I know Paul and Jill want a large family, even if I find a wife and mother for the twins, they'll still need your help while they have young ones. I know in life there are no guarantees, but for your sake I'd prefer to arrange a secondment from ITP with six monthly reviews giving you options of employment with your pension and national health contributions paid."

With a shrug Rosemary commented, "As you wish! But as your father said, I'm more interested in doing the job than the salary, and am quite content to just have a roof over my head, and food to eat."

"Oh Rosemary, I believe we can do better than that. And we'd be very happy if you'd…" amused he took hold of his labels and burst into song, "*Consider yourself at home, consider yourself one of the family, We've taken to you so strong, It's clear we're going to get along, Consider yourself well in, Consider yourself part of the family, Where we go, you go, Whatever we do, you do, for you're part of us.*" At the altered lyrics from the musical 'Oliver', Rosemary laughed. That was so unusual, so unexpected, it made him feel so joyful he bantered, "Shall I take that as a 'yes'? At her nod, he made a sweeping bow, and said, "In that case Madam, it is with great pleasure and on behalf of the twins, I thank you. Jane would be so pleased." Rosemary's eyes filled with unshed tears. To deflect that he cautioned, "You'd better get that chocolate to Jill before it goes cold. We can discuss terms and conditions another time."

On his way up to his flat it dawned on him that, with Rosemary sharing the twin's lives with him, there would be wifely elements, but without the status, comfort and companionship. How essential it would be for them to show their appreciation, make her feel part of the family and know she'd the security of employment when she wanted to return to ITP. Gerald might be fifteen years her senior, but his gentle, slow manner did seem to be breaking a hole through the wall Rosemary had erected around her life. Perhaps that relationship, and her caring of the twins, would bring her to blossom into the woman she was intended to be.

Ten days later from his office window he watched the large white flakes falling against the black sky. The predicted white Christmas looked on its way. Thank goodness he wasn't going to Bath. They'd decided, with the twins and new baby, it would be more sensible this year for the family to congregate in London. A few days earlier, he and Paul had erected a large tree in his lounge. Rosemary handed up lights and baubles while Jill, feeding Luke, acted as forewoman and decreed their placement. The three children, starry eyed, sat together on Joshua's playmate, but it wasn't long before William was up and eager to help. Rebecca waving her hands gurgled happily, but his boy did his upmost to follow William, in something akin to press-ups, before crying with frustration because he went backwards instead of forwards!

Last night, Rosemary, for the first time in his memory attended ITP's Christmas party accompanied by Gerald. Inebriation probably accounted for the audacious way he'd commented, "Rosemary you look stunning. Red suits you. I wonder how you found time to buy a dress with working here, and the Christmas preparations at home." At Gerald's appreciative smile Rosemary had blushed prettily.

Tossing her curtain of hair, she'd uplifted it, tilted her head, and with a rather endearing smile had commented, "Jane insisted I buy and wear it." Taken aback his smile had turned to frown. Rosemary's brow puckered, "Do you think it's too flamboyant? But it is more suited to this occasion than the river trip two years ago."

Quickly he assured her, "I can't fault Jane's taste, the dress is perfect for you." And with a genuine high-wattage smile he gave a courteous bow. "May I have the honour of the next dance?" Rosemary's equally courteous smile, and response in taking his outstretched hand, drew him to wonder if she'd imbibed alcohol to give her courage to join the party. However she didn't falter in stepping into the rhythm, executing a perfect foxtrot and proving she was as an accomplished dancer as Jane. But she wasn't forthcoming to tell where she'd learnt the skill. Rosemary's continual secrecy he found irritating, but perhaps with the family over Christmas she'd open up more.

A brief tap on his office door before it opened interrupted his musings. Grace spoke from the doorway, "Wilhelm is downstairs. Stan's waiting to lock up. We're looking forward to being with you on Boxing Day, and seeing baby Luke. I still can't get over Jill delivering a 9lb baby in about two minutes. Is she up to cooking the Christmas lunch, or will Rosemary do it?"

"I've left that to the women folk to arrange, I'm just footing the bills." He gave a last look around, turned off the lights, and as they moved through Mavis' office he thanked her and Wilhelm for volunteering to look after the skeleton staff in the days between Christmas and New Year."

Along the corridor to the main staircase Grace responded, "David, it's us who want to thank you. You have made us so welcome, and who would have thought one day I'd be married to a director of ITP? What a Christmas present. It will be good in the New Year to get our teeth into forming the new Overseas Department. We were delighted by the staff's approval when you announced those decisions at lunch time."

David with a smile admitted, "Even I didn't expect them to give you a standing ovation, but that proves how in a short time they've come to like and accept you both."

Grace tucked her arm in his as they descended the stairs. "Helped no doubt by the generous amount of wine they'd all consumed, reminding me of a Christmas lunch four years ago!"

He sighed, and squeezed her arm against him, "It feels like yesterday, and yet a life time ago. As they turned, to descend the final staircase his mind was imprinted with past times he'd come down these stairs. Today, there was no cheeky young girl chatting to the Receptionist, or hundreds of people watching him and Jane descend as Mr and Mrs Reinhardt. It was empty except for Wilhelm and Stan, the caretaker, who chatting looked up at their approach. Stan grinned at Grace, "Who'd have believed you'd be back Grace, and a Director's wife as that. And Mr Reinhardt, I thought the days of you being last out of here were gone. Get home to those twins of yours, forget work, and God be with you."

"And you too Stan, see you in the New Year."

The smell of Christmas food assailed his nostrils the moment he entered the house. He took a deep breath and inhaled, the specific aroma he recognised as the roast gammon they'd eat tonight, and cold on Boxing Day. With two kitchens the cooking and storing of food wasn't a problem. He took the stairs two at a time. The routine was William would have his tea, as Jill fed Luke. Rosemary had pointed out that it was good for them to have a family time in their part of the house, just as it was good for him to come home and find his children waiting for him in his."

But tonight, his lounge, the tree and dining room were in darkness. There was a lingering smell of cooking, the kitchen obviously used earlier, but now all was silent. He stowed his briefcase, hung up his coat in the hall cupboard and experienced a deep pang of sorrow. Last year Jane curled up on the settee would have leapt up at his homecoming to hug him. A small tree with lights had made the room warm and welcoming, the smell of dinner cooking and the table laid ready with candles had started with him kissing that delectable little neck, patting that sexy little bottom and... It wasn't good to dwell on those memories so he ran down the stairs to the basement to hug the twins.

Delightful smells made his stomach rumble in hunger. Jill made a beautiful picture of motherhood as she breast fed Luke while reading a story to William cuddled up next to her. At her feet the twins were sitting on their play mats and appearing to listen. At his arrival she looked up with a small smile, as Paul emerged from the kitchen with William's tea. William slid off the settee ran to hug his knees as two small pairs of eyes lit up with expectancy. As he picked William up he asked, "Have the twins been good today?" William nodded, then frowned before saying, "Oosie gone."

"Has she, I expect she'll be back in a minute. Shall we sit you in your chair to eat your tea?"

Behind him Jill cleared her throat. Paul took William from him, and declared. "I'm afraid Rosie has gone."

Puzzled he picked up Rebecca, made her giggle with his kisses, and then asked, "What do you mean, 'gone'?"

He sat opposite Jill and encouraged Joshua's crab like crawl towards him as Paul answered, "You tell him Jill because she spoke to you." Joshua arrived by his knee, he pulled him up, rocked and heartedly kissed him, and when Joshua's giggles had subsided he looked expectantly at Jill.

"It was about three o'clock. Paul popped out to the shop for some last minute things. Rosie appeared with the twins saying she'd fed them and could we amuse them until you came home? She told me the twins' bottles were ready for their next feed, their food mashed and just needed heating up. She said she'd checked everything was up to date and she'd be back on the 2nd January.

Bewildered he boomed, "What! Why? I thought she was spending Christmas with us?"

With a rueful expression Jill agreed, "So did we, brother dear, so did we."

"Did someone upset her?"

"Only perhaps in our omission of not inviting her to stay and enjoy Christmas with us. Because she'd said nothing to the contrary, and was part of the preparations we just assumed she'd be here."

Bewildered David queried, "But it was only two weeks ago I told her to consider herself one of the family. She laughed at my song. The words, 'so where we go, you go, what we do, you do…'" He raked his hair, "It didn't occur to me… Her family lives…it's too late for her to go to India for Christmas. Where has she gone? Did you ask her?

Jill's face contorted to a cringe. "I did, she looked puzzled, so I said we'd expected her to celebrate with us, she looked surprised. Then I said how sorry I was that no-one had conveyed that to her, she looked upset, and when I said we'd assumed as she was so much part of our family she'd be here, she looked ready to cry. But you know how aristocratic her manner gets if she's upset, her reply was so stiff upper lip. I quote: 'Oh Jill, this is a time for families. You don't need me here. I do have a home to go to.' I commented, that I'd assumed, if she were going home she'd have told us, and received that cold stare. Then as if to excuse herself she went on, 'Every employee, even nannies, are entitled to a Christmas break. Don't worry I'll be back before the men return to work.' She then disappeared into her bedroom and came out with her suitcase, wished me a happy Christmas and said she'd put our presents under the tree. At that I jumped up, and said, "You can't go without taking your presents, and thrust Luke into her arms so she couldn't leave before I'd gathered them up. Fortunately I'd wrapped ours last night. I knew David you'd tied her gift to the tree, so I went and got that too. I put them all in a bag and said, "We love you, we'll miss you, but have a happy Christmas." At that I'd swear her lips trembled, so I asked, "Why don't you stay?" Her reply was to tilt her nose in the air and state, "To do so would let others down." With that she handed me back Luke and left.

"I've thought about those words, 'I've got 'a' home to go to' and 'letting others down'. When we talk of 'home' we interchange that with seeing 'the parents,' but where is this 'home' and who are the 'others'?

Paul helping William collect up the food on his plate commented, "Perhaps her parents have come home from India."

Irritated, and feeling let down at Rosemary's lack of trust to talk of her home and family he said bluntly, "It's her life, and business. We aren't her keepers!"

Jill burping Luke grimaced as she voiced the truth. "But we see her loving our children, and want her to know we love her. I don't understand why she's so secretive, and suspect Gerald knows more than we do, but even him she keeps at arms length."

That was true, for he'd seen Gerald try to capture a kiss under the mistletoe at the Christmas Party, but Rosemary had ensured all kisses landed on her cheek. Four Christmas' ago, without giving her opportunity to turn from him, he'd very publicly he'd kissed her. The fear in her eyes had led him afterwards to take her aside to apologise, but he'd then needed to restrain her from gouging out his eyes as she spat, ranted and raved at him like a demented animal.

Paul said quietly, "Let's not speculate. Even little people have ears! And she's entitled to her privacy, we'll just make her feel very welcome when she returns."

CHAPTER 25

Startled David awoke. His dream and reality collided as he saw a reflection of Jane's face in the water of the lake. The explanation wasn't supernatural, but because he'd been revisiting the photo albums and scrapbooks of Jane's life. Today marked one year since her death. And just before falling asleep he'd stared at her photograph, talked of how much he missed her, and supposed he always would. A glance at the clock showed 3.33 am. Padding into the twins' room he peered into the cots that sat side by side. It was incredible how twins could look so different. Curled up with her thumb in her mouth Rebecca looked so small and petite. When not asleep her brown eyes were constantly sparkling with love, fun and mischief and with blonde shoulder length hair often in pigtails, she knew just how to wind her Daddy around her little finger! Joshua splayed out on his back with arms outstretched was heavier, broader, longer and had black hair. Awake his dark eyes were serious, and protectively watchful of his adored little sister, often striving to mimic her ways, knowing to do so would bring amusement and laughter.

It had been several months since David last had his recurring dream. Then, the horses having slowed, had come to a halt in a large oasis in a desert. Within the dream he'd felt compelled to dismount, to rest, to take refreshment from the lake's water and wait for the imminent dawn to rise over him. Tonight, he'd been sitting alone on a stone, contemplating the water as the sun came up, and in that he'd seen Jane's reflection. It had jumped him awake, perhaps with the hope she'd be there in reality. God spoke in many ways, was there a correlation in time and God's Word? Slipping back into bed he picked up his Bible, it opened at Jeremiah, there was no 3:33, but there was a 33.3 and it was strangely fitting. 'Call to me and I will answer you, and will tell you great and hidden things which you have not known.' He made a rueful face, he'd not found the clues to those things Jane spoke of in the maize field. Was Jane, or the Holy Spirit trying to communicate something? He prayed, and remembered he'd noted the time in the maize field as 11.40 am. Did that have a relevant biblical match? There were sixty-six books in the Bible. Having asked the Lord, he sensed the New Testament, but the verse didn't exist in Matthew and Mark. There wasn't a message in Luke 11:40, but John 11:40 read: "Jesus said to her, 'Did I not tell you that if you would believe you would see the glory of God?' Excited he wanted to shout, 'I have, I have experienced that glory cloud. But knowing preachers didn't recommend taking Biblical verses out of their context he read on, and found this was said in the midst of Lazarus' death and resurrection! It felt like confirmation of his witnessing Jane's eternal resurrection. How good of the Father God to bring these reassurances on the anniversary of her death? But the message today still talked of God wanting to reveal hidden things, Jane had talked about clues and treasure. Could it be possible Jane, without realising it, had written down God's clues? Expectant, he jumped out of bed. Dragging the top two boxes from the wardrobe containing the photo albums and scrapbooks he'd put away only hours before, he grabbed and pulled out a third box. He'd not opened it since reading Jane's diaries, and that then, as now, seemed an intrusion. David drew out, and hugged to him the Bible he'd given Jane that first Christmas. It had represented the beginning of his hopes and dreams. Inside he'd written the words of Ps.37:3-4. Those verses had become so relevant to their lives! Jane's hearts desire was much the same as his, to serve the Lord, her God with all her heart, soul and strength. He thought of Ian who'd admired Jane, and his letter last week informing him of his engagement to a Christian girl he met at the church he attended. Jane, the great romantic, would have been thrilled to know that.

Propped up against the pillows he opened the Bible at Ps.37, he knew it, oh so well, and then noticed tucked deep between the pages a thin slip of paper. Gently pulling it out he read in Jane's writing, 'Take delight in the Lord, and He will give you the desires of your heart' Ps.37:4, and on the other side two words, 'Remember Rosemary'. He smiled. Jane said she often planted as 'seed faith' her prayer requests in the relevant passage in her Bible. At least he was 'remembering Rosemary in that for the past six months she'd been working happily alongside Jill running the household and looking after four children. But the desires of Rosemary's heart, he wondered what they might be beyond loving the children. If it was romance, then it wasn't to be Gerald for he'd not been around the house for months. Jill had inquired about him, the answer like so many was ambiguous, 'his work keeps him busy'!

Laying the Bible beside him he considered again Jane's

cryptic words, 'but you still have treasure to find in earthen vessels, follow the clues, and enjoy the journey'. If 'earthen vessels' meant people then the twins were indeed his treasure and delight, and their growing up could be the journey. Where there clues he was missing, perhaps 'remember Rosemary' was one of those?

After the Christmas fiasco they ensured Rosemary was always invited giving her the option to chose whether she wished to be included. The Friday after New Year had been her thirtieth birthday. The previous year Jane had taken her out to lunch at the Serpentine Restaurant, but with the children, and looking after a new born baby, Jill couldn't do that. And seeing her embarrassment at having to thank him for the large bouquet of flowers he'd had delivered, anything more would have stretched their friendship. Beatty had been staying, and with more people to feed, the cooking and meal each evening was in his flat. Jill made Rosemary a birthday cake with thirty candles and she'd been visibly touched, but tears had spilled over when on behalf of the family William presented her with a box containing a gold watch. In a choked voice she'd thanked them saying, "This really is too much!" to which almost in unison they'd disagreed with her. Obviously pleased she wore it frequently as she did the necklace he'd given her at Christmas. There was no doubt, Jane would be pleased that they were 'remembering Rosemary'.

Their desire in feeling Rosemary should feel comfortable and at home with them they'd discussed with her the 'nanny' role. Her request had been she didn't want an official role, set hours or pay, but just do whatever was necessary whenever necessary. The family had considered her proposal, but agreed that when David arrived home, around six o'clock, Rosemary's official day finished. If she wanted to help, or join in their activities that was her choice, but her evenings and weekends should be free for her to pursue her own life. David had insisted that Rosemary accept the option to stay employed by ITP who would pay her a half salary with sixth month options to return. And when the new department was up and running she would be offered a responsible and well paid position. His father had insisted he recompense ITP the cost of Rosemary's secondment, while he and Paul covered Rosemary's share of household expenses and food. From David's point of view it was working well. He arrived home in time to play with the twins for an hour before bed time, and on bath nights Rosemary stayed to help because she wanted to. She smiled more often, and on occasions laughed! Weekends, she'd join in with shopping, a walk to the park or a visit to the zoo, but he noticed only if Jill or Paul were part of the plan. And she might not enter into conversations, but the giving of such appropriate Christmas and birthday presents revealed she listened. Jane, would also be delighted that after William had taken to calling 'Osie, the family began calling her Rosie, and she didn't seem to mind.

On a yawn David stretched across the empty bed. Only ten percent of his life he'd spent with Jane, but how she'd changed it. It was unimaginable that anyone would fill her place, especially in his bed where they'd experience such pleasure and laughter, yet he'd the rest of his life to live. But Jane's name would live on with the 'Jane Mckenzie Fund' that was slowly being established. In his mind's eye he saw Rosemary's startled expression when, at his birthday dinner in January, his father had inquired, "Rosemary, what do you think of my proposals! And oddly, he'd felt proud when she'd not only met his father's challenge and agreed with his match funding, but gone on to talk of the growing number of Charity Shops on the High Street, and an idea of shipping our unwanted goods to the poorer nations. Undeterred, by his father's gruff cross-questioning, she'd suggested Inharts' personnel in foreign lands could find local citizens, help them set up a small business, and on receipt of the goods, sell them to their own people at affordable prices. She'd also pointed out, that would provide employment, finance and if profitable, help pay for future shipments. From his father's interest he wasn't surprised when he boomed, "I like it! An excellent idea, young lady. Well thought out!" But the final accolade was his father proclaiming, "You're wasted as a nanny." Rosemary blushing had denied that, but they'd all watched with astonishment at his jovial enthusiasm in concluding, "But, my dear, you won't always be a nanny, children grow up, go to school, so think about it, there's a future in this for you and our family." David received a hard look from his father that he read as his need to also consider and think beyond Rosemary caring for his children!

At Easter his mother had persuaded Rosemary to join them in Bath by saying David needed someone to accompany him with the twins on the long journey. But it was obvious his mother had determined Rosemary wouldn't spend the whole time acting as 'nanny' to four children, but enjoy and be part of the family weekend. The conversation with Rosemary on the journey had been spasmodic, but putting on the radio had helped, and provided their conversation when they stopped for lunch. When drawn she'd talked of her creative ideas which went beyond play mats and the waterproof bag she'd made that doubled as a nappy changing mat. In knowing it was in business conversations, or those centred on the children where Rosemary seemed most at ease David had led her to discuss how her ideas might be developed.

At the Board Meeting, later today, he knew they'd be discussing how the plans for ITP's new Overseas Department might be developed. Rosemary's six month secondment was nearly over. Would she want to return to ITP? Feeling sleepy he turned out the light. Then grinned into the darkness considering how William's name of 'Oosie' had started them calling her 'Rosie' and how she was becoming more 'rosie' by nature. It just went to show that in the right conditions their Rosie's hard, prickly stem could form a bud, and that however tight it would one day open into a delicate bloom. A picture came into David's mind of soft petals in tight layers protecting and covering the centre. Rosie, had a gentle, loving heart and what appeared inexhaustible patience with the four children.

A telephone ringing penetrated his sleep. Opening one eye to look at the clock, his body jumped into gear quicker than his mind. Tussle headed, bleary eyed and unshaven, he staggered down the stairs as Rosemary emerged from the dining room. Taken back, she gave his state of undress a disapproving stare, and stated, "I thought you'd gone to work." Picking up the phone he muttered crossly, "Overslept", and then barked into the telephone receiver, "Reinhardt".

Wilhelm commented, "Ah David, you're there. Shall I cancel the scheduled board meeting that was due to start at nine thirty?"

His answer was abrupt. "I had a disturbed night and overslept. Maud's got the figures. She'll fill you in on the financial implications. I'll be there in about thirty minutes, traffic permitting." He dropped the phone back in its cradle and raked his hair. With no excuse, but his stupidity at staying awake half the night, he scowled hating to be late.

In the lounge the twins sat on the floor of the play pen

building up bricks, with Luke sitting and watching them. All three faces looked up as David entered. Joshua gave a little cry, pulled himself up against the wooden bars, and able to put one foot before the other determined to reach him by holding the bars and walking round. Encouraging him, David admitted to himself Mrs P's expression was right, "'e's a chip off the ole block'! Rebecca crawling across dragged herself up to stand, her little bunches bobbing up and down on either side of her face, as she gave him a toothless, cheeky 'I got here first' grin. From photos, Rebecca was the image of Jane at the same age. With arms outstretched wanting to be lifted out, David complied, and those same arms wound tightly around his neck as Rebecca's little body snuggled into him. Joshua impatiently rattled the wooden bars, not for a cuddle, but to being thrown up in the air and caught. But all David had time for was a quick hug before returning them both to play pen, and say to their disappointed faces, "Daddy's late for work." Fortunately Rosie entered with segments of apple to placate their cries, and as he left he ordered, "Be good for Rosie today." But as Rosie followed him out the room he turned to ask, "Why didn't you call me, you know I never go to work without saying 'goodbye' to the twins."

Without expression Rosie replied, "I'm the nanny to your children, not your keeper."

At that succinct retort he stalked out, but as he dashed upstairs to wash and dress he had to admit she was right! Out of time, he bound down the stairs and passing the lounge called 'goodbye' to no-one in particular. Still feeling disgruntled he walked into ITP, said an abrupt 'Good morning' to those he met on his way, and marched through into his office to say as he took his seat, "Apologies for the lateness. Now, to the business in hand?"

Chris empathised, "If it isn't one of the children keeping me awake, it's the wife wriggling to get comfortable." Wilhelm coughed, frowned at Chris and drew their attention to the spreadsheet before them. Several hours later Wilhelm began reporting on their successful head hunting of two men, one to be responsible for the US and the other Australia, both to start in September. Through hunger from missing breakfast, and tired through missing sleep, David's mind wandered causing Wilhelm to say his name twice before he drew his attention. "In line with Rosemary's six month secondment we now need to offer her employment, and outline what her job could entail. Eventually, London with be the Head Office for the Overseas Division, but until we get a European representative, she could continue to administer the London and Brussels Exhibitions. In another six months her job description will change again, but if she takes up that role now, it will mean I can concentrate on the overseas development, and just be ITP's representative for the duration of those exhibitions. And before you ask David, Grace is happy with that arrangement, preferring to help me develop the Overseas Division, and sometimes travel with me. Susie is a good worker, she's enjoying experiencing ITP's different departments, and assuming Rosemary returns and is happy about it, I feel Susie could become her secretary. My plan, once all the continents have their representatives, will be that Grace and I retire. Ideally Rosemary, with her languages will easily be able to oversee and liaise with the overseas representatives, and be ready to head up the Division from London. The hope is she'll gain in confidence enough to travel to the various continents and meet with our representatives to encourage and expand the vision."

In comparison to the exciting and challenging job being offered to Rosemary he felt he'd become ITP's housekeeper! And his heart sank, for if Rosemary chose to accept that extremely good offer, how would they manage at home?

Maud stubbed out her cigarette in the overflowing ashtray. "I assume when Rosemary's job comes to its full potential it will have the salary to match, just as I insisted when I took Carlton's place."

David's voice was gruff. "That goes without saying, that's assuming she wants a career."

Wilhelm gave him a questioning look. "I hope David you're pleased. I feel I've fulfilled your mandate by orchestrating a job that will stretch Rosemary's skills, give her good career prospects, and without the need to socialise with the men who dominate the industry."

Chris chortled, "Rosemary would have to be very keen on looking after your kids to miss a job opportunity like that!"

Despite the feeling of abject dismay David spoke the truth. "She'd be a fool to refuse it. Wilhelm when do you envisage her starting?"

"I'd like her in post by the end by the August so I can

prepare the way for the US and Australia representatives visiting us mid-September."

David stifled panic. He hadn't expect it to be so soon. "What will we do if she doesn't want the job?"

Wilhelm raised his eyebrows. "David, my understanding was that her secondment to you was the opportunity and space needed for ITP to acknowledge Rosemary's loyalty in tailor-making a job for her."

David repeated Rosemary's earlier words, "But I'm not her keeper."

After exhaling a deep breath, Wilhelm said, "Our agreement was to offer Rosemary a position in six to twelve months. In which case David, if she refuses this, we'll see what we can offer her in another six months. But after that we'll have to put someone else in that post."

Injecting enthusiasm into his voice, David said, "Thank you Wilhelm, and you really have accomplished much in a short time." Glancing around the table, he gave a tight smile, "Next on the Agenda is the discussion of who to appoint as director, but I've no suggestions, and as I missed breakfast I'd like to take a break for lunch." In their nods of consensus he sensed their sympathy, they'd probably noticed his distraction, and didn't seem surprised when he excused himself from going to the canteen, but asked for a meal to brought up to the office.

The moment they left his office, he walked to the window and looked down through the persistent driving rain to the wind-swept drive. His life felt like that, swept along by a tide of events with a persistent hammering of need within and without. Four years ago today, in this place, he'd married Jane on a bright and sunny day believing they'd their lives stretching before them. Of course he'd the twins, and his family, but he wanted to weep at the nonsensicalness of it all. And if Rosemary took the job, he'd loose the only mother figure his children knew, and he'd be stuck in this boring job. Disappointment and dismay weighed heavily upon him, he tried to think positively and attempted to pray, but finally he sat behind the mahogany desk, put his head in his hands, and wept. The telephone rang several times, he ignored it. At a tentative knock at the door he wiped his eyes on his handkerchief, and feeling drained and dejected called, 'Come in' guessing it was Mavis bringing him his meal.

Instead it was Grace with a tray, and a gentle smile. "Doreen, in the canteen, has sent up one of your favourites. Can I get you anything else?"

At the shake of his head, she slipped into the chair opposite his desk. "David, I can see you're upset, and understandable it being the anniversary of Jane's death. You've coped admirably, but with barely a break. Grief takes different forms, it's a painful business, but needs to run its course. I'll get you a pot of tea while you eat that, you'll feel better for it, then take my advice and go home."

Grateful for her obvious care David nodded, and asked, "If you could rustle up a couple of headache tablets that would help."

An hour later, with food in his stomach, and the pain killers relieving the pressure in his head, he took up Wilhelm's offer to drive him home, with the proviso they use the car and go somewhere nice for the evening. Grace readily agreed, "I'd like to do a big shop, it's so much easier with a car, but we'll put it back on your drive tonight for parking around the Mews is a nightmare."

It was the middle of the afternoon, the house was unusually quiet. The play-pen in his lounge empty, and with no-one in the basement flat he looked in the garage. The pram and William's push chair were gone. With the heavy rain clearing they must have decided to go out. The truth was he did feel exhausted, and he didn't want to dwell on Jane dying in his arms. Slowly, he climbed upstairs, lay on the bed, and promptly fell asleep. His dream was full of expectancy and excitement. Unable to rest he walked around the desert oasis as the sun's rays began to touch the trees and bring a sparkle to the small lake. With the glory of dawn, permeating darkness, were chords of love, like soft music. The sound permeated his consciousness, and as he basked in the melody he began to recognise it as a piece of classical music, the composer one of Jane's favourites. That thought catapulted him into reality. It was on his piano the symphony was being played! It was real, not a dream! Joy filled his heart. He jumped up from the bed. Hadn't Jane's blown kiss over the piano with the silent message, 'Won't be long. See you soon'? Had she persuaded God, on the anniversary of her death, to allow her again to break through the veil?

Even as David considered these things he was rushing down the stairs. Bursting into the lounge he boomed, "Jane, Jane..."

In that instant the music stopped, and his sanity returned. In a stultified whisper he said, "Rosemary! I thought, I thought…" Quickly she arose to face him. Bewildered he stated, "But you… you, don't play the piano." Her expression was one of sadness, and he realised the stupidity of his remark. The initial shock turned to anger, his voice to steel, his face to scowl as he challenged, "How dare you play this piano. This is Jane's piano!" At Rosemary's dazed look he stepped forward with an irrational desire to shake her. Apprehension leapt into her eyes, as fiercely he demanded, "What did you think you were doing?"

Head up, her lips pursed, she took several steps backwards towards the children in the play pen, saying quietly, "Entertaining your children. Classical music brings culture into their lives."

"And who told you to do that?"

Puzzled, her brow furrowed. "Jane loved music" She turned towards the play pen, "They do too." In the tense silence she stepped back further, and added, "When they become skittish it calms them down."

Irrationally, he snapped. "This is Jane's piano. She is the only one who'll play it." To indicate that intent, he slammed down the lid, and glaring at Rosemary, accused, "How dare you take such liberties in my home." Even Rosemary's mortified expression didn't stop him booming, "What else do you get up to when I'm not here?"

Luke's sudden howl from the play pen took his attention. And then he noticed the wide-eyed expression of two little people as they grasped the hem of Rosemary's calf length skirt through the wooden bars. At a sudden hug around his legs David looked down on William. Worried, but appeasing, bright blue eyes stared up at him. And, as Rosemary retrieved Luke, William said, "Uncle David, Rosie play, we like Rosie play."

Now it was David, who was mortified! To hide his tears of remorse he picked up and hugged William, and moved forward to assure the twins everything was alright. Luke in Rosie's arms was still crying, and because he was the same size as the twins it was easy to forget he was only six months old. Behind him Rosemary spoke with a quiet intensity, "I'm taking Luke downstairs."

William wriggled from him. "I go Mummy, too." To Rosie he said, "Uncle David upset. Why, not like Rosie play?"

Rosie. in the doorway sent him a pinched look, before saying to William "Hold my hand William as we go down the stairs."

Disappointment, despair and dismay filled him. Two pairs of eyes looked curiously at him. With false joviality he began playing peek-a-boo, while reflecting on his behaviour. How could he have been so nasty, and to accuse Rosemary…and not even apologise? Would she understand? That kind of behaviour would certainly drive her back to ITP. Tired, he turned on the television, and sat with a twin under each arm to watch the Magic Roundabout. And as that came to an end, Jill arrived, the look on her face told him he was in trouble. Arms folded his now rather tubby sister came to stand before him. "So brother dear, Rosie is clearly upset, I know little beyond William's few words, and that you had one of your Jane fantasies."

Cross, he retorted, "I don't have Jane fantasies! And I didn't know Rosie played the piano, so you can't blame me for thinking it was Jane."

Jill gave a heavy sigh, "That I understand, especially today" But here's no excuse for making Rosie feel an intruder in your home."

"I know. I'm sorry. I will apologise."

Concerned, Jill sat beside him. "Why are you home early? And where's your car?" Joshua slid off the settee to walk around the furniture. Rebecca snuggled into him.

David grunted in embarrassment before replying. "I had a bit of a breakdown. Grace and Wilhelm bought me home."

"Oh David, I'm sorry, but not surprised after all you've been through in the last year. How kind of them. We could all do with a proper holiday. If we all went together, everyone would have an opportunity to relax. It would give you time to perhaps consider those clues and treasure Jane spoke of."

"It was considering Jane, and our lives, that kept me awake during the night causing me to oversleep this morning!" David went on to tell her the pattern of his thoughts during the night and Jill, at the end, made a rueful face and commented, "Let's pray then brother dear, that our 'remembering Rosemary' hasn't been harmed by today's events."

With his all too familiar hair raking gesture, he added, "Believe me, this couldn't have happened at a worse time. Wilhelm has more than fulfilled my mandate for Rosemary, and ITP are about to offer her a wonderful job with amazing career prospects."

Worried, Jill asked, "Do you think she'll take it? She really loves being at home with the children?"

"She'd be a fool not to! But perhaps we could quickly organise a family holiday with her, before she starts her new job."

"Are you saying she'll be starting soon?" At his nod, Jill groaned, "She does so much. She's always here, and available over evenings and weekends. I've come to depend on her."

"So have I! Don't say anything about the job. The offer won't come for several days in the interim let's book that holiday, and keep telling her how much we value and appreciate her."

By the time he'd fed the twins their tea, read them a story and put them to bed, it was seven o'clock before he went downstairs to eat the dinner Jill had prepared for him. Her first comment on his appearance, "Rosie's out with Gerald Maysfield. You'll have to apologise another time."

"I thought she wasn't seeing him these days?"

"I don't think she was ever seeing him, in the way you think of it. With such an age difference, I think she sees him more as a father figure, although I'm not sure that's what he hoped for."

Wilhelm and Grace brought back the car about nine o'clock. Not accepting his offer of coffee, Wilhelm produced a letter from his inner pocket. "Rosemary's job offer. I thought I'd leave it for her. The start date is the first week in August, we can delay that, but the latest would be the beginning of September."

Grace, probably noticing his scowl of dismay, tapped Wilhelm's sleeve, "Let's leave David to get his rest. After the rain, it's a lovely clear night, we'll enjoy a stroll back to the cottage." Smiling at him, she asked, "Just before we go, I've been meaning to ask, do you know our landlady?" His mind on Rosemary he shook his head. "That's fine I was just interested."

Wilhelm patted his shoulder, "Take some time off. The place won't collapse without you."

Closing the front door he sighed, that was the problem, he'd been back at work for six months, and there was little in his job that Mavis wasn't capable of doing. Wilhelm with his contacts and expertise had quickly brought his vision of an Overseas Department to pass, and the career Wilhelm had tailor made for Rosemary was similar to that he'd originally hope to carve out for himself. Of course, as Director he'd the ability to invent his own job, but what did he want to do?

The next morning, even after a night of undisturbed sleep, he didn't feel any less weary. Heavy eyed and groggy, he staggered from bed just before seven-thirty to look in on the twins. They were happily interacting through their cot bars, while waiting for Rosemary to get them up. As he washed and dressed for the day he thought how rare it was for Rosemary to see him in a state of undress, and never bare-chested as he had been yesterday! Yet, another transgression, needing an apology.

Tentatively, he smiled at Rosemary as he joined her and the twins at breakfast. Joshua was on the last few spoonfuls of porridge so he helped him to scrape the dish. There was a palpable tension in the air. Joshua having finished wriggled to get out of his high chair, but not wanting to be distracted, he ignored him. "Rosie I'm so sorry about yesterday. It was…a difficult day. Forgive me for shouting at you. Please play the piano whenever you wish. You…you play well."

With a nod she continued feeding Rebecca. David helped himself to a cup of tea and asked, "Shall I make the toast? I'm not in a hurry. I've taken the day off."

Rosie's look was cold, her reply polite. "No thank you." Picking up an envelope she said, "This was on the sideboard addressed to me."

"Oh, you weren't meant to find it."

Angry eyes challenged him. "Why?" Before he could speak she went on, "I saw Wilhelm and Grace leaving last night. I suppose you discussed how he could make me an offer I couldn't refuse?" She thumped the letter down on the table, "An offer so ridiculous, it's unbelievable! Me, heading up the Division when he retires, oh come on! What is this? A way to placate me because my services are no longer required." Bewildered, still holding his cup, he put it down and looked at her with consternation. "Originally you didn't want a nanny in your flat touching Jane's things, when you asked me to take on the role I didn't think that would apply to me. Obviously it did. And equally obviously by coming downstairs half naked yesterday and demanding why I didn't wake you, you don't need a nanny, but a wife. At least with me out of the way I won't cramp your style." Joshua's wriggling took his attention, he loosened the chair straps. Rosie continued "The promises in this letter are stipulated by a proviso that everything is subject to the future development of the Division and no guarantees can be given." Curling her lip she snarled, "So barely worth the paper it is written on." Desperate to interrupt he tried to talk over her, but she wasn't listening as though unable to stop the bitterness and resentment spilling from her.

"No, I'm not Jane. Jane was special. Jane was my friend. I loved Jane, I love her children, I miss her, but I'm Rosie, not to be shouted at in your frustration or desperation. I'm sorry I touched your precious piano and…"

A scream rent the air. David turned to see Joshua splayed out on the carpet. In unison they jumped up, almost banging heads, as they dived in to pick him up. Rosemary pulled back, and Rebecca, frightened at Joshua screaming, and seeing the blood pouring down his face, began yelling. From his pocket David pulled out his handkerchief to stem the flow and with Joshua on his lap, tried to assess the damage. Above the din, Rosie's voice filled with anxiety and fear asked, "Is he alright? I'm sure I strapped him in."

Equally anxious to reassure her, he looked up at where she stood comforting Rebecca. "It's just a nose bleed. Like his Dad it's the thing that sticks out the most from his face!" He gave a rueful smile. "And it wasn't your fault, you did strap him in, but I started to release him and got distracted."

Horrified Rosemary acknowledged, "By me!"

"Forget it, accidents happen, look the blood has already stopped flowing." Joshua, still crying, was wriggling in an attempt to get away. "I'll get Paul later to check him out, but I doubt noses at this age can be broken." Still struggling Joshua extended his chubby little arms towards Rosie in clear indication of wanting to go to her. Unexpected jealousy arose, but David quenched it seeing Rosemary's longing to soothe him, but perhaps because of their previous conversation, was reticent to take him. Guessing she needed as much comfort as Joshua David gave a rueful grimace, and declared, "I think Joshua wants a cuddle, so before he falls off my lap and does further damage I suggest you take him." Rosemary carefully lowered Rebecca to the floor, showed her how to hold on to the chair, before taking Joshua from him. About to bend down and retrieve her, David stopped. For Rebecca had taken a step away from the chair toward him. Encouraging her, she took another tentative one, but as she wobbled on the third, he caught her up to exclaim, "You walked, well done!" Joshua stopped crying to look at his sister. With that David observed, "With both children walking they're going to need careful watching." Rosemary didn't reply, and went to make the toast, as he ate his cornflakes.

Once the children were nibbling on the toast, he re-opened the conversation. "Rosemary I'm afraid you misunderstood the intent of that letter. I explained to you about the arrangements made for your six month secondment. And I asked Wilhelm to tailor make a job for you, so you had a choice. He has exceeded my expectations in giving you a career structure and a goal to reach. Believe me it is a genuine offer, and one you deserve. I am convinced, and in full agreement with him, that you are fully capable of doing it." Seeing Rosemary was about to speak, he pre-empted her by saying, "Please hear me out. This is in fairness to you, but it does give me a serious problem, a conflict of interests." At Rosemary's stare, he continued, "You would be a fool not to take such an amazing job, but equally I am a fool, for not letting you know the value we place on you and enormity of the hole you would leave in our lives, if you accept it. Yesterday I struggled, not just because it was the anniversary of Jane's death, but because of what I saw was the futility of my life, and worry at how the children would cope without you. Grace, in understanding my depression, suggested Wilhelm bring me home to rest. Later, on returning my car Wilhelm gave me the letter to give you, you weren't meant to find it. It's obvious you love all the children, they adore you, and I wanted to apologise for my disgraceful behaviour yesterday before giving you the job offer. I wanted to tell you how much you mean to us."

At his praise of her, Rosie's hair had fallen as a curtain over her face, and there was silence, as she sat cuddling Joshua who was nearly asleep. With Rebecca now wanting to get down, he suggested, "Let's settle the children, and I'll get another cup of tea."

As he headed toward the door with Rebecca, Rosemary called, "David." Big brown eyes, awash with silent tears, looked up at him, "I-I, well, I'm not used to being wanted." About to bluster, 'oh I'm sure that's not true' he stopped, and after a brief silence she went on, "I'm sorry for my reaction. I've known empty promises and rejection. Jane was a wonderful friend. Your family has been good to me. But I still have insecurities." David walked back and sat down. "Children are accepting, loving and don't ask questions. They don't have hidden agendas. I'm grateful for your faith in me." Rosie gave a small smile, "But I'd rather be a happy fool, surrounded by people who want me, and children who love me, than be a career woman and head up any department or division."

David reached out toward her, then awkwardly, retracted his hand. "Rosie, please don't be hasty, this is a big decision to make in a few minutes."

A shy smile touched Rosie's lips. "David there's no conflict of interests in my mind. As I said before, all I need is a roof over my head and food to eat. Your family have given me so much more in friendship. I have all I want or need. And when the children grow, should I want a job, your father has offered me several!" She sent him an amused look. At that moment David, in knowing it wouldn't be acceptable, resisted hugging her. A huge weight seemed to have fallen from him. Rosie didn't want the job and the children would be cared for in the foreseeable future.

CHAPTER 26

"David this needs to go in?" Bent inside the Rover having managed to stuff yet another Christmas present under Joshua's car seat he backed out, shivered in the cold wind, and looked at the size of the parcel Jill was carrying.

"There's no room for that! You should have taken my advice and hired a car. You know the problem we had in the summer with suitcases and equipment for the children."

Under the weight her voice was strained as she explained in a conspirator's whisper, "It's our 'remember Rosie' gift!"

Eyebrows raised he took it from her. "Ouch it's heavy! At five months pregnant you shouldn't be carrying it."

"Oh brother dear, it's no heavier than William. Now be quick because I've been hiding it and this is the only time I've distracted Rosie long enough to get out here. She tapped the boot lid, "Open up! I'll make space."

With a heavy sigh he complied, but complained. "At this rate Paul will have to return by train, for what goes to Bath, has to come back."

"Except brother you've forgotten Rosie isn't coming back with us."

He looked at the packed boot. "Nevertheless, what do you suggest we leave behind, the double buggies, our suitcases, that bag of presents?

Jill hoisted out the presents, "Right, put it in there. Stop scowling, you just need a woman's ingenuity." After obeying he stood back as Jill scattered the presents across the car boot and as he protested, she instructed, "When we get to Bath we'll put them back in the bag to carry in. Right try the boot lid?" It closed with room to spare. And, as Jill said cheerily, "Smile, brother dear, it's Christmas" Rosie appeared, her dark shiny curtain of hair held in place by a pink and grey knitted hat and wearing a long matching scarf. Beside her and holding hands were four similarly attired little people. William and Joshua carried a small rucksack of their special toys, while Luke grasped Rosie's hand as not yet steady on his feet. Each boy had a look of his father, but Rebecca at eighteen months was a little Jane, her heart-shaped face was animated, her smile cheeky and her attitude confident. Her pink bag was overflowing with toys her teddy bear sitting on the top, and bewitchingly she called,

"Daddy, help me."

Joshua and Rebecca were his treasure in earthen vessels, his boisterous boy loved a rough and tumble, his little girl melted his heart with a smile and from the day she called him Daddy he was besotted, as were the three boys standing with her. In two strides he crouched beside her, his tone serious. "If the princess needs a lift to the car with toys and Patch bear, the payment will be a cuddle and kiss?" Instantly giggling she ensnared his neck with her little arms and planted a smacking kiss on his mouth. But before he could convey her to the waiting carriage Joshua hugged his legs to demand, "Me too, me, me Daddy."

"Let me put Rebecca in her seat, and then I'll fly you round the car to your seat." Joshua hugged his legs tighter. He spoke more firmly, "Joshua, let go."

Rosie bent to say quietly, "Let Daddy take Becky, then your turn." Joshua frowned, but obeyed. Free to move he sent Rosie a thankful smile.

A minute later he whisked Joshua off his feet through the air, nose dived him several times before a final turn, big cuddle and a backwards thrust into his car seat. Before he could wriggle out he had him buckled in his seat. "Daddy, want more, more plane."

"We'll have time for those when we get to Grandma and Granddad's. At seeing the little face begin to crumple he asked, "What's in your bag?" That distraction gave him opportunity to close the door. Across the roof of the car he grinned back at Rosie, who having lifted Luke was about to put him in the Morris Minor as William looked on. Her response was a tender smile, "It's lovely to see the children's personalities and characters emerging."

Immediately, he thought of how that remark could be applied to her. In the last six months Rosie had flourished in their encouragements of her creative skills, her capable handling of the twins and at his father's obvious interest in her business acumen. David moved round to pick up William. As Rosie backed out of the car his thoughts tumbled out in words, to which he added, "The matching hats and scarves are lovely, especially yours for it offsets the austerity of your black calf length coat and long boots. He might have said more if her face hadn't reverted to what he termed her 'pinched' look so he whisked up William, swung him through the air and nose dived him into his car seat.

As the radio played quietly in the background, David speeded up on the M4 to Maidenhead, and considered when that linked to Bath and beyond, the journey would be a great deal quicker. This Christmas, he hoped, wouldn't be like the last, which had borne a similarity to negotiating a minefield! On several occasions grief had overwhelmed him. Jill, weary from three hourly breast feeding, was short tempered and during the Christmas lunch Joyce barely coped, and once the presents were opened Ted asked him to return them home. His Mum had spent much of the time in the kitchen, and while Paul tried to help and pacify everyone, his father scowled and bemoaned about her being a skivvy, but offering little assistance. And the children either picking up the tension, or missing Rosemary, were tetchy. Fortunately on Boxing Day his father had taken an instant liking to Wilhelm, and his mother to Grace who had insisted on helping. But that week had highlighted how valuable Rosie was with her quiet efficiency and calming influence.

And why, today Rosie was travelling with Jill because both William and Luke were loveable handfuls! A glance in his rear view mirror showed Rebecca hugging her teddy, her thumb in her mouth contentedly looking out of the window, while Joshua nosily pushed a toy car around his seat and bag. Jill, driving his reliable Morris Minor was keeping up his steady pace, but it would be good to break the journey by lunching with Paula and Jim in Theale. David smiled. Jane had thought his parents lived in Berkshire, so when he'd stopped en route to Bath, she'd wondered why Paula and Jim seemed so at home, and his parents' not there! She'd blamed him for misinformation on the night he'd suggested she work for him, while he retaliated by saying she'd drunk too much wine! That had caused a friendly bicker that had turned into… He swallowed hard. Sometimes the simplest of memories opened up the void within. There were also times, when afraid he'd forget her, he'd delve into the scrapbooks he'd made of her life. He rechanneled his mind to his constantly changing and challenging life.

After Rosie's refusal of her tailor-made job, the Directors considered, and readjusted their responsibilities, allowing him to work with Wilhelm in ITP's expansions plans. Now, there were only two continents left. Wilhelm hoped at the end of 1972 to retire, leaving him to head up the new Overseas Division in London.

Slowly he negotiated a roundabout to ensure Jill was near enough to see which turning to take to Jim and Paula's new house. This Christmas they'd also ensured Rosie was invited, but her acceptance had come with the request she'd have time off to go home. To which he'd teased, "Of course! You aren't a slave, you're part of the family. You don't have to ask, just let us know when. We always miss you, but that mustn't be a pressure." And he'd gone on to point out that she'd only taken off four weekends in six months. Jill had used the opportunity to ask where 'home' was, and received the usual succinct reply, 'Hampshire' before Rosie had sidetracked the conversation.

The sight of two boys on bicycles sidetracked him as they waved him down. Grinning he lowered his window. Saluting Richard said, "Here to escort you to your rendezvous, Sir. Please follow us."

In saluting back, he spoke with an air of authority, "Excellent idea chaps. On your way, we'll be right behind you." Those boys who had once been terrors were thankfully developing into respectful and helpful human beings.

Three hours later, fed and watered with the children exhausted from playing with their cousins, they embarked on the remainder of the journey. As the twins fell asleep in the back, he considered how easily, Rebecca, with five boys in the family adoring her, might become over confident and obnoxious. On holiday last August, despite being unable to express herself in speech, she'd Richard and Philip vying to push her swing, build her sandcastle, and pander to her every whim.

The holiday with the three families in a hotel in Boscombe had been a great success. In the relaxed atmosphere there had been much fun and laughter. Rosie obviously adoring the children seemed to have infinite patience, yet with a quiet firmness brought peace to any situation. But bright, blue eyed, cheeky and loveable William at two and a half was becoming a handful that even she struggled to control.

As a family they agreed with the Bible edict 'spare the rod, and spoil the child', but only as a last resort. Paul hated administering that, but sometimes it was the only deterrent William understood. That same discipline would apply to the twins, but for now a stern face and tone still brought remorse.

His thoughts drifted to Boscombe, the sunny days walking down the chines to the promenade, where the sea was blue, but bracing to swim in. Rosie in a swimming costume, had revealed long legs and a very shapely body that every testosterone male would be attracted to. But, any interest in Rosemary by him, or perhaps any man, was doomed to failure. Her words echoed through his mind. 'loving his children is one thing, but him…' However she'd happily joined in the family activities, and accompanied him, when in couples they doubled up to visit the theatre and cinema. Yet her life away from them remained a mystery.

It was becoming apparent that some of the single women at church, and in the business arena, would have no reticence in going out with him. A vivid picture exactly five years earlier jumped into David's mind. The memory still made him cringe, and probably why Rosemary shuddered when she thought of him. Slightly inebriated and having public kissed Jane, Rosie's nasty gossip challenged him, and in reprisal he'd singled her for similar treatment. Initially her eyes had filled with blazing rage, then disdain, but realising he was about to kiss her they'd reflected terror. Trapped in a scene of his own making, he'd tried to act chivalrously to woo, rather than plunder her mouth, in a form of punishment. After nuzzling, teasing and cajoling her stiff lips into being pliable and moist he released her, but seeing her dazed eyes he'd felt obliged to remove her from the caterwauling and jeering crowd. In steering her through the door into the corridor towards her office his intention had been to apologise. But she'd twisted towards him, her whisper a sneer. "You hateful beast!" Through clenched teeth she added, "You self-righteous, supercilious, pompous pig." In finding her voice it grew in volume "Let go of me, you rotten swine." Taken aback at her venom he'd glanced through the glass partition of the switchboard room to see the temporary telephonist's mouth open in astonishment. He could still remember Rosemary's eyes blazing with rage and hatred, and to waylay her flaying hands, he'd practically bulldozed her backwards down the corridor, while she accused, "You hypocrite! You take what you want without thought of the consequences." Thrusting her into the end office, she'd backed against the photocopier, as he kicked the door shut. About to speak, she'd yelled, "Touch me, and I'll sue you for rape, as well as assault." Those words instantly brought him to his senses, and furious at her, and himself for being so stupid, he'd turned, wrenched open the door and marched back down the corridor. Re-entering the hall he'd determined to forget the incident and resume the party spirit, later to dismiss it as a simple kiss to a disturbed, Grace, a bit of fun to Jane and Rosemary over-reacting.

Once married to Jane, Rosie seemed to have forgotten the unfortunate incident, for she'd agreed to work for him, live in his house, and now looked after his children. But to him, Rosie had revealed betrayal, or perhaps physical abuse, at the hands of a man. At that thought, David's hands tightened on the steering wheel. Male arousal was quite normal for a man seeing an attractive woman. As was being upset at seeing someone you know knocked down by a car, but before he could delve deeper into his feelings for Rosie, his attention was taken by an awakening Rebecca, then a crotchety Joshua. The only way to divert that was to sing their songs as he negotiated the remaining miles. By the time he'd stopped the car outside his parents' house, he felt as irritable as the children!

Rolling out of the car to stretch his legs, the porch light came on, the front door opened, and his parents spilled out on to the drive where Joshua was wailing loudly, and Rebecca demanding to be set free. His father moved around the car to Joshua, and his Mum reached into Rebecca, just as Jill pulled in the drive behind him.

"Phew it's cold out here." His Mum urged them inside. "You can unpack the cars later."

Once inside and the door closed, the hugs Jane had instigated into their household began. And he noted his Mum was quick to welcome Rosemary, and to say, "It's good to see you again dear. I'm so pleased you could join us."

Over the din of excited children Rosie replied as she caught William's hand, "Thank you, Mrs Reinhardt, for the invitation. I'm glad to be here."

"Now Rosie I've told you before, I'm Margaret, so please call me that."

Rosie's response was a small smile. Hand outstretched, having released Joshua his father boomed, "Yes Rosie it is good to see you again. Are you keeping that son of mine in order?"

Rosie gave him a wide-eyed look, but replied, "That, Professor Reinhardt, would be beyond the call of duty."

At that he gave a gruff laugh, "Point taken, and remember, I'm Franz" with that he bestowed upon her a smile, looked across to frown at him, and then continued, "Be clear young lady there is no call of duty here, you are our house guest, not a servant."

If Rosie replied he didn't hear it because his Mum was instructing at his elbow, "Put all the coats in the hall cupboard David. You all look a bit frazzled, it's a long journey. I'll make a cup of tea."

Smells of mince pies, roasted ham wafted in the warm air and made the kitchen the obvious place to congregate. Despite his father's decree, Rosie was busying herself working alongside his mother to get the drinks. "It smells, Mum, as though you've been working hard, we're all here to help, and hopefully do better than last year!"

From her diminutive height his Mum smiled up at him to declare, "Your father has a programme worked out, everything will be done with military precision. If you're lucky there's time off for good behaviour!"

Jill snorted, "Oh great! The only one to appreciate that will be Rosie."

Franz jumped in, "That's what I like, people who understand the benefits of organisation. Last year, Rosie, without out you, was a shambles."

Glaring at her father Jill retorted, "In that case instead of complaining you could have organised us. Mum did a sterling job in the circumstances."

Rosemary looked upset. "I'm sorry. I tried to make everything ready before I left."

Not wanting her to feel guilty David stepped in. "Rosie you did all that was possible. It was an emotional time, tempers were frayed. You were best out of it, and I'm sure far happier with your own family."

Rosemary gave her enigmatic smile and his Dad said abruptly, "Yes Rosemary, do tell us about your family? I hope they don't mind you being with us." The kitchen fell silent. Was everyone, like him, holding their breath for the long awaited answer? He watched as the expression in her eyes hardened, she stated flatly, "They're away."

Jill, attempted to disguise her frustration in a bland observation, "But they'll be back by Tuesday."

"No, I'm visiting friends." Rosie's attention went to William, who'd latched on to her skirt. "Do you want to go to the

352

toilet?"

"I want to see the fish in the pond?"

Crouching to his level she explained, "It's too dark to see them. I'll take you in the morning." She arose, took William's hand and looking at Franz said, "Shall we ask your Granddad if we could look at pictures of fishes in the Encyclopaedia Britannica." In response his father gave a stiff nod, and after she'd departed Jill whispered, "She did it again! What is she hiding?"

Clearing the cups his mother said sharply, "Whatever it is, it's none of our business. If she felt she could trust us, she'd tell us."

Folding her arms Jill declared, "She knows that, she was there at the Ben debacle." When no-one spoke, his father took the opportunity to draw several sheets of paper from the corner of the work top. Handing them around he announced, "This is the rota for the holiday, you can swap, but please ensure your duties are covered." David's glance at his mother brought the receipt of a wide-eyed look with a quirky smile, but after the groans and grumbles and several swaps, they accepted their allotted tasks.

Paul arrived the next day, just in time to be whisked off to the Christmas Eve Carols by Candlelight service in the local church. Feeling it was only fair, David stayed back with Rosie, who'd happily volunteered to look after the children, and he sat as interested as the children as Rosie talked very simply of the gift from God to Mary of the baby Jesus, and how each of them was a gift from God, to their parents. Out of a bag, she produced four large red velvet socks trimmed with white fur, and on each she'd appliquéd a name. On receipt of their sock, each child's eyes grew wide with excitement as Rosie explained how Christmas was a celebration of Jesus' birth, and God loved and gave good gifts to all His children. And if they hung up their stockings they'd be filled with treats in the morning. The children over excited the previous evening had taken ages to settle, but only William remained awake when his parents and grandparents returned. And once William had shown them his big red sock, he swiftly cuddled down and fell asleep as Paul read him a story.

The table set with candles gave the large dining room a pleasant warm glow, and without the distraction of children it was an enjoyable, slow and relaxed meal. Even Rosie after several glasses of wine giggled like a school girl in the whispering stealth of retrieving, filling and returning those socks to the right beds. From that he also gleaned that Christmas stockings hadn't been part of her childhood, but further probing had ended in the usual cul-de-sac.

Little voices and shrieks of joy from above heralded in Christmas morning! The illuminated dial of his watch read 6.13 am. By the time David, with his parents reached the second floor Paul and Jill had already gathered the children in the twin-bedded room where William slept. As little voices in unison began calling Rosie's name, Jill knocking on her door called, "Don't get dressed, just come and join us." Already seated next to the twins on one of the beds, he looked up as Rosie, in her matching lavender satin nightdress and negligee, stood shyly in the doorway. Jill invited, "Come on in. We can't start without you. Dad move up so Rosie can sit next to the twins. As Joshua clambered on to David's lap, Rebecca scrambled across to Rosie and the intimacy of sitting next to each other on a bed in their night attire felt rather strange. His Mum sent him an amused look. Jill suggested, "As the stockings contain similar things shall the children open them together?" William anxious to know the contents of his immediately tipped it out on the floor, while Paul helped Luke, he and Rosie shared in the twins' squeals of delight.

In anticipation of an early morning, and a late lunch, a full English breakfast was on the menu to be cooked and served by Margaret and Franz, and in complying with the rota he and Paul washed up and cleared away. Rosemary and his Mum were assigned to oversee the lunch, as others took turns to peel vegetables, lay the table and occupy the children. The smell of the enormous turkey was already wafting through the house, and at precisely ten forty three cars left to drive to church. And equally precisely at twelve noon, four cars turned one after the other into the drive, as with perfect timing, Jim and family arrived for sherry and nibbles in the lounge. Despite Rosie's attempts at distracting them, the children sitting in the wooden pews had been fractious throughout the forty minute service, and now free, the three that could, egged on by Phillip and Richard, ran screaming like banshees around their legs. But after an upturned sherry glass into a dish of crisps, the children were banished to play in the library with the men supervising them. Unlike the restful meal the night before lunch was a chaos of spillages, noisy children and the banter Ted referred to as 'Reinhardt entertainment'. Richard and Philip's delight at seeing Rosie with them in Theale had alerted David to warn them to keep their thoughts and prayers to themselves. But he noted their exchanging of looks whenever he and Rosie communicated, usually over the children, but especially on his telling Rosie to put her feet up, enjoy her coffee and the Queen's Speech.

It had become tradition in the Reinhardt household that present opening was after the Queen's Speech because then everyone was free from cooking, eating and clearing up. Conveniently the children having gone down for a nap straight after lunch, didn't awake until the 'speech' was well over, and then such was their excitement they gave them their presents first. Rosie, sitting on the floor with William and Joshua racing their wind-up cars was so preoccupied, she looked quite startled when Jill announced, "A present for Rosie."

And when she saw the size of the heavy box Paul was dragging out from under the tree, wide-eyed Rosie exclaimed, "That's for me?" Paul nodded, and indicated she come forward. Getting off her knees, she tiptoed in stocking feet across the carpet to avoid the toys and other debris.

As she did Jill added, "It's from us, and David and the twins. We hope you'll be pleased with it, but you can change it. Would you like William to help you?"

On her knees before the package, her head tilted slightly, her look bashful, Rosie beckoned an eager William over, and ripping off the paper quickly revealed a cream coloured plastic case.

Rosie, realising what the present was, shook her head and promptly burst into tears.

Paul, being the nearest, rested a hand on her shoulder, "Hey Rosie that wasn't the response we were expecting!" Bewildered William threw his arms around her neck. The other children stared at her. And in catching his father's meaningful look, and nod in Rosie's direction to 'go and comfort her,' David shook his head, Rosie wouldn't appreciate that! Paul unhooked William from Rosie so she could extract her handkerchief from the sleeve of her cardigan.

Wiping her eyes she stuttered, "I'm sorry...my crying...it's just... I've never...it's the best... I can't believe it...a 'Bernina' sewing machine." Hugging a bemused William she went on, "Sorry, so silly, but…well…just well…so generous. Thank you." A frown etched her brow, "None of my presents match this!"

With a smile, Jill chided, "Rosie, there is no better time than Christmas to show our appreciation?" Turning to Paula and Jim, as Rosie was examining and exclaiming over the electric machine, Jill explained, "Rosie used that old, hand sewing machine, and made a play tent to fit over the play pen. We felt such talent deserved a machine to match her skills." Turning to Rosie, Jill smiled, "And, you're going to need it." Rosie looked puzzled, "I took some of your creative ideas to that exclusive boutique in Knightsbridge."

Frowning Rosie asked, "Why?"

"I thought, if they were interested, it would boost your confidence. And believe me they were. They want to meet you to discuss selling the things you make. And I'm sure the extra income would come in handy."

Franz piped up, "Good heavens, if Rosie needs confidence, or an income boost, I'd want her to head up and run the 'Jane Mackenzie Fund', not skivvy over a sewing machine for a pittance."

Fascinated, David watched as Rosie's back stiffened, her mouth pinch, and by her aristocratic tone and succinct words he knew she was cross. "Jill, as much as I appreciate my present, I've no wish to make money in selling my creations. Franz, thank you, but I have a job as nanny to the children. When they no longer need me I'll think again." Jill looked slighted. His father thoughtful. In catching Paul's wink David knew that Rosie's stand would gain her esteem in his father's eyes. The slight awkwardness dissipated as the present opening continued. At the end of which no-one was in any doubt of Rosie's creative skills. Each child cuddled a soft toy and wore the clothes she'd made them. He and Paul received black leather Bible covers that zipped on three sides making a case for easy carrying. Jill had a similar one made of hard-wearing navy and red woven material. Paula and his Mum received a tissue box covered in a pretty material, its frills hiding the metal poppers that allowed it to be removed for washing or the box changed. The exclamations of the ingenuity of the items brought Rosie a 'rosie' glow of pleasure. For Jim and Franz she'd made a box out of heavy duty card, the inside covered in cream satin and the outside with black velvet. On receipt they'd looked puzzled, although admiring the handicraft, and relieved as she explained, "Use it for your cuff links, oddments, lose change when you empty your pockets at night." Only Philip and Richard's present wasn't homemade. The three dimensional noughts and crosses game made out of clear Perspex, was three layered, with nine holes in each layer and green and blue marbles to make the line up. It was instantly popular and also a challenge to the adults.

About seven o'clock, with a cup of tea they cut the Christmas cake, the younger children had their supper and went to bed. Richard and Philip stayed up until after the buffet supper around nine, and several times David caught their grins as after a couple of glasses of sherry, and then wine Rosie's inhibitions began to disappear. However, the alcohol didn't affect her ability to play Monopoly and outwit the astute businessman, his father, by winning! Eyes shining, a healthy bloom to her cheeks, Rosie glowed with joy, borne out as they broke up to go to bed by her profuse thanks which included her 'feeling part of the family', 'the best Christmas ever' and 'one she'd never forget'. With tears in her eyes she ran up the stairs leaving them to stare after her. No-one commented, but David couldn't help wonder what kind of Christmas she usually experienced.

CHAPTER 27

Next morning the schedule billed a light breakfast at 9.00 am. Once seated, beside each of them, Rosie placed a gift, wrapped in yesterday's discarded Christmas paper. Rosie's delight at her sewing machine had caused his Mum to find the remnants of material from the burgundy satin dining room curtains, and it was from this Rosie had made a tie for each man, including smaller ones for Richard, Philip and William. Ties, his mother commented were notoriously difficult to make. Jill was delighted with her tissue box cover, and although apologising to Paula and his Mum who already received one, his Mum was quick to reassure Rosie by saying, "It's ideal, it matches the curtains in here." For each child there was a drawstring bag containing several chocolates with Rosie apologising again for taking the sweets from the tin in the lounge! Bombarded by praise, and unable to flee, she gave a shy smile and her attention to the children.

Just before Paula and Jim, with two very disgruntled boys, left to 'have Christmas again at Jim's parents', David saw Richard beckoning him into the empty lounge. And after joining him, David struggled to look serious, as the boy said, "Phillip and I wanted to tell you we're still praying. We thought you'd like Auntie Rosie better if she was more fun, like Jane. I think God's answering, don't you?"

Speaking with the gravity needed, he replied, "Richard, it's not a case of whether I like Rosie, or if she likes me. I don't mind you praying, and it's good to see Rosie happy, but remember the Lord's prayer, 'Your will be done, your Kingdom come'. Jesus might have other plans." Disappointment etched Richard's face, and before he asked, David answered. "No there isn't anyone else, but you can ask for the Lord to bless us." To reassure him David patted his back, as he went to rejoin his parents. Worried, he'd upset Richard, he was grateful for his 'thumbs up' sign through the car window as they left.

The rest of the morning was a chaotic juggle between playing with the children and helping prepare and carry food into the dining room for the Boxing Day buffet lunch to which his parents had invited a dozen friends.

At noon, he was in the hall taking guests' coats, when he was rooted to the spot at seeing Felicity arriving with her parents.

Indignantly, he hissed at Jill, "What's she's doing here?"

Leaning toward him she replied, "Probably still got her eye on you brother dear, and of course Daddy's millions."

The smile he plastered on wasn't far short of a snarl as Felicity sashayed toward him. A quick move of his head waylaid the kiss aimed at his mouth to his cheek. Undeterred she gushed, "Oh David darling, how delightful to see you again. Now where are those wonderful twins of yours?"

A desire to laugh bubbled up within him as behind her they appeared from the kitchen, their little hands and faces smeared with chocolate sauce from licking out the saucepan. He nodded to indicate them, and turning Felicity screamed and jumped back. "Oh my goodness! What a frightful mess!"

It was impossible not to compare Rosie's bright eyed, pink cheeked, fresh and alive look, to Felicity's over bloomed, over indulged one. With an enigmatic smile, Rosie apologised, "Sorry to startle you. The children are on the way to wash their hands. Once clean I'm sure they'd appreciate you playing with them." Felicity barely disguised her shudder, and he caught the laughter that flashed through Rosie's eyes before she ushered her charges down the hall.

Possessively Felicity slipped her arm through his and asked the same question as he'd asked of Jill, "What is she doing here?"

Deliberately sliding out from her arm, he said, "I was wondering that about you?"

"Oh that dry wit of yours!" He winced at the tinkling laugh and drew back when, almost rubbing herself against him, she purred, "I'm in between photo and film shoots. I came home for Christmas to keep the 'oldens' happy." In seeing the hostility in his eyes she pouted. "They said I'd be welcomed. Surely you're still not cross with me over those things I said in the park. I've forgiven your rudeness." In danger of being rude again, he sidestepped and scowled. Puzzled she queried, "Doesn't your religion decree you have to forgive and forget?" Then as if that were a joke, her laughter jangling in his ears, she gave him a bewitchingly look and lent toward him. In believing she was about to kiss him he put his hands on her shoulders to keep her at arms length. Not bothering to mask his dislike he said in a cold voice, "My parents will be polite, but you will have to excuse me." With that he strode off down the corridor. Forgiveness surely didn't mean he had to like, or be near her. Drawn by excited, chattering little voices, he put his head around the downstairs cloakroom door where Rosie was helping them wash their hands and faces. Amused he asked, "And who likes chocolate?"

"Me, Me!" the four children chorused.

And who loves Rosie? The reply was the same.

Rosie smiled, and tussling the hair of each head before giving William a towel she instructed, "Here, dry your hands and face."

An idea jumped into David's head. After a quick assessment he decided there was no harm in asking! "Rosie can I ask you a big favour?" Bent over wiping Joshua's face with a flannel, she looked questioningly up at him. "I can't believe that wretched Felicity woman would show her face here!" Rosie gave him a sympathetic look before concentrating on the little people before her. "I fear I might be very rude. And being my parent's home it wouldn't be right to upset their guests."

Puzzled, she glanced up to ask, "And the favour…?"

Not knowing her reaction he took a deep breath to request, "Would you appear to be with me?"

"I am with you." Her brief impish smile surprised him. "To prove it you can take this towel and dry Joshua's hands and face."

A curl of pleasure unfolded at her teasing, so he pressed on, "Can you help me avoid her?"

Drying hands and faces Rosie said thoughtfully, "Felicity obviously doesn't like messy children. Probably not noisy ones either. Eat with the children, and suggest she play with them afterwards."

The children pushed past him, and as they ran down the passage he risked pushing his suggestion further. "I was thinking that you could appear to be more than a friend of the family?"

"As in 'with you'?" A frown creased her brow.

"Oh dear, is that so dreadful a thought?"

"That would depend on how far you wanted to go?"

He grinned, "As far as you'd let me." At his taunt he received a disparaging look. Undeterred he added, "A room full of people won't give me much scope!"

"And what would your parents think?"

"Disappointment when they find out it's only a ruse."

Rosie raised her eyebrows, but conceded by saying, "You'll have to do all the talking." To that he readily agreed. "And no more than hand holding, or putting an arm around me."

Playfully he retaliated, "Spoilsport." Rosie pursed her lips and raised her eyebrows to which he cautioned, "If this is to look authentic you'll need to appear fond of me."

Rosie gave him an odd look, and for sheer devilment he asked, "Do you want to practice?"

The retort was quick and sharp, "No I don't! And be aware, this is only an act for Felicity's benefit." A slender hand slipped into his large one. Her stony look had him chuckle, but that unusual contact brought an urge to protect her. He sent her a wry smile for it was she who going to be protecting him! As they walked down the hall he bantered, "Time to paste on the smile. And you never know, you might find you like me!"

With that he gently squeezed her hand, she acknowledged with a shy smile as they entered the dining room where the guests had congregated. Paul seeing them sent him a questioning look, to which David gave a slight shake of his head to indicate it wasn't what he thought. Still holding hands they moved into the crowd as Paul spoke to Jill who turned, her eyes meeting his with a question. With a glance at Felicity, he winked, let go of Rosie's hand, and as Rosie instinctively turned towards him, he gave her a loving smile and drew her closer by putting his arm around her waist. A brief look back at Jill revealed her puckish grin of understanding, her nod, her acquiescence to convey the real situation to the family. David moved Rosie forward to introduce her to several of his parents' friends with no further explanation than her name, until Ron and Gwen began to ask her questions. Practised at avoidance, Rosie quickly excused herself to help Jill with the children's lunch. Ron patted his arm. "Nice girl, attractive and likes children too, quite understandable. Ron gave him a knowing smile, "That'll put paid to Felicity thinking she was in with another chance!" Without comment David excused himself to offer people drinks, and for somewhile avoided both Felicity and her parents. But the moment he began making polite conversation with them, a hand slipped through his arm. Believing it to be Felicity he quickly turned, and found it was Rosie moving in closer, her eyes smiling into his. The extraordinary jolt of pleasure was such he wished this wasn't a charade, and it was easy to respond with a loving look, and draw her near to introduce her. "Gordon, Sandra, Rosie has been here several times, but I don't think you've met." Felicity's eyes narrowed, while curiosity reflected in those of her parents. Rosie, with an enigmatic smile nodded, and he couldn't resist saying, "But Felicity of course has had the pleasure several times." He sent Rosie a sexy smile before deliberately focussing on her beautifully sculptured mouth. However, the pinching of skin on his forearm gave him warning that wouldn't be acceptable, yet his upward gaze was met by Rosie's expression of shy adoration, causing him to consider pinching himself! The dislike in Felicity's eyes was so hideously clear he'd a strong urge to move Rosie away. In a protective gesture David slid his arm around Rosie's waist as he talked affectionately of her care and love of the twins, and her efficiency in running his home. Throughout Rosie looked coy, and then with a sweet smile said, "David exaggerates!" Felicity's jealousy was almost palpable.

A push against his legs brought him to look down on an uplifted and adoring little face. Blonde bunches bobbed up and down as she said fervently, "Toilet, Daddy." At that he picked Rebecca up just as his father announced lunch was about to be served. Pleased to escape, he and Rosie left the room, but when he returned he felt Felicity's eyes were constantly upon him.

The next time he saw Rosie she was playing with the children in the lounge. "Have you eaten?" At the shake of her head he offered, "I'll keep an eye on them. Go, eat, drink and enjoy yourself."

Not looking at him she said, "I'd rather not."

He slipped into the seat beside her to taunt, "I'd rather not… what? Eat, drink, or enjoy yourself?"

"No, go in the dining room." Before he could ask she elaborated. "Felicity is in there. I've had the sarcasm. I'm only 'the nanny', convenient always for a flirtation." He scowled. Rosie continued, "Next, the warning! Inveigling myself into your affections, or family is foolish. You won't marry again beneath your station in life."

Outraged, but with guests around he could only growl, "What utter rubbish."

"Finally, the threat! If I don't back off, she'll ensure you won't want me associating with you, your family, or your children."

Incensed he shot up. "That's preposterous!" Not caring

about the people in the room he went on, "Party or no party I...?" Rosie caught his hand and pulled him to sit back down. Seeing Rosie's worried face he obeyed, and listened to her plea. "She's jealous. And wonders, as I once did how Jane, a jumped up no-body, could worm her way into your affections? I hated Jane because she was confident, happy and bright. Life seemed to treat her well, whereas mine was totally opposite."

That was interesting comment, but still fuming and puzzled, he asked, "So how would you want me to respond?"

Distracted by the children, she admitted, "I don't know. I've been asking the Lord."

Abruptly he said, "Then I'll get you a plate of food and do the same." As he walked away, it was now Rosie's eyes, boring into his back. Furious, he wanted to challenge Felicity, but this wasn't the time and place for a row! To threaten Rosie she must have something on her? Praying about that, and what he should do, he tried to remember what Rosie liked to eat and for that awarded himself nought out of ten for observation.

Jill sidled up to him as he filled up a plate, "Surely brother dear, you aren't still hungry?"

Cross, he snapped, "It's for Rosie."

Jill lowered her voice, "You're both making it a good love parody, the only one not enjoying it is that obnoxious bitch, Felicity?"

Irritated, he growled, "The latter is not the sentiment that should come from the mouth of a Christian!"

To that Jill retaliated, "Tell Dad, they're his words! He was crestfallen hearing it was only an act to ward Felicity off." With a grimace, David quickly reiterated his conversation with Rosie. "What's Rosie's response?"

David shrugged, "To avoid Felicity. But she didn't show any emotion."

"We have to agree, Rosie keeps her past under wraps, does Felicity know something we don't? But whatever it is don't think anything would change Dad's high opinion of her." Jill giggled, "Mum said she was so cross at Dad's constant singing of Rosie's praises, she asked if he'd prefer to be married to her! Apparently Dad was shocked, and explained he was merely trying to open your eyes to Rose's potential as a good wife, and suitable mother to your children. So, I think, I'll put the word into a few ears about how we all love and appreciate Rosie, and that Dad would be delighted to have her as a daughter-in-law."

Worried, he responded, "Don't over do it, we don't want to scare Rosie away. Remember, the thought of marriage to me makes her shudder."

"I don't know why you keep saying that. And no-one, after today's charade, would believe it."

"Believe me Jill, she's acting. I'll admit I wanted to kiss her, but she pinched my arm to warn me off!" The roar of Reinhardt laughter emitting from Jill turned all eyes upon them, and at that he departed to the lounge.

Rosie gave him an appreciative smile as he handed her the wine glass and put her food on coffee table. "That looks delicious, just as I would have chosen, thank you." Delighted, he grinned happily for it seemed in asking for wisdom to deal with Felicity, he'd received it for Rosie's lunch. And seated by Rosie as she ate, he enjoyed appearing as a couple when people came in to talk to them. When he next saw Felicity she wore a disgruntled expression, but seeing him she plastered on a smile and made a beeline toward him. Deliberately he turned on his heel, and guessing Felicity would follow him, he bent to hand Rosie her cheesecake so he could whisper in her ear, "Felicity's on the prowl so I'm going to kiss your cheek." Rosie gave a shy laugh giving the impression he'd said something romantic, and put out her hand to touch his knee as he did so. His Mum, with a knowing smile arose so he could sit by Rosie and as he did, he bent forward to say, "She's still there." To his astonishment, Rosie took a spoonful of cheesecake and in a provocative gesture, indicated he open his mouth to receive it. His response to that was genuine, and he watched Felicity scowl, turn, and push past her mother who was standing behind her. He didn't bother to inform Rosie, because he was enjoying the flirting that had initiated a coil of desire, shut down since Jane's death. Eyes locked on Rosie, he didn't look away when Jill touched his shoulder, and he heard her amusement as she bent to quietly report, "Felicity has left, her excuse an appointment elsewhere. But don't stop. Felicity's parents are still here. And best that people don't know they've been caught up in a charade authenticated by Mum and Dad." With that she walked away, but with a backward glance, she sent him the naughtiest of smiles.

Frowning, Rosie admitted, "I didn't think this through. I don't want to embarrass your parents. We've put them in an awkward position."

David rubbed a nub of his finger down her cheek. "Don't worry about it. Just because two people create an impression of interest in each other, it doesn't lock them into a long term relationship." But after that he made the most of holding her hand and putting an arm around her. And felt sad when Rosie said bluntly, "David you can stop now, the last of your parent's guests have left." But that didn't stop him teasing, "I know, but I was enjoying it. Perhaps we could do it again sometime?" Turning to help his Mum, she ignored his remark, but Jill sent him an amused smile.

For the rest of Rosie's time with them he was sure she was more relaxed, especially after the children were in bed, where she enjoyed the challenge of playing board games. And in dropping Rosie at the station his Mum reported she seemed sad to leave them. And after in picking up Maria, the three women took the opportunity to go to the 'sales' while the men looked after the children. The twins particularly loved 'hide and seek', and with his Dad knowing all the best places, it was only the children's giggling that gave them away. But although Maria was good with the children, by late afternoon they'd begun fretting over Rosie's absence.

During a leisurely dinner the conversation turned to the charade between David and Rosie, bringing laughter, and Paul to comment, "Rosie is always more comfortable with a role to play."

His mother gave a sympathetic smile, "It's more than that, she only sees her value in what she does, not who she is."

Jill piped up, "And that's the million dollar question. David, tell Dad what Felicity said to Rosie." He shook his head, but having caught the interest of those around the table, they goaded him into repeating it.

Outraged his father roared, "Margaret, ensure that woman never enters this house again! How dare she threaten my guests? Who cares about Rosie's past?" Grimly, he stared at those around the table. David saw his mother touch his father's knee at his over reaction. In a gruff voice, his Dad resumed more calmly. "I know people. I can judge them. That woman has a brilliant mind, works hard, is honest and totally genuine. I'd have no qualms employing her."

David chuckled, "Dad you do. You pay for her to be our

nanny."

Displeased, his father grunted, "Nanny! It's time that you made that farce into a reality."

"Really Dad, well let me tell you Rosie has made it abundantly clear that 'farce' was all it would ever be." And before his father could say more, he followed his father trick of diverting an unwanted conversation elsewhere.

After another exhausting day with continually distracting the children from wanting Rosie, they were only fit in the next evening to watch a film on television, and pig out on left-overs. Paul indicating to Jill she shouldn't have another chocolate reminded him of Jane watching his weight. Memories triggered of Christmas' with Jane, and to her ditty, '...the children will show on whom your heart to bestow'. It was evident the children loved Rosie, and by the way his body had stirred with desire, he wasn't adverse to her either! Was he, like the song's words, finding the 'lake of pain draining', and 'coming back to life' again?

"David, are you listening?" He dragged his thoughts away from how to nurture Rosie's acting ability into reality, to stare blankly at Jill.

With a sigh, Jill explained, "I was just saying that when the new baby arrives, we'll have an accommodation problem in London. Maybe, it's time to move nearer Beatty?"

Before David could voice his opinion his Mum asked, "How would you manage without Rosie, she's such a treasure?"

"I don't know. We all argue at times, but I love the way we live separately, yet work together as one big family."

Vaguely he heard Jill talking about Paul being away, but his mind fixed onto the word, 'treasure'. Had Jane meant more than the twins being 'a treasure in earthen vessels'?

Thoughtfully, Paul rubbed his beard. "The baby can sleep in our room for the first few months, but we really need Rosie's bedroom, for three children won't fit in the other bedroom."

In a desire to help David suggested, "William could have my study. I've a big bedroom that could accommodate my books and desk."

Jill countered, "Or Rosemary could have it, it's a similar size room to the bedroom she has now?"

At that his mother voiced her concern. "I'm not sure that would be right."

Considering space, David added, "It would solve the immediate problem, and we could extend into the loft space."

There was silence as they consider the possibility, out of which his father concluded, "The best solution would be for the boy to marry Rosie." As eyes turned to see his reaction, his father proclaimed, "You're almost living together, so why not make it official. Oh I know you loved Jane, but Rosie is attractive, intelligent, loves your children and for eighteen months has efficiently run your household. Good grief boy, you won't find a better woman than she."

There was no denying the truth, but aggravated by his father outspokenness he blurted out, "Because Dad, she wouldn't have me!"

The retort was a loud derisive grunt before his father barked, "That's ridiculous. You're an attractive man, own a beautiful house, have a good job, any girl would be pleased to marry you."

"Believe me, not Rosie! Our relationship is on a purely business footing. And she certainly doesn't find me attractive. The beautiful house doesn't impress her, oh and my good job was first, offered to her! The only benefit I could bestow is for her to be mother to two adorable little people who have her heart. But, sadly, she's made it quite clear, I'll not win hers."

"Rubbish boy! I saw with my own eyes you and Rosie together."

He grinned, "Dad, she was acting as a favour, but I'll admit to enjoying playing my part."

"Well, keep playing it until it becomes a reality. Good heavens boy, you dithered over Jane, now you're dithering over Rosie?"

That observation caused him to stiffen, and contradict, "I didn't dither! I assessed the situation so as not to blunder in and ruin everything. Rosie could be the 'treasure' Jane spoke of, but it will have to be in the Lord's way and timing."

His mother squeezed his father's arm. "David is right Franz. You only see a solution, but Rosie is very different from Jane. We've already talked of Rosie needing to know she's loved for who she is, and not what she can provide." Across the room his Mum, her eyes filled with love and an understanding similar to his own, said, "Rosie is prickly and a closed up bud. But David, I believe, if she knew an abiding, unconditional love, she'd blossom and respond. So different from the baiting and bantering, passion raging love affair, you and Jane enjoyed, but nevertheless together you could develop a deep, rich and enjoyable relationship."

In the midst of her words, Paul agreed, Jill giggled and Maria slipped out of the room. Embarrassed, but looking less belligerent, his father muttered, "Margaret really, do we have to talk of such things?"

His Mum patted his father's knee. "I loved Jane's cheeky bounce, the way she didn't care where and what she said, it was honest and refreshing. I agree with your father about Rosie's qualities, but only David knows if he has the patience and understanding to offer her that abiding, and unconditional love."

"I don't know, but it would be a major challenge to gain Rosie's confidence." As they paused to consider that, he knew a second challenge would be to keep his awakening libido in tight check. But he didn't speak of that, instead reminded them of the line of Jane's ditty, written several days before her death. 'The twins will show on whom your love to bestow'.

Jill put forward, "There is no doubt the twins love Rosie, and Jane's desire was to 'remember Rosie'. And there's no better way for the twins to know their 'birth' mother, than through Rosie."

Paul interrupted their musings. "I think it was amazing, she agreed to pretend you were a couple. And it revealed that she knows about love. Whatever the reason for locking away that side of her life, I believe the twins could be, maybe are already, the key to unlock it".

His mother interjected, "Yes, but marriage goes beyond the children. David, have you enough in common to grow old together?"

"It's possible." David contemplated, "And, with Rosie unable to have children it would…"

Jill gasped, "I didn't know. Did you Paul?"

Paul nodded, as David continued, "…this would fulfil the desires of her heart which she thought would be denied her. Psalm 37 was where Jane planted the words, 'remember Rosemary'. She loves children, and the twins will know no other mother but her!"

Still taken aback Jill asked, "David, why didn't you tell me about Rosie?"

"I thought you knew. Jane said she had an abortion that went wrong."

"Oh how awful, but I can't imagine her…well, that explains a few things…" Jill trailed off in thought.

Paul glanced around the family, "That information should be kept confidential."

After a short silence Jill piped up, "I'm sure we can organise things so Rosie and David spend more time together."

"Hold on Jill." The eyes of the family moved back to Paul, who looking serious chided, "That's something I can't condone. It's a Reinhardt trait to manipulate and control, David admitted to it when wanting to attract Jane's love." Paul appeared to ignore his father's hard stare, and David had no grounds to refute that.

With a sympathetic smile his mother pointed out, "I think Rosie is well aware of her welcome in this family. Let's just encourage and include her in all our family events."

Jill retorted crossly, "That's what I meant."

Paul put his arm around her, his voice firm, "Good. If it's right the Lord will reveal when David should speak to Rosie about the future."

"But, Paul we haven't solved our accommodation problem."

"Don't worry my love, it's not urgent, let's see how things pan out."

Yet despite Paul's advice, in the following days Jill was full of ideas and suggestions of how she might assist him to woo Rosie.

CHAPTER 28

Back in London after New Year, with only days to Rosie's birthday, Jill organised an afternoon party to celebrate with the children. Beatty was staying with them so she baked a cake, and later babysat, when they took Rosie to an exclusive restaurant. There Rosie was able to wear the dark green cashmere dress she'd admired in Bath, given to her by Paul and Jill, and the jacket that went with it, from him and the twins. With the pearl necklace and gold watch she looked so serene and beautiful he found it difficult to keep his eyes off her.

At the end of January for David's and his father's birthdays Rosie joined the family gathering for dinner on the Friday, and Jill engineered it that Joyce and Ted would volunteer to babysit the following evening, so Rosie could be included in their theatre trip.

Two weeks later on Valentine's Day, Jill wanted the four of them to go to a restaurant. Paul feeling it was too pointed, suggested with Jill's burgeoning body that the four of them have a quiet dinner, followed by Scrabble, at which Rosie excelled. But it was David, who orchestrated the two dozen red roses to be sent Rosie, with a card on which he'd written, 'To our very special Valentine, We love you.' Joshua, Rebecca and David.' On his arrival home, she'd casually thanked him, so he teased, "I bet the children had a hug and kiss, where's mine?" But at the wary look in her eye, he added, "Only joking!" But she did dress up for their candlelight meal, relaxed with the wine and over the Scrabble game teased and disputed Paul's medical words which he insisted were in the dictionary. At the end of a very pleasant evening, and having said they must do it more often, David handed Rosie a small bag. "It's a newly released record I heard on the radio, and felt the words appropriate!" Bemused, Rosie frowned, and then politely thanked him. That was three weeks ago, but he'd neither heard her play it, nor had she commented on it.

David turned the car right into Church Street, and considered how Jill was rapidly gaining weight, and with the baby's birth about seven weeks away, it was doubtful she'd arrange any social event in the near future. Jill wanted a girl this time, and as Rebecca was becoming a bossy little madam, it would do her good to have some competition! And there, along the street, was that little girl, sitting in the double buggy with her brother. He pulled into the kerb. "Hello people where are you going?" The surprise had them chorus "Daddy" and the glee on their faces brought joy to his heart.

Rosie bent to the window to explain. "Jill fancied marmite and banana sandwiches, we've run out of marmite so I thought we'd take a stroll to the shops before they shut."

He made a face, "How can she eat that?"

Rosie shrugged, "It's beyond me, but at least it's less fattening than the Mars bars and salted peanut phase! Anyway I'll be back in about half an hour to start the twins' tea."

He was still considering his sister's weird food combinations as he put down his brief case and hung his coat on the hall stand. Mrs Perkins appearing behind him made him jump! "Sorry Sir, but I's glad to see you…"

Concerned, he frowned, "Oh dear, is there a problem?"

"Oh no Sir, no problem! Just wanted to tell you how brilliant Miss Rosie is with them's babies. Lovely girl, different from Jane, but pure gold, just the same. Quiet, keeps herself to herself, yet…" In knowing Mrs P's ramblings, he nodded rapidly in the hope she'd get to her point. "Them roses you sent, well I fought Sir, you'd like to know brought tears to 'er eyes, 'appy ones, of course!" Now he was interested. A gleam of conspiracy entered Mrs P's eyes. "She likes that record you gives 'er. Plays it so much I know words off by 'eart. All about 'Not being able to forget the evening, 'er face when leaving, the smile in 'er eyes, but the sorrow it shows, and 'can't live, if living is without you'." Not the usual kind of music you'd normally buy, is it Sir? It's now in the 'it parade." Mrs P gave him a wily look, "I guess it's a message to 'er?" Shrewd eyes looked up into his, and she grinned at his wide-eyed, but inscrutable expression. "If you's forgive me saying, Sir, you're just the man for 'er. She'll be a lovely mother for them twins, and 'er 'aving been a friend of Jane's, seems right to me."

Mrs P had enjoyed conspiring with him over his romance with Jane, so he drew nearer to her to say confidentially, "Rosie never complains, but I'd like to be more supportive. I worry that she doesn't tell me of problems with the children and takes much of the responsibility upon herself. If ever you think she needs help, please don't hesitate to tell me, or ring me at work and let me know."

The front door opening had Mrs P sending him a 'knowing' look and after a nod and wink he turned his attention to the little voices shouting, "Daddy, Daddy." And for the rest of the evening he was caught up with the twins and his thoughts of Rosie as their mother.

In building up the Overseas Division, he and Wilhelm, had put aside appointing two new Directors. The Board meeting this morning was to discuss potential candidates. From the French windows of his office, he wistfully watched Grace and Wilhelm coming arm in arm up the drive. Grace had waited a long time for that kind of companionship. Could he and Rosie enjoy something like that? His mind drifted over the latest instalment of his dream. The army had dissipated, the dawn had fully broken, and he was alone, slowly riding up a mountain path. It was quiet, peaceful, relaxed and he'd paused on a crag to look out at the green vista of undulating hills before him. The only building was on a far horizon. It looked like a castle or walled city. It would take several weeks journeying to reach it, but there didn't seem much else to head for. A knock at his door jerked him back into the present, and as the three Board members entered Maud queried, "Where's Mavis?"

"At the dentist. I've primed Susie to bring us another tray of tea at ten-thirty, and told switchboard to hold my calls until lunch time."

It was nearly mid-day before, as Chairman, he was able to conclude, "We are in agreement that..." The shrill of the telephone cut across his words. He stared at it as if to do so it would stop.

When it didn't, Maud suggested while knocking the ash off her cigarette into the ashtray, "I'd answer that. Trudy wouldn't ring, unless it was urgent."

With a grimace he walked over, picked up the telephone, barked his name into it as Grace entered. She glanced at him and went to speak to Wilhelm as he refocused on the voice, that was saying nervously, "Sir, it's me, Mrs Perkins." Irritated he closed his eyes. Oh no, surely his encouragement two days ago to call him didn't mean she'd do so at every small crisis within his home. More sharply than intended he asked, "Yes, what is it Mrs Perkins, I'm very busy."

"There's been an accident. Rebecca fell down the stairs. Miss Rosie took Joshua with her in the ambulance but..."

He cut across to boom, "Ambulance! Distressed he raked his hair. "Is she badly hurt? Why didn't Rosie ring me? Where's Jill?"

"Ah well that's it, Sir. This all started when Mrs Jill fell over Master William's tractor …"

"Yes, yes, but Rebecca?"

"The ambulance men said she was more winded than unconscious, but…"

Horrified he bellowed, "Unconscious" and then snapped, "Which hospital, tell me?" He whirled around to see his colleagues standing in the centre of the room looking anxiously at him.

"St Mary's, same as Mrs Jill?"

"What do you mean 'same as Jill?"

"After the fall Mrs Jill was in bad pain and bleeding."

Closing his eyes he took a deep breath and endeavoured to ask in a calm voice, which belied his rising panic, "Where are Jill's children?"

"I'm with thems Sir. I said I'd look after them, but I can't stop William screaming for his mother and he's making Luke cry. I've had to shut them both in the bedroom to ring you. I need 'elp." As his mind raced to find a solution, he assured her, "I'm on my way" and put the phone down.

Grace moved towards him. "Trudy told me Mrs Perkins was calling to say there'd been an accident. I told her to put it through to you and came to see how we could help." On overdrive his mouth relayed the situation as he moved toward the door. "You need to go to the hospital. Wilhelm and I can look after the children."

Wilhelm nodded. "David, the simplest solution is I drive your car, drop you at the hospital, and we go on to the house. You can contact us there." It made sense he went with it, his mind filled with questions and worse case scenarios.

Twenty minutes later, in frustration, he tapped his fingers against the hospital reception desk, causing the woman to look pointedly at them, and him. Finally, she directed him towards the examination room, and having rushed along the corridor he burst in to see the back view of the doctor bending over his child. Rosie, who was standing next to him turned, her face white, her voice coming out as a hoarse whisper as she exclaimed, "David!" Without hesitation he pushed between them to see Rebecca.

Big blue eyes stared up at him before they filled with love, and in a voice of adoration, she announced, "This is my Daddy."

The young doctor smiled. "Mr Reinhardt I presume! I'm pleased to report there's no evidence of broken bones or internal damage." Rebecca giggled as he tickled her. "There may be some external bruising, but children of this age have little fear of falling, so don't tend to get badly hurt."

"Daddy, cuddle." The doctor stepped back, and as he bent forward over the examination couch a pair of tiny arms wound tightly around his neck. Relieved he hugged her close before Rebecca pulled back to declare, "Joshua push me."

He glared at Rosie. "Where is Joshua?"

The doctor answered, "With a nurse in the playroom. Although there's no sign of concussion I think it wise to keep this little one in overnight. Now excuse me, I'll send someone to take your details and organise a transfer to the ward."

"We'd like a private room."

The doctor gave a slight bow. "I'm sure, Mr Reinhardt, that can be arranged."

The moment the doctor left, and anxious to find out what happened, David snapped, "What happened? Did you forget to shut the stair gate?"

In a choked voice, Rosie spluttered, "No, no it was..." Arms outstretched Rebecca struggled toward her. Still angry, he didn't want to hand her over, but had no choice.

The moment she was in Rosie's arms she was touching her face saying, "No cry 'osie, 'becca, no damage!"

David stroked Rebecca's hair as she buried her face into Rosie's neck. Rosie murmured, "Oh my little love, that's so good to hear."

Still upset he accused, "No thanks to you, it seems. Where were you? More to the point what were you doing?" Desperation filled his voice, "First Jane, now this?

Weakly, he rested against the examination couch, and groaning he put his head in his hands, as an older voice said cheerily, "Don't upset yourselves, these things happen, children will explore. I'm sure it wasn't anyone's fault. Mum's can't have eyes in the back of their head. and with twins double the trouble." David frowned at the reference to 'Mum'. Nurse Drew continued, "If you'd like to follow me, we'll join your son." Irritated that Rebecca continued to bury her face in Rosie's neck, he strode behind her, but ahead of them.

The moment Joshua saw him, he left his drawing to run and grab his legs, his face crumpling as he cried, "Daddy, Daddy, Becca, fall, Becca hurt." Drawing the little body upwards, he cuddled him, and turned to show him Rebecca in Rosie's arms. For a second Joshua stared in amazement, before declaring as a question, "Becca better now?"

Nurse Drew dismissed the woman who'd been looking after Joshua, and indicated they sit. Rosie moved to engage the children in play, and he was left to fill in their details. Looking across the room the Nurse asked, "I assume Mrs Reinhardt, you'd like to stay with Rebecca tonight?"

Rosie raised her head and gave him a questioning look. He shrugged and gestured with his hand to indicate it was up to her. Lips trembling she said fretfully, "I'm sorry." Silent tears rolled down her face. Not knowing how to respond David frowned. And Nurse Drew having glanced at him, said briskly, "Come, come, now Mrs Reinhardt, accidents happen in the best of homes with the best of mothers. I know it's been a shock. I'll give you time alone."

With that she left, but not before she sent a sympathetic glance towards Rosie who was rocking Rebecca on her lap. Annoyed, as being seen as hard-hearted, he challenged, "Why didn't you tell them you aren't my wife, or the children's mother?"

Nervously she stuttered, "I, I only left them a few minutes. I thought they were safe."

Sarcastically he retorted, "Safe where, playing on the stairs?"

Rosie winced, and further tears rolled down her cheeks. "I closed the stair gates and the doors."

Frustrated he barked, "So what did happen?"

The answer was a shudder, grimace, before she straightened and composed herself to explain. "Jill fell over William's big truck. She hit her stomach on the wooden arm of the settee. Mrs P found her doubled up in pain. I told her to put Luke in his cot, and shut William in the bedroom with him. The twins often play in the hall of your flat, so I shut all the doors believing them to be secure. When I got to the basement Jill was bleeding heavily, I helped her upstairs to her bedroom, grabbed towels and told her to lie down with her feet up. I was just coming out of their flat to ring for an ambulance, when there was a scream…" She hesitated, closed her eyes, and obviously reliving the event, said in a strained voice, "Rebecca fell in heap at my feet. She was silent and unmoving, Joshua, looking down through the banisters, was screaming hysterically. Afraid he'd fall through too I shouted for Mrs P, ran upstairs, hugged him and made the call. When I returned Mrs P was hovering between keeping Jill calm in the bedroom, and watching Rebecca laying in the hall, her eyes open, but glazed. The ambulance men arrived in about five minutes. They quickly reassured me Rebecca hadn't broken anything, and had probably passed out due to knocking the air out of her body. They were far more concerned about Jill who was in agony."

Less cross, but still upset he demanded, "Why didn't you ring me?"

"In the short time between the ambulance arriving, and leaving I had only time to make one call." At his questioning expression, she pursed her lips and said, "To your father, believing contacting Paul in Ghana and getting him home was the priority." At every stage Rosie had done the right thing, he scowled at his wrong assumptions. "I was going to ring you, but with Jill, and Rebecca to deal with, there hasn't been time." About to apologise for his brusque manner she pre-empted him by asking, "How did you find out?" When he told her she repeated "Mrs P!" in surprise.

"She's worked for me for years, and has my number in case there's an emergency." Mrs P's words echoed in his mind, 'that girl, like her name, is like a sensitive flower, easily bruised, damaged and crushed'. Now the shock of the situation was dissipating, he realised in his anxiety he'd virtually accused her of neglect, blamed her unjustly, had spoken sarcastically and no doubt scowled throughout to a woman who'd virtually given up her life to love his children.

Those big brown eyes, that at Christmas sparkled with life, had returned to their doleful state in a dour face. As she murmured, "Events overtook me and were out of my control" an inner voice told him those words covered an anguish that went deeper than today's situation. The curtain of her hair obscured her face as she bent forward to cuddle Rebecca, but he knew she was crying. Jane's reaction would have been challenging, Rosie looked deflated and defeated. Not knowing how to comfort her, he put his hand on her shoulder and felt her cringe from his touch. Desperate, he prayed for wisdom. How would Paul tackle this? He was quiet and gentle, yet equally firm and commanding. He crouched at Rosie's feet, his voice soft and encouraging. "Rosie, look at me?" Slowly, she looked up. "Please stop crying. I over-reacted, my behaviour and attitude contemptible. If there is an excuse it was a reaction from being sick with worry." Rosie stared at him. Emotion choked his words, "Please forgive me? I can't imagine how anyone could be a better mother to the twins, and if you were my wife, I'd be proud to acknowledge you as that." The truth that slipped out caused a frown to pucker across Rosie's forehead, and her eyes fill with disbelief. Quickly he went on, "Would you like to stay with Rebecca?" She nodded. He stood, "I'll go and tell the nurse our decision and ring Wilhelm to collect me. He and Grace are looking after the children. Here's my pen, make a list of the things you and Rebecca will need, then Jill can…" Appalled, he realised he'd forgotten about Jill. "Do you know how Jill is?" Rosie shook her head, her eyes filled with such fear it caused dread to rise in his heart. "I'll find out."

At the Reception Desk the same woman gave him a small smile. "All well now?"

"My daughter, yes, but I'm afraid my sister came in the same ambulance. Can you tell me how she is? Her surname is Stemmings."

"Oh, Dr Stemmings' wife? He nodded. "Such a lovely man. If you'll take a seat I'll find out for you." Several minutes later she pointed out a man in green theatre garb coming towards him. Hand outstretched he introduced himself. "Julian Standish, the Obstetrics Consultant. I believe you're related to Dr Stemmings' wife."

"Yes, I'm her brother. Paul's in Ghana, he's been informed, and hopefully on his way home."

"That's good for when she wakes up he'll be here to support her."

Alarmed he repeated, "Wakes up? Is the baby alright?"

"I'm afraid her fall caused problems. The baby was distressed. We took the decision to operate. Obviously, this has been very upsetting for her, but she will recover. Their daughter weighed in a healthy 5lbs 2 ozs, she's breathing well, her heartbeat strong, but we'll need to monitor her progress."

Relief and joy flowed through him. "Oh, a girl, Paul will be so pleased."

"We've put her in the private wing, but she'll not be up to visits today."

Rosie's lack of response when he returned to give her the news of Jill's baby revealed her shock, her hand trembled as she handed him his pen and the list. What could he say to comfort her except, "So all's well." And with no response he said, "Right I'll get on to this. The nurse says she'll put you a private room near Jill. Now I'd better take Joshua home."

Rebecca looked up from her jigsaw, "Me, Daddy, come too." Rosie said nothing, so he picked her up to kiss, cuddle and explain to her, "You and Rosie are going to share a special bedroom here tonight." It was obvious Rebecca liked that idea for she didn't complain. To Rosie he explained, "With three children at home I'm not sure I'll get back, but if Wilhelm keeps the car he can bring Grace over with the things on this list."

The nursing station was empty so he and Joshua wandered down the corridor, but he stopped short when around a corner he heard his name. "...Reinhardts' are in the play room. She's beautiful. He's attractive in a sexy rugged way, but totally devoid of empathy or understanding. Angus said he arrived like a raging bull, pushed him out of the way, and then instead of comforting his distraught wife, spoke sharply to her. But the children obviously adore him."

Joshua pulled at his hand wanting to walk on as the voice of the Receptionist confirmed, "Once he'd established his child was here, he dismissed his chauffeur. I'd say he's a high-flying business man, not used to waiting, but I took that as anxiety, not annoyance."

"I'd say the latter. When I walked into the examination room he was berating his wife, and before putting his head in his hands, he said, 'First Jane, now this' I'm not sure if she was white with shock from the accident, or from his fury that she'd allowed the accident to happen. From my observation she's good with the twins, but frightened of him, he's in charge, he answered all my questions. They only have the twins, so whatever happened to Jane, my impression is he blames her for it. Not once has he touched her, offered comfort or ..." Joshua tugged at David's hand, he let him go as Nurse Drew finished, "...expressed any sympathy for her distress." In catching up with Joshua he made it appear he was chasing him. Whipping him off his feet he zoomed him up and down, causing him to chuckle with delight as he came face to face with his critics.

Nurse Drew's guilty blush was already rising as she declared, "Mr Reinhardt."

A wicked thought entered his mind, he turned on his high-wattage smile, and still playing with Joshua he commented, "He's such a little imp. He takes after his mother, Jane. Since she died her friend Rosie cares for them, but as they grow, they are becoming more of a handful." There was a certain satisfaction in seeing the women's embarrassment as they exchanged a glance. And he couldn't resist adding, "As you can imagine I'm terrified of something happening to the twins, they are all I have left of my wife."

But seeing the tears jump into the Receptionist eyes, and hearing Nurse Drew clear her throat before saying, "I am so sorry to hear that, what a terrible shock this must have been for you, and such beautiful children" he felt perhaps he'd overdone it.

"Thank you. Rebecca is the image of her mother at that age, Joshua I fear might inherit my rather intimidating looks."

Nurse Drew looked him squarely in the eye and said, "Well as the saying goes you can't always judge a book by its cover."

"No indeed." And with that he winked, "Much the same as 'eavesdroppers never hear good of themselves'. Believe me, after my initial shock and wrong assumptions I've done my best to reassure Rosie of my appreciation. And she'd like to stay with Rebecca. I have to go. My sister has just had a Caesarean, and her two children are being looked after by my friends."

The Receptionist smiled and informed Nurse Drew. "Mr Reinhardt's sister is married to Paul Stemmings." Knowing the expected response David smiled, told them that Rosie had the forethought to send a message to Paul in Ghana, and he should be home in twenty-four hours. After a self-deprecating smile he asked, "Now I'd better get some change? I need to telephone my friend to collect me."

The Receptionist sent him an approving smile, "If you'd like to come with me, just this once, I'll let you through to use the office telephone."

CHAPTER 29

David had no stomach to eat, but Joshua enjoyed the sandwiches Grace had prepared. And Wilhelm told of how he'd calmed William and Luke by playing Teddy Bear Hide 'n Seek they'd introduced to the children on their previous visits. With three boisterous boys, David suggested the run off their energy at the park, and while he and Wilhelm accompanied them, Grace offered to delve through Jill and Rosie's female things to pack Rosie's list. In considering whether to move Joshua's cot to the downstairs flat so he could sleep in Paul and Jill's room and be near William and Luke, Wilhelm and Grace offered to stay. And once all the boys were asleep, David drove to the hospital, discovered Jill was still under sedation, and saw Rosie had reverted to silence unless directly addressed. Rebecca's welcome lifted his heavy heart, but still despondent he drove home knowing that his behaviour and words had fed Rosie's insecurity of not being wanted, or being good enough!

After a disturbed night, pacifying Joshua who missed Rebecca and worrying about Rosie, he felt rather drained as he returned to the hospital to first visited Jill, and then disturbed to see her propped up, in a painkiller daze, crying and rambling. The nurse explained, "She's convinced she's lost the baby. We've tried to explain her daughter is in the special care unit, and when she's well enough we can take her to visit, but she doesn't believe us."

With that David boomed, as if Jill were hard of hearing, that he was off to see her little girl, and returned to report, "Well, despite your daughter's traumatic arrival she's quite beautiful, holding her own, and about the same size as Rebecca when born." Jill appeared to understand, so he added, "Due to Rosie's prompt action Paul's flying home. I haven't spoken to him, but Dad has told him he's got a little girl, so he's looking forward to meeting her tomorrow!" Rosie also took the opportunity to visit the baby and reassure Jill while he played with Rebecca who seemed unaffected by her fall the day before.

On the drive home he praised Rosie for her quick action which probably saved the baby's life, and went on to reassure her, "It's inconceivable that Rebecca's could squeeze her body through so narrow a space, but I've roped the banisters through, it won't happen again."

Rosie said nothing. Concerned, he glanced in her direction and asked if she was alright. He received a curt nod, and her face remained pinched. However, on arrival home and seeing the three little boys in the basement lounge Rosie let out a choking sob, and fell to her knees hugging, kissing and crying over them. Such was her reaction Grace, he and Mrs P exchanged a worried glance. "There, there luv, don't upset yourself so, accidents 'appen and alls well that ends well. How's Jill? I 'ears she's 'ad a lovely little girl." When Rosie didn't answer, he told Mrs P the latest news and Mrs P, believing every trauma deserved a cuppa, went to put on the kettle, and Grace indicated to David to follow her upstairs.

Once in his lounge she shut the door. "David, I think there's more to Rosie's over emotional state than you being upset with her yesterday."

David waved Grace to sit. "I agree. It's as though something has resurfaced in her past, bringing guilt, or perhaps shame." Upset he ran his fingers through his hair. "And my words yesterday exacerbated, and confirmed that." Lowering his voice he sat forward to confide, "My family like Rosie, she loves the twins, and would be a wonderful mother. I wouldn't be averse to marrying her, but know she would be."

Grace looked thoughtful, and then asked, "Do you care for her?"

Vehemently he straightened to boom, "Of course I do."

"Think about it. If she became a mother to your children, she also becomes your wife, and the promise you make is 'to have and to hold...until death do you part'." David shuddered at the word, 'death'. "Besides the children, do you have anything in common? From business you know it's foolish to enter into a partnership without knowing what you are getting into. Could Rosie's continual silence about her past be a lack of trust?"

"I do trust her. I admire her abilities, her integrity. Good heavens I let her look after my children."

Grace sighed, before quietly stated, "David, I was talking about her trusting you!"

Appalled to think Rosie wouldn't trust him, he listened as Grace continued, "You've seen the problem in part. The old acerbic Rosemary, in fearing rejection, rejected others first. You would have rejected her except Jane stepped in and befriended her. Rosie knows the Lord won't reject her, and that knowledge is changing her, but she's still fearful of man's rejection. Immediately she has a personal problem she retreats behind a wall of silence. Your family's acceptance and appreciation is gaining her confidence, but you've seen how easily that deflates. If you feel, because of your mutual love of the children, you could nurture and love her, perhaps, if it were on her terms she'd be open to a 'marriage of convenience'." With a wide-eyed look Grace added, "Her terms! You'd need to be prepared for a long and arduous road, and only you know if you want to travel that, but security, stability and belonging would eventually break that lack of trust, and maybe bring a reciprocating love."

The path of his dream came into mind, it led to a castle! Could that be Rosie's heart? But when yesterday, he told Rosie if she'd been his wife he'd have been proud to acknowledge that, he'd seen her expression of disdain and disbelief. Grace, as though reading into his silence, added, "Rejected people often have a defence mechanism that twists the positive to negative. It makes an emotional minefield for others to walk in. I said to you once before, if you are going to get embroiled, remember this is someone's life, and you need to think carefully about your actions and the consequences if it doesn't work out."

Immediately David retorted, "I was right, with Jane." Grace raised her eyebrows and clicked her tongue. To help reassure Grace he told her about their Christmas charade, and ended, "I knew then I liked Rosie enough for it to be a reality. And to help Rosie think of me as a good friend, we've been involving her more in our social lives. I felt she was growing more comfortable around me." He sat back and steepled his fingers against his mouth as he said, "But now I've spoilt it, and don't know if Rosie would even consider a 'marriage of convenience'. But I can see it would be a solid foundation on which to build that mutual love of the twins into a mutual love of each other. I like the idea."

Grace asked bluntly, "Do you? Well, you'll need to give Rosie time to get over her present emotional state, and work towards it, not spring it upon her."

Hours later, laying in bed, he pondered Grace's words, but soon his eyes grew heavy and he slept. He knew that he and his horse had cantered up hills and down dales for many days, and at times he'd thought he'd lost his way. The forest he was now in seemed never ending, yet, just as he was giving up hope of finding a way through and out, the trees began to part. Before him a gentle, grassy slope headed down to a moat, beyond which towered old, yellowed stone walls. He cantered around, and stopped to view the raised drawbridge. Slipping from his horse he lay on the bank in the warm sun to consider his alternatives. Nearby his horse champed on the grass as outwardly he felt weary, but inwardly was a strong urge to find a way inside. To tunnel under the moat and walls would be hard work and take years. He could swim the moat, climb the wall, but if construed as attack he'd lose all he'd gained. The simplest way would be to hide, wait and pray that next time the drawbridge came down he could slide across unawares to observe, and then strategise to ensure a warm welcome. Looking at the height of the walls, he murmured, 'Lord, you made the walls of Jericho tumble down.' Instantly came the reply, 'True my son, but in this case we don't want any fatalities!' Coming back into consciousness he was still querying what 'this case' was?

Opening his eyes, the time on the clock read 3.33 am. This couldn't be coincidence, it had to be God referring again to Ezekiel 33.3. So he called upon the Lord for an answer? The promise of Psalm 37 came to mind. 'God gives you the desires of your heart'. Was the castle and Rosie connected? Eyes closed he pondered on that. Rosie hid behind the wall of her past. The family had tried digging and got nowhere. In friendship they'd tried climbing her walls. They'd not been repelled, but not welcomed into Rosie's personal life. The drawbridge had lowered to allow Jane access, as it had for the twins, could this be his way of slipping in undetected? Rosie blossomed in a need to be needed! He hadn't cajoled her to stand with him on those two occasions against Felicity, but afterwards she'd retreated. He stretched across the bed and grinned into the darkness. His ticket then was to make her feel needed, and 'this case' was to do so through love. Rosie's drawbridge was always lowered when the twins had need. Anticipation and desire began to rise, but instinctively he knew that any intimacy, even in marriage, would have to be at her pace, and he'd need to be sensitive to that. And enjoying challenge he felt ready for that. The mystery was Rosie's past beyond the fact that An older man, her employer had taken advantage of her, and the consequences of that had ruined her hope of a family life. But the Lord was into redemption…he smiled, closed his eyes, and while considering how he might woo Rosie, slipped back into sleep.

A few weeks later, David observed to Paul that life in the Reinhart household had lost its atmosphere of well-being. Paul nodded, but looked preoccupied, the children, perhaps a reflection of the general tension, seemed tetchy.

Paul, returning home from Ghana, had been thrust into ten days of supporting Jill in hospital, and coping with William and Luke at home. Everyone had pulled together to help, his parents, Joyce, people at church, Beatty, and he'd been leaving ITP at lunch time, and working at home in the evening. Last week, he'd taken holiday, believing as he helped Rosie this would be a prime opportunity to observe, and strategise his next move. But he'd been disappointed for she was very withdrawn, and even with the children, seemed a little distant. Jill and Paul were becoming more fraught because Rachel Beatrice wasn't the contented baby William and Luke had been. Jill, occupied with the baby, and still weak, wasn't up to housekeeping and cooking, so it mostly fell to Rosie. Paul, with sleepless nights, was beginning to look drawn, and David, sensing his worry, had asked, but felt brushed off when Paul replied, "It's early days, it'll sort itself out."

The last two Saturdays David's job had been to chauffeur the cook! Shopping on Saturday in Tesco wasn't a pastime he enjoyed, but it was a chance to build a bridge of companionship with Rosie. With four adults, and four children needing three meals a day, shopping and cooking was no mean task. The Morris was always available, but either Rosie didn't drive or didn't want to. On his broaching the subject, she'd skilfully sidelined the need to answer. This week's shopping was larger than usual, because the family was coming for the Easter weekend. And on Sunday Maria, Paula's family and Jane's parents would join them. David piled the bags from two trolleys into the car boot as Rosie went off to the post office. His mind vied between dread of the extra workload the weekend would bring, and the pleasure of a lively household. With the entangled domestic arrangements, he and Rosie could have been married. It certainly gave him insight as to how difficult, if he accepted it, the challenge could be. His few angry words, said in anxiety, seemed to have caused irrevocable damage to their relationship.

Through the windscreen he viewed Rosie walking towards the car, her hat and scarf making her look younger than her thirty-one years. He jumped out to open the car door for her, and polite as usual, she thanked him and slid into the passenger seat. On the way home he talked, and every reply was monosyllabic. Irritated, he gave up. Under instruction he manfully hauled all the shopping upstairs, and having put it on his dining room table, he clenched his jaw as she decreed, "I'll manage now. Thank you."

What was the matter with the woman? Afraid he'd say something that might bruise a delicate, but very prickly Rosie, he saluted saying, "Yes Ma'am!" before hurrying downstairs to see the twins. The beautiful scene in the basement lounge over-rode his frustration. Jill was feeding Rachel, and Paul, sitting crossed legged at her feet, had four little faces gazing up at him, as he read a story. Joshua spotting him, let out a whoop of joy, and leapt forward to hug his legs, saying, "Story! Come, hear story."

Rebecca joining him, smiled up at David in adoration, then with palms up, her head on one side, she frowned to ask, "Where's Rosie?" The child and her gestures were so adorable he just had to whip her off her feet and kiss her, and as she giggled delightedly, Joshua was insisting he wanted to be lifted up and become a plane.

"Did the shopping go well?" Jill asked, adjusting Rachel to her other breast.

In between his zooming noises, David answered, "If you mean did we buy all we needed, yes! But after my usefulness I was dismissed, my help not wanted, thank you very much." He made a rueful grimace, "Perhaps it's my imagination, but Rosie seems more uptight than usual."

William climbed up to watch Jill feeding Rachel. Paul, with his rapt audience depleted, picked up Luke and asked, "Why do you say that?"

"Just a feeling. You're the doctor, what do you think?"

Paul ushered him towards the kitchen. "I'll make some tea. Rosie's made a delicious apple cake."

Jill called out, "Don't be too long in there. I haven't got five pairs of eyes!"

Filling the kettle Paul said, "We're all overstretched. We thought we could cope with Rachel in our bedroom until we move in June, but her coming seven weeks early, and constantly crying, keeps us both awake. We've no extra bedroom now to either put Rachel in, or to use so we can get six hours sleep. We don't want Rosie to feel pushed out, this is her home, but we could do with her room."

Leaning back against the work surface David stated, "I'm still happy for her to sleep in my study, but being so touchy these days, even that suggestion, might be just too much. Paul, with so much going on, we've had no time to chat, but when Grace was here we talked about Rosie."

Paul nodded thoughtfully as David repeated the conversation, and commented at the end, "I can see billing it to Rosie as a 'marriage of convenience' could have potential, but Grace is right, about being prepared for a difficult, and maybe long haul." Ruefully he added, "You might need the room, but now isn't a good time to approach Rosie. She's barely speaking to me after the incident with Jill and Rebecca. But, I have hope! Let me tell you the latest scenario in my recurring dream…" The kettle had boiled, the tea brewed, the cake cut, before he ended, "…so I feel the drawbridge will be the children, but recently, even with them, Rosie seems subdued."

Paul hummed, then jumped as Jill, opening the door, demanded, "Where's the tea? Rachel needs changing. The children need supervision!"

They exchanged a glance. Picking up the tray Paul explained to Jill, "David's happy to give up his study. I know you don't want William to sleep there, it's too far from us, but how about Rachel stays in our bedroom, and we use David's study to get six hours sleep a night? It's only for a few weeks."

Jill argued, "But what happens if I need your help during the night?

In a placating tone, Paul asked, "Now, how often has that happened? And Rosie would be quick to help you, or get me." Jill pursed her lips, and arms folded gave Paul a belligerent look as Rosie appeared on the stairs.

David rushed forward, "I said I'd bring the bags down."

Brusquely, her tone plummy, her nose in the air, Rosie stated, "I needed to sort them. These are for this fridge." She moved past without a glance in his direction. "There are four more bags upstairs, you can get those."

Was she being deliberately rude? Instinctively words of challenge came, but he clenched his jaw, took a deep breath and invited her retreating figure to join them for a cup of tea and a piece of her delicious cake. At Jill's frown, he raised his eyebrows, Jill shook her head as though to say more would make matters worse. Did he care enough to tolerate and not challenge Rosie's moods? Surely Jane's ditty would have meant that the woman the twins bestowed their love on would also love him? Pathetically, he blinked back tears and consoled himself with his dream. It brought the hope and belief that one day Rosie would lower the drawbridge, and allow him to enter and heal her heart. Cynically his mouth twisted, that sounded like a fairy story.

The following day in church, he remembered how his father, when last visiting, had commented on the number of single females who, in cooing over the twins, seemed interested to befriend him! But none of them interested him, he didn't encourage their chatter, and like his father frowned on Nurse Brown giving the impression she was a family friend! When his father had queried why Rosie no longer attended the morning service, he'd shrugged and suggested it gave her opportunity to be away from the Reinhardt clan, to which his father had scowled, and given David to consider that Rosie didn't give the impression of being a family friend.

It was Thursday, the day before the Easter holiday, and David, preoccupied, head down, left his office and nearly bumped into Wilhelm. Seeing Wilhelm's worried expression he jokingly commented, "You look as I feel. What's on your mind? Do you want to come in?"

Wilhelm acknowledged Mavis, and once David's office door closed, he came straight to the point. "Grace and I have been given notice to leave the cottage." David indicating the easy chairs by the French windows let Wilhelm continue. "Rosie, acting on the landlady's behalf, was very apologetic, but said that for family reasons the landlady need us to leave as soon as possible, but at the latest the end of April."

David responded, "It's a pity because it's so cosy and convenient, but with house prices rising why not buy a place? You could double your investment in a few years." On a broad smile he added, "And, there's no reason why you couldn't have an extended holiday in Germany, while waiting for the purchase to go through."

"Wilhelm sighed, "I know, we're considering all those things, but our worry was more about our landlady, and the nature of her 'family reasons'?"

Puzzled, David commented, "That's kind of you."

"We were wondering if you knew the landlady's identity?"

With a grimace, David shook his head. "Sorry no. Rosie never talks to us about her family, or friends."

Wilhelm focussed inwardly. David looked out the window and watched as one of the three attractive women, in their late twenties, walking up the drive, glanced up at his window. He knew they couldn't see him, but lately he'd become aware, as an available man he was again an attraction to the female staff. In seeing further glances, he guessed he was the subject of their conversation, but none sparked a challenge sufficient to catch his attention. Wilhelm as though following his thought pattern asked, "How's Rosie? It doesn't seem much of a life for an attractive, and adept young woman to be a nanny to five children, under four years of age."

"Oddly Wilhelm, that 'attractive and adept young woman', is uppermost in my mind. I can't fathom her out."

"David, I've had two wives, a daughter, and three grand-daughters and believe me I've still not fathomed them out. But my experience tells me they are driven by their emotions. Grace told me she'd spoken to you regarding Rosie."

Grimly he nodded. And as he bemoaned his lack of progress, Wilhelm sat back to listen. David finished, "Everyone knows she'll make a wonderful mother, and me a good wife, but the drawbridge to her heart is definitely up, and the walls impenetrable! The question is, what is best for Rosie?"

At the analogy Wilhelm chortled, "I see your dilemma, but how do you know she doesn't observe you from the ramparts of her castle?"

"If she does her eyes are sending daggers into my heart." Wilhelm laughed. David responded with a smile, what do you suggested, "I become her knight in shining armour and rescue her from herself!"

"Didn't Jane think you were her guardian angel?"

At that David laughed. "Oh Wilhelm, I don't think Rosie would prescribe to believing in either of those."

"Grace told me you warmed to an idea of 'a marriage of convenience', but the need to give Rosie time. Personally, I'd be scaling the walls, and going over the top to tell her of how much I appreciated her, the love and care she has for my children, the way you've always worked well together, and that mutual respect and honesty is a good basis for marriage. If she's worried about the intimate side of marriage. tell her compatibility is good, but often over-rated and termed as love, which in most cases it isn't."

Playfully he retorted, "Did you say that last bit to Grace?"

Wilhelm gave an ironic smile, "No! But we don't consider that side of our marriage as important as our companionship and enjoyment of life. Look at this situation with Rosie from another perspective. She still appears upset at your angry response to Rebecca's fall. Could it be she so highly values your opinion of her, that she's afraid of letting you down again?"

"Doubtful, but I'll consider what you've said. But changing the subject, what makes you interested in your landlady, and her 'family reasons'?"

Wilhelm sighed, "Grace, is a woman in a million, and she has gut feeling about it, right or wrong, only time will tell. Anyway assuming we need to leave England at the end of April, we need to discuss how I can take that time out without impeding our expansion plans."

Later, driving home, David began to evaluate the situation with Rosie. He needed to assemble the facts, revisit, dissect, clarify, make specific points for analysis, be ready to step forward. Experience told him observation of the smallest detail could often be the key to bring about a satisfactory conclusion.

Feeling more confident to tackle Rosie, and the situation, he arrived home believing even if Rosie didn't respond, he could exude love and care, with that thought he took the stairs two and at time. But Rosie wasn't sitting in his lounge Paul was. William and Joshua were doing a large piece jigsaw on the coffee table. Luke was using the border of the carpet as a road on which to run his car, and Rebecca who was drawing opposite the boys, looked up. Head on one side, her hand palms up, she said in her cute little voice, "Rosie's got lost."

Laughing he picked her up, "Then we better go and find her." But before he could move anywhere William and Joshua grabbed his legs, Whoa boys, you don't want me falling over, let me put my briefcase down and take off my coat."

A smile at Paul, showed his consternation, his words like the sounding of a death knoll, "I'm afraid, we have lost Rosie."

Dread, like a heavy stone dropped into his stomach. Ridiculously, tears pricked his eyes. But he managed to ask, "Lost, in what respect?

"As in left us, and not wanting to be found." Unable to comprehend, David frowned, and sunk onto the piano stool. Paul took a deep breath to explain, "After lunch I was talking about our lack of sleep, and Rosie piped up, 'You can have my room. I've been planning to move out.' Before I could tell her she'd no reason to, she was telling us that our decision to relocate to Kent had brought her to consider her position here, and the future. Surprised, we didn't know what to say. She told us how she'd enjoyed living with us, being included in our family, and looking after the children. Her voice cracked, she swallowed, said it was better to go sooner, rather than later and she'd go home for Easter and not come back. Jill tried to talk it through with her, her words, 'it's better not to prolong the agony' and then she excused herself. Two hours later she appeared to tell me, 'I'm going now, I'll send for my boxes. Thank you for everything'. I tried to placate her, but backing away she said, 'Please understand why I have to go' and ran down the stairs and out the front door.'

Dumbfounded, David stared at Paul as Jill spoke from the doorway. "I'm still in shock." Clearly upset, Jill, with Rachel in her arms she sat beside Paul. "David, I did my best to change her mind. I told her she was like a sister, more than a friend, she couldn't just leave. We'd have asked her to live with us in Kent except it would have taken her away from the twins. She blanched at that, but said she loved all the children. I said surely she wasn't going to walk out of our lives, we thought of her as family, the children loved her. At that she murmured, 'Thank you, but to stay in touch…' she trailed off, we waited for her to finish. Then, sounding like a well thought out speech, and in a business tone, she said, 'It's for the best we cut the ties now. The children will soon forget me. Imagine how difficult it will be for the twins when David remarries, to have the children with divided loyalties and love. His wife will become the children's mother, it wouldn't be fair on her, or the children, to have to replace me in their affections'. David it was awful, even if a blind man couldn't see the pain in her eyes, he'd have heard it in her voice. Taken aback, we were at a loss to know what to say."

The first shock, the fear that 'lost' meant dead had worn off, and David knew what he had to do. "Jill, Rosie might think she can disappear out of our lives, but Wilhelm told me this morning, the landlady of the cottage has given them notice to leave for family reasons. I've no doubt Rosie is those family reason, the landlady must…"

Paul butted in, his voice sharp, "David you didn't hear me, Rosie doesn't want to be found."

Rebecca looked up to parrot, "Rosie lost, Rosie found." Drawing her to him, David debated his next move. Upset Paul continued, "I'm so sorry David. We didn't know what to say to her fait accompli, and we could hardly ask her to marry you. I did mention there were other options to consider, she should wait to talk to you, that was when she said, 'You'll have to excuse me' and went to her room. Jill exhausted went to lie down, and I brought the children up here so as not to disturb her. When Rosie came up to say 'goodbye', she kissed the children, and avoided my hug. When I looked out of the window, a taxi driver was hauling a large suitcase in behind her."

David groaned. "I'd hoped this weekend, with the family again, she'd relax as she did at Christmas. And the cottage won't be free until May so, as we've no idea where 'home' is, it seems I'll have to wait until then to talk to her, and sort this out."

Jill's expression was grim. "David, this isn't a sudden whim, Rosie has obviously been packing her things into boxes over several days, and her room is bare. And you'd better read this." She bent forward to hand him a lined sheet of paper covered in Rosie's bold script.

'*Dear friends, I'm sorry if my decision appears sudden, but I've been considering the situation for some weeks. Thank you, Jill for allowing me to live in the flat, being a friend to me and letting me stay on when you married Paul. David, I've loved looking after the twins they are special and precious. But I see to entrench myself further in your lives will only lead to greater heartbreak in the future, for them, and for me. Please thank your family for me, they have made me so welcome, giving me memories I shall always treasure. The appreciation I've had from you all has built up my self-worth and confidence, but I'd appreciate it if you allow me to start a new life. I have had to put the past in the past before, it's hard, but I can do it. And this time, I have the Lord as my strength and my salvation, and it is in Him I put my trust, so please don't worry about me. Blessings and thanks to you all. Love Rosie*

The piece of paper fluttered to the floor, he put his head in his hands and wept. His world had just caved in, not just for him, but for the children too. How could he have failed so miserably to show Rosie he cared for her?

He felt a small person's tug on his arm. Paul said quietly in his ear, "David you are upsetting the children. I'm sorry, I misjudged the situation. I didn't think this would hit you quite so hard. Let's go into the dining room."

David, wiped his face with his hands, smiled lovingly at the four concerned little faces, hugged Rebecca who, with her hand on his knee, had been stretching up to comfort him. "Daddy cry, don't cry Daddy. Rosie, she come back."

Brokenly, he put her down, and said, "Daddy will be back. I'm just going to talk to Paul."

Wisely, Rebecca nodded, "Paul, good man."

It was impossible not to smile, and he agreed, "Yes darling, he is."

That good man now asked his wife, "Jill can you manage here? I promise I won't be long." At her nod, they left to sit in the dining room.

Despair had him raking his hair. "Oh God Paul! What am I going to do?"

"This may seem a clinical approach, but we have to deal with priorities. First, we need to pull together for the benefit of the children. Second, we need to cobble a meal together, feed and put them to bed. Third, your parents arrive tomorrow. I don't want your mother exhausted in trying to take Rosie's place. Beatty could give us extra support, but she's tends to overdo it when she comes here. Maria can help on Sunday. We've all come to depend on Rosie. This isn't just your problem, but I do see your attitude and desire will influence the future, and you could have a major role in solving it."

Cross at Paul's lack of sympathy, he retorted sharply, "What? By choosing one of those women who surround me every Sunday in church. Paul shook his head, and clicked his tongue. "I have no desire for any of them. What I see in Rosie is everything I, and my children want and need."

"But, my friend, you have to consider what Rosie wants and needs. She has made a choice, which, whether we think it right or wrong, we have to respect. However, she doesn't know that you were thinking of offering her marriage, so let's gather the wisdom of others, and decide how best to go from here. But now, let's get the kids in here, and put a meal on this table."

CHAPTER 30

Alone with his thoughts, David negotiated the Saturday traffic on his way out of town. The last eight days had been a rollercoaster of emotions. Grief at losing Jane had been rekindled by losing Rosie. He determined to believe Rosie wasn't lost, and grappled with conflicting reasons as to why she'd left before speaking to him. Mrs P said she cried over the flowers, she liked the record, yet left it behind on his turntable. He'd thought she was warming to him until his anger changed that. Was she afraid of him? Surely not! At one point his remorse converted into anger at Rosie, she'd left the children she said she loved. Had she no compassion for Jane's children, that in missing her, there were times they could not be consoled. Then, he blamed himself for being unaware Rosie would contemplate just upping and leaving, in knowing the grief of sudden lose. That returned him back to the yawning hole of grief, making the Easter story even more poignant this year as they as a family, including Ted and Joyce, gathered and rallied round.

That first evening he'd looked again at Jane's photos, the stories, her ring, the bracelet with 'the twins' charm, and then put them away. That part of his life was over. This week before God he'd been assessing his manner, his attitudes and behaviour. After much heart searching he'd felt Rosie had more to offer than he to give. And as with Jane, he came to a place to accept that if Rosie didn't want to marry him, the Lord would be with him and provide for him.

On Good Friday, when his parents arrived for a late lunch, he'd broken to them the news. His father's immediate response was to blame him, but seeing David's distress he said more kindly, "Don't let that woman slip through your fingers. Go after her, do all you can to get her back. You have the ability to plead a case in court, now is the time to plead your case to her. Prepare your defence, you know Rosie's weakness is the children, use it to cut through argument, thrust your point forward, and be determined to win!"

His Mum countered, "Franz dear, a court of law doesn't equate to courting a woman, especially one who finds men a challenge, and with remarks like that I can empathise with her." Then turning she'd advised, "David, Rosie might appear quiet and unassuming, but she's a woman of integrity and intelligence.

I admire her strength of character to leave when she realized it wouldn't be fair to you, or the children, when it wasn't a nanny you needed, but a wife."

At that he'd sighed. "A role I hadn't discussed or offered her, but perhaps she didn't want to be considered for that. And until I know where she is, I can neither fight my cause, nor prove my case, that she is the only one I want to mother my children, and be my wife."

"I think dear, before you get into that, you will need to change your priorities from wanting a mother for your children, to your desire for her to be your wife."

Franz chortled, "I like that Margaret. The children are the bait, but Rosie needs to know that David's fallen for her hook, line and sinker!" Although they groaned at his father's humour, it brought him to realize that he relished the challenge to hook Rosie, to reel her in to become his wife, and sink her in such love that she'd bloom into the woman she was destined to be. It was love, but different from that he'd had for Jane.

To get through the Easter holiday, his father didn't hesitate in drawing up one of his regimes. Rosie was uppermost in David's mind, if he was suffering, how much more was she in having given up the children she loved? And that made him desperate to find her. Speaking of that at Sunday lunch, Jill responded by saying, "My experience of God is He's never in a hurry, and all things do eventually work together for our good." Was Jill thinking of Ben, who she'd needed to let go?

Richard having attracted his attention, tapped the side of his nose with forefinger, and pointed upwards. But Philip voiced the sign, "Don't worry Uncle David, God knows all about it!"

Paula frowned, Jim studied his sons over his glasses, and Maria piped up, "Dad could give you some tips, after all, he had to woo a woman who wasn't interested in him."

Amused Jill retorted, "Oh I was interested, but so messed up I couldn't believe Paul would want me." She paused, "Perhaps Rosie feels like that." David was just considering whether that remark could be true when Jill continued, "At ITP David has been likened to Mr Darcy. I've seen with my own eyes women going weak at the knees at his smile."

Amused, his mother pointed out, "Mr Darcy was also known to frown, scowl and prowl disinterestedly among the ladies. I rather think, David and Mr Darcy have much in common! And believe that extends to their hearts. Once set, they found ways to overcome all the obstacles."

David nodded, and noticed Ted nudging Joyce. No doubt he was providing more entertainment. So he boomed, "So Ted, have you any advice to offer?"

Ted's face reddened, but he admitted, "I'm afraid my wooing of Joyce, was to be there whenever she needed me. And I hoped that one day she'd realize she couldn't do without me. But it was two years before I felt brave enough to ask her to marry me."

Eyes bright, and as the women cooed, Joyce snuggled against Ted, and full of affection she looked up at him to say, "It worked because it's impossible not to love someone who serves you so unselfishly."

Thumping the table David announced, "Then that's what I must do! But to accomplish that the first priority is to find her." Inspired, they began to pool together what they knew about Rosie: thirty-one, loves children, excellent administrative skills; creative; enjoys music, plays the piano; relative owns cottage in Kensington; home in Hampshire; parents live in India; doesn't drive; well educated; speaks fluent French and German; has an aristocratic voice and bearing. Richard chipped in with 'she's a good cook', and Philip not to be left out, added, 'she doesn't like brussel sprouts'. Laughing he'd commented, 'Now we really are scraping the barrel'. But the truth was they knew little considering Rosie had lived under their roof for three years!

The novelty of a personal treasure hunt drew the family together. His parents stayed the week in their desire to help with the children, and were enthused by seeing the pieces come together. Jill rang Directory Enquiries and received the numbers of three 'Dawes' in Hampshire. Paul admitted to seeing Rosie's medical record at St. Mary's, and felt it wouldn't be breaking patient/doctor confidentiality to narrow their search to the area near Petersfield.

Jill had huffily retorted, "You've known this, and not told us?" Paul gave her a wide-eyed look, and then Jill confessed, "Sorry David, but I once delved into Rosie's file at ITP. There was only the cottage address, her date of birth, but there was a reference from an army brigadier, turned politician. He lived in Langrish, near Petersfield, he gave Rosie a glowing reference."

Having delved into the same file, David added, "Brigadier Frederick Greenhaigh who had 'no hesitation in recommending

Miss Dawes, who had been a tireless and efficient worker in his election campaign'. Before you ask, I've checked, he has an ex-directory telephone number, but 'Who's Who' gives his address and says he's recently retired." What David didn't add was his suspicion that Greenhaigh was the employer who'd dumped Rosie when she was pregnant. Was it because he was Rosie's employer, and in living closely with him, she feared, he might take further advantage of her?

Paul suggested Gerald Maysfield might know more. David arranged to meet him after work on Thursday, in the Pig and Whistle pub a few streets from ITP.

But Mrs P, delighted to be involved, came up trumps by telling them Rosie surname wasn't Dawes, but Doughty-Dawes. She'd seen envelopes in her waste paper bin. And that she'd asked Rosie why she didn't go by that name, and the reply had been a double-barrel surname set her apart, so she only used it when necessary. That led them to enquire again for a Hampshire telephone number, but frustratingly the only Doughty-Dawes was ex-directory, and the 'Who's Who' didn't have an entry under either or both names, but then it wasn't conclusive, as not all who were invited to be in it, wanted to be listed.

Wilhelm and Grace on hearing Rosie's full name were surprised David didn't know it, and said they paid an all-inclusive rent into a Coutts bank account and the bills arrived addressed to that name. Rosie it appeared knew the landlady well enough to allow her to sub-let the cottage to others. Wilhelm then worked out that Rosie had given them notice to leave three days after Rachel was born. That confirmation gave David to think they were getting somewhere and to that Jill commented, "Rosie's landlady has to be a friend or relative, look how accommodating she was only taking a week's notice when Rosie moved in here. And she kept the cottage free for Helen until she came out of hospital. If we could find out who she is, she might help us."

David then began to wonder if Rosie having unconsciously revealed she'd suffered similar fate to Helen, had been given a long tenancy agreement of a cottage in upmarket Kensington as a pay-off? But all these tit-bits of information were of no real use. Each day was like another stroll around the walls of Rosie's castle, with no clue or clear indication of ever finding it, or a way in!

By Thursday he'd begun to feel Maysfield was his only hope, and had to sit through the news of those involved in Jill's debacle. Chris, Sanchez half brother had been caught slipping into the country on a false passport. And Sanchez alias Mallory was hating solitary confinement, but rumour had it someone was out to get him. Worried, that Jill might get drawn into that again, he was relieved when Gerald assured him they'd enough to convict Chris for several life sentences without her input. It was only after Gerald had drunk four pints to his two, and was halfway through his fifth he brought up Rosie's disappearance. Gerald's immediate reaction, "You've no need to worry about Rosemary, she's a survivor."

Carefully he dropped a hook into his reply, "You're right, after all she's reinvented herself before. What was it - nine years ago?"

Gerald between gulps of beer said, "Eight."

He added the bait. "At least dropping the double-barrel name helped her to go into obscurity."

At that Gerald grunted, "I suspect her parents not wanting anything more to do with her influenced that!"

Incensed at her parent's treatment, so like Helen's experience, he had to batten down his emotions, and carelessly throw out the line, "At least she had the mews cottage to recuperate in."

Grim faced, Gerald observed, "Bradford only gave her that to make himself look like a rich, benevolent benefactor, rather than the despicable lying sod that he was."

At Gerald's knowledge of Rosie's past David fought the rising resentment and jealousy, and in a need to know more he fished, "A cottage is hardly recompense for ruining her life."

Gerald downed the remainder of his pint before agreeing. "What I find amazing is that she seems to have forgiven her parents, him, and… but that's this Christianity thing of yours, she explained it to me."

Forgiveness was not something David was feeling at that moment, but he did manage to ask casually, "Did you know about this at the time?"

"Good heavens, no. The police were never involved. I reckon with Bradford's high profile, he had it hushed up under the pretext of protecting her. My connection, surprisingly, came through the Mallory fiasco. Rosemary came into the Police

Station to identify Sanchez's voice as Mallory's, but the doctor, who'd sewn up Mallory, heard, and identified hers. The doc became quite agitated in thinking we were gaining evidence to convict him. But by then we'd promised him immunity in order to convict Sanchez, so it went no further. However, the doc confessed he'd been forced to perform the abortion, just as Rosemary had been forced to have it. But Rosemary's distress, the need of restraint, and her horrific screaming had so unsettled him, he'd botched it. A day he said that would be etched on his mind forever."

Horrified at the picture Gerald painted he'd thumped the table, causing Gerald to jump and spill his beer. Furious, he retorted, "Etched on his memory, what about Rosie's scarred and ruined life? And that same man, that doctor, my father helped to go abroad and start a new life. You should have told us."

Gerald looked around, bent forward and said quietly, "How could I? The information was confidential. His evidence convicted Mallory, staying here would have been his death sentence. And what about Rosemary, would she have wanted her past dragged up? If it's any consolation that same doctor, knowing the damage he'd caused, followed her taxi home, rang for an ambulance and probably saved her life!" At that news he gave a derisive grunt, but Gerald continued, "His story was similar to Ben's, and why your father also helped him disappear. Anyway, when Rosemary had that car accident it was an opportunity to reconnect with you." Gerald gave a rueful grin. "I'll admit the curiosity of Rosemary's past isn't all she arouses." David's response was a thin smile. Gerald continued, "When she agreed to have a drink with me, I told her I knew her story and admired how she'd built herself a new life. With that enigmatic smile of hers she said, "If you can't trust a Member of Parliament, twenty years your senior, who can you trust? I'll not trust any man again!"

Appalled to know that the man was Bradford, who'd been a member of the Cabinet, David declared fiercely, "We have to find a way to bring that man to justice?"

Gerald shook his head. "Too late! Bradford died of a heart attack two years ago."

"Do you know if Brigadier Frederick Greenhaigh was involved?"

"Good heavens no! He's a very decent man. Rosie said he

tried to stand against the establishment, and uphold her character and morals. There was another couple, in a difficult position, who felt it more expedient to keep in the background, and be there for her rather than get embroiled in the lies and deceit, but it's her story to tell, not mine."

In a dour voice he admitted, "You, Gerald, know a great deal more about Rosie than we do." He pulled her note from his pocket, "She wrote this and I need to find her."

Gerald read it and commented, "I can understand her perspective. She's developed a strong bond with your children. And from my observation, her concern tends to be more for others than herself, so sees how difficult it would be when you remarry."

"And that is why I need to find her." Gerald raised his eyebrows as he declared, "I want her to be my wife."

Tapping the letter, Gerald pointed out, "From this I'd say Rosie doesn't want to be found." But at David's groan, he grinned, and said in an amused voice, "Yet I'd say she should be. And by you. If for no other reason than she should know, that you, and your close knit family, care enough about her to find her. I'll be interested to hear how she responds to your proposal! Frederick Greenhaigh will have her parent's address, if he won't give it to you, I can find it, but I doubt Rosie will be there."

In reporting that back, the family was agreed it would be expedient to visit Brigadier Greenhaigh, and find out what he knew. The clues, the answers were coming together, the treasure was in sight, and he was determined to become the man Rosie could wholeheartedly trust.

And today, he was only a few miles from his destination. The windscreen wipers going backwards and forwards against a sudden downpour of rain echoed his nervous heart beat. Yet as he turned off the busy main arterial road, the sun broke through, bringing hope his journey wouldn't be in vein. The house in Langrish was set back off the main thoroughfare, behind a three foot stone wall. He parked in the road, knocked on the door, nervously straightened his tie, and within a few seconds the door opened to a pleasant smile from a tall, white haired, portly gentleman in his late sixties. In returning the smile, he asked politely, "Are you Brigadier Greenhaigh?"

The man replied, "I am indeed, and who is asking?"

"My name is David Reinhardt. I'm a friend of Rosemary

Doughty-Dawes." A shadow passed over the man's face so he hurried on, "I live in London, and have worked with Rosemary for many years. But after my wife died Rosie has been helping me look after my twin babies. Unfortunately, with flawed thinking she decided to up and leave believing I needed a wife, and when that day came she'd be in the way."

In seeing the muscles in Brigadier Greenhaigh's jaw twitch with laughter, he paused and felt foolish to have blurted all that out. "Go on son, you're doing very well."

"I'm sorry, it just, well, your name was on a reference from years ago, and frankly you're the only clue I have as to where she might have gone. So please, can you help me find her, because she is the one I want for my wife?"

"I think you'd better come in and meet mine."

With that the Brigadier stepped back, allowing him to enter the narrow hall, and closing the door he called, "Jennifer, I think we may have your answer to prayer."

From the kitchen, wiping her hands on her apron, the motherly figure of Jennifer appeared with a somewhat sceptical expression, while he was already asking, "Answer to prayer, does that mean you're Christians?"

"It does. We've prayed for years that a man would come to appreciate, love and care for Rosemary, and of course restore her trust in our species!" Happily he chortled at his remark, while Jennifer wide-eyed looked him up and down as the Brigadier informed him, "Rosemary, or as you call her Rosie, was badly done by. Didn't deserve that, and although we haven't seen her since that time, we've never forgotten her."

Encouraged, as he was ushered into their lounge, he explained, "You'll be delighted to know, four years ago, my wife Jane helped her commit her life to Christ. He sat in the chair indicated by the Brigadier and continued, "A year later Jane organised for Rosie to live with my sister, who subsequently became a Christian." The Greenhaighs unashamedly held hands as they sat together, their faces alight with happiness. "Rosie has become a friend of my family. I'm sent out by them with their love and prayers to find her."

"I think David, if I may call you that, as you have come all the way from London, we must give you a cup of tea or coffee, and Jennifer, love, as it's nearly lunch time, perhaps we can have a bacon and egg sandwhich to go with that?"

Jennifer smiled loving at her husband, "Freddy uses any excuse to eat, but you're very welcome, and we'd certainly appreciate hearing about Rosie, you, and your family."

Two hours later, in the nicest possible way he felt like the bacon, thoroughly grilled. He'd given them his story, had learned a little beyond that he knew about Rosie's earlier life. Rosie's parents, Daphne and Leonard, preferred warmer climes and lived most of the time on their tea plantation in India. At that Jennifer shook her head and clicked her tongue, but didn't share the reason for her disapproval. Freddy in giving him directions to their house, cautioned it was possible Rosie wouldn't be there. Jennifer's last words as they stood at their gate to wave him on his way were, "We'll be praying for you. Keep in touch."

The road began to rise up the hill, a forest of trees lined both sides of the road. He watched carefully for the right-hand bend in the road, as just before that the nearly hidden drive entrance would be on the left . Despite slowing he nearly missed it, it's angle such, it was difficult to manoeuvre the car between the two rather battered, dark grey stone pillars, on which he presumed gates had once hung. A well weathered board fixed to one of the pillars indicated, 'The Grange', his destination, but the remaining words he felt described Rosie, 'Private Property. Keep Out'! Between the trees ran a single-track, well-worn and potholed road, before a clearing in the trees revealed a fork, in the midst of which was a small grey, derelict cottage. Automatically he took the left one, which after a few yards turned at a right-angle and slightly uphill. The trees remained thick to his right, but began to thin out on his left. In first gear he carefully negotiated the potholes, not wanting to end up in the ditch that was running with water, probably due to the heavy rain.

A brief glance ahead showed the trees ending in a grassy area and beyond that a large grey stone house. How extraordinary, at the top of the building the stones were castellated. Up until then his face had been set in grim lines of concentration, but now he chuckled. Rosie really did live in a castle. He could only hope the ditch beside him wouldn't turn into a moat, and he'd have need of a drawbridge! He whistled, and exclaimed, "Not an ancestral home, but impressive Rosemary Doughty-Dawes." The large, well-proportioned house was built on three sides around a large courtyard with a centre stone basin and a fountain at its centre. He drove around that, and parked just beyond the front door, leaving his car facing over parkland. Childishly he muttered, "My daddy could buy two of these, but he prefers a home to a high ceiling mansion."

Conscious of the large windows, and unknown eyes that could be watching, he walked purposefully towards the large oak door. But his eyes didn't miss the black water and green slime in the basin pond, the mildew of an unused fountain, and the general run down look of the place. What had once been a brass knocker was dark green, the bell handle was broken at the end, and as he pulled it, the ringing bell echoing within made him shudder. It reminded him of the TV programme, 'The Munsters', and the sound of bolts being slid back, along with the shudder and creak of the door opening, he expected the person behind it to have a bolt through his neck! Instead a tall, thin, white-haired man stood before him, his stern expression one of enquiry. Believing that Rosie's parents had treated her badly, caused David to put out his hand and say stiffly, "Mr Doughty-Dawes I presume?"

Faint amusement crossed the man's features as he proclaimed, "No Sir! Sir Leonard and Lady Daphne are away. I'm Hawkins, the butler." Dumbfounded at learning Rosie had titled parents, and embarrassed he let his hand fall away, as Hawkins added with a warm smile, "Otherwise known as Jack, very fitting as I'm a worker of all trades, but master of none'!" David's eyes took in Hawkins navy blue tool apron over his dark trousers and white shirt, as Hawkins enquired, "And you are, Sir?"

Jolting back to life, he boomed, "Reinhardt, David Reinhardt. I'm looking for Rosie, I mean Rosemary? Is she here?"

"Perhaps Sir, you would care to step inside." Hawkins stepped back with a courteous bow to allow him to enter the large stone tiled hall with it's magnificent stone fireplace, opposite which began a wide imposing staircase rising up to a glass dome two floors above. David imagined when the sun shone through the huge glass chandelier hanging below it rainbow colours would be reflected on the stone floor. At David's bemused expression the butler enquired, "Was Miss Rosemary expecting you, Sir?"

"No, I…well I need to talk to her."

"I'm afraid Miss Rosemary is out, but due back in about half an hour. May I suggest you wait, Sir?"

Inside came the urge to laugh, but with a straight face, feeling like an actor in a historical play, he replied, "Thank you Hawkins, that would be most kind."

There was no doubt about the twinkle of humour in Hawkins' eyes as he requested, "Follow me, Sir" before turning on his heel to head right along the well-worn red carpet runner in the centre of a wide stone tiled corridor. On the wall David recognised a Gainsborough painting, was it an original? Further along he noted several light rectangles indicating pictures had once hung there. Near the end of the corridor Hawkins opened a door to his right and revealed a high ceilinged room filled with shelves of books. Standing back, Hawkins indicated he enter the room, and announced unnecessarily, "The library, Sir."

As he strode purposefully into the room, his eyes took in the chairs around the large central table, where magazines and books were in neat piles. An antique desk stood by the window overlooking the courtyard, and two winged back chairs resided by the stone fireplace, that had no fire. By the large windows overlooking the parkland and drive, four more chairs were clumped together around a small table. To bring the back of the room more light, Hawkins was switching on the two table lamps by the fireplace, while saying, "I'm sure Sir, as you wait for Miss Rosemary, you will find something here to interest you." Despite the warm glow from the lights, the room felt cold, smelt of damp, and looked unlived in. As if reading his thoughts Hawkins continued, "I'm afraid with Miss Rosemary out during the day, and her parents away, we don't light the fire in here, but I can offer you a pot of tea."

Politely he responded, "Thank you that would be very kind." As Hawkins left he strolled down the room to look out of the large, stone bay window. This place must cost a fortune to heat. He glanced around, there weren't any radiators! Had the Doughty-Dawes fallen on hard times, or were they away so much they just didn't care about the run-down appearance of their property? Hawkins comment about being a 'jack of all trades' caused him to wonder if he was the only one looking after the place. And just how big was it? He seen opposite the door to the library a long corridor with a narrow staircase at the far end, it would seem the house was H-shaped. Slowly he perused the books. Most were literary classics, including the entire works of Shakespeare, Charles Dickens, and the 1911 edition of the Encyclopaedia Britannica renowned for its scholarship and literary style. Finally, having strolled around the room, he thumbed through the magazines. The most recent was an Illustrated London News two years out of date, but taking that he moved to a chair by the window to watch for Rosie's return.

Half an hour later, feeling the room's chill, he wondered if they were boiling the kettle over an open fire, for how long did a pot of tea take to make? He was changing his magazine for the third time, when he saw emerging slowly from the trees a 1930's Mark V Bentley. A car he recognised as it was one much admired by his father, who'd scoffed at buying it believing it to be 'too pretentious'.

To his knowledge Rosie didn't drive, but perhaps her parents had a chauffeur, or were they returning home? Hawkins drew his attention by entering with a large silver tray containing delicate chinaware and large silver tea set. So he asked, "Is that the Doughty-Dawes Bentley?"

Carefully placing the tray on the table, Hawkins took a moment to reply, "Indeed it is, Sir."

Nervously David moved to look out, but stayed far enough away from the window not to be seen as the forty-two year old, but immaculately kept car, drew to a halt in front of his. "I thought you said they were away?"

Hawkins, concentrating on pouring the tea commented, "Indeed they are Sir". The driver's door opened and a pair of long sleek legs appeared, followed by a fashionable short tight skirt and matching boxy jacket in a warm shade of apricot. Rosie always dressed in dark greys, brown and black and this woman, although resembling her, had short, layered hair, cut in spikes around her face which dramatically highlighted her refined features and attractive face. He watched, as with an air of the aristocracy, her head held high, she strode purposely to the car boot to retrieve her shopping. Without taking his eyes off her David queried, "Have the Doughty-Dawes two daughters?" As the woman headed for the front door, she directed a brief glance at the library windows. In realising Hawkins hadn't replied to his question he turned to find the room empty, but the door left ajar.

Not wanting to be at a disadvantage he headed across the room, and as the front door opened and shut, Hawkins' announced in a sonorous voice, "Miss Rosemary, you have a guest. I have shown him into the library and served him tea."

"Yes Hawkins. Thank you. I've seen his car."

He blanched at 'Miss Rosemary's' imperious tone. That aloofness had been less prominent in recent years, but it appeared her aristocratic voice and bearing were genuine. So perhaps being offered a Morris Minor to drive rather than a Bentley had been beneath her!

"Will you be needing anything further Miss Rosemary?"

"Not at present Hawkins. Thank you. I'll ring when I need you."

Stilleto heels clicking across the tiled flagstones of the hall fell silent, indicating Rosie was heading along the carpet towards him. To appear casual he picked up the delicate china cup from the tray, and in sipping his tea he peered over the cup as she entered.

"David!" The tight mouth and clipped business tone expressed her displeasure. She came straight to the point. "Why are you here?"

Was this reinventing herself, or reverting to type? Undeterred by either her acting ability, or the façade of aristocratic confidence, he gave a rueful smile and teased, "Not the welcome I would have hoped for, but perhaps you'd allow me to answer that as we sit and take tea? At her curt nod and wave towards the chairs by the empty fireplace, he made himself comfortable, as she, with her back toward him, poured tea into the cup Hawkins' had provided. Once seated, the lamp light gave Rosie's face a delicate glow, but her expression was far from warm. And those often doleful eyes held a cool and challenging gaze. Observing her, he emptied his cup and waited for her to speak. When she didn't he said nonchalantly, "I'd like another of those, if you don't mind I'll help myself."

The pursed lips and pinched expression showed her displeasure, but she granted his request with a nod. Challenge had attracted him to Jane, and although the real Rosemary might take time to uncover, he felt energized and determined to run with whatever persona she wanted to embrace. Christmas had revealed Rosie was an accomplished actress, did she think she was fooling him now? Returning to his seat he commented, "That colour, Rosie, really suits you. I don't think I've ever seen you look quite so beautiful." With eyes narrowed in scepticism Rosie watched him as he sat down. In response he raised a questioning eyebrow over his teacup.

"David, why are you here? I made it quite explicit I didn't want to be contacted."

With a wry smile he replaced the cup on the saucer to taunt, "You didn't say 'goodbye'." Rosie clicked her tongue. "You gave a reason for your departure, but as I, and the family, think of you as a friend, I felt, at least, you'd allow me the opportunity to show my concern for you in the same way you did for Helen." At that she flinched, inwardly he smiled. Rosie stood, and crossed the room to replace her cup on the tray. When she turned, she took several steps toward him, and said stiffly, "Thank you for your concern. As you see I'm fine. When you have finished your tea, you can go on your way." She turned to head for the door.

At that he boomed, "Is that so? Then perhaps you would be good enough to sit again for I have several matters yet to conduct." He relaxed further into the chair, and gave her an inviting smile.

"What matters?" She asked sharply.

"If you come over here I'll explain." He watched curiosity and defiance vie in her eyes. Having given in to curiosity, Rosie perched on the edge of the chair opposite him, crossed her long legs and appeared oblivious to the sexual frisson she was creating within him. "Rosie, the bottom line is both I, and the children miss you." Pain flashed through her eyes, she moved as if to leave. "But I can understand the reasoning behind it." Her back straightened, her lips curled in cynicism. Paul had strongly advised against saying anything that would manipulate Rosie's emotions and control any decisions she might make, but he longed to tell her of the twins' constant misery in wanting her, his deep ache akin to grief that had followed her departure, and the hole she'd left in all their lives. But instead he arose to replace his cup and saucer on the tray, and could almost feel her eyes boring into his back. Heading back toward her, he took out his cheque book from his inner pocket. Rosie's face was expressionless, but anger, and perhaps disappointment, flashed through her eyes. "Your bank will receive this month's salary, but we all felt you'd provided us with such sterling service that it should be rewarded." He tore out the pre-written cheque, and held it out. Rosie dipped and turned her head, but without her curtain of hair he saw the tears brimming in her eyes. Yet knew he must press on. Still waving the cheque he announced, "When you accept this, your role as nanny to our children, will be officially terminated. I'll no longer be your employer."

Leaping up she shouted, "I don't want your money!" She pushed past him, and then turned to accuse, "You didn't need to come here. I don't need a Reinhardt payoff. There's no reason to feel sorry for me."

David stood to proclaim gently, "But Jane wanted us to always remember Rosie."

After glaring at him, Rosie marched to the door, and directed as she took hold of the door knob, "Well, now you can go, you've done what you needed…"

Walking towards her, he interrupted, "No Rosie, I haven't done all I need, or want, to do. And it may be some while before I can." Puzzled, and in looking wary at his advance towards her, she was perhaps remembering another time! Her reaction was much the same as then, her lips pursed, her back straightened and she stood her ground. But as he neared her hands came up, as though to ward him off. About three feet away he said softly, "Rosie this is a present from us all, not a payoff. Please take it."

Something akin to anguish filled her eyes as she plucked it from his outstretched hand, and said without looking at it, "Thank you, please thank the others too" and turned to open the door.

Gently he requested, "Please Rosie, can we sit again? I also have a proposal to put to you."

In exasperation she bit out, "David, how many times do I have to say it, I don't want you here! I don't want your money! I don't want to hear your proposals! Please, understand, I have to distance myself from you, your family and…" her voice caught as she finished, "the twins." With only a slight pause, she added firmly, "And as kind as you've all been, I need to think of my future. I explained the reasons in my letter. Don't worry about me. I'll easily find a new job."

"And I'd be the first to give you a glowing reference, but Rosie, you may think that is for the best, but I don't agree." Ignoring her clenched fists of frustration he continued, "I see you as a friend, but I've also been your employer. I've given our situation considerable thought, but found it difficult to broach the subject with you."

"Oh yes, I'm sure you have! You wanted me to have your

study as my bedroom and live in your part of the house."

"It was discussed, but not what I had in mind." At that Rosie looked confused. "Now you are no longer dependent on me for either employment or accommodation, you've made it's easier for me to simply state my mind. Rosie, my children couldn't have a better mother than you, so please, would you consider becoming my wife?

Disbelief chased through Rosie's eyes. The cheque fluttered from her hand to the floor. Her mouth gaped, with furrowed brow she whispered, "Me? Your wife!"

Without taking his eyes from hers he stepped forward, and in taking her cold hand, he held it to ask, "Is that so terrible a request?"

Snatching her hand from his, she splayed it across her chest as she stepped back to state, "But you don't know me?"

With a shrug he informed her, "I know all I need to. I've lived in close proximity to you for nearly two years, and am very happy with what I see and know."

Anxiously she insisted, "I meant you don't know anything about me."

"Jane told me a little of your history. There have been occasions when you have revealed deep hurt. And it's obvious a man inflicted that."

Looking at the floor, Rosie murmured, "It's not just that."

"Oh Rosie, there's much about me you don't know." Rosie avoided his outstretched hand. "None of us are perfect. In marriage Jane and I were happy, but we had our differences. I appreciate you, and have every desire to treat you well." He grinned, "And if I don't, I'd have my family to answer to."

Bewildered eyes met his. "Why…Why me? You have so many choices. It's not as if you love me."

To that he gave a rueful grimace. "Rosie I've come to see there are many facets to love. If you wish, look upon it as a 'marriage of convenience'. He repeated the benefits Grace had listed, and finished, but I truly believe it can blossom into so much more. My message was in the words of that record I gave you, and your disappearance proved that I, and the children, can't live without you." Shaking her head, Rosie looked down at the carpet. Stretching out his arm, he gently lifted her chin with his finger. "Rosie, I can understand your reticence. I know I can be difficult. I've upset you. I've accused you wrongly. As your employer, beyond an apology, I didn't know how to repair the damage caused. As a friend, I asked for forgiveness and wanted to hug you, but guessed that would unacceptable." Unable to read Rosie's expression, he gave a self-deprecating smile and said sadly, "I don't even know if you like me. Coming here I also have risked rejection."

He drew back his hand, but Rosie's troubled gaze held, and softened at his vulnerability. "You can be intimidating, even infuriating, but I've never disliked you. And with Jane, and the twins, I've noticed you changing." Hesitantly she added, "I get angry...I've learnt to distance myself, or close down."

"Was that because of the way Bradford treated you?"

Fear leapt into her eyes. "How do you know about him? I've told no-one."

"I'll admit to barrister tactics on Gerald Maysfield to get information."

Before his eyes Rosie seemed to crumple. Worried, he took her elbow and led her to the nearest chair. Crouching before her, he stated, "Rosie if I cared about your past I wouldn't be here proposing to you. And let me assure you I abhor men who treat women badly."

At that she looked at him to state, "But sometimes you frighten me."

Aghast, he raked his hair. "I don't mean to. Jane said I often scowled, but most times it's not anger, but contemplation. We had heated arguments, and maybe we'll have them too, but I'd never hurt you." David's mouth twisted into a small, secret remembering how he and Jane had made up. And then realised Rosemary was staring at him he went on, "I'm sure you haven't forgotten that Christmas when I picked you out from the choir?" She nodded. "When I saw your contempt turn to fear at my intention to kiss you, I tried to be gentle. My leading you away afterwards was to apologise, but you didn't give me the chance."

Her gaze fixed on his tie, she said, "I–I thought, you were going to..." blushing she trailed off.

Distressed he leapt up to boom, "Good grief woman! Have you thought that all these years?"

With hands fluttering nervously, Rosie looked up at him. "I don't know... Jane adored you." Embarrassed she wrung her hands together as she admitted, "Jane told me, you'd never force her to do anything against her will." Glancing up she added, "But that you were excellent at persuasion!"

To that he gave an amused grunt, and asked as he crouched before her again, "Did Bradford force you to do things against your will?"

Rosie bit her lip, her eyes filled with tears, evidence he felt of her pain and shame, but her reply was firm, "Perhaps another time?"

He dared to hope. "Does that mean I can come again?"

A faint, but familiar enigmatic smile appeared with the word, "Maybe."

Cold, long fingered hands trembled as he gently took them in his own. With his eyes fixed on hers, David slipped onto one knee to declare, "Rosemary Doughty-Dawes I'm asking you to be my wife, not because of what you do, or because you love my children, but out of desire to see you blossom fully into the Rose you were intended to be." Tears filled her eyes and overflowed down her cheeks. "When I first knew about you, you were sharp and prickly. After Jane nurtured you, you began to quietly grow and bud. But in calling you Rosie, you are becoming a rose among women. At first a tight blossom, but in being nurtured you've been gradually opening up, revealing the fragrance of your presence, filling my home with love, children's laughter, and..." he grinned, "delicious smells of cooking". Unbelief, bewilderment, happiness chased through her eyes at his words, the reward a small smile. Encouraged he added, "And last Christmas...I so enjoyed seeing you happy, and especially loved the ganging up against Felicity, could we practice until it becomes real?"

Visibly shaking, with silent tears dripping off her chin, David stood drawing her up with him. Determined that she'd know he could be trusted, after giving her his handkerchief, he confessed, "Rosie, right now I want to take you in my arms to comfort and kiss away your tears. But, as I once said to Jane, I am a gentleman and only take that which is offered." Rosie, dabbing her eyes, didn't move or speak. Believing it was time for him to take his leave he concluded, "I hope you'll now forgive me for not following your explicit instructions, but that needed saying. Should you agree to my proposal, every step will be at your pace, and in your way, but I'd appreciate knowing what you decide."

He strode to the door and opened it, saying, "I'll show

myself out" and with that nearly bumped into Hawkins. Had the man been listening, or just loitering by the door in case Miss Rosemary needed a protector? At David's quizzical expression Hawkins recovered well. "Ah Sir, you are leaving. Let me show you out. I've removed the Bentley so you can drive away."

From the library came an imperious voice. "It's alright Hawkins. I'll see David to the door." To David's astonishment Hawkins winked and mouthed, "You're just what she needs" before entering the library to reply, "Yes, of course, Miss Rosemary. I'll deal with the tea things."

Rosie didn't speak as she accompanied him to the front door, but on opening it she said softly, "Thank you for coming, and saying the things you have. But I think it best you withdraw your proposal."

Feeling sick in the pit of his stomach, he barely managed to ask, "Why?"

"We've worked together, some might say lived together, but becoming man and wife goes beyond the years of mothering your children. Have we enough in common to be life-long friends? To leave the twins was very hard and painful, and I suspect it is for them too. But they are young enough to forget me."

Afraid, this was final, he thought quickly. "Rosie, couldn't we at least try courting for six months? If it doesn't work out, the twins will still be young enough, as you say to forget you."

Rosie processed that. "Would you want me to come back as the twins' nanny?"

"Yes, but no. That's why I proposed to you. Engaged to be married, you'd be looking after them as their potential mother. There's security in that. Have your room back, we'd date, go out, talk, relax together. I wouldn't have asked you if I didn't believe it could work."

"David, it's tempting, but too firm a commitment. Engagement means announcements, a ring, and devastation, if it doesn't work out. When you know all about me you may not want to marry me. We might not make six months, but if we do, and you still want me to be your wife, you can ask me again."

How he admired this woman! His heart soared, but he said calmly, "Could I extract a promise from you?" At her quizzical expression he asked, "You'll not run at the first hurdle, you'll give me regular and truthful feedback, and unless our relationship becomes completely untenable, you'll stay six months. The children opened my eyes to see the real Rosie, and I need that time to become the desire of your heart, so you can have the family you so deserve."

Tears filled her eyes, "David, thank you. I will give your offer consideration, and do appreciate all you are saying." Rosie swallowed hard, "I left the twins to protect myself, and them, from the pain of loving, it's a risk."

To that David pointed out, "But there is no other woman. And even if I fail to make you love me as you do the twins, a 'marriage of convenience' would be a foundation on which to build, and I'm sure we've enough in common for a reasonable life of companionship."

As if unable to grapple with that Rosie asked, "Who's looking after the twins?"

"Ted and Joyce agreed to stay until I return. Dad proclaimed that without you we were reverting into chaos, and asked how could I have let such an incredible woman slip through my fingers? Everyone is behind this and helped me track you down."

Rosie gave a small smile. "It seems I am the only one then to make up my mind."

Eagerly he asked, "So you'll come back?"

"David there is much to think about. I'm not sure coming back to the house would be right. My cottage will be free at the end of April. I could come back then."

"But it has two bedrooms." Rosie gave him a puzzled look. "Grace and Wilhelm have been very supportive of me in this, and they might be willing for you to stay until they leave?"

The wind blew, Rosie backed into the doorway, "Brr... it's getting cold. I'll ring and let you know my decision."

He stepped forward, she didn't retreat, so he kissed her cheek, and near her ear spoke with quiet anticipation, "I'll look forward to hearing from you." With that he strode across the gravel, and with a final wave of his hand, he slipped into his car believing that the drawbridge to Rosie's castle had been lowered. There was hope he'd gain her permission to cross, and one day she'd let him fully enter in.

July 2012

Dear Reader,

I hope you have enjoyed this third book, and hopefully it won't be too long before I've written 'Rosie' and you can discover what happens next.

All the supernatural events in this story have either happened to me, or to someone I know. The Holy Spirit delights to reveal truth in pictures, words, dreams and visions. This book being published coincides with my celebrating forty years since I became a Christian. And it is through a daily reading of God's Word that I have come to know something of the personality, and character of God, and enjoy a relationship with Him that surpasses all others.

I can assure you that through the deepest difficulties and sorrows, the Lord promises are true, He has never left or forsaken me. The Father knew each of us before we were conceived in our mother's womb, He knows our name, He has a plan, purpose, future and destiny, for everyone He has created. The deepest joy comes in understanding just who you are in Christ, and who He is in you. It is then you really step into understanding His Kingdom coming on earth as it is in heaven.

I hope after reading this you will, as the Bible says, 'taste and see that the Lord is good'. If you haven't given your life to Him, I urge you to do so. (See next pages) And if you have, then in these days all 'David' experienced is open to you, if you take time in His Presence by listening, reading His Word and speaking to Him.

RUTH JOHNSON

THREE GOOD REASONS TO TRUST IN JESUS

1. Because you have a past
You can't go back, but He can. The Bible says, 'Jesus Christ the same yesterday, and today, and for ever.' (Hebrews 13:8) He can walk into those places of sin and failure, wipe the slate clean and give you a new beginning.

2. Because you need a friend
Jesus knows the worst about you, yet He believes the best. Why? Because he sees you not as you are, but as you will be when He gets through with you. What a friend!

3. Because He holds the future
Who else are you going to trust? In His hands you are safe and secure – today, tomorrow, and for eternity. His Word says, "For I know the plans I have for you…plans for good and not for evil, to give you a future and a hope. In those days when you pray I will listen' (Jeremiah 29:11-13)

The Bible says, 'Taste and see that the Lord is good.' ask Him to help you understand, prove Himself to you. There are places to find more information mentioned opposite.

Or take a step further and begin a personal relationship with Jesus today by praying the simple prayer below. And once you have done it, allow Him to become real to you.

Dear Lord,

I am sorry for the things I have done wrong in my life. I ask your forgiveness and now turn from everything which I know is wrong. Thank you for dying on the cross for me to set me free from my sins. Please come into my life and fill me with your Holy Spirit and be with me forever. Thank you, Lord.

FOR MORE INFORMATION:
Access the website run by United Christian Broadcasters at
www.lookingforgod.com

Need prayer: UCB prayer line is manned from 9.00am – 10.30pm
Monday to Friday on 0845 456 7729

UCB *Word for the Day* – daily stories of ordinary folk touched by
an extraordinary God. It has Bible references for each day and
when followed means you get to read the whole Bible in a year.
Telephone: 0845 60 40 401 to get your copy.

IF YOU HAVE PRAYED THE PRAYER:
To fully receive all the blessings God wants to bestow upon you,
I'd advise you do the following:

1. Get yourself a Bible - New International Version

2. Ring UCB for *Word for the Day* to be sent to you.

3. Ask the Lord to become real to you and even if you don't
understand what you read follow the plan for each day asking
God's Holy Spirit to open it up to you. It took three weeks at about
15 minutes a day before it began to make sense to me.

4. Try out the churches in your area. Find one that you feel
comfortable in, then join it and get to know the people in it.

5. Please email me: Ruth.Johnson@theartsdesireseries.com as I
would love to know that this booked has helped you, and I shall be
thrilled to hear if you've found the Lord through it..

If you would like to make contact with a local Christian, or would
like further help from someone living locally to you please write
giving your full name, address, telephone number and email —
include your age group, to:

3 reasons, FREEPOST, WC2947, South Croydon, CR2 8UZ

OTHER BOOKS IN
THE HEARTS DESIRE SERIES
Www.heartsdesireseries.com

Book 1 JANE
Jane's sheltered existence is disturbed by the caresses of a stranger in a darkened room. Haunted by the incident she determines to experience life. Her encounters and challenges bring fun and fear as she searches for the reality of love. But love is gently hovering awaiting release and its unexpected arrival encompasses all her heart's desires...

Book 2 JILL
Jill, despite failed relationships, is looking for Mr Right. A chance encounter sets off a chain of events which threatens her, her friends and family. In this, Jill discovers there are many faces of love, but there is only one who will bring her the fulfillment of her heart's desires....

Book 4 ROSIE
Rosemary has found love and contentment, but anguish squeezes her heart as history seems to be repeating itself. Hurts and fears taunt her as she struggles to decide if a marriage of convenience is too high a price to pay for the joy of motherhood. The tenacity of love draws her to confront her heart's desires....

Book 5 JANICE
Janice, battered and homeless finds an unexpected refuge. Her arrival causes shock and dismay, her attitudes and behaviour lock those involved into a battle to hold onto love. Even as she holds them to ransom, she experiences an unforeseen love growing within her, making her rethink her heart's desires....

Book 6 MATT
Matt's past haunts him across continents, in spite of unexpected friendship, love, provision and fulfillment in his chosen career. His caring heart brings a chance encounter and brings rewards he hadn't envisaged, unveiling that love that has no bounds as he is set free to know his heart's desires....

FURTHER INFORMATION AT
Www.emanuel-publishers.com